T0148700

THE
HALF
EMPRESS

ADVANCE PRAISE FOR THE BOOK

'A historical novel, well-researched and imaginatively written, resurrecting the life of exceptional beauty, and the obsession and ruination of a king. [Raskapoor's] story was all but expunged from history'—Gaj Singh, former Maharaja of Jodhpur

'I was fascinated as I read the tale of the Half Empress. She was an amazing woman whom history had forgotten. Now, fortunately for readers, Raskapoor has been brought to vibrant life for us to enjoy'—Chitra Banerjee Divakaruni, author of *The Last Queen*

'A compelling tale of love, lust and intrigue, of splendour and pageantry, betrayal and heartbreak—a story that negotiates some lost pages of history'—Namita Gokhale, author

'Tripti Pandey's latest book combines romance, intrigue, history and court politics in a fascinating way that looks at the life, and death, of Raskapoor. Raskapoor . . . either admired or loathed by the courtiers and populace, was a powerful, beautiful woman who was, allegedly, bestowed the title of "Ardhrajan" by Maharaja Sawai Jagat Singh of Jaipur. The title signified that she held mastery over half the kingdom of Dhoondhar, which had Jaipur city as its capital. Raskapoor rose to the heights of royal power as the favourite of Maharaja Sawai Jagat Singh. But time plays strange tricks on humans, and eventually, the same Raskapoor fell from her position to become a prisoner-for-life in a fortress that overlooked the city of Jaipur. A city that had once been at the feet of the Half Empress, later lay literally beneath her prison walls but out of her reach. There are different versions of how she died, but, as Tripti Pandey notes in her book, she is mainly remembered today by tourist guides. For the majority of others, Raskapoor has long remained a shadowy figure: beautiful, scheming and somewhat damned. That picture is altered the minute one opens *The Half Empress* and follows the story of Raskapoor. A woman who was ambitious, well versed in poetry and the arts, a brilliant conversationalist, concubine to a maharaja, rich beyond imagination with the gifts given to her, and at the same time, vulnerable—and a product of her surroundings and her times. *The Half Empress* makes for a compelling read. Get your copy today'—Rima Hooja, historian and author

'*The Half Empress* takes readers on a fascinating tour of the unfortunate, tragic, twisted fate of a dancer, Raskapoor, who, defying all norms, rose to be installed as the queen of half a dominion, the "Ardhrajan" of Amber, by her paramour king. In this novelized biography, Tripti Pandey has successfully interwoven palace intrigues and prevailing social norms to deliver a gripping tale of the concubine Raskapoor, an exceptional beauty, talented dancer and an able administrator, yet much vilified and deliberately omitted by historians from the annals of history'—Shovana Narayan, eminent Kathak dancer and Guru

THE
HALF
EMPRESS

TRIPTI PANDEY

EBURY
PRESS

An imprint of Penguin Random House

EBURY PRESS

USA | Canada | UK | Ireland | Australia
New Zealand | India | South Africa | China

Ebury Press is part of the Penguin Random House group of companies
whose addresses can be found at global.penguinrandomhouse.com

Published by Penguin Random House India Pvt. Ltd
4th Floor, Capital Tower 1, MG Road,
Gurugram 122 002, Haryana, India

First published in Ebury Press by Penguin Random House India 2023

Copyright © Tripti Pandey 2023

All rights reserved

10 9 8 7 6 5 4 3 2 1

This is a work of fiction. Names, characters, places and incidents
are either the product of the author's imagination or are used fictitiously,
and any resemblance to any actual person, living or dead, events or
locales is entirely coincidental.

ISBN 9780670098286

Typeset in Sabon by MAP Systems, Bengaluru, India
Printed at Thomson Press India Ltd, New Delhi

This book is sold subject to the condition that it shall not, by way of trade
or otherwise, be lent, resold, hired out, or otherwise circulated without the
publisher's prior consent in any form of binding or cover other than that in
which it is published and without a similar condition including this condition
being imposed on the subsequent purchaser.

www.penguin.co.in

Dedicated to my late parents, Mrs Bhagwati Pandey and Mr Indra Narain Pandey, who introduced me to the world of words extending from poetry to novels

'In the height of his passion for the Islamite
concubine, he formally installed
her as queen of half of his dominions, and
actually conveyed to her in gift a
moiety of the personality of the crown . . .'
                                    —Col James Tod

Contents

Prelude

Among the rulers of Jaipur, only a few are talked about besides Sawai Jai Singh. Apart from him, people of the walled city still remember his son and successor Sawai Ishwari Singh and two later rulers, Sawai Pratap Singh and Sawai Ram Singh II for the monuments they built and their contribution to the performing arts. The rest find a home in the annals of history, their stories requiring more coaxing to emerge. However, one other ruler whose name is uttered often is Maharaja Sawai Jagat Singh, who ruled from 1803 to 1818. But his name is taken with contempt because of his affair with a courtesan (or tawaif), Raskapoor. All the other rulers before and after him had such affairs, but he was the only one to share his empire with his tawaif.

He defied all norms as he bestowed upon her the title of 'Ardhrajan' or 'Half Empress' before a specially summoned gathering of the feudal lords of his state. The shocked court watched as Raskapoor was given the jurisdiction of the erstwhile capital of Amber. No one could fathom how their ruler accorded such a title to her—a title with which one could even take over the reins of the entire state.

Gifted with extraordinary beauty and wisdom, along with an incredible talent for music and dance, Raskapoor captured Jagat Singh's heart, leaving no space for anyone else to come close to him. His overwhelming love for her ignited hate, jealousy and intrigue not only in the *zenani deorhi*, or the ladies chamber, but also among the Thakurs, or the nobles. The combined force of the two factions left no stone unturned in attempting to get Raskapoor away from their Maharaja.

Up in arms over her influence on their ruler, they hatched plans and designed strategy after strategy to outwit each other's groups. Raskapoor must have been a very gifted thinker with diplomatic skills, as she successfully and resiliently navigated her way through the cobwebs of the royal life for many years. But pitched against a fleet of plotters in an atmosphere filled with deceit, she finally fell into their trap.

Even the prolific writer on the princely states of 'Rajpootana' of that period, Col James Tod, skips the details and comments on the reign of Maharaja Sawai Jagat Singh with disdain. Tod not only found him 'the most dissolute prince of his race or of his age' but also went on to say, 'We shall not disgrace these annals with the history of a life which discloses not one redeeming virtue . . .'

While writing about Raskapoor, Tod only reflects his contempt. 'In the height of his passion for the Islamite concubine, he formally installed her as queen of half of his dominions, and actually conveyed to her in gift a moiety of the personality of the crown, even to the invaluable library of the illustrious Jai Singh which was despoiled, and its treasures distributed amongst her base relations. The Raja even struck coin in her name, and not only rode with her on the same elephant, but demanded from his chieftains those forms of reverence towards her which were paid only to his legitimate queens.

This their pride could not brook, and though the Diwan or prime minister, Misr Sheonarayan, albeit a Brahmin, called her 'daughter', the brave Chaand Singh of Doonee indignantly refused to take part in any ceremony at which she was present. This contumacy was punished by a mulct of £20,000, nearly four years' revenue of the fief of Doonee!' He even talked about how the daily journal (*akhbar*) featured 'the scandal of the Rawala (female apartments), the follies of the libertine prince with his concubine Ras-caphoor'.

Forgotten by the people, mentioned in records only when it was mandatory, and deliberately omitted by historians, Raskapoor's life and death turned into an interesting fable. There are many stories about how her life ended, though all agree that she was eventually convicted on charges of betrayal and attempting to take over the throne from her paramour, the Maharaja, and imprisoned. According to some, the compassionate prison chief allowed her to flee; others suggest that she committed sati by discreetly joining the group of wives who flung themselves on to the pyre of Jagat Singh. Perhaps she is best remembered by the guides who routinely mention her as a celebrity prisoner at the Sudarshangarh Fort, popularly referred to as the Nahargarh Fort.

I heard Raskapoor's name for the first time many years ago when I visited that fort. Later, one of the well-informed men who owned the haveli diagonally opposite the City Palace talked about her while giving me a tour of his house. Triloki Das Khandelwal was the owner of the haveli known as Nawab Sahib ki Haveli. He had been a family friend for a long time, and given my role in the promotion of tourism, asked me to visit his palace. Taking great pride in his historic abode, the first sentence he uttered on that visit was, 'You know, Raskapoor wanted this haveli to be gifted to her.' He also directed me to the Kaanch Mahal where Raskapoor lived before moving to the palace.

When I went to her abode, I could visualize her and her mother standing in the pavilion built over an arched gate strategically raised in the middle of that bylane, commanding the view of the lane from where it began. I looked for the entrance leading to the pavilion, and a fruit vendor there directed me to the old mansion. I rang the bell and the man who came out was surprised, but delighted to see me. 'How come you are here?' I had no clue that a person I knew so well would lead me to that pavilion.

Raskapoor's home was later allotted to his forefathers, the Rajput nobles of the Jaipur State. Finally, there I was, warmly seated in the pavilion, imagining the days when it was the dwelling place of Raskapoor. After talking to him for a while, I went to the temples she used to visit. At the Krishna temple, the over-enthused young man boasted about the beauty of the legendary Raskapoor. 'She had a neck like a sarus (a large non-migratory crane) and her skin was transparent like glass. One could actually see the water trickle down her throat.' I smiled at his exaggeration, but I also admired him for talking about her with so much respect, and without any trace of contempt.

I had visited the lonesome zenani deorhi (the ladies' quarters) at Amber many a time, and each time I could not help but imagine the lives of the women who lived there, from the maharanis to the concubines. It was much later that I visited the zenani deorhi in the City Palace, Jaipur, which is now under the jurisdiction of the Governor of Rajasthan. Lying in ruins, those dilapidated structures still haunt my thoughts. The first occasion was a rather emotional one when I went to pay a floral tribute to the Queen Mother, the legendary beauty, Gayatri Devi.

Her mortal remains were placed in the apartment allocated to her post her marriage. Two other wives of Maharaja Man Singh II were also living in the zenani deorhi. Those must have been the last days of princely rule before the State took charge, following the merger of princely states.

I visited again during the Gangaur festival when a portion of the zenani deorhi was decorated, bedecked with the image of the Goddess standing in the courtyard and an embellished canopy with a velvet seat awaiting the arrival of Diya Kumari, the granddaughter of Maharaja Man Singh II who would offer prayers and send off the image in the grand procession. I was drawn to the place again to shoot some images for my book *India's Elephants: A Cultural Legacy*. Every time I visited, my thoughts revolved around the women history was determined to forget, such as the concubine Raskapoor.

I had a chance to discuss Raskapoor with Thakur Rajvir Singh of Dundlod, one of the erstwhile Rajput nobles. A few days before his demise, he called me about his work on the genealogy of the Shekhawats. As our conversation was drawing to a close, I couldn't resist asking him about Raskapoor. He summed up her life in just a few words, 'She was a concubine who was trying to take over the princely state of Jaipur, and it was only because of her that Maharaja Jagat Singh was disgraced. He even gave her half of his empire with the title of Ardhrajan.'

The woman in me protested by questioning him, 'Why blame only her? Why not the Maharaja, who was a much-married man with not one but many concubines before she came into his life? Don't you think that she must have been not just an extraordinarily beautiful girl but also, an extremely bright one to earn that confidence?' He immediately conceded, 'That she must have been!'

A couple of months later, I met Thakur Rajvir Singh's brother Ranbir, who is well versed with the history of the region. Sharing my last conversation with his late brother, we ended up speaking about Raskapoor again. He was very sure about his point of view and said with certainty, 'She could not have been allowed to perform sati as a concubine,' as some of the records stated. When I cited mentions of other concubines committing sati, he elaborated his view further, saying that as a convict and a prisoner, she could never have been given the honour to immolate herself on the pyre of the Maharaja.

As I followed Raskapoor down the corridors of history, I became increasingly curious to know how her life ended, especially in view of her being part of the Early Modern Period of Indian History. During her lifetime, the Moghul Empire was declining fast while the French and the British were trying to cage the 'golden bird' Hindoostan, as India was then called. This period of the late 18th century and the beginning of the nineteenth century witnessed immense upheaval and changes. The princely states of Rajputana were experiencing their share of unrest and conspiracies.

Raskapoor appeared in the palace of the Maharaja at such a time. This is her story, a person who belongs to history but has been turned into a fable. I decided to tell her story, framing it within the history of that period. It is fictional, as I imagine the thoughts and conversation of the characters, and it is history when I recall the past of Kachchwahas as well as the events that connect to Maharaja Jagat Singh.

The book spans many years, from Raskapoor as an offspring of a Brahmin father and a courtesan mother, to finally emerging as an influential lover of the Maharaja. It moves from the intrigues of palace life to Raskapoor's innate love for mythological tales, being herself an ardent follower of Lord Shiva, Radha and Krishna. Those tales provided her solace, for she assimilated her fate as a concubine with that of another dancing girl, Mahananda, who could spend a night with Lord Shiva but not marry him, and to Radha, who could not be married to Lord Krishna and had to live without him, because he was a royal and she a commoner. The tale starts with 'Camphor Enkindled', moves on to 'Camphor Enlightened' and culminates in 'Camphor Extinguished'. In the course of my writing, I consulted several books on history, culture as well as mythology to weave the storyline.

One big task was to find an image of Raskapoor for the visuals of that period that could only be found in the miniature paintings. Portraits and miniature paintings of her lover Maharaja Sawai Jagat Singh were available but nothing on her was easily discovered. I contacted the miniature painting artist Shakir Ali, a recipient of the prestigious national level Padma award. He did have a painting displaying her, but never completed it.

He then narrated the story of the painting, which was a second copy of the painting in the collection of the Jaipur's City Palace Museum. He was provided a print to paint a fresh copy by then army chief, General Sunith Francis Rodrigues, presented to him by yet another army man, the Late Maharaja Bhawani Singh. Shakir Ali started the second painting for Lt Gen. Moti Dar, an artist himself but like Raskapoor, it remained an unfinished story. It was during that search that I found the name of one miniature painter in a press review referring to his painting on Raskapoor displayed in an exhibition.

With some effort, I succeeded in contacting the artist Gulab Chaandra Chcheepa. I manoeuvred the bylanes of the old city and reached his home. He was humble and proud of his work. He took his precious painting out. It was indeed a splendid miniature painting, which captured her phenomenal beauty, the romance of the lovers and the opulence of the period very minutely using gold and natural colours.

I shot a few pictures, and he willingly wrote down a note of permission for me to use the pictures in any form. He would part with the painting only at the time of the wedding of his daughter to meet the expenses. Suddenly, one day while reading the book of the late Gopal Narain Bohra, in charge of the library at the City Palace, Jaipur, I saw a small photograph of a fresco painting with the caption mentioning Jagat Singh and Raskapoor on the wall of the residence of Ratnakar Pundrik, head priest of Sawai Jai Singh II. I went there and the small room had not one but a couple of paintings depicting the lovers, all fading away with time.

Part One

The Essence of Camphor

The Sacred Mantra

Karpur gauram karunavataram
Sansarasaram Bhujagendraharam
Sadavasantam hridayaravinde
Bhavam bhavani sahitam namami

Oh Lord!
As pure as camphor
You are the embodiment of compassion,
You are the essence of this universe
You adorn the serpent king as a garland,
You always reside in the lotus of my heart,
To you, Lord accompanied by Goddess Parvati,
I bow!

That is the last prayer offered to Lord Shiva at his altar when the arti or the flame in the lamp is lit with camphor or kapoor or *karpur*, as it is called in Sanskrit. The fire is offered in a circular motion to remove darkness all around. Chanting the favourite mantra of Shiva, who is considered as pure as the White Lotus, the devotee reaches out to his deity. The flame of camphor lights up instantly and extinguishes within seconds, leaving no residue.

The chant is meant for the devotee's illusions to be extinguished, leaving behind a feeling of gratitude.

Shiva, who is considered the god of gods in the Hindu trinity, has been worshipped from time immemorial, and so the camphor in the ritual is wrapped in a timeless history. In ancient India, this pure white crystalline substance was derived from the vapour that arose on roasting the bark and wood of the camphor tree. It is also used in Ayurveda Rasshashtra, which involves extracting the essence of herbs. Camphor was used for many more health benefits, even to increase sex drive in men. Above all, spiritual practices have also recognized the power of camphor from time immemorial. Camphor could work wonders, but the overuse of it could be fatal.

Camphor Enkindled

The aroma of camphor lingered in the air. It came from the terracotta lamp lit at the tiny Shiva temple on the corner of the road leading to the home that he had been frequenting for the last couple of months. Today was different for him, though, as he was going to see his baby. Right at the entrance of the courtesan's home, he could sense the excitement. They were celebrating the birth of a girl child . . . his child.

One of the women saw him entering the main courtyard, and from the terrace above congratulated him at a loud pitch, 'Badhai ho (congratulations) Mishraji, what a beautiful baby . . . hoor ki pari (a fairy from paradise)! She is like a glittering star . . . no . . . no, her face is like a full moon . . . or like a sheer drop of dew . . .'

Before she could search for another expression, Mishraji smilingly interrupted, 'Will you go on and on or let me in to see my baby?' But she was not going to let him in so quickly, 'No Maharaj, how can I ever allow any man to see her, even if you are her father, without any incentive? You have to first reward me,' and with a mischievous smile, she stretched her arms to cover the narrow steps leading to the room.

Familiar with the customs of the courtesan's world, he took out one of the pouches of gold coins he had come prepared with and handed it to her. She looked inside and smiled at him before she led him up. Filled with many emotions, Mishraji, a Brahmin, entered the chamber of the new mother resting in bed with her eyes closed. His child was lying next to her. It was a different feeling for him, who till then had been the father only of sons. He was overawed by the beauty of the baby, in wonderment that he and his beautiful love had a baby like that . . . a fairy tale princess fit to be in a palace.

Her marble-like, tiny feet would get blisters walking on a velvet carpet, mused the awestruck father. He put his hand on the head of the baby's mother. She opened her eyes, but they bore a blank look. She, on the other hand, had been dreaming of the future of her baby. She knew the reality of her world, and the fear it gave rise to, worrying her enough to stop admiring the beauty of her baby girl. She had so much longed to have a boy instead!

Mishraji thought she was too tired, so he picked up his baby instead for the first time. He kept looking at her, and suddenly the baby opened her eyes. As he saw her sparkling almond-shaped eyes, Pandit Shiv Narain Mishra spontaneously sighed, '"Raskapoor"! Yes Chaand, my love, I am naming this beautiful baby of ours Raskapoor!' A moment that would carve her destiny.

It seemed as though her learned father had forgotten the 'Naamkaran Samskar', the elaborate Hindu ceremony they should have had to name their baby. When a baby was born, it was he who professed the importance of 'Solah Samskar' (the sixteen rituals from birth to death). It was he who drew the astronomical charts for new-born babies and sought the blessings of the family deity. It was only after the horoscope had been drawn, calculations made based on the positions of the planets at the time of the birth, that the first letter considered auspicious was decided.

In the end, a 'hawan' was performed to seek the blessings of the deities and the ancestors to protect the baby. The child was then placed in the lap of the father, who would whisper the selected name in its ear. It was he who saw to it that the sanctity of this ceremony was kept alive, and the parents understood that the name not only gave a unique identity to the child but also impacted its whole life. Today, however, the keeper of these rituals seemed oblivious and instead whispered the chosen name to the baby, 'Raskapoor . . . aha, my Raskapoor . . . my little girl.'

Little did he realize that he was giving his little girl a name, the 'essence of camphor', that would go on to create history, one that would be remembered for a journey from the courtesan's home to the palace and inspire intrigue in the zenani deorhi and finally be exiled in a fort overlooking Sawai Jai Singh's dream city Jaipur.

Zenani Deorhi: The Hidden World of Women

Like all royal abodes, this one too had an area away from the public eye where the women of the family lived. This design had trickled down from the influence of the Moghuls to the Kachchwaha rulers of Amber. While the Moghul rulers had used the term harem for the ladies' section, a term that had its origins in Arabic terms 'haram' and 'harim', which denoted a prohibited place with restricted entry, the rulers of Amber called the women's apartments the zenani deorhi. Another commonly used name for that area was 'zenana'. It was also known as the 'rawala'.

The majestic Amber Palace was situated amidst the Aravalli range in north-western India on the 'Hill of Eagles'. Maharaja Man Singh I of Amber, who had been declared one of the Nine Gems or Navaratna by the Moghul Emperor Akbar, built a zenani deorhi in the fourth courtyard of his palace. Man Singh's mahal had a rawala or an apartment for each of his twelve or fifteen wives. His concubines too lived within the compound. In the centre stood the barahdari, or the twelve-arched pleasure pavilion. The Maharaja was the only man permitted to come into that area, which was restricted to the women of the palace. To guard that section, the recruits could only be taken from the community of eunuchs. They also served as first-hand informers of politics and intrigue among the women, playing a significant role in state affairs.

The zenani deorhi was a world on its own, with constant struggles of power among the wives. It was duly fuelled by the fleet of Paswan and Padadayat, the women who enjoyed proximity to the Maharaja as short-term companions. There was also the entourage of maids, serving as spies gathering information from rival groups. Col. James Tod was so taken aback with the proceedings of this secret world that he even went ahead to observe, 'it is within the rawala that intrigue is enthroned.' On the other hand, in times of peace, many of the women rejoiced in poetry, dance, music and even drama; and during the wars, they proved to be accomplished tacticians.

Sawai Jai Singh II was born and raised in such environs. When he decided to shift his capital from Amber to Jaipur, he held a chain of discussions and meetings on the plan of the new abode with the chief architect Diwan Vidyadhar Chakravarti. He gave a clear-cut direction, 'Diwanji, while adhering to the blueprint made by you in which seven squares will provide space for the people of my state and the two squares in the centre will have the main palace, you need to pay special attention to one area.' Vidyadhar was a bit lost and pondered the plan rolled out in front of them. Appreciating the dilemma of his brilliant architect, the Maharaja smilingly told him, 'Do not look so worried. All I want is to handle the section earmarked for women very carefully. Adequate space and privacy are an absolute must for all the maharanis. There has to be enough space even for the other ladies, the concubines, and the maidens.' Pausing for a few seconds with a mischievous look in his eyes the Maharaja remarked, 'You do know how they all play their games. Their life revolves around power play.' Vidyadhar was amused to see the insights of his master who came to the throne as an eleven-year-old boy, and left Emperor Aurangzeb stunned with his smart response! No wonder he was granted the title of 'Sawai', thought Vidyadhar. The zenani deorhi in the Jai Niwas (now known as the City Palace) was thus well laid out next to the majestic Chandra Mahal.

Interestingly, the entrance to the ladies' chamber was always winding and angular so that the outside world could not get even a small glimpse of it. The entrance gate to the area would have a passage leading to the apartments placed in a row. Perhaps being almost one and a half times longer or 'dedhaa' than the other passages within the palaces, the term deorhi was added, and the area came to be known as zenani deorhi.

Sawai Jai Singh had twenty-seven queens. The hierarchy among the various wives was prescribed, but at times, the ruler himself could declare a favourite queen as Patrani, or Chief Queen. Life in those apartments was woven with the warp and weft of intrigues in a bid for supremacy. The main bone of contention was the gaddi or the throne whenever the issue of succession came up. Marriage was a critical instrument for forging alliances with the different princely states; but it created problems in the well-prescribed system of hierarchy and succession duly backed by the state that the princess came from. Even farsighted Jai Singh II could not escape from that when he married the princess of Mewar, the state wielding more power and influence. In the hierarchy of queens, the Mewar State insisted that its daughter be the Chief Queen, not the queens from his earlier marriages; and if she had a son, he would be the successor and not his eldest brother.

Somehow not much information is available on the zenani deorhi of Sawai Jai Singh. The only fact mentioned about it is connected to the Chief Guard Panna Miyan, who hailed from the community of eunuchs. His community, too, played its games to gain more mileage as well as subjected the women who fell out of Maharaja's favour to cruel treatment. Panna Miyan was brought to Amber by Jai Singh's father.

After the demise of Sawai Jai Singh, it was Sawai Pratap Singh who added to the grandeur and glory of the Kachchwahas. He built the beautiful complex of Hawa Mahal and the temple of Lord Brijnidhi. A romantic at heart, he loved music, dance and poetry. He himself wrote poetry under the pen name Brijnidhi and extended extensive patronage to the performing arts. During his regime, the department of Gunijan Khana, which nurtured virtuous artists, became particularly famous among the other princely states.

Drifting sounds of music and tinkling bells would serenade the Maharaja throughout the day as artists honed their skills in the green pavilion or Hara Bangla located in the palace arena just above the Pritam Niwas Chowk, the courtyard. Extravagant sessions filled with music and dance, or mehfils as they were called, would go on all night, at times in a barahdari, a pavilion open on all four sides each with three arches or the embellished personal apartments.

Noormahal was a performer at one such session. Her talent and beauty held Pandit Shiv Narain spellbound. It was Sharad Purnima, and the mehfil was held under the autumn full moon on the open terrace with two barahdaris. After a harsh summer, the air felt fresh as the winter cold, and the dancers were inspired to romance their esteemed audience with their sensuous but elegant dance. As the tradition of the palaces directed, everyone was bedecked in the day's dress code of motia gulabi, or pearl pink. All the dancers were given a special pink odhani, or veil. Noormahal remembered the first time her eyes spotted the handsome Brahmin. His gaze was fixed on her. He smiled, and their eyes didn't leave each other. He was smitten by her beauty and grace.

Middle-aged Mishraji could not help but initiate the first move. Her paramour then became a daily visitor at her place, and she never looked again at any other man. Their love blossomed, and soon she gave him the news.

'Mishraji, you are going to be a father again!' His happiness knew no bounds. But Noormahal worried—what if she had a daughter? Months later, when the nurse delivered the baby and her friends excitedly told her, 'We have a new addition!', her world shook, because she knew she had given birth to a baby girl.

Noormahal had heard all the tales of the walled city of Sawai Jai Singh. So much deceit, torture, and even murder, lurked behind the walls. After the demise of Sawai Jai Singh, the issue of who would be his successor had shaken the state, for the Sisodia Queen had married him on the condition that her son would succeed to the throne. However, she could not stop her stepson Ishwari Singh, who was older than her son, from laying claim to the throne. Several attempts were made to dethrone Ishwari Singh in his absence and replace him with her son to the throne.

Ishwari Singh could not trust anyone in the zenani deorhi or his administration. Finally, the poor man ended up with a barber and an elephant keeper as his confidants. Those frustrating circumstances led to him finding solace only in the ladies' quarters. Unable to deal with the mounting pressures, one night, he ended his life by ingesting poison. His three wives and even his favourite concubine died along with him.

This horrifying episode had been recounted often by the tawaifs Noormahal lived with, particularly each time a new person joined them, to remind them about the fidelity expected of them. Noormahal couldn't get this story out of her head, and she stared at her beautiful baby girl with glassy eyes.

Kaanch Mahal: The Glass Palace

When Noormahal discovered she was expecting, she was in the employment of the lady who operated the *kotha* where the dancing girls entertained their clients. How Noormahal ended up there and where she came from remained a mystery even for her lover as she had vowed never to talk about her past. She had accepted her fate and focused only on charming her elite clients. Chandramukhi, the owner of the kotha, took full advantage of her dedication, driving up the offer from her clients. One evening, she was shocked to see Pandit Shiv Narain coming through the chilman, the glass bead curtain. She rose from her velvet seat, throwing the pipe of the hookah she was smoking to one side, and asked the first-time visitor, 'Brahmin Maharaj, how come you are at this poor lady's establishment? The sun indeed rose from the west today!' She continued in her inimitable manner—taunting yet welcoming, 'Of course, I do know that you are a regular at some other venues like this one.'

Mishraji did not take even a minute to answer her question. He said, 'For my love!' She was even more surprised. 'Your love? You have not come here before.' Mishraji mischievously responded, 'But I saw her and know she is the new girl.' She laughed, 'Oh! you mean, Noormahal!' Mishraji nodded with a smile and handed over a big bag to her. 'Take this and advise all her suitors to keep away from her. Count the gold coins and look at the precious jewellery, which all of them put together cannot offer,' he said. 'It was the night of Sharad Purnima when our eyes met and our souls connected. If you do not believe me, ask her.'

She was left speechless. After a few minutes of silence, she summoned Noormahal and told her to usher in Mishraji. She then started counting her money, admiring the guts of the Brahmin in manoeuvring his way through the bylanes to her place. As she counted her coins, she soon put him out of her mind and was glad that the goddess of wealth, Laxmi, had blessed her.

In the first meeting, Mishraji tenderly held Noormahal's soft hand and asked her about her mother. She steeled her beautiful, young face before responding, 'You are a Brahmin and must be reading Ramayana every day. Do you remember the Laxman Rekha that Sita was told not to cross? But Sita unwittingly crossed it and then suffered severe consequences. So, I must tell you that I too have a Laxman Rekha between my past and my present. When you decided to come here to express your love, did you know who my mother was? So please do not cross the line set by me, or else we will not meet again'. Mishraji was taken aback, but he saw the firm resolve in her face. He never asked her again about her past. But he was still smitten by her, and it marked the beginning of the day her life changed. He smiled at her and said, 'Your name is too long. I will give you a new name.' Noormahal smiled.

'A new name! How many times will I get a new name? It is just a few months ago that I got this name when I entered this place,' she said.

'Don't feel that only courtesans' names are changed. Empress Noor Jehan got her name from Emperor Jahangir, replacing her maiden name Mehr-un-Nisaa. You are my empress. This will be the last time, my love . . . my moon . . . my *Chaand*. Yes, Chaand will be your name for now and forever. When I saw you the first time, I wondered if the moon had descended. I could not stop looking at you. You had surpassed even the beauty of the full autumn moon. My name is Shiva, and you know Shiva wears a crescent moon on his head to protect the moon. From this moment you will be protected by me, Chaand, my love.'

On his way out, he happily told Chandramukhi, 'Now you have a Chaand in your house. There is no Noormahal,' he smiled and walked away. Noormahal turned into Chaand from that day, longing for her new name to give her a new lease of life, away from the kotha.

Over the next few months, Mishraji visited every night, and the owner of the kotha got richer by the day. When Chaand discovered that she was pregnant, she was very concerned about how the kotha would affect her baby. She wanted her child to be born away from that house, to breathe fresh air, and start a new life. One evening she asked Mishraji if he could give her whatever she wished for. He could not believe his ears, for, in all these days, Chaand had never asked for anything, unlike the other girls he had met. She would even dissuade him every time he tried to bring her something. On his insistence, she would honour the presents, but in return, she would smile and say, 'Panditji, all I need is your love and protection, not these expensive gifts.'

So, he didn't hesitate for even a moment when he heard her request and immediately promised her whatever she would ask for. He wondered what it would be, as being a tawaif, she would not ask him to marry her. She had told him this on the day of their first meeting.

She took a deep breath. 'I want our child to be born away from here; where there is a new dawn with fresh air free of the culture of tawaifs. The new home will be the beginning of the new life we are going to bring on this earth,' she said, tentatively waiting for her lover's response. Admiring her sensitivity, he smiled at her and said he would make sure their baby didn't grow up in the kotha.

The house was carefully selected and in the vicinity of temples so that his frequent visits there would not raise any suspicion. Pandit Shiv Narain left no stone unturned to get the place ready within months of the day she asked him. It was not an ordinary home, but a lavish haveli embellished with exquisite paintings, glasswork, well laid out courtyards and balconies. The most lavish part of her new abode was the apartment built over the arched gate, standing tall right in the centre of the road.

Once it was all set to usher in his love, he told Chaand, 'Tomorrow will be a new dawn for you.' Chaand had not reminded him even once after the day she had asked him for her new abode. But she knew that it would be there soon, so she was all ready to leave the kotha. When she saw her new residence, she was wonderstruck. She could not believe her eyes, and her first remark was, 'This looks like someone's palace!' Mishraji said, 'The palace is yours, and that is why it is named "Kaanch Mahal".'

'Look at my fate! I became a tawaif, and now I stand in this palace fit for a queen,' thought Chaand, staring around in wonderment.

'Come in, my dear,' her lover held her hand, leading her through the main entrance, startling Chaand out of her thoughts. Mishraji smilingly remarked, 'Often I notice you are not with me even when you are here . . . you seem to be lost in your world.' How could she tell this generous man that the future of their baby scared her? She had never wanted to have a baby and had prayed to god to save any child coming into her world, the hopeless world filled with gloom and despair. However, Allah had a different plan she realized when her pregnancy was confirmed by the local midwife employed to check the health of the dancing girls every day. The check-up was done to prepare the list of names of the girls who would entertain the clients. Those not on the list were confined to the inner yard till after they had given birth and recovered.

Chaand was initially sad about the news of her baby, but how could she not but accept the decision of Allah, her divine master? Her intense faith gave her one relief that she was not confined to the backyard and continued to spend the nights with Mishraji in that beautiful room. Mishraji paid a hefty amount to ensure that arrangement. She was grateful to him for bestowing the abode upon her where one could only hear echoing chants and the divine bells from temples on either side. Once she had had time to admire everything, she began praying to the almighty that no shadow of the culture of the tawaifs would reach her majestic abode.

Life in the glass palace was filled with a fleet of servers to make the mother-to-be totally comfortable. This surprised her group of friends, all tawaifs. Shabnam, Gulbadan, Heera, Hasina and the ever-conniving Nargis came to visit her at the first dawn. Chaand was surprised to hear their loud voices. 'Ya Allah, they are not sleeping here after their exhausting night duty,' she mumbled, moving away from the arms of her lover. Mishraji resented their visit and wondered if Chaand could ever be taken away from the world of tawaifs she had joined.

The first dawn was not the only day that her friends came over. Shabnam and Gulbadan convinced her that during the daytime when her lover was gone, she would need company in her condition. She could not be left alone to brood. For the sake of her child, she had to be happy. They offered to move in with her, assuring her that they would go back to the kotha for night duty. They had done much for her, stood with her in moments of crisis, and were her confidants, and so convinced, Chaand shed all her apprehensions. They moved in quickly, without giving her the time to give the idea a second thought. During the daytime, other inmates also started coming in to rejoice in the setting and comfort of the house. How would the priests of the temple around and neighbours not know that Kaanch Mahal was the den of the dancing girls? They could not raise their voices, knowing that the respected Brahmin, Pandit Shiv Narain, came there nearly every night. Besides, many of the tawaifs were ardent followers of Hindu gods, like Shiva and Krishna, and donated money and jewels to the temples.

Once the group of friends moved in, their accompanists were not far behind. Gradually, sitar player Fateh Mohamad, sarangi player Mohmmad Ali, singer Rahim Khan and tabla player Aladdin came almost every day. For the girls, Chaand's home was an ideal escape; to have a conversation away from the restrictions of the kotha, where even riyaz to rehearse and polish their singing and dancing skills were held under strict vigilance. This was because Chandramukhi knew that her girls could slip up even for a small sum offered by the shrewd accompanists. The friends talked about everything, from the intrigues of the palace to the pursuits of Maharaja Sawai Pratap Singh. As time flew by, their visits became longer, for they began to rehearse there. Chaand knew the instinct of musicians and dancers to burst into improvisations so did not object to their prolonged sessions. At times, she even enjoyed lying in bed listening to the songs of those gifted singers and sent requests to them to sing musical compositions like a thumri or a tarana. On the other hand, Mishraji was getting anxious to see the lingering presence of the tawaifs in the haveli, and wondered how she would be able to keep her child away from the life that she had left behind.

Dhruv Tara: The Pole Star

Kaanch Mahal was filled with the excitement of having a new life within it. The baby looked divine and the glass palace beamed with a new ray of hope. Pandit Shiv Narain made it a ritual to chant the Vedic hymns every evening as he rocked her to sleep in his arms. Chaand often asked him, 'Panditji, are you going to make this baby a priest?' He brushed that question aside with a smile, for the ambitious and shrewd Mishraji had no such pious intentions. Instead, he was already charting the route to be the most influential man in the royal court someday. The day he saw her face, that desire took over him, which he knew only his daughter could help him realize—if all went the way he imagined. Mishraji wanted to groom her into a highly cultured girl who would not only be extraordinarily beautiful but also have a magnetic personality. The priest in him knew how significant the sound of the holy chants was, right from the birth of a child.

After putting the baby to sleep, they spent the night together. Days passed by. The baby seemed to be growing fast, listening to the chants and mythical stories of her learned father on the one hand, and on the other, the music and the dancing bells of her mother's friends, whom she called mausis (maternal aunts). Her mother never allowed her to go to the area where they sang and danced. They came to see their adorable doll every day, not forgetting to buy beautiful gifts for her. Nargis Mausi, however, was the one who got her the most expensive gifts. Chaand worried. She did not want Nargis to lure her princess, for she knew how Nargis had manoeuvred to reach Gunijan Khana at such a young age.

The little girl was the star attraction of the glass palace. Her father rightly called her, 'Tara . . . my Dhruv Tara,' as he lifted her in his arms. Mishraji was farsighted enough to get the little girl to address him with a word that did not denote her relationship with him. Opting out of Abba and Pitaji, he chose to be addressed as 'Guruji' or teacher. It took a while for her to pronounce it correctly as Mishraji went on teaching her, and she babbled Guluji . . . Guluji . . . Guluji! Her teacher pursued and succeeded and was thrilled the day she was able to utter 'Guruji' clearly. When she was about five, she would eagerly await her father's arrival at sunset, as she longed to sit in his lap and hear his fascinating stories. One evening she asked him, 'You tell me stories of the sun and the moon but why not of a star? Today, you tell me a story of a star.' Well-versed with the Puranas, the religious Hindu texts, he decided to narrate the story of Dhruv Tara from Vishnu Purana. He smilingly told her that he was going to tell the story of the boy Dhruv who became that bright star Dhruv Tara, pointing his index finger towards the sky.

'But if Dhruv Tara was a boy, then why do you call me by that name? I am a girl, not a boy,' was her quick response. Mishraji was stunned but also proud of her intelligence. He mumbled, 'After all, she has the genes of a Brahmin like me.' He responded, 'See, Dhruv Tara is the brightest star of the sky, and you are bright like it, so I call you my Dhruv Tara.' She was thrilled to hear that and then wanted to listen to the story. He said, 'There was a king named Uttanapada who had two queens, Suniti and Suruchi. Suniti was a tribal girl whom the king met when he went for a hunt. She was stunning, and the king could not help falling in love with her. Soon, he decided to marry her, and together they had a son whom they named Dhruv. The second wife Suruchi, however, was from a wealthy family. King Uttanapada and Suruchi too had a son whose name was Uttam. Suruchi wanted her son to become the king and not his elder brother Dhruv.'

Intently listening to the story, Raskapoor interrupted, 'Guruji, you say I am very pretty, and Ammi says it too. Will I get to become a queen and live in a palace?' He was intrigued by that question, but told her to first listen to the story and then tell him what she would like to be. Continuing the story, he told her how the pretty lady got the king to banish Suniti and Dhruv to the forest. 'Living in the forest, Dhruv became a devotee of Lord Vishnu. When Dhruv grew a little older, he asked about his father and discovered that he was a king. Dhruv then longed to meet his father. His mother, who was apprehensive of Suruchi's reaction, tried to dissuade him each time he expressed his desire. Finally, one day, Dhruv managed to get his mother to concede and allow him to go to the palace. Inside the palace, as he saw the stepbrother sitting in his father's lap, he was overcome with a longing to sit there too. He yearned for the love of his father. Unable to resist his desire, he walked straight towards the king's seat. He told his father who he was and of his desire to sit in his lap. Upon hearing this, the queen was outraged. She intervened and insultingly asked him to return to the forest where he belonged. Humiliated, Dhruv went back to his mother. Feeling the agony of her son, the mother asked him to worship god, who would one day grant him justice. Dhruv decided to find his God Vishnu. He went deep into the forest and meditated to reach out to the almighty. Finally, Vishnu appeared before Dhruv and told him that he would not just get his rightful place in the palace but after his death would become a permanent star in the sky, shining bright forever,' ended her father.

Raskapoor clapped her hands when her father finished the story and told him, 'Now I know why I am your Dhruv Tara!' That night she fell asleep dreaming of the stars.

Chaand wanted her to shine with dignity happily married to a man from a respectable background; Nargis wanted her to shine and dazzle royalty when she grew up. She was in no hurry as the prince, the son of Sawai Pratap, was just a few years older than the little girl. Her father Pandit Shiv Narain too started dreaming of his political career, confident of the spell she would cast on the growing prince. Oblivious of all those dreams, Raskapoor, inspired by the story of Dhruv Tara, became an ardent devotee, but of Lord Shiva instead of Vishnu.

The first time she had asked why her father was called Shiv, she became drawn to Shiva. She often insisted on visiting the temple of Shiva just around the corner, but her superstitious mother wouldn't let her. Her repeated requests were turned down on the ground that only married Hindu women went to the temple of Gupteshwar Mahadev. Intrigued, Raskapoor could not resist her desire as Shiva appeared in her dreams in a faceless form from time to time. One day, determined to ask her father why she could not visit a temple where he went regularly, she posed the question to him as soon as he walked in. Mishraji told Chaand that, like many other ill-informed lay people, she too was perceiving 'Linga worship' as touching the male organ, whereas the altar represented the creation of the Universe or Srishti. Seeking a piece of charcoal from his daughter, the father started sketching the Shiva Linga to explain the symbolism of phallic worship to both his daughter as well as her mother. Chaand did not want her daughter to see the sketch and asked her to go inside to see the new dress she had just put on her bed.

Mishraji very firmly asked both the mother and daughter to stand right there as he began. 'The sanctum sanctorum, where the statues of the deities to be worshipped are placed, is called the 'Garbhagriha', which means womb chamber. The lower part of the pedestal represents the creator of the Universe, Lord Brahma, and the portion a little above that represents the preserver of the Universe or Lord Vishnu. The base on which the Linga is placed represents the Mother Goddess, while the Linga represents the Destroyer or Lord Shiva. The temple denotes the cycle of birth and death,' Pandit Shiv Narain finished with a smile.

'So, now tell my mother to take me there,' pleaded their daughter. 'Tomorrow is the third Monday of Sawan, the day and month in which Shiva's blessings are especially invoked, and your mother is going to take you there,' Mishraji told Raskapoor as he looked at Chaand firmly. After all, he was the father, and Chaand knew nothing could stop her daughter from visiting the

Shiva temple. While her excited daughter fell asleep quickly, so she could dream of Shiva to tell him that she was going to see him the following morning, the mother could not sleep a wink with the world of courtesans haunting her.

They were delayed! Chaand wanted to follow the directive given by Mishraji to take their daughter to the temple but only before sunrise. Filled with many apprehensions, she did not wish her precious treasure to be seen by anyone. Accordingly, she decided to go there just as the priest arrived when hardly anyone else would be there. But when she heard the lightning and thunder with which the heavy monsoon rain hit, she thanked her Allah, imagining that the temple visit could be deferred at least that morning. Restless Raskapoor brought out two umbrellas, but the mother showed her the heavy rainfall from the window. Raskapoor chose to plead to Shiva instead. She went on chanting 'Om Namah Shivay', praying to the deity to stop the rain. After three hours of torrential downpour, suddenly the rain stopped and the sun came out. Perhaps Shiva had heard her prayer. She called out to her mother, 'Now we can go!' Chaand was forced to walk her to the temple. Despite the rain, there were a lot of devotees waiting for their turn to make an offering. A few of them had a glimpse of the little Raskapoor walking towards the temple holding the hand of a lady in a veil. Nothing seemed to go right for Chaand that day— some of the devotees had already seen them come out of Kaanch Mahal. They knew then and there—the beautiful little girl was the courtesan's daughter.

Unaware of the stir she was causing and brimming with devotional excitement, Raskapoor seemed to be in a great hurry to see her lord. While her mother stood by her, she made the offering as the priest directed. He was amazed to hear her clear diction while she chanted the Sanskrit shloka:

Om Triyambakam yajamahe sugandhim pushtivardhanam,
Urvarukmiva bandhanan mrityur-mokshiya maamritat.
(We worship the three-eyed One, who is fragrant and who nourishes all. Like the fruit falls off from the bondage of the stem, may we be liberated from death, from mortality.)

As she was leaving, the impressed priest asked her, 'My child who taught you this?'

'My father, Pandit Shiv Narain Mishra,' replied the innocent Raskapoor. Her mother quickly grabbed her hand to rush back home. 'Pranam Pandit Ji.' The thrilled Raskapoor did not forget to take leave of the priest before going out. The priest was moved to see the devotion of a courtesan's daughter, but he recognized her father, who was well known for his profound knowledge of all Hindu scriptures, from the Vedas to Puranas.

'Pranam beti,' he said, returning her respectful greetings and asking her to come again.

Coming out of the temple, Ras was thrilled with the darshan or glimpse of her Lord Shiva. 'It was so beautiful, Ammi. The priest was so happy to hear my mantra. He has asked me to come again,' said the little girl, trying to strike up a conversation with her mother. She could sense by her mother's tight grip on her hand that she was angry with her. Ras, however, continued, 'Ammi, please bring me here again next Monday.'

'Once was good enough. You talk too much,' Chaand replied firmly.

Raskapoor still did not give up, 'He even called me beti—daughter—just as you do. We will come again,' she reasserted. Her big sparkling eyes dazzled as she spotted a rainbow in the sky and burst into excitement, 'Oh! The same *Indra Dhanush* that Shiva showed me in my dreams! He also showed me Lord Indra, who was riding a white elephant with many trunks. You know Ammi, he even asked Lord Indra to give me an elephant ride.' She expressed her strong desire to ride an elephant one day. Her dreams worried Chaand. They returned to the glass palace, but it was not the same Raskapoor who had gone out. She felt different. She wanted to go out every day now, at least to the Shiva temple and the Krishna temple. Chaand could read the thoughts of her daughter, who was sensitive like her, and firm like her father.

The next day, Nargis Mausi came with glittery glass bangles, a pot of henna paste, a box of the special sweet ghewar and the beautiful lahria, which is worn for festivals, for the following day was the celebration of Teej. Raskapoor's excitement knew no bounds seeing so many gifts. She sat down with Nargis Mausi, who decorated her soft palms with henna patterns. Chaand knew her daughter's day was made but also realized that it would be hard to restrict her from visiting the temples anymore. She went inside her apartment, leaving her daughter and Nargis in the courtyard. Raskapoor was delighted to share the story of her first temple visit with Nargis who was wonderstruck to see the little girl's devotion towards Shiva and decided to narrate the story of the Teej festival, which celebrates the marriage of Shiva and Parvati.

'Can I also marry Shiva?' asked the innocent girl. Like her mother and the priest, Nargis too was reminded of Mahananda. She thought about that intriguing question for a few minutes and then replied, 'Yes, maybe you can, like Mahananda.'

'Really? What did she do to marry Shiva? What can I do to become Mahananda and marry Shiva? Mother wants me to marry a nice man.' Raskapoor showered Nargis with questions. Amused with the girl's desire, her mother's plans, and then her own plan to groom her for the palace, Nargis told her first to learn music and dance. Farsighted Nargis did not let the opportunity slip away to inform her that before meeting Shiva, Mahananda was a well-known dancer in the royal court of Kashmir. Deviously, the seed of the idea was implanted in the innocent devotee's mind to commit herself to blossom into a dancer and singer par excellence.

Lost in a World of Dreams

Chaand saw a significant change in her daughter with each passing day. Often, she saw the little girl lost in her own world. Her visits to the Shiva temple became more frequent, and she chanted at sunrise and sunset. Driven by a divine frenzy, she even visited the Krishna temple nearby. Chaand tried to dissuade her and often conveyed her displeasure to her father, but to no avail. 'How can you stop her from seeking the supreme power? She is a Brahmin's daughter, don't forget that,' would be Mishraji's reply. Raskapoor knew when she wanted her special wishes to have her mother's approval, she first had to ask her father. She even managed to get a parrot and a rooster, as Nargis Mausi had told her that Mahananda used to have them as pets and taught them to chant 'Om Namah Shivay'.

Nurturing her dream to be Mahananda so that she could marry Shiva soon, Raskapoor took permission to learn music and dance. Mishraji not only granted the wish but approved Raskapoor's idea to have Nargis Mausi as her music and dance teacher. She believed that Nargis Mausi alone could make her Mahananda, the woman she wanted to emulate, even though she did not know the most significant fact about her. When Raskapoor's first musical notes echoed in the courtyard, and she danced to the beautiful song of Nargis, Chaand gravitated to the window of her room to witness that magical session through the thin curtain. She was amazed to see her daughter's phenomenal talent but was equally saddened to realize that her daughter had inherited her genes. She wanted to stop her then and there, but she could feel the reins slipping away from her hands. She wished her daughter to remain a small girl, but time seemed to be ticking away, and Ras was growing by the day. Her figure was changing, and even at eleven, she appeared to be well into her teens. Nargis, on the other hand, became increasingly convinced that she was a jewel to be showcased in the royal palace.

One day when Ras entered the temple, her gaze met that of a young boy, a few years her senior, and they both smiled spontaneously. She was captivated both by his chanting and his looks. He, too, could not help noticing the beautiful girl, and it created a ripple in his heart. Confident Raskapoor asked him his name. She laughed as he told her his name was Rudra Narain Mishra. 'Like Rudraksha, the bead of Shiva that I put around my parrot and the rooster.' She continued to laugh.

'You must be a silly girl to tie a Rudraksha bead on your parrot and rooster,' replied the sober and intelligent boy.

'Why do you call me silly? Even the dancer Mahananda did that and married Lord Shiva. Everyone at home tells me I am a brilliant singer and dancer. Wait and watch for the day when Shiva will come to my doorstep to marry me,' she replied with a firmness that surprised Rudra.

'Who told you that? Do you even know who Mahananda was?' he asked.

'Yes, I do. She was the wife of Shiva,' she replied, hurrying out of the temple as her mother was calling her to go back home. Inside, the priest wondered about the future of that innocent and beautiful devotee of Shiva. Pretending to be in deep meditation, he had heard every word of the conversation between Raskapoor and Rudra.

'Why were you taking so long?' questioned her visibly upset mother. Raskapoor told her mother about the wonderful boy she had met, describing him as being a devotee of Shiva who was very friendly and good-looking too. Chaand's heart missed a beat or two to see the first seeds of interest in a boy sown in her daughter's mind. Taking charge of her emotions, she asked her daughter about his age and name.

'Rudra Narain Mishra. He is a few years older than me, Ammi. Do you think he can be my friend?' The boy's name inspired Chaand to thank Lord Shiva. As a Brahmin and a devotee of Shiva, that boy could perhaps bring a ray of hope into their glass palace and free her daughter from the destiny of being a courtesan.

Convinced, Chaand readily told her, 'Yes, he can be your friend. You can even invite him to our home. Maybe you can chant together along with your parrot and the rooster.' For the first time, they laughed together after visiting the temple. They both started dreaming of the change that a boy would bring in their lives.

Rudra was looking forward to meeting that beautiful girl ever since their first meeting. While he pondered about her words on the marriage between Mahananda and Lord Shiva, she was haunted by his question of whether she even knew who Mahananda was. She became increasingly curious to know more about Mahananda. She decided to ask Nargis Mausi a critical question: if by being a good dancer and singer Mahananda could get married to Lord Shiva, then why was she, Nargis, not married, despite being the best dancer and singer of Jaipur? The very next day after the rehearsal, she posed that question leaving Nargis shocked. She did not know how to answer her, and without realizing it, she just said, 'Because like your mother, I am a tawaif, and tawaifs do not get married.'

A bit shocked and confused, Raskapoor wanted Nargis to tell her who a tawaif was and why could tawaifs not get married. Nargis knew that she had dropped a bombshell without even realizing the repercussions of the words she had uttered a short while ago. The expression and the questions left Nargis speechless, and after pondering for a few moments, she found the escape route as she made her way out. 'Look, Ras, since I do not have any more time right now, the best person to answer your questions will be your Ammi or Guruji.'

That day was devastating for Raskapoor. She had found out the well-kept secret about her parents not being married. What was upsetting her even more was that this revelation came to her from

an outsider and not her parents. Her soul was restless to find the
reason and answers to the questions Nargis Mausi did not answer.
She took refuge in praying to Lord Shiva to pull her mind out of
the turbulence and grant her peace. For the moment, she was able
to calm her mind down thinking both her mother and Nargis did
not worship Lord Shiva as she did, and like Mahananda, she only
had to continue to pray to her Lord. In those hours of prayers, she
realized that soon it was going to be her father's turn to answer
some difficult questions. How could a teacher not answer the
queries of his disciple who was his child and who he had told one
day to address as Guruji for he would be her teacher all his life, she
wondered? She made the decision of not asking her mother, who
would not only try and divert her attention as usual but forbid her
from asking her father the questions that would raise a storm.

Two days later, Rudra made his way to Kaanch Mahal after
completing *abhisheka*, an elaborate ritual, at the Shiva temple.
Raskapoor and her mother had invited him to their house. He
knew very well that he was entering the home of a courtesan; that
Raskapoor's mother had entertained clients before moving there,
and that after some years that house too started reverberating with
music and dance through the night. Chaand had been unable to
stop the lavish rooms of her house from being opened up for the
clients of her friends. They paid her, and she needed the money
as Mishraji no longer spent time with her, preferring to spend an
hour or two with his daughter and then leaving. Chaand knew his
next destination. She, of course, kept to herself despite some of
the clients sending requests for her well-known musical sessions,
giving their full assurance that they would not demand anything
beyond music. It did not matter to Rudra what impression his
entry would create. Unlike the clients of that home who came and
left manoeuvring in the darkness and never during the day, he had
come in broad daylight. Shiva did not differentiate between the
status of his devotees—after all, he had made his way to his ardent
devotee Mahananda, a prostitute—thought Rudra, a true devotee
of Lord Shiva.

Rudra's visit delighted everybody. Chaand asked him to come again any time before sunset. She did not want his young mind to be influenced by the elite of the society, and he knew that. Chaand let Rudra accompany Raskapoor to the temples. That day it was Janmashtami, the birthday of Lord Krishna. Raskapoor had already planned with her friend Rudra to set up a *jhanki*, the scene of Krishna's birth. On such festive occasions, clients had to join their family celebrations, and the courtesans' homes were left quiet and empty. So, when Raskapoor apprised her mother of their plans, she readily agreed. Both Chaand and Rudra joined her flight of imagination as Raskapoor told them she would become Radha, Krishna's love, and Rudra would become Krishna, and they would dance to celebrate the divine birthday.

The next day, when Nargis Mausi came, Raskapoor told her what a beautiful celebration they had at night when she and Rudra danced as Radha and Krishna. Nargis felt her plans would be waylaid unless she made Raskapoor experience the grandeur of the palace.

'Great, now I will take you to the palace on Sharad Poornima. I am singing on that full moon night,' said Nargis, laying the trap by reminding Ras of how Mahananda used to dance and sing in the palace before marrying Shiva. As planned, Raskapoor started dreaming of the palace that would bring Shiva to her doorstep and then how she would invite Rudra to come for their marriage!

Stepping into the Royal Arena

Raskapoor longed for the full moon of autumn, but she knew she would have to negotiate permission to go with her father. Her mother avoided any conversation about the palace whenever a reference was made to it. That evening, just as Pandit Shiv Narain entered, it started raining heavily. Realizing he would not be able to go to his next destination for at least a few hours, Chaand romanticized the idea of being in her lover's arms after a long gap. She loved the rains and enjoyed the lovelorn dance of the peacocks in the backyard from her balcony. All this wrapped Kaanch Mahal in romance and excitement. Chaand read those signals well. She sensed that this would be a night to remember for both of them.

She decided to pamper her lover and entered the kitchen to make hot *pakodis,* which he liked to have with his drinks whenever it rained. Raskapoor, like a tigress, was keeping an eye out. She wanted to catch her father alone and curled her arms, showering all her affection on him. The father was totally in the grip of his daughter's love. He knew she had some special mission, so moving her arms away, he tilted his head up, asking her to whisper what she wanted in his ear. Folding her palms around his ear, she asked him to keep an eye on her mother and whispered, 'Nargis Mausi wants to take me to the palace on Sharad Poornima. It will be so beautiful to see her perform before the Maharaja on the full moon night. Please tell mother and permit me to go.' Pandit Shiv Narain Mishra could not help but marvel at the cleverness of Nargis. She had pre-empted his plan of bringing his beautiful girl to the palace and realizing his political dreams.

He smiled and looked into the pleading eyes of his daughter in which he could see his future. He assured her, 'Don't worry, you will go.' Her evening was heavenly, but Chaand's was wrecked as sipping the saffron wine from the silver goblet, he put his arm around her to start the crucial conversation. He told her, 'I still remember that full moon night when I first saw you dancing at the party on the terrace of the palace. Our love, at first sight, gave us this extraordinary gift—Raskapoor, our daughter. We have to fulfil all her wishes.'

Chaand was alert, and putting his arm aside, asked him what was it that their daughter had asked for when she was in the kitchen. 'I can see she is becoming too smart for her age and bypasses me knowing that you would grant her anything. Mishraji please, I want our daughter to be happily married,' she said, taking her stance.

The shrewd operator Mishraji again put his arm around her, telling her that it was too early to worry about Raskapoor's marriage. He told her about the plan for the upcoming celebrations on the full moon night. It was going to be more lavish than ever before as the venue would be the beautiful courtyard of the newly built Hawa Mahal. That Nargis was going to perform there was news to her. She was shattered to hear that Nargis was the one who had invited her daughter.

She got up, but Mishraji made her sit down, 'Why do you worry? I am going to be there. I am her father, and I will keep an eye on her.' Chaand wanted Mishraji to leave immediately but also knew that she had no other option but to let Raskapoor go. After a very long time, he spent the whole night there as it rained till morning. After a couple of drinks, when her lover fell fast asleep, the sound of his snores pierced her heart. She thought scornfully—was that man sleeping so comfortably her daughter's father? How could any father let a vulnerable child step into the palace where fairy tales met tragic ends? She knew very well that although he might assure her that he would keep an eye on her daughter, at the end of the day the world would see Raskapoor as a tawaif's daughter. For Mishraji was never going to officially acknowledge her as his own. In the morning, they did not exchange any words, but coming out of the chamber as he glanced at his daughter chanting, he put his hand on her shoulder and silently communicated using sign language that her mother had been told and that she would get to the palace. Standing behind the thin window curtain, Chaand witnessed the scene and felt defeated as both the father and daughter exchanged smiles.

When one day Mishraji met Nargis on the steps of the glass palace, he complimented her. He said, 'You are one step ahead of me. Well planned, my dear. You are taking Raskapoor to the palace even before I could work out my plan.'

Nargis laughed and teased him, 'Don't I know the men who take pride in proving their manhood, but not in the result—the children? The fact is that when a daughter is born, they feel they have struck a gold mine! Not just the men Mishraji, even tawaifs like myself start seeing a girl like your daughter as a lucky charm. We have both chartered the same plan for her—'Jai Niwas'—the palace of the Maharaja of Jaipur.' Both burst out into a peal of echoing laughter that reached the ears of Chaand. A stream of tears rolled down her eyes, and all she could see was the blurred face of her fairy, who seemed to be flying away far into a distant horizon. The thought struck Chaand in her core and she lost consciousness, falling to the floor in a tragic heap.

From the courtyard, dangling bells echoed. 'Wake up, mother! Why are you sleeping again? This is no time to sleep. Open your eyes. See what father got for me.' Raskapoor dangled the anklets near her mother's ear. Chaand slowly opened her eyes to the loud sound, regaining her consciousness. As she gathered herself, she was shocked to see the pair of anklets right above her eyes. They were anklets just like hers! She had worn them the first time she had gone to the palace. Those were the anklets that Mishraji mentioned in their first meeting while stroking her feet with a smitten gaze. 'You know my sweetheart, I was first dazzled with those anklets when you were twirling abundantly. I saw your face only when you finished your hundred and one chakkars, and stopped to take the bow. All along, everyone admired your spinning movement while I was mesmerized by those anklets and your delicate movements before seeing your moonlike face.' At the time, Chaand could not help but admire his sharp eyes.

Was it that same sharp eye that had admired her newly born baby? Was it the same day that he decided he would present the anklets to her so she could walk into the royal arena and be a tawaif like her mother? These were the questions hammering at Chaand's head. If her child were not standing in front, she would have relieved the pain by hitting her head against the wall, but all she could do was silently gaze at the anklets in her daughter's hand.

'Why, mother, you don't like these anklets? He came at this time because he was on his way to the palace to perform the hawan for Ashtami Pooja after which, Brahmin girls of my age are worshipped like Durga Devi. He explained to me all about the nine-day-long festivities in honour of the deity. Then he gave me the anklets, for I am his little goddess this day. Father also told me these are just like the anklets that you were wearing when you danced in the palace, and he saw you. See, like Mahananda, you found your Shiva and married him the same way. No wonder his name is Shiva Narain. Mother, now I am sure I too will find my Shiva someday when I dance and sing in the palace. These anklets are for the full moon celebrations in the palace. Still, Father told me for the day of my first performance, he would make you gift me yours,' Raskapoor narrated the entire conversation with her father in breathless excitement. Chaand just gestured to her credulous daughter to leave, closing her eyes.

Chaand realized for the first time that day how her lover used intelligence and words to manoeuvre his plan without anyone being the wiser. He called Raskapoor Durga Devi for one day, knowing very well that a courtesan's child never inherited the father's status! She was struck by the thought of how he found the opportune moment to give the anklets just a week before the full moon. Hope only flickered when Rudra came over, and he and her daughter spent hours together chanting and sharing delightful conversations. He, too, was a Brahmin like Mishraji but not drawn by the sensual pleasures. Chaand could see a growing love for her daughter in his eyes. She thought if someone could foil the plan of Raskapoor's father, it would be that young boy and prayed to her Allah that it be so.

The day before the full moon night, Raskapoor asked her young friend, 'Have you ever been to the palace?' His answer surprised her—he did not even want to go to the palace. She asked him why, and he simply said, 'For me, the Shiva temple is my palace.'

She could not help but laugh aloud, 'That small temple is your palace?' She then told him that she was going to the Maharaja's palace the next evening for the big dance performance along with her Nargis Mausi. Older and wiser, Rudra realized where that first visit would land this extraordinarily beautiful girl with whom he was falling in love, and to whom he could not express that love, as she was not at the age to feel that emotion. She was an innocent bud but was getting close to the dawn to bloom like a fragrant flower. He was eagerly awaiting that day. He felt a strong desire to keep her away from the fatal attraction of the palace, telling her that those evenings were not meant for young girls like her. 'Nargis Mausi is going . . . my father is going,' she argued. A bit irritated, Rudra told her that her Nargis Mausi was a dancer while she was not, and she did not have to follow in her footsteps. 'I am only following the footsteps of Mahananda to find my Shiva to marry me,' insisted the resolute girl. He then offered to narrate the story of Mahananda, but she wanted to hear it only after the visit to the palace.

On the full moon night, as custom had it, Chaand was making kheer. It had to be put under the moonlight to receive the nectar that was believed to shower down from the rays of the autumnal full moon.

'How am I looking?' asked her daughter, entering the kitchen. She was dressed in a pale pink outfit embellished with silver sequins. Chaand was spellbound to see her and spontaneously responded, 'Poonam ka chaand . . . yes, indeed you look like the full moon today.' She looked at her daughter from head to toe, but as she saw those anklets on her delicate feet, she felt her child was trapped! She turned her face back to the fire, pretending to cook. Excited, Raskapoor ran out, and as Chaand heard her anklets jingling down the steps, she could think of nothing but Jai Niwas.

A Walled City within the Walled City

The first time Chaand went to Jai Niwas, the City Palace had felt like an imposing walled city. Gate after gate had opened to lead their group to the arena of the performance. Walking there, she was reminded of the stories that echoed beyond those walls. That evening when her daughter was within those same walls, those stories kept coming back to Chaand, and she was lost in the maze of memories.

Dreaming of peace and prosperity for many generations, Jai Singh moved to the well laid out palace of his city Jai Nagar, as Jaipur was initially named. It later became known as Sawai Jaipur. But after Jai Singh's demise, peace eluded the palace. Chaand wondered why, if the astronomer prince drew the horoscope of the city, was he not able to predict the palace intrigues and remedy the dire consequences that followed? The fate of the town was ordained only by succession disputes, untimely or unfortunate deaths of the rightful inheritors, political marriage alliances and above all, the defaulting and ambitious vassals who were from the Maharaja's clan.

Chaand seemed to be having an endless, silent conversation with the full moon as she had not slept a wink awaiting her daughter's return, who had never been up that late. Her mind wandered from the mehfil to the moon. The full moon of autumn possessed all its sixteen traits according to her lover, when he explained to her the significance of the position of the planets and their relationships to the constellations in Hindu astrology. She had laughed to hear that the sky was divided into twenty-seven sections as the separate dwelling places for the twenty-seven wives of the moon, which waned and waxed on his visit to each of them as a punishment for extending all his love to only one wife, Rohini.

Recalling all those tales, she wanted to pose many questions to the moon: was the sky your zenani deorhi? Why did you rape Tara, the wife of Brihaspati or Jupiter? Was it love or revenge? Why did Daksha plead with you to marry all his twenty-seven daughters whom you had raped? How could marriage condone the act of rape? Why was sexual indulgence on earth affected by your movement and the constellations so far away in the sky? Moon seemed to smile and come closer to her to respond, but a creaking sound interrupted them. She emerged from her deep slumber as the main gate of the glass palace opened. Trembling with her fears, she ran down to see if her daughter had returned.

She was surprised to see Pandit Shiv Narain Mishra carrying his daughter—who was rather tall for her age—and climbing the steps of the house. She was almost on the threshold of becoming a young lady. Putting his left-hand index finger on his lips, he conveyed to Chaand to be quiet. He then laid his daughter in her bed, covering her with a light quilt, and then made his way to Chaand's room. She could not but admire the fatherly instinct of her lover. Feeling grateful, she joined him in bed, and after many months they spent the night in each other's arms.

He slept, but she did not. She was waiting for her daughter to wake up and hear all about her experience at the palace. In the morning, all three got up around the same time. Chaand was waiting for the two to begin narrating the story of the special moon night at the Hawa Mahal. Both the father and the daughter seemed reluctant to talk about it. She was all ready to greet them with her offering of two glasses of hot milk stirred with saffron and dry fruits. Inside, Raskapoor was turning her bed upside down, folding and unfolding her pink ensemble and shaking her delicately embroidered pink jootis, or shoes, over and over, desperately searching for one of her anklets, which seemed to have fallen off.

'Maybe it dropped off my foot when I fell asleep, and my father lifted me in his arms through the tunnel, or maybe in the covered carriage in which we returned home.' Debating with herself, Raskapoor decided to hide the one that was with her. She did not want anyone to know that she had lost one of her anklets. Feeling upset and sad about losing what her father had gifted, she was having trouble holding back her tears. She wanted to cry, but good sense prevailed, and she realized that her swollen eyes could reveal her loss. She hastened to put on kohl before coming out. Flashing her captivating smile, she reached out for the glass in her mother's hand. As she slowly sipped the milk, her thoughts revolved around the splendour of the palace.

Her mother, who could not hide her eagerness anymore to hear her daughter talk about her maiden visit to the palace, asked, 'How was the evening? Did you keep awake through the celebrations? Did your father introduce you to Maharajadhiraj?' Unable to appreciate her mother's anxiety, Raskapoor replied: 'Let me first finish the milk, then I will tell you all.' Just then Mishraji came out, drank his glass of milk in one go, and wiping his mouth with a handkerchief, rushed out telling them that he would come later in the evening. His strange attitude and lack of sensitivity struck Chaand deep in her heart. How could he not sense her eagerness to hear all about the evening at the palace?

In the meanwhile, Raskapoor read her mother's expressions of disgust as her father hurriedly made his way out. She then chose to keep the glass aside with a bang to draw her mother's attention. Raskapoor started her narration of the experience, which then went on through the day with breaks in between.

'Such a big palace! You go in circles through the gates and the dark tunnels to reach Hawa Mahal. I also saw beautiful horses and exotically painted elephants with howdahs in the courtyard. I so much wanted to touch the elephant and sit on a howdah. Ammi, we could see all the riders, but no one could see us get in there as we were in a palanquin. It was great fun to sit in a palanquin. Hawa Mahal is something to be seen. Ammi, you will not be able to take your eyes off it, just like I couldn't. I looked at it each time when I was falling asleep. The moon was waxing brilliantly on the facade of the Hawa Mahal, making it look like the divine crown. It reminded me of Shiva and Mahananda,' said Raskapoor, finishing the first round and chanting the morning hymns to invoke the blessings of Lord Shiva.

Chaand worried about where her daughter's fascination with Mahananda and Shiva was going to lead her. At about midday, she started the narration again. 'Mother, I did get to meet the Maharajadhiraj, and he knew you!' Astonished, Chaand asked her, 'Did he tell you that? How did you get to meet him? Did your father introduce you to him?' Raskapoor smiled and replied, 'No, Ammi. It was Nargis Mausi who took me along when she went to greet him. He gave her a big pouch of gold coins in appreciation of her beautiful singing. He looked at me and asked Nargis Mausi, 'Who is this lovely little girl?' Nargis Mausi told him that I was Noormahal's daughter and then he smilingly took your name, saying, "Oh! Mishraji's Chaand". Ammi, I did not know you had another name?' Before she could go any further, Chaand stopped her, rushing to the bathroom to pour her heart out, crying inconsolably for a short while. It was heart-wrenching for her that her daughter was discovering the facts that she had carefully managed to keep away from her for so long. So as to not give any indication to her daughter of her sadness, she quickly wiped her tears and went into the kitchen. What must be going on in her daughter's head worried her.

She felt she was standing alone in the centre and these dreaded thoughts were encircling her. First, a small circle, then a bigger circle, and then several circles, one bigger than the other, seemed to drag her into a whirlpool. Her throat choked, and she felt suffocated. She wanted to reprimand the irresponsible Mishraji, but then realized how cleverly he had avoided the confrontation by choosing to leave so abruptly. From her daughter's elaborate description, she could imagine the moment when Raskapoor was introduced to the Maharaja.

He was standing just behind Nargis when she told the king who that beautiful little girl was. Maharaja had then looked straight into his eyes as he spoke those words with a mischievous smile, 'Oh! Mishraji's Chaand'. Those vivid images cast a gloom in her mind. Mishraji, who knew well that his daughter must have told Chaand all the details of meeting the Maharaja, chose not to show up that evening. Raskapoor's duly upset mother, on the other hand, chose to maintain a haunting silence. Raskapoor was yearning to share the thrill of the mesmerizing full moon night but had no one to turn to.

Dancing Divinity

She woke up early, had a quick bath, and sat down to chant to Shiva to find an outlet. After chanting for an hour, Raskapoor seemed to be hearing Shiva's voice, 'I know, little girl, that you need to talk to someone. I think the best person will be the priest at my temple. He, too, has just finished his puja. I can see him sitting alone. He will tell you stories about the autumn full moon.' Raskapoor quickly folded her prayer mat, and taking the guidance from her lord, decided to head straight for the temple to meet the priest. Overtaken with excitement of finding someone to share the experience of her lifetime, she quickly informed her mother from the courtyard only that she was going to 'Gupteshwar Mahadev'. Without giving her mother a chance to respond, she ran down the steps, dragging her maid behind her. Since Raskapoor was strictly prohibited from stepping out alone, she made sure to take the maid along, not giving her mother yet another reason to be upset. She knew her mother was already quite disturbed after her visit to the palace. Raskapoor made her escort sit outside while she entered the temple. 'Beti, I was waiting for you today,' smiled the priest.

Surprised, Raskapoor said, 'Today is not Monday. I decided to come on the spur of the moment.'

The priest again smiled and surprised the little girl furthermore, 'I also found out you were coming only a short while ago. Your

Shiva informed me.' Raskapoor laughed and said, 'Then you also know you will have to tell me all the stories about Sharad Poornima.' But before that, she insisted on sharing with him the special celebrations at Hawa Mahal.

'You know Panditji, it was the first such celebration at Hawa Mahal, and for the first time, they had Maharaas—the dance of circles. It was enchanting.'

Panditji asked her if she knew what that dance was all about. 'That is the problem,' he said. 'Many do not know that our music and dance have a spiritual connection. These days, often both the performers and the onlookers see it as only entertainment. Let me tell you the story of Maharaas. It is a spiritual dance. Lord Krishna embodies divine love, and he is the god considered to have all sixteen traits which make a perfect human being. Even Lord Rama is supposed to have only twelve. You have witnessed the Janmashtami celebrations when the temple celebrates the birth of Lord Krishna. All indications at birth were signalling the birth of a spiritual child. He was playful and enjoyed tricking and teasing ladies, including his mother, as well as the milk maidens. Maharaas is described both in Bhagwat Purana, as well as in Geet Govind.'

'But how can a god do that?' interrupted Raskapoor.

'You must be a patient listener before passing judgement, my little girl. Our mythology is filled with mysterious and magical tales reflecting what human minds can do. All lead to one truth: that both god and the devil live within you.'

Raskapoor requested the learned priest to pardon her for the interruption and continue the story. He assured her that he was not angry with her and resumed the story of Krishna.

'He would play his magical flute when he wanted to play the mystical trick. Once, when he was eight years old, he went to the territory of Barsana, not far from our city. On Sharad Poornima, the full moon night, the *gopis*—the young milk maidens—decided to bathe in the holy Yamuna river. Soon, seeing the reflecting rays, they began dancing around those rays in a bid to catch them. Krishna was sitting on a tree branch about to play his magical flute. Before he could start doing that, he heard the laughter of the

gopis and decided to play a trick on them. He began to play the
flute, and one of those girls was drawn towards the drifting sound.
She asked the others if they heard it, but they said no, resuming
their amusing game and delighting in catching the reflections in
the water. Watching their expressions, he played his flute again,
but this time a bit louder. The only person to hear the loud sound
was that one girl yet again. Do you know who that was?' asked the
priest, to see if the girl was listening to his story.

'Must be Radha,' replied the engrossed Raskapoor. She asked
him not to break the story as she was listening to it raptly. To
assure him, she even offered to repeat the words uttered by him
so far. He laughed and continued, 'Seeing her friends not believing
the girl, he decided to pull them out of the river in search of the
flute player. He played the flute continuously. His melodious music
hypnotized the girls, and they ran to grab their clothes hung on
the tree in front. Each time they stood on their toes and stretched
their hands to pull down the dresses, they would disappear and
reappear again. Finally, they realized someone was sitting up on
the tree.'

'Seeing them almost on the verge of tears; he lowered the
branches for them to dress up. They wore their beautiful dresses,
and Krishna played his magical flute. They teased Radha, "Your
Kanha is here." Krishna manifested himself into many Krishnas to
dance with each one of them. Mischievous Krishna was playing yet
another trick as each gopi of that group of milk maidens believed
that she was dancing with the real one. They formed many circles
around Radha. She stood alone in the centre but knew that the real
one was yet to come! She closed her eyes and called out to Krishna,
saying, "Bade chhaliya!"'

Krishna was amused to hear that she had called him the
biggest trickster. So, he decided to appear before her the moment
she opened her eyes. Seeing him standing next to her with a
mischievous smile, she started dancing. They all danced together
through the night and extended the night for a time equivalent
to a billion years. The sound of the Maharaas echoed through
the Universe.

Your Shiva, too, heard the jingling sound of that dance sitting up in the Himalayas. Shiva, in his avatar as 'Natraj' the King of Dance, was surprised to visualize the magic of Maharaas. He came down to join that spectacular dance and asked the boatman on the river to take him to the spot. The boatman, however, told him that he could not go there as the only man allowed to participate in that dance was Kanha. The only way for Shiva to join the dance, according to him, would be to dress up as a woman. Then your Shiva took no time in dressing up as a gopi and danced abundantly.'

The story finished, and they both chuckled. 'I would love to hear more stories of all these fascinating gods and goddesses,' she told the priest, and he asked her light-heartedly if she wanted to take away his work and become a priest. She laughed again. 'You are funny. You know very well that only men become priests, not women.'

He calmly explained to her that to become a priest, the main concern was the knowledge of Hindu rituals and scriptures and not the gender of the candidate. 'Maybe it will take centuries for that day to come when priests will realize this basic fact and give up the baseless prejudice against women,' he said, appearing to be talking to the deity in front. Then turning to the girl, he narrated yet another story of the autumn full moon relating to Laxmi and the moon. She even learnt a new word from him— Kaumudi—meaning moonlight. Before her curiosity led her to another question, he advised the girl to leave. He reminded her of the moon at home, her mother!

Raskapoor hurried back, and Chaand was standing at the door of the glass palace. Enlightened and excited, Raskapoor did not worry about her questioning gaze and held her hand leading her mother back to their courtyard. 'I have heard stories that even you have not heard before, Ammi.' Chaand was filled with anxiety. One evening in the royal arena had made her daughter indulge in gossip too, she thought. However, she had no option but to sit down at the insistence of Raskapoor. The daughter, however, startled her with the offer to tell a fascinating story about the full moon. Already upset with the idea of Raskapoor witnessing the party meant for adults, the mother refused point-blank. 'I am not interested in hearing any story from you or your father.' The rest of the day went by in an unusual silence in the courtyard. Riyaz, or her daily practice session, had been cancelled well in advance since the team of her Gurus was going to perform at the palace till late. Rudra, she knew, would not come, being upset with her excitement over going to the palace. Mishraji also did not show up that evening. She remained intrigued by the story of the dance of her Lord Shiva and Krishna all through the day.

At night, looking out of the window, she addressed the moon, 'So you and the Goddess Laxmi are brother and sister! All along, my mother has been telling me that you are my Chanda Mama— my maternal uncle! Does it not mean that my mother is your sister too? Tell me then, why does she not hear the fascinating story about how you and Laxmi became brother and sister and the Kojagiri festival? For sure, she does not know that story; otherwise, she would have included it in my bedtime stories. The priest told me that Goddess Laxmi was your sister because the two of you emerged from the ocean when it was churned to empower the gods, who were threatened by the demons.

The priest knows all the stories from far-off places as he goes on long pilgrimages. He has visited all the major Hindu shrines. How fascinating that your sister Laxmi, the goddess of prosperity, is also worshipped on a full moon night. I loved the story of a queen praying to your sister all night to restore the wealth of her husband, who became too poor to take care of his kingdom . . . and your sister answered her prayers. Now I know why the Maharaja had a late-night party to keep awake all night. He wants to be rich and look after his people.' Raskapoor's innocent thoughts wandered all over the sky as she was gradually slipping into her dream world. 'Did Mahananda know about the dance of her husband? How funny, he even joined the Maharaas dressed as a woman with Krishna . . .' Thinking about that dance amused Raskapoor and she finally fell asleep.

The Inspiring Cosmic Dance

'What if the learned priest was joking with me about Shiva joining the Maharaas dressed as a woman to dance with Krishna?' thought Raskapoor. She had woken up recalling his words 'your Shiva'. She decided first to meet the priest in the morning before starting her daily routine. She got ready, informed her mother and walked to the temple with the same maid who had not hurried her back the previous morning. Right at the entrance of the temple, she smelled the lingering aroma of camphor and knew the priest had finished his ritual. She felt she was in luck and would be able to strike yet another enlightening conversation with him. But before that, she had to find out if he was joking about Shiva dancing like a woman! She greeted the priest and asked him her question. The priest knew that she would come back to him with this question. And because of that, he had decided to carry a special gift for her. He took a small bronze statue out of a sling bag made of red cloth. 'See, this is dancing Shiva,' he said. 'Natraj—the King of Dance. Have you ever heard of Tandava? It is the dance Shiva performs to maintain the balance of this Universe. This statue was presented to me by a priest from the southern part of our country. We met during a pilgrimage to Shiva's shrine in Kedarnath up in the Himalayas.'

The young girl was amazed to learn that Shiva not only performed the Maharaas but also the Tandava; and had yet another name, Natraj! Raskapoor had not seen this sort of statue ever before. She was captivated with the sheer grace and vigour of his imposing posture, and the priest noticed that she couldn't take her eyes off the figure.

'This is yours now, Raskapoor. The first time you offered prayers here, I could see that you were a blessed devotee of Shiva. But let me first explain what this statue signifies. The circle is the ring of fire. It represents the cycle of life—birth and death. His flowing hair symbolizes the river Ganges, which he brought down to earth entwined in his matted hair. In his right upper hand, he has the divine drum to dance rhythmically to balance the rhythm of life on this earth. See Ras, he holds a flame in his left hand, which destroys to recreate. Do you see a cobra?' he asked, turning towards her. Raskapoor, who was listening to him intently, nodded her head in affirmation. The priest explained further, 'That cobra is the cosmic energy known as "Kundalini Shakti". It is within all of us and is awakened with meditation. Now, observe his hands. The hand facing the devotees is to bless them, removing all their fears, while the lower hand, pointing towards his foot, is suggestive of an elephant trunk to remove all evil. Next, pay attention to his legs. The raised left leg is to invoke devotion and respect, and the right foot on the dwarf conveys his presence all around us.'

Raskapoor could not resist asking, 'But why is he crushing the poor dwarf?'

He explained to her that the dwarf was the symbol of ignorance, which needed to be crushed to liberate devotees from all kinds of sufferings. Elaborating on the dance, he described its variations. 'His cosmic dance has many expressions depicting creation, destruction and preservation. When he is angry and violent, he performs Rudra Tandava, and when he is blissful, he performs Anand Tandava. The statue I have given you represents Shiva dancing in bliss. Do you feel that, Ras?' She again nodded her head smiling. The priest continued, 'He is the one who connects all the arts with religion. Our classical music and dance connect with god. All professional artists first worship Natraj. Not just the dancers, but singers and actors also pray to him, for he was also a great singer and actor. You know, one of the very popular ragas, Raga Bhairav, is believed to be his creation.'

Suddenly he asked her, 'How are your music and dance classes going?'

Surprised at his question, she asked him, 'How do you know about my classes?'

He replied with a smile, 'Nargis told me that you were taking regular music and dance classes. She was amazed by your talent and progress. I know you will win many hearts one day.'

Before he could go any further, she shocked him with her question, 'Will I win Shiva's heart? I only want to win one heart, like Mahananda, and marry him. Tell me, will I get to marry him?'

The learnt Brahmin did not know how to reply to her curious question.

'Now no more stories and no more questions,' he said and stood up. She knew that was her cue to go back home. As she came out, she saw Rudra making his way to the temple. She was sure in their next meeting Rudra would perform Rudra Tandava expressing his anger! He had not seen her, and she was in a hurry to get back home.

Chaand saw her daughter rushing to her room, holding her skirt. She thought her daughter was in need to answer the call of nature and smiled. Inside, Raskapoor was looking for the appropriate place to install the statue of Natraj. She found a spot in the corner, away from the eyes of others, and then she released the dress from the grip of her left hand, bringing out the statue of Natraj. She invoked his blessings to be an accomplished singer and dancer like Mahananda so that she could marry Shiva!

She eagerly waited for Nargis to start her class that day. But Nargis did not come, knowing that she needed to give a much-annoyed Chaand a little time to calm down over Raskapoor's visit to the palace. Chaand, on the other hand, was waiting for Rudra to bring some respite in her life. Rudra himself was taking time to come to terms with his last encounter with Raskapoor. Chaand silently went ahead with her daily chores, while determined Raskapoor spent several hours in her room trying to master the dance posture of the divine dancer. She lost her balance innumerable times, lifting her left leg to the same height, as she tried to stand in his fearless posture. She prayed to Natraj again to bestow her with balance, vigour and grace. After spending hours on it, she was delighted to be able to finally stand in that posture for a good five minutes. She could not wait to display her success to someone. Who could that be? She knew her mother was in no mood to appreciate anything, leave aside a dance posture, the teacher was yet to show up, and her friend Rudra had to be appeased!

Just then she heard familiar footsteps entering the house, and was delighted with the entry of the right person who could admire her achievement. She ran to the courtyard and stood in the pose of the dancing Shiva to greet the connoisseur. Mishraji was wonderstruck to see her in that graceful stance of Shiva.

'Natraj!' Her father was overwhelmed. He asked, 'Who taught you that?'

Promptly she replied, 'Lord Shiva.' Seeing the expression of disbelief on his face, she told him all the details of the day.

Mishraji realized that his daughter was no ordinary girl. 'Brilliant, Ras, I never knew you are so talented!' He gave her a warm hug. Walking into the room, he asked her if the priest had told her that Shiva danced on the Sanskrit verses composed by Ravana.

'Really? Father, you really mean that Shiva danced to the compositions of a demon?' Raskapoor asked with disbelief writ large on her face.

'Yes. Ravana was an ardent worshipper of Lord Shiva, but because he was a demon, he thought himself to be a bigger destroyer than Shiva. One day, to prove his power, he lifted Mount Kailash, the abode of Shiva, in one hand. Shiva then decided to crush his ego and brought down Ravan's hand on the ground so fast that he could not pull it out from under the mountain. Hit with the terrible pain and fear of losing his hand, the demon cried, "Shiva . . . Shiva".'

'He composed several verses in admiration of Shiva's traits and his infinite power. Those verses are known as Shiva Strota, my dear little girl,' he said. He then narrated the whole Shiva Strota to her, explaining the meaning of each verse. Totally mesmerized with the overpowering chant, Raskapoor insisted her father teach her all the verses.

He knew his daughter, who had perfected the Natraj posture on her own, was not going to give up. 'Even Ravana took fourteen days to compose these seventeen verses to appease Shiva,' he said, trying to convince her. But driven by the lure of Natraj, she was not going to yield and settled down to learn at least two verses that evening itself. Her father ensured that she perfected the pronunciation of each word, explaining how important it was in deriving power from words. After spending a few hours, he decided to chant with her. Their resonating chants filled the environs of the glass palace, and Chaand's anger melted away.

The night was ecstatic for all three of them. Chaand and Mishraji relived the romance of the days when their courtship had just begun, while Raskapoor silently recited the two verses again and again and recalled the beautiful explanation her father gave her of those two verses of the Shiva Strota:

'From whose matted hair, like a thick forest, the river Ganges flows purifying his neck.

One who wears the cobra as his garland.

Damat damat damat damat he plays his drum and dances the vigorous Tandava.

One who blesses all is Shiva . . . you Shiva.

That Shiva may bless me every moment. From whose creeper-like hair, the Ganges is flowing. On his forehead, fierce fire is crackling and blazing. He adorns the crescent moon.'

A Leap towards History

It certainly was going to be a unique day, as all three of them got up early with a smile on their faces. While Chaand offered Namaz in her room, Raskapoor and Mishraji chanted Om Namah Shivay outside in the courtyard. Their faiths did not collide. A kind of solace prevailed that morning.

As Chaand served hot milk to the two of them, Mishraji asked Raskapoor, 'So, did you like the evening at Hawa Mahal? And meeting Maharaja Sawai Pratap Singh?' Her clever father, who had first observed Raskapoor's deep inclination to hear spiritual stories caught the expression in her eyes as she nodded a couple of times, flashing a smile. She was thrilled to have stepped out of the glass palace for the first time after sunset. Enamoured, Raskapoor already thought that the Maharaja was a very affectionate and kind person. She was grateful to her father for getting her to see the palace where she was able to meet a real-life king for the first time.

Suddenly her head turned upwards as she gazed towards a butterfly taking off from the lemon tree in the courtyard, which in no time erratically gained height and disappeared up in the sky. 'Did you know a butterfly can fly so high so fast?' amazed, Raskapoor asked her father. 'Yes, with those wings she can,' he replied. 'But those are tiny wings to fly that high,' she countered. 'Ras, my beautiful butterfly, it is not about the size of the wings. She also has a dream to fly high and explore the colours and

51

fragrances; otherwise, she would have died in this small courtyard only. All of us can fly high if we have the wings of dreams,' he subtly tried to lead her to the world beyond that courtyard. Now, he felt the time was ripe to kindle her interest in the life that he had envisaged for her, a presence in the royal arena. Knowing what a great story listener his daughter was, he decided on combining the royal fables with spiritual stories to get her hooked.

Mishraji began his discourse on history with Pratap Singh, who was a devout worshipper of Lord Krishna and wrote poetry under the pen name 'Brijnidhi'. 'Hawa Mahal took nine years to build. You know Ras, he has dedicated this palace to Lord Krishna and his beloved Radha,' the father said, igniting her curiosity. Her teacher had hit the perfect chord to interest her in learning about the history of the palace, tapping into Raskapoor's innate romance with the spiritual world. He knew it was the best way to apprise her of the intrigues and politicking, which she would have to deal with one day.

'To me, the sidewall looked like the crown of Krishna,' the excited Raskapoor told her father. Her observation amazed him. It reminded him of the couplet the Maharaja wrote about the building. He admired the phenomenal imagination of his daughter and then chose to recite that couplet in his resounding voice: 'Hawa Mahal is created, you all must know, it is with the feeling, Radha-Krishna will appear here.'

Raskapoor was mesmerized both by the ruler's devotion, as well as her father's soul-capturing rendition. So, the first question she wished to ask was if the Maharaja had built a temple as well at Hawa Mahal. 'He had built the temple of Govardhannath Ji just as he commissioned Hawa Mahal. He was also the one who constructed the beautiful Brijnidhi temple in Chandni Chowk,' her father informed her.

'How nice! I only knew that Maharajas were warriors! Has the king fought wars? How old was he when he became the king?' Raskapoor wanted to know all about Pratap Singh. She requested her father to tell her all about him, but the next day, as she expected Nargis any minute for her practice session.

'Oh! She will not come today. I forgot to tell you. I met her in the market yesterday with her guest when I was coming here.'

Mishraji had meticulously planned his conversation with Ras after advising Nargis to remain absent for one more day. He chose to spend that whole day trying to pacify Chaand and share stories of royal life with his daughter. As their mission was the same, Nargis joked, 'If you say, I will not come even tomorrow.'

Seeing his daughter a bit disappointed on missing the dance and music lessons, he chose to divert her attention. 'Never mind. Today, I will spend the whole day here. We will get more time together.' After the morning prayers and the delicious breakfast, Mishraji called Raskapoor in the living room.

Just as she stepped in, she stood still, taking a deep breath and enjoying the fragrance inside. She had entered the room that was filled with the fragrance of sandalwood! Raskapoor was surprised to see him sitting with a board with toy animals. Carved in sandalwood, the toys appeared like two armies. Laughingly, she enquired how come he was playing with the toy armies like a little child. Seating her opposite him on the other side of the board, he told her, 'Ras this is no ordinary game. I got this especially for you to learn this ancient game, which is a mind game and needs a lot of planning to be a winner. This game, now known as Shatranj, was developed from Chaturanga, designed by a Brahmin. That game was named after the four limbs of the royal army: elephants, infantry, chariots, and horses.' He also told her how, once played by the Indian kings, the game became a passion with the Moghul kings and was then picked up by firangis, who called it chess!

The father had already initiated her in the traditional racing game of Chaupad, which they could only play when Ammi and Nargis Mausi were available as the game required four players. Mishraji observed the winning streak in Ras, as within no time, she had mastered all the skills to play. Each time she played intending to win, warning the other three to be ready for defeat even before the game began. Sure enough, more than often, she was the winner, and her shrill voice could be heard by the maids in the courtyard down below.

Curious as she was, she reached out for the big piece and went on smelling it, delighted with the fragrance. Her reaction made

Mishraji smile, who then asked her to put it back in its place and sit across. She was delighted to get the first news that the game needed two players only, unlike Chaupad, as she remembered how difficult it was to get the other two players to agree to play. Her father explained that the game was a war game between the two armies and introduced each piece of the contingent. 'Ras, do you realize what you picked is the Raja, and the whole game is about protecting him? Of all the other pieces, the most powerful is a woman. Rani gets her power from the freedom to move in different directions: horizontally, vertically, and diagonally to protect her man.' Her father had articulated his words very carefully to make an imprint on the mind of his little girl at this tender age, making sure that his words would guide her later in life. With all the details given to her, she stunned her father with the remark on dice. She observed that unlike all the other board games like Pachisi and Chaupad, the new game did not use any dice. They played the first game of chess, and the father chose to lose out to his little girl. The twinkle in her eyes requesting him to play each time that he came was convincing enough to know that the girl was hooked on to the game forever.

'After this wonderful game, I have many fascinating stories for you. So, let me tell you the story of our Raja,' he said, to turn her thoughts back to history. 'Pratap Singh was just a few years older than you when he became the Maharaja of the kingdom of Kachchwahas. His kingdom is not just our city of Jai Nagar. It covers a vast region,' he began. He knew that this start would make her want to know the whole story. Sure enough, Raskapoor was surprised to learn about such a young boy becoming the Maharaja of a big state.

She instantly interrupted her father, saying, 'How can a boy who is just a little older than me become a Maharaja?' 'Yes, Ras,' said her father, 'He became the ruler as a thirteen-year-old boy. But do you know, his grandfather was even younger than him when he was crowned? Sawai Jai Singh, the founder of this beautiful city, was two years younger than his grandson!' Thus saying, he got her engrossed in the tale. Rapt with wonder, his daughter shot yet another question at him, 'Did these young boys ever fight wars?' 'Yes, Pratap Singh's grandfather did, not one but many,' replied her father. 'As a young boy?' she further asked.

'Yes, Ras, as a young boy. He is best known for his campaign of Khelna against the Marathas. Who do you want to hear about first—the grandfather or the grandson?' the smart Brahmin asked the young girl, to sustain her interest in history.

Raskapoor surprised him with her reply, 'Obviously about the grandfather first. He was so brave to fight wars, and as the priest told me, a great genius to plan our city. Where is my grandfather?' Her father was stunned to hear her question. How could he tell her that the children of nautch girls and mistresses had no family on their father's side! To stop her from raising any questions about his family, he safeguarded himself with a lie. Maintaining a sad look, he regretted his inability to tell her where her grandfather was, as he was an orphan raised in the ashram of a yogi.

Raskapoor's heart reached out to her father, and she tried to console him, 'Do not worry. Now you have a daughter.' Chaand, who was hearing this conversation between the father and daughter, was deeply troubled with his stance. She mumbled to herself, 'Strange! These elite men can bear children out of wedlock with women from the lowest strata but not own them!' She decided to serve lunch to collect herself. Raskapoor let her father take an afternoon nap, only on the assurance that he would begin their next conversation with stories of Pratap's grandfather. When he awoke from his rest, he saw Ras sitting just outside his bedroom.

While recommencing their session, he asked her from which point he should start. She promptly replied, 'From the campaign of Khelna. You said that he was best remembered for this one particular war. All afternoon I was thinking about it. How could he do it? He was so young.'

Her father sat next to her and began. 'When Jai Singh came to the throne, the all-powerful Moghul empire was breaking apart. His ancestors had been friends with the mighty Moghul Emperor Akbar and came to the aid of the Moghuls in wars. They benefitted from aiding them, and in return, received a big chunk of territories or jagirs, special powers and a lot of wealth. But as the Moghuls started losing their grip, the fortunes of Jai Singh's ancestors started dwindling. It was the genius of Jai Singh that retrieved the glory of the Kachchwaha kingdom. Nobody could ever imagine that the young boy, soon after coming to the throne, would be able to fight the tactics of the Marathas in their difficult terrain and achieve success. When Emperor Aurangzeb was trying to take over the hill forts of the plundering Marathas, he needed to muster the help and resources of all the rulers from the north. He laid siege on the impregnable fort of Khelna, and young Jai Singh commanded the post on a hill facing the post of the enemy.'

Raskapoor was once again rapt with wonder, and exclaimed, 'Really? Was he so brave?' Mishraji told her to keep listening. 'That historic campaign earned the young Maharaja the title of Sawai. The location and the size of the massive fortress posed a considerable challenge even for the warrior king Maharaja Shiva Ji to conquer it. He finally had to work out his attack by manipulating the Adil Shahi commander. Jai Singh was taken aback by the sheer size of the Khelna Fort, and he named it "Vishalgarh" or the colossal fort. When the over-ambitious Moghul Emperor decided to annex the hill forts of the Marathas, he was totally clueless about how arduous his mission was going to be. He had neither considered the hardship of manoeuvring the hazardous terrain nor the harsh weather conditions of the Western Ghats. The siege dragged on for months together, and the Moghul army was suffering heavy losses.'

'Ras, see how smart Jai Singh was and how equal to this formidable task. He secretly got one route cleared for his contingent to take over a Maratha post little before the fort. His strategic plan finally resulted in the capture of the targeted post of the enemy. Jai Singh was not impatient like the emperor and did not enter the fort right away. He planned it well, and after nearly three months, he decided to scale the fort. The Marathas, taking advantage of the height gave Jai Singh's army a tough time, but he was determined to take charge of the fort. Finally, he succeeded, and the first thing he did was to fly the five-colour flag of Amber on the tower of the fort.' Raskapoor celebrated Jai Singh's victory, and her loud claps resounded in the courtyard.

After a short while, she got back to him with yet another question, 'You said that the emperor was so impressed with Jai Singh that he called him Sawai, what did that mean?' Mishraji replied, 'It meant Jai Singh was one and a quarter times cleverer than the other rulers of Amber. Another story tells that the young Jai Singh was given that title in his first meeting with the emperor. Aurangzeb summoned the Maharaja to appear in his court, and the Maharaja complied after an inordinate delay, upsetting the emperor. As Jai Singh came before him, the angry emperor held both his hands in a tight grip and asked him if he was not aware of the consequences of non-compliance with the emperor's orders. Instead of being scared, Jai Singh smiled and replied that traditionally holding someone's hand signified protection and affection and since the mighty emperor held both his hands, he need not worry about anything. Jai Singh's witty and intelligent reply amazed the emperor. He immediately realized that the genius standing before him was way ahead of the other rulers, and he awarded him the title. No wonder he was granted the title of 'Sawai', declaring him to be one and quarter times wiser than the rest of the boys his age.'

As she listened to the salient historical episode, Raskapoor was reminded of the flag on the palace fluttering in the autumn breeze! It was a two-piece flag. She immediately caught the reason behind the distinctive design of the flag to be the title bestowed upon Jai Singh as the piece above was a quarter of the big one. However, Raskapoor needed to confirm it with her learned father. 'Is the design of the flag also based on his title?' The father marked that his daughter was well ahead of other girls her age. 'Yes, you are right,' he confirmed. His confirmation encouraged Raskapoor to know if the rulers before him also had a flag.

Mishraji told her not only about the original white flag of the rulers of Amber, that had a tree marked on it and was called *Jharshahi,* but also how in the sixteenth century it was changed to *Panchranga,* the flag with five different coloured bands. When she learnt that Raja Man Singh had decided on giving up the white flag, choosing the five-coloured flag instead after defeating the five tribes of Afghanistan, she was keen on knowing what the importance of an ordinary thing like a flag was. Mishraji then chose to describe the significance of a flag or *dhwaja* as it was known in Sanskrit, talking about *Gaurud dhwaja*, the flag of Lord Vishnu. She was surprised to discover that even gods had their flags for identification, and that practice was adopted by the rulers as well as the temples, which constructed Dhwaja Stambha or the pillar standards in the ancient period. Mishraji even explained the significance of worshipping the flag before proceeding for warfare to seek blessings for victory, as well as capturing the enemy's flag on the battlefield. Raskapoor was in awe of her father's immense knowledge but then shifted her focus from the war to Jai Singh's family asking about his wives, his children and who came to the throne after Jai Singh died.

After a short break for evening refreshments, she was ready for the continuation of the 'Jai Singh' episode. Wondering where to start the next session, he decided to talk about the benevolence of the ruler; how he came to rescue the starving people from an unjust financial burden. 'Hindus are indebted to him for what he did for them.'

This again piqued Ras' curiosity. 'In the territories of Muslims ruled by Islamic law, the non-Muslims had to pay a special tax if they did not embrace their religion. The tax was known as Jizya. When they came to our land, they imposed the same tax, but Emperor Akbar withdrew it. Years later, Aurangzeb, who was a fanatical Muslim, levied it back.'

Upset, Raskapoor intercepted her father, 'It was not right. If the tax was for the territories of Muslims, then why did they bring it into our land? We did not go to their territory!'

His daughter was again proving to be as smart as young Jai Singh, who gave the same reasoning to the emperor. A sudden thought struck him, 'This girl could have been a queen and perhaps, powerful like the empress Noor Jahan if she had been born a princess!'

She was surprised to hear him call her his little Noor Jahan! She asked him who that was.

'Emperor Jahangir's wife! She was an intelligent girl like you,' he told her with a sense of pride. He knew his little angel loved elephants, so he told her that Noor Jahan rode a war elephant to defend her husband. At that moment, however, Raskapoor was keen only to know what happened to that unfair tax and diverted her father back to it. Mishraji then applauded her argument, 'Yes, Jai Singh thought the same. He tried to convince the emperor but to no gain. A few years later, when a big famine hit the land leading to starvation, and people had no money to pay the tax, intelligent Jai Singh decided to argue their case once again. He took it up with the then emperor Muhammad Shah. The Maharaja pleaded firmly on one basic fact that the Moghul rulers came to rule Hind where Hindus had been living for centuries. While reasoning out with the ruler, he carefully underlined the loyalty of his people to the crown. With his profound argument, he finally succeeded in convincing the ruler not to differentiate between his subjects on religious grounds.'

Impressed, Raskapoor commented, 'This means a ruler has to be intelligent, brave, and kind!'

Mishraji said, 'Yes. Ras, you can see he had all these qualities and I am sure he will be remembered as the best Maharaja of Jaipur.'

His inquisitive daughter immediately asked, 'So after him, Pratap Singh's father became the Maharaja? Was he as nice as Jai Singhji?' She was surprised to hear that it was not Pratap Singh's father Madho Singh but Ishwari Singh who succeeded Jai Singh. 'But why could Madho Singh not succeed?' she inquired.

'As per tradition, the oldest son of the Maharaja is the one to be crowned. Madho Singh had two stepbrothers older than him, Shiv Singh and Ishwari Singh. Shiv Singh died a few years before the death of Jai Singh, so next in line was Ishwari Singh,' Mishraji explained.

Raskapoor asked, 'If Madho Singh had two stepbrothers, then how many wives did Jai Singh have?' He was running out of steam to prolong the history session, which by any standard was rather too much for such a young girl. However, he could not have ended it with an unanswered question. 'Jai Singh had twenty-seven wives,' he replied in brief and concluded, pointing towards the setting sun, 'Time for my evening prayer.'

That girl, who was cruising between cascading history and mythology was suddenly reminded of Shiv Strota as her father mentioned the evening prayer. 'Fine. After the prayer, you have to teach me two more verses of Shiva Strota.' To strengthen their relationship, her father had no choice but to yield to her wish. He decided to teach her two hymns only on one condition—that she would then let her parents have their own time together. For more than one hour, she chanted with him:

'Shiva, who rejoices in the delightful glance of Parvati, Mountain Himalaya's daughter.

Shiva in whose mind the universe and the living beings reside.

Shiva, whose merciful glance removes all troubles.

Praying to that Shiva, my mind is filled with eternal happiness.

My mind is absorbed in seeking Shiva.

Shiva, from whose hair the matted snakes illuminate the universe with their shining hoods.

That Shiva who adorns the skin of an intoxicated elephant.'

Inside her room, a delighted Raskapoor mumbled, 'What a beautiful day I have spent with my father. I thank you, Natraj, my dancing Shiva.' Standing in the same posture, in awe of his anger that could even scare a demon like Ravana, she instantly thought of Shiva's namesake Rudra, her friend!

A New Dawn

She felt rejuvenated with the warmth her father was extending as never before and teaching her so much history in such a short time, as well as the exciting game of Shatranj. And above all, teaching her the difficult Sanskrit hymns with perfect pronunciation. While Raskapoor was over-awed with his teaching skills and deep knowledge on different subjects, he admired her intelligence and her quick understanding. He became an inspiration for her to gear up as a willing disciple of all her teachers. She decided to surprise her father with her pace and her varied skills. As Mishraji was leaving early that morning, she begged him to first play another game of chess. Mishraji willingly gave in but asked her to set up the board. He was astonished to see that Raskapoor had not taken any time in setting it up without making any mistake. It was certainly an accomplishment for such a young girl who had learnt the game just one day before. She moved all in the right directions but then to give her a taste of defeat, the second time he did not choose to let her win. Looking at her disheartened face, he told her to think more before moving the pieces, anticipating the option of different moves the opponent could make after her one move. Mishraji then got up to leave and she let him leave on the promise that he would come early every morning to tell her more history and teach her the hymns of Shiva, as well as play one game of chess. The father willingly gave her his word as he too had a mission to accomplish! The shrewd Brahmin, while going down the steps told her, 'Ras, first you be ready for your music and dance classes. Nargis is going to come.'

Her mother, on the other hand, was keen to keep her daughter's friendship with Rudra alive. She wondered why he had been missing for the last couple of days. 'Did you meet Rudra the last time you went to the temple?' she enquired, just as Mishraji stepped out of the glass palace.

'No. I only saw him there,' Raskapoor replied. The mother could read the disappointment in her daughter's eyes. She instantly strategized a plan to take her to the temple before Nargis came. 'Let's go,' she said, taking her daughter's hand.

'Where, Ammi?' the surprised daughter asked.

'To the temple,' Chaand told her. Ras was surprised at her mother's suggestion. They both smiled and headed to the temple, hand in hand. Raskapoor was amused to think of Rudra for if he were already there, her mother would bring him along to the glass palace. Chaand on the other hand, was praying for the first time to her daughter's Lord Shiva to grant a meeting with Rudra.

They heard the voice of the priest from inside. 'Rudra, you really chant the Shiva Strota so well. Come again.' Raskapoor knew her mother was a devout Muslim and would not go inside. She made her mother sit outside and headed towards the entrance of the temple. As she was stepping in, she almost collided with Rudra, who was stepping out.

She laughed aloud and asked him, 'Did you think I was Ravana?' Rudra apologized but decided to ask her why he would think that she was a demon. She smiled, 'I know you are angry, and you have just recited Shiv Strota composed by the demon Ravana.'

In a sarcastic tone, he expressed his surprise over her knowing that, for she seemed to have an interest only in dancing in the palace. She knew he was upset so retorted, 'I don't know. I just know that right now, you are in a mood to perform Rudra Tandava. How can you do it in this small temple! You are most welcome to come to our palace with the big courtyard.'

Teasing him, she dragged him out while the priest wondered where their friendship would lead them. 'Ammi, Rudra wants to come home just now. He will show us the dance of angry Shiva. Can he come?' she asked.

'Of course, my son. I have actually been waiting for you to come,' was the instant response of her mother. Left with no choice, Rudra silently walked with them, thanking Shiva for answering his prayers for an opportunity to meet Raskapoor. He had been missing her ever since the day she had gone for the celebrations at the palace. Many questions rattled his thoughts. He wanted to know if she was yearning only for the palace or sometimes thought of him too. The young man could feel his first love blooming in his heart but could not express it to her, for she was still too young to feel that emotion. Chaand went inside to get some sweets for her special guest.

Raskapoor was waiting to find Rudra alone to confront him about why he had not come all those days. She rushed inside to bring the statue of Natraj to show to him and then stood in the same dancing pose. Rudra could not help but smile, admiring the perfection of both. She certainly was a divine dancer, endowed with phenomenal beauty and grace, he thought. Coming out of the pose, she recited all the four hymns taught to her by her father.

'So, now you can dance to my hymns, my angry Shiva. Shall we start?' she teased him again. Rudra burst out into loud laughter and then the two of them laughed together for a few minutes. Chaand came out with a silver tray filled with sweets. She told them how much she loved to hear their resonating laughter, which she had been missing all those days. As he was leaving, she told Rudra, 'You must come every day around this time.' He not only willingly accepted but literally took it as her directive, coming almost every day till Raskapoor left the glass palace.

Next to come was Nargis. She came all set to begin the music and dance lessons. She had come along with two new faces and introduced Ras to them, saying, 'You are lucky to have two much sought-after teachers. Kundan Lalji is an exponent of Kathak, and Ustad Hafiz Khan is one of the finest masters of classical Hindustani music. They were attached to princely states near Banaras for many years. When I told them how talented you were, they accepted to teach you for two months before going back to

Banaras. You are a raw diamond that will shine like a star within no time as they polish your inherent qualities.'

They were both stunned to see the beauty of the young girl and were all set to start the session. Ras opted for the dance class first, placed the statue of Natraj on a table and bowed before it to seek his blessings. She stood in the same fearless posture as that of Shiva and smiled at Nargis. Her two teachers admired her flawless posture thinking that she was born to be a dancer. After being initiated by Pandit Kundan Lal in Kathak, Ustad Hafiz Khan asked her to sing the seven ascending and descending notes. He could not believe the depth of her voice and her unusual breath control. On their way back, the two teachers discussed whether she would excel as a singer or as a dancer. They looked forward to the sessions and mutually decided never to miss one.

Finally, well before sunset, her father came in. He had brought hot jalebis to have with her. Ras was thrilled to see that her father had kept his word, while the father could see the unusual happiness radiating from her sparkling eyes. Relishing the Jalebis, she gave him details of the proceedings of her hectic but exciting day, including how impressed her two new teachers were with her dancing skills as well as her singing talent. She had, however, excluded Rudra's name on the strict advice given by her mother to avoid any restriction on their meetings.

'I have always believed in your talent and now even your intelligence,' he complimented his daughter, admiring his clever move to get the two great teachers to Jaipur in order to hold exclusive sessions with Ras! He wanted to maintain the pace of grooming her for the day when she would steal the heart of the young prince. His next move was to commence the history lesson, and he continued from where he left off the previous evening.

'Ishwari Singh was crowned after the demise of his father, but it was a crown of thorns,' began Mishraji. 'Why a crown of thorns?' asked Ras.

'Jai Singh had twenty-seven wives,' explained her father. 'One of them was the princess of Mewar, and she was married to him on the condition that her son would be the Maharaja of Jaipur, not the eldest son.'

'Oh, she was like the queen Kekayi in Ramayana who did not want Lord Rama, the eldest son, to be the king. Instead, she wanted her son Bharat, the third in line, to become the king. Madho Singh was also the third son of the king,' said Ras, citing the parallel episode from mythology. Her level of knowledge of mythology was expected, but to cite a parallel example was yet another surprise for him.

'You are absolutely right. The princess from Udaipur continuously hatched plans with her uncle, the Maharana of Udaipur, his allies, the rulers of Jodhpur and Bundi, and the factions in the Kachchwaha baronage. Ishwari Singh did not have peace even for a day during his reign of seven years. Constantly, Madho Singh pushed his demand to divide Jai Singh's kingdom in half, and Ishwari Singh rightly did not want to give up his legal right. Was he right?' Mishraji wanted to see his wise daughter's reaction.

'Yes, he was right. How sad that the royals fight like that!' Raskapoor was upset, but then asked, 'Did the two brothers fight a war?' He then told her about not just one but many battles between them and even explained to her how the feud resulted in bringing both sides under heavy debts. They had to pay big sums due to the support they had generated from the powers in Deccan. The final disaster struck after the failure in the battle of Bagru and the demise of Ishwari Singh's learned ministers one by one. The worst was that his once very trusted businessman associate, Natani, cheated him, which led him to commit suicide.

Anxious, Raskapoor wished to know how he got cheated. 'After Bagru, Ishwari Singh fell into such despair that he confined himself to the four walls of the ladies' quarters. When he got to know that the Marathas were coming to collect the arrears of the battle of Bagru and were closing in, he directed his minister Natani to collect all the troops of his kingdom. Natani kept assuring him that all the troops were in his pocket each time Ishwari Singh asked. When finally, the news came that the enemy was right before the city walls, he called Natani who shocked him with the reply, "The pocket got torn." Ishwari Singh then committed suicide.' With that, her father ended the story of the succession of Jai Singh.

Raskapoor was not just sad, but disgusted. Getting up, she told her father, 'It means nobody is reliable in the palace.' Mishraji felt a sense of achievement in conveying that message to her.

She went inside. Her mind was tired and filled with a variety of emotions. She wondered how in one day she could feel so excited and also so sad. She stood before her Natraj and prayed to him. All she wanted was for him to marry her like Mahananda.

The Unique Marriage

Post that eventful day, her days seem to fly away on wings. She started her day chanting Om Namah Shivay with her parrot and rooster. Some days she went to the temple to meet the priest who was delighted to hear the verses of Shiva Strota from her, and he too decided to teach and explain the next verse to her whenever he could. The dance and music lessons were being conducted at a whirlwind pace, and her incredible talent made the two teachers return after a few months to teach their unique disciple.

Rudra came nearly every day, rejoicing in their meetings filled with exciting discussions and funny riddles. When one day Ras asked Rudra if he knew how to play chess, Rudra feigned complete ignorance, requesting her to teach the game. She quickly ran to her room, grabbed the chess box, and sat down to set up the board. Ras began introducing the game the same way her father had done while inducting her. Rudra seemed to have a lot of difficulty in picking up the nuances, which she had done so quickly, and she wondered if she was missing something in his attitude.

After losing two games to her, when he saw Ras a bit disgusted instead of enjoying her victory, he burst out laughing. Shocked to see the defeated man laugh, she asked what was wrong with him. Rudra then told her the fascinating story of the board game that Lord Shiva and Parvati used to play and Shiva would lose the game, not using the divine power. 'You know like you, Parvati too was convinced that Shiva did not know how to play the game. Actually, he enjoyed her company and allowed her to win. I am doing precisely that, as both of us are Shiva devotees,' Rudra teased her. Raskapoor was embarrassed about being so naïve not to realize that Rudra was tricking her.

The third game was a learning game for her. Rudra not only won it but gave her some winning tips on how to get the king out of check. Those playful moments spent together led him to dream of having her in his life as a wife. He had always detested Mishraji for not taking Chaand as his wife and coming out before the world as the father of his little fairy. To foster a stronger bond, he too took it upon himself to teach her the verses of the Shiva Strota, which made Raskapoor look up to him. She at times wondered if Shiva was like Rudra when he was as young as her friend.

Her father came every evening, continuing the history lessons from Ishwari Singh onwards. She was turning out to be rather inquisitive about what went into the making of the Maharajas, how those women from the four walls of the ladies' quarters meddled in state affairs, the role of the ministers as well as Marathas, and dealing with constant warfare. It was the Marathas led by Malhar Holkar and the ministers who got Madho Singh to rush back from Udaipur to finally wear the crown. Holkar negotiated a support payment for Rs 10 lakh, which was not acceptable to his senior master Jayappa Scindia, so he also arrived on the scene demanding a much higher ransom for freeing the throne. Raskapoor was taken aback to hear, 'Four thousand Marathas entered the walled city slyly. They desired to see the new city, visit the temples and buy the camels, horses and the saddlery for which Jai Nagar was famous all over Hindustan. When they wielded their arms to demonstrate their one-upmanship, Rajput fury knew no limits, and the Marathas were attacked. For nine hours, the carnage continued, resulting in bending the Marathas and the demand was reduced.'

In the narration of the regime of Maharaja Madho Singh, intelligent Raskapoor concluded that he certainly was much smarter than his stepbrother. In the next one and half years, after coming to the throne, he did not face any attack from the southern powers. He also forged a truce between the then emperor, Ahmad Shah, and his rebellious minister, Wazir Safdar Jang. However, he too could not keep away from the advances of the southern armies who kept on appearing from time to time to extract arrears. Towards the end of his regime, he was able to establish a friendship after paying a major part of the money due. It was yet another discovery for Raskapoor that the last battle fought by Madho Singh was not against the Marathas but against the Jat ruler Jawahar Singh of Bharatpur, who had the martial Sikhs in his army. Madho Singh valiantly fought and defeated the Jat army. Soon after, he fell sick and died.

The history lessons were suspended after a few days for some time, as the Diwali festival was approaching. Mishraji was directed by his family to get the house painted. Knowing it would take him weeks together, he said to his daughter one evening, 'Ras, my dear, I will not come for a few weeks as I have to perform some special rituals for the Diwali festival in the palace, undertake the holy pilgrimage to Pushkar and be there till the full moon.' He had built such a bond with her daughter that she did not doubt his story, but Chaand knew the truth. How could she tell his dear daughter that the father whom she adored was lying to her. He, in fact, was going to rejoice in the lavish pre- and post-Diwali parties held across the state with wine, women and gambling!

One day, when her best friend Rudra invited her to a unique wedding, she readily accepted. It was four days before the full moon of the lunar month Kartik.

'Are you getting married?' she teasingly asked him. 'You keep guessing,' Rudra said, making her even more excited. She anxiously awaited the day of the wedding, thinking of who the bride and the bridegroom would be. Finally, together with Chaand, they headed for the wedding venue, which to her surprise was the Krishna temple nearby. The temple was decorated all over with earthen lamps and outside, the musicians were playing the ceremonial wedding music on the shehnai accompanied by the double drum called the nagada.

Chaand let the two walk into the temple, dreaming of the day her daughter would get married. As she entered the courtyard and spotted the bride adorned with a red veil with gold embroidery under the wedding pavilion, Raskapoor could not believe her eyes.

'Look at her beautiful veil, Rudra,' she exclaimed. It was the wedding of the basil plant tulsi with Lord Vishnu. She was thrilled to witness the whole ritual of 'Tulsi Vivah', and was eager to know the real story. Rudra told her that he would narrate it to her afterwards at home. When they reached the glass palace, Chaand invited him inside to have some sweets. Rudra wished to leave then, but Ras insisted on his coming in to narrate the story, reminding him that he would tell her the story behind this grand wedding. Rudra yielded, and they had the sweets together, but again got up to leave.

'What about the story?' Ras enquired. Rudra asked her to wait till the following day and left with the naughty intent of letting her think about it the whole night. At night, before going to bed, she prayed to her Natraj and shared with him her reaction to the unique wedding she witnessed. 'All gods are fascinating. You, Shiva, married Mahananda, and today I discovered Lord Vishnu married Tulsi.' That night she dreamt of becoming Mahananda and getting married to Shiva. The ceremonial sound of the shehnai filled her dreams through the night till she woke up with the chant of her parrot and rooster. She never told anyone that dream, believing that the dreams of the early morning came true if not shared with anyone.

The Divine Ecstasy

The very next day after the Tulsi Vivah, Nargis came in to announce that from that day on, Raskapoor's music and dance sessions would go on for the whole day, breaking only for lunch and the prayer time of her Muslim music teacher. Raskapoor tried to plead with her that the schedule should change on the return of her father. Her mother, however, knew that Nargis would not have extended the timings without being instructed by the ambitious Mishraji. She recalled one evening when while admiring her talent and beauty, he had told her, 'I wish I could have arranged these two teachers for you as well.' She had known then that the teachers had arrived at the glass palace because of him.

In the meanwhile, the two teachers noticed that their disciple was not as attentive as she usually was. They did not know that she was longing for Rudra to come in to complete his story. At the end of the day, she was very upset as he did not come. But Rudra had come only retracing his steps upon hearing the sound of music and the dancing bells. Standing on the balcony overlooking the entrance gate, Chaand had seen Rudra turn around and walk back.

Before the cunningly planned revised schedule crashed her dreams, Chaand decided to get Ras and Rudra to meet. That night, she told Ras that Rudra had come, but did not come up because of her classes.

'Never mind, Ras. We can go to the Shiva temple before Nargis and the party come. Maybe Rudra will be there, or else you can ask the priest to tell him to come to our house on the full moon day around sunset.' The next morning when they reached the temple, Rudra was already there as he too was looking forward to seeing Ras at some point before her classes.

On that full moon day, Rudra told her not just about the Tulsi Vivah but also about Mahananda's wedding to Shiva. Chaand had arranged the seating on the top-most terrace of the glass palace. Evenings had become cooler, announcing the arrival of winter. Rudra came in a little before sunset and Chaand was all ready to welcome him. Leading him to the steps, she told him, 'My son, these days Ras gets very tired because of her music and dance classes and sleeps early. Today, because you were coming, she slept for an hour after the classes. She has just got up and gone to get ready for your story and chanting session.' When her daughter came up, Chaand went down to cook dinner for her special guest. Sitting down, Ras immediately asked Rudra to narrate the story of the Tulsi Vivah first.

'See, here is something for you,' he took out the red veil cloth from his bag and handed it to her.

'Exactly like the one that Tulsi wore for her wedding! Very nice but I am not getting married,' she smiled.

'This is to celebrate this evening and for you to remember it. So now no more questions if you want to hear the story,' said Rudra, firmly, allowing his voice to display the affection he felt for her for the first time. He explained to her how Hindus consider certain trees and plants to be sacred and worship them on certain days. He then told her the tale.

'Throughout the month of Kartik, the basil plant Tulsi is worshipped. According to the Padma Purana, the demon king Jalandhar was married to a very pious woman called Vrinda, who was also an ardent devotee of Lord Vishnu. It was because of her devotion and piousness that the demon became so powerful that even the gods could not destroy him. They then sought the help of Lord Vishnu to limit his power. Vishnu disguised himself as the demon king and appeared before Vrinda, who, because she took another man as her husband, lost her piousness. This resulted in the weakening of the all-powerful demon king, who was then killed by Lord Shiva.'

'When Vrinda discovered how Vishnu had tricked her, she got furious and cursed Vishnu that he would turn into a black stone, and then drowned herself. Vishnu, although ready to face her curse, blessed his devotee that in her next life, she would be married to him. He became the black stone shaligram and gods turned her soul into the Tulsi plant.'

Raskapoor looked puzzled. She asked Rudra, 'Can an ordinary woman curse a god? And can her curse come true?' Rudra said, 'Yes, any woman who is betrayed the way Vrinda was can curse, and that curse will be very powerful. The day of the wedding of Vishnu as shaligram and Vrinda as Tulsi is celebrated on the eleventh day of the bright half of Kartik month. You know this day is considered very auspicious by Hindus as the wedding season begins from this day.'

Raskapoor immediately commented, 'All these gods have strange marriages in different incarnations. They can transform and disguise themselves in different forms like Krishna in Maharaas.'

Rudra looked up at the full moon of Kartik. He said, 'Our gods have human traits as a reminder to us that we too can become divine, as well as turn into demons. Gods disguise themselves, dance, marry, and even celebrate festivals as we do. You know Ras, today the gods are celebrating their Diwali.'

'Their Diwali? What do you mean? Diwali is already gone fifteen days back. Don't fool me,' she said to him disbelievingly.

Rudra then told her the story of Dev Diwali. 'What we celebrate is Devi Diwali, in honour of Goddess Laxmi; but on Dev Diwali, the Gods descend to take a holy dip in the river Ganges. On this day, your Lord Shiva slew yet another demon, Tripurasura, who ruled over the three worlds.'

Raskapoor was in awe of his knowledge and asked him how he knew so much. 'Unlike you, I do not spend time in meaningless celebrations at the palace,' he teased her, with the intention of keeping her away from the fatal attraction of palace life.

Raskapoor, who was lost in the world of gods and goddesses, retorted, 'You say that because you have never been there. It is another world—exotic and beautiful beyond your imagination. Let's not talk about the palace.'

Rudra calmed her down, 'Let's get back to Shiva.' Talking of dance and gods, she was reminded of Mahananda, and she enquired if he knew her story too. 'Yes, I do know. Do you want to hear that as well?' he asked her, having heard of her intense desire to become Mahananda and marry Shiva. 'Mahananda, in some ways was like you. An ardent devotee of Lord Shiva, a very talented dancer, and gifted with extraordinary beauty—but she was a wealthy prostitute,' he began.

To pull her out of the world of tawaifs and prostitutes, he explained to her that prostitutes earned their wealth by being in the company of not one but many men. Mahananda was a special woman who had taken the oath to be faithful as a wife to the man in whose company she was, who shared with her his fortunes as well as misfortunes. No amount of temptation could make her betray that man. So much so, that even the immense charm of Lord Indra could not break her oath when he wanted to lure her away.

He said, 'Mahananda was basically a pious lady. She observed a fast on Mondays as well as Maha Shivratri and donated food and money to the needy. One day, a handsome young man came to her doorstep. She was instantly attracted to him as he had a personality that she had never seen before. She asked him to sit down. When she admired his divine bracelet, he took it off and extended it to her. She told him that she did not accept anything from a man if she did not serve him as a wife. He took her as his wife for three days. He then handed her a very special phallic stone to keep safely, explaining his vow that any damage to the stone would result in him sacrificing his life. That young man was none other than Shiva, who had come to test her devotion for him. At night he himself set fire to her palace. Compassionate Mahananda rushed to set her parrot and rooster free before she and her guest came out. Within no time, her palace turned into ashes. The guest asked her to give back the stone, which she had unfortunately failed to retrieve from the flames. She begged him for his forgiveness, but he told her he had to keep his vow and entered the fire. She too did not forget her vow to be with the man who she had accepted as a husband and jumped into the fire with him.'

Raskapoor was immensely moved by this tragic tale and asked, 'Did both die?' He saw tears rolling down her eyes and responded in a comforting tone, 'No, my dear Ras. How can a god die, and how would he not protect such a devotee? From the blazing flames, the young man emerged as 'Chandramouli Shiva' holding Mahananda in his arms! For the first time, Mahananda felt the divine ecstasy that was the meaning of her name. So now wipe your tears and laugh.' She laughed and Rudra joined her. The sound delighted Chaand, who called them down as their meal was ready.

Back to the Palace

Till her father returned, Raskapoor rehearsed through the day, spending the evenings in conversation with Rudra, who also helped her master the complete Shiv Strota. She was indeed looking forward to the return of her father to recite all the verses with perfection to him. The idea of surprising her father was exciting but not at the cost of the evening sessions with Rudra, who the mother and daughter knew would not like to be present in the company of the likes of Mishraji. Raskapoor seemed to be getting fonder of Rudra with each day. She admired his intelligence and ability to strike up an engaging conversation every day. Time flew by in his company and whenever he got up to leave, she asked him to stay back for a few more minutes.

When after a few weeks, Mishraji arrived with some gifts of jewellery for both mother and daughter, neither felt excited, wondering what would happen to Rudra's visits in the evenings. Her father asked Ras how the classes were going, but Chaand replied, 'Panditji, she is a swift learner, but the day-long classes tire her. I would like you to schedule the lessons for half a day as they were before.'

He laughed. 'I know my daughter. She has a lot of energy. Chaand, my love, the teachers will leave in three weeks. Let her learn as much as she can.' Chaand and Raskapoor knew that they had no way out.

It had been quite some time since he was gone, and he was not very sure if his daughter remembered all the moves and the game rules of chess. To check her memory, he invited Ras to play a game of chess. She quickly got the chess box, and after setting the board, she challenged him to be ready for a defeat. Remembering the guidance of Rudra, who had told her that the one who made a move first had an advantage, she surprised her father by not flipping the coin to decide who would go first. She had already set the light-coloured sandalwood pieces towards her side and placed the ebony set for her father to follow. Mishraji noticed the smartness of her daughter but did not insist on the toss. But when she moved the pieces tactfully and checked his king, he could not resist enquiring who her teacher was in his absence. Before Raskapoor could open her mouth, the mother who was watching the two play intervened, not letting Rudra's name come up. 'She is your daughter, and she practised when you were gone, playing on your behalf too. She is a very fair girl, many times, making you win in your absence. I saw her do that many times from her window.' Chaand's words caused him to admire her passion for the game. Applauding her victory, he gave her a standing ovation in appreciation of her sharp mind.

He left a little before the time for the teachers to arrive, telling Ras, 'My beautiful daughter, practice well. I am going to come back in the evening.' The teachers worked with their disciple throughout the day, having been instructed in advance by Mishraji. At dusk, as he was heading towards the glass palace, Rudra saw Mishraji a few steps ahead of him, walking in the same direction. Much as he did not want to, Rudra turned back. Ras and her mother saw Shiv Narain step into the courtyard and realized that his visit was going to dissuade Rudra from coming. They exchanged a glance of disappointment over his entry.

Unaware of this, Mishraji excitedly handed some sweets to his daughter. 'So, let's get back to the palace.'

'Back to the palace?' she asked, and laughed when he told her what he meant—they should return to the lessons in history he had been giving her before he left. Much as she yearned to meet Rudra, her mood changed, as Raskapoor was waiting to hear about the Maharaja who succeeded Madho Singh.

'Did Pratap succeed to the throne after the death of his father?' she asked. 'Well, do you remember as per the norms, the eldest son of the king was first in line?' inquired the father. 'Like Madho Singh, did he also have a stepbrother?' Raskapoor asked. Her father smiled and told her, 'Yes, a stepbrother older than him. His name was Prithvi Singh, and he was all of five years when he came to the throne.' 'What? Just five years old!' Ras laughed out loud and then asked on a serious note as to how such a small child could rule.

'Indeed, such a small boy could not even comprehend what was happening around him! The regency was in the hands of his stepmother Maji Chundawatji, Deogarh Thakur's daughter. Soon, her father himself appeared in Jaipur to run the state on Prithvi Singh's behalf in league with two ever-conniving ministers and Firoz, the elephant keeper.'

The innocent young girl was unable to understand how an elephant keeper could be involved in running the state. The father refrained from explaining the close relationship between the young Maharaja's mother and the keeper. It was a well-known fact even outside the palace, but he knew that such facts were better not talked about. Mishraji, therefore, chose not to divulge such details in case she chose to share it with others as, like him, she loved storytelling.

Manoeuvring his thoughts, he told her that the elephant keeper was a confidant of the family. He explained to her how the local barons of the Kachchwaha clan got upset with his interference, which undermined their authority. They too started working on getting control of the administration, giving rise to two rival groups. While the Nathawat Rajputs gathered under the leadership of the barons of Chomu and Samode, the baron of Jhalai led the Rajawat group.

'However, Prithvi Singh's regime ended in just ten years when he died a sudden death due to a fall from a horse. But, according to many, this was not the real story.'

Raskapoor immediately asked, 'How did he actually die?'
Mishraji answered her question with caution, as he explained
to her that no one ever really knew what transpired behind the
walls of the palace. But most believed the cause of the death to
be poison as his mortal remains bore no sign of injuries from a
fall. Disturbed by the sad and unfortunate demise of the young
Maharaja, Raskapoor was not going to let her father continue
further until she knew who poisoned him and for what reason.
Failing miserably in his attempts to divert her attention, he
realized that he could not make headway until he told her what
she wanted to know.

Mishraji then explained that not just the outside world, but
many insiders too suspected that the Maharaja was murdered at
the behest of his stepmother, who wanted her son Pratap to be
the ruler.

'Another Kekayi! How old was Pratap Singh when he became
the Maharaja?' she asked her father.

'Thirteen years old.'

'So, somebody else controlled the throne till he grew up,' she
observed. Mishraji told her that she was right. He then related
the whole story to her. When Pratap Singh was a minor, power
remained with his mother, her trusted elephant keeper and her
chosen set of ministers, leaving the disgruntled barons grabbing
villages and playing their game of intrigues. Every time a new
Maharaja acceded to the throne, he had to pay a succession fee as
a tribute to the Moghul Emperor. Shah Alam II, the emperor, had
settled for Rs 20 lakh, of which only Rs 2 lakh could be given as an
advance. The remaining amount due from Jaipur State provoked
the emperor to attack the defaulting state time and again to coerce
them to pay.

'That was too much money to pay. Could the emperor not be
requested to reduce the amount peacefully?' asked Raskapoor as
she pondered over the excessive and unjust tribute.

'Pratap Singh, after coming out of his minority, did try to settle
the matter to govern his state peacefully but failed. When he came
to the throne, India was witnessing a great upheaval. The Moghuls

were decaying, the Marathas were upgrading their military might with the help of the French, and the British who came to trade were spreading their political wings. Within eight years of his succession, the tribute got as high as Rs 60 lakh because of the chief negotiator Rao Pratap Singh Naruka's double-dealings. Despite being a small vassal holding just a couple of villages, Naruka was able to draw the ruler's attention with his intelligence and mannerism. Ambitious and smart, Naruka had a firm grip over the Kachchwaha administration without holding any responsible office, but later, he moved away to forge an alliance with the Maratha camp.

Deeply aggrieved, Raskapoor insisted on getting a detailed account of the game plan of Naruka, whom she even called a traitor. Mishraji continued further, 'The emperor had appointed Mahadji Scindia as the Imperial Regent as well as the Commander in Chief. After being selected as the Emperor's Wakil-i-Mutlaq and Amir-ul-Umara, Mir Bakshi Scindia became very powerful. The first task assigned to him was to recover the money due from Jaipur State. Scindia got the Moghul Emperor to march towards the territory of Pratap Singh. Initially, even the over-ambitious Maratha wished to settle the dues peacefully. Knowing of Naruka's proximity to the Jaipur ruler before joining the Maratha camp, Scindia chose him to start the peace process with the Maharaja. The much-pressurized ruler gave his consent without any hesitation. He was a wheeler-dealer who had even managed to oust the Queen mother and her brother out of the administration and connived first to get the influential Mahout arrested and later set him free on the payment of a huge ransom. Naruka had also taken a big loan from the treasury as well as acquired some land through deceitful means. He knew that a peaceful settlement would mean loss of that property, for till the time the state was under pressure, no one would dare the man in crisis. So, he convinced Mahadji to hike the amount given the presence of the emperor himself, insisting that settling for a smaller amount would undermine the very authority of the emperor. He even went a step further. He proposed that they dislodge the

Maharaja if he did not pay, appoint a new ruler, and make him the Regent. For this, he would pay Rs 50 lakh.

Correctly judging his mediator's unreliable character, Scindia negotiated the terms with a representative of the Kachchwaha ruler, but the amount was the same as proposed by Naruka. As a way out, Rs 11 lakh was reimbursed, but Pratap Singh knew that the settlement could not be adhered to. He also knew that his army could not match the army of Scindia, which was equipped with modern artillery and aided by the tactical intelligence of the French. He then decided to send one of his emissaries to Lucknow to get the English soldiers to challenge the Maratha invasion. The new Governor-General Lord Cornwallis could not be convinced as the British policy of non-intervention was in place in the Indian States, which were always at loggerheads.

Pratap Singh decided to face the Marathas and formed an alliance with the martial Rathores of Jodhpur and directed his own feudal subjects not to pay anything to the Marathas. Finally, the Marathas and Rajputs fought the famous battle of Tunga, in which the Marathas were forced to retreat from the territory of Sawai Pratap Singh.

Raskapoor was thrilled with the courage of Pratap Singh. She asked if the Moghuls came back again to collect the tribute. Her father informed her that they did return after three years, as the disloyal and jealous forces of his regime connived and proved to be his greatest enemies.

'Pratap Singh was a very nice human being, and all these crooks took advantage of that,' continued Mishraji. 'He even tried to dislodge the Deccan powers when he got the news that the allies Holkars and Scindia had fallen apart. He set aside the negotiation on the dues, which resulted in another battle about a year ago. Though victory eluded him, it ended in a peace accord. The full moon night celebration at Hawa Mahal, in a subtle way, celebrated some moments of peace. Now let's pray and hope for peace in our kingdom!'

As he sipped his drinks, Raskapoor hurriedly finished her dinner and came back. She asked, 'How many wives and children does Pratap Singh have?' She wanted to figure out who would be his successor. He told her that there were about twelve wives and one son Jagat, who was sitting next to the Maharaja during the celebrations at Hawa Mahal.

Chaand was quick to notice that he had skipped mentioning Pratap Singh's other children. They were the offspring of two tawaifs like her, and lived in the palace too. Pratap was known for his weakness for dance, music, and beautiful girls. Deedarbaksh, his favourite nautch girl, was the mother of his two sons, Mohandas and Kandas. Rangrai was the mother of Pratap Singh's son Balbhadradas and his daughter Mohan Kanwar. Chaand was also upset to hear of the presence of the young prince at the full moon celebrations. The sceptical mother was filled with apprehensions about her daughter's fate and could not sleep a wink.

Leaving her parents alone, Raskapoor got back to her room. Why could the Maharajas and Maharanis not live happily? Why did they trust the untrustworthy? Why did the feudal lords connive against their masters? Why did the queens only want their sons to rule and get the legitimate ruler dislodged? She brooded over all these questions as she lay awake in her bed. She began worrying about the fate of all the princely states fighting among themselves. She feared this would result in them being taken over by foreigners someday. The thought of foreign rule was too scary, and suddenly she sat up to pray to Natraj to grant wisdom to all the princely states to unite and not fight among themselves.

Winter and Spring Time at the Glass Palace

Raskapoor's teachers gave her a beautiful gift before they headed for Banaras. 'You are our divine disciple. Together we decided to give you this statue of Goddess Sarasvati, the goddess of art and wisdom. We both worship her every day, and it was with her blessings that we could excel in our art. You should start praying to her from Basant Panchami, the first day of the beautiful spring season dedicated to her,' they said and handed her the statue.

Ras held the beautifully carved figurine in her hands. She admired the deity's string instrument Veena, her mount, the swan, and her lovely eyes for a few minutes. The teachers observed her expressions and then asked her how she liked their gift. Raskapoor opted to raise a point instead of replying to their question. 'You just said that you both worshipped her, but then Muslims don't worship any statue. Am I right?' she questioned the two senior masters. Amused with her observation, the Muslim teacher chose to respond, 'For artists, the religion is their art. Since she is the goddess of art, all artists practising classical art forms of Hindoostan invoke her blessings.'

Her Hindu teacher endorsed his view. 'Just as Hindu artists go to Sufi shrines to make an offering, Muslim artists seek blessings of Devi Sarasvati. We make no difference in rendering devotional songs, be they the work of a Sufi saint or a Hindu poet.' She was then informed that their two assistants would continue to teach her and that the two teachers would return in the course of the spring to see her progress.

Winter was rather severe. The days became shorter and the nights longer, with the result that Raskapoor's life was confined to the glass palace. Her day was spent on dance and music classes, and before it got dark, her father would come to keep an eye on her like a hawk. All through winter, Ras and Rudra could not get the quality time they both longed for. However, their rendezvous at the two temples continued.

Ras gradually realized that the only man she could trust was going to be Rudra. One day, when she showed Rudra the statute of Sarasvati and shared the advice given by her teachers on seeking her blessings, his enthusiastic response astonished her. Usually, he needed to be coaxed into participating actively in any such event, but this time, they joined hands in planning the celebrations from that very moment. It was going to be an occasion just for the two of them, witnessed only by her mother. Raskapoor did not want the two assistant teachers and her father to come that day. She discussed her feelings with Rudra and asked him to pray with her to grant her two wishes. He yielded to the innocent request made by her. Initially, he was surprised to see the change in himself that had led him to make such a dubious pact with Raskapoor; but for the first time, he loved that childlike change.

She could not believe her ears when a few days later she heard her father tell her mother that he would be gone for nearly two months. He had decided to take dips in the holy river Ganges in the month of Magh, considered to be the most auspicious ritual by Hindus. He would return only after Maha Shivratri, the last day of the bathing ritual. Raskapoor, who was longing for Basant Panchami, also found out that it fell in the bright half of Magh. She could not wait to divulge the news to Rudra that one of their wishes was being granted. The moment she saw him, she told him, while asking him to continue to pray earnestly for the suspension of her classes as well for that day.

It was Makar Sankranti, the day the sun transited into the zodiac sign of Capricorn. And with it came a crucial transition in Raskapoor's life, too. She was getting irritable by the day. Often, she complained of back pain, fatigue and soreness in her breasts. Her dance classes were cancelled off and on. Experienced Chaand read the signals and knew that her daughter was not sick but going through the turbulence of premenstrual syndrome. A few weeks later, the red dots on her daughter's skirt drew Chaand's attention. On that day, Raskapoor moved from her childhood into adulthood. Her ever-alert mother explained to her that from that day, she would not visit the temple for the four days of her monthly cycle following Hindu custom. She had already prepared her daughter for this day, knowing that if she did not, it could result in mental agony. Chaand felt pleased to observe that her daughter was not shocked to see the bloodstains. On the contrary, when the mother took her inside to change, she smiled, 'Ammi, so now I am a big girl.' Behind the closed door of her room, instead of feeling uneasy with the significant change in her life, Raskapoor was thanking her Shiva. He was the one who had scheduled the change in her life in a way that it did not disturb her plans. She was delighted to realize that she would be able to celebrate Basant Panchami, which would fall nine days later as she finished counting the number of days bending her fingers. Raskapoor was ready to seek the blessings of Goddess Sarasvati to become a virtuous singer and dancer so that she could surpass Mahananda and marry Shiva!

Her farsighted mother sewed clothes that were long and loose for her daughter so that her striking figure did not attract any attention. Initially, Raskapoor complained about the sudden change in the dresses her mother was designing for her. Chaand, however, convinced her tactfully. She informed that those outfits were prescribed as suitable for growing girls when they visited temples.

Realizing that her daughter would take a little time to feel at ease with the new change in her life, Chaand decided to suspend her classes for the next ten days. She quickly sent out a message to Nargis informing her about her daughter's ill health. For shrewd

Nargis, this was heartening news. She knew then and there that her disciple had turned into a young woman, for she had already sensed the day was not far away noticing the symptoms Ras showed in the past few weeks. This was what she had been waiting for from the moment Raskapoor was born.

On Basant Panchami day, when Chaand handed over the two yellow dresses to her daughter, she was thrilled. 'Ammi, you made a dress for my Goddess Sarasvati too,' she cried. Chaand then gave her yet another packet, saying, 'And I have some ornaments for her too.' Raskapoor dressed up the statue in the clothes and all the ornaments. 'See Ammi, how pretty she looks with the tika on her forehead and the nose ring.' Chaand smiled and urged Raskapoor to wear her outfit. As she put it on, she wondered what was wrong with her mother. She had made a clingy blouse, which was also a bit above her waistline. She came out complaining, but her mother told her that she desired her daughter to look like the goddess. 'Today, apart from Rudra, no one else is coming. He will be here any moment. You can change after worshipping the goddess. You are looking so divine, my child,' Chaand said, making her daughter feel elated. She put a nose ring on her daughter's sharp long nose. Ras looked extraordinary in that yellow outfit with kohl highlighting her sparkling almond eyes. Both mother and daughter waited for Rudra to come.

When Rudra entered the courtyard and saw Raskapoor holding the statue of Sarasvati in her hand, he was spellbound. He could not take his eyes off the young lady standing before him in place of the child he knew. He had not been able to see Raskapoor for a while, as according to the message sent to him by her mother, she had not been feeling well. Raskapoor had not stepped out for the past few weeks, and he refrained from coming over since he knew he was invited to join the celebration on Basant Panchami.

Chaand was delighted to see how he kept looking at her daughter just as she had hoped he would and prayed for their blissful life. She drew his attention, asking him to conduct the prayer. 'My son, you are our priest today.'

Rudra performed the ritual, and once it got over, Ras's mother asked her to keep the statue in her room and change.

'Wait Ammi, let me ask Rudra how I look in this new dress,' Raskapoor said. She had noted how Rudra had admired her, staring at her as if in a trance while chanting hymns.

Rudra was embarrassed but managed to say, 'Just like Bani Thani.' 'Who is that?' asked Raskapoor, instantly curious.

Her mother intercepted her, directing her first to do what she had advised her to do. She changed quickly into one of her loose outfits and rushed out to get Rudra to tell her who Bani Thani was.

'A witch,' Rudra replied. While Chaand knew he was joking, Raskapoor was not amused to hear this.

Seeing her expression, Rudra told her, 'Do not get upset. Bani Thani was an exceptionally beautiful woman and a great singer who was always dressed up. When I saw you, I instantly thought of her.'

She relaxed then but wanted to know when he met Bani Thani. He laughed, telling her that she died many years before he was even born. As expected, she wanted to know how he was reminded of her if he had not even seen her. 'I had seen a painting of her two years ago in Kishangarh when I went with my father to the Kartik fair at Pushkar. We had halted in Kishangarh for a few nights, and I went to Nagri Kunj Temple and saw the two chhatris, one of King Sawant Singh and the other of Bani Thani.'

Raskapoor asked why Bani Thani's cenotaph was built next to the Maharaja's. Rudra then told her the whole story.

'The real name of the beautiful lady was Vishnu Priya, and she was employed in Kishangarh palace by Sawant Singh's mother. He was absolutely smitten by her beauty, singing and above all, her devotion to Radha and Krishna, just like him. They fell in love. The old priest at the temple told me that first, she was the mistress of the Maharaja, but as their love blossomed, he took her as his wife. She was always decked up, following the desire of the king, and her name Vishnu Priya turned into Bani Thani. He considered himself to be Krishna and her to be Radha. Both expressed their divine love under the pen names Nagri Das and Rasik Bihari, respectively. He got his court painter Nihal Chaand to depict her beauty in his art, and he created an extraordinary portrait. The priest arranged with the court priest for me to see that painting, and I have never been able to forget that elegant and graceful face. Their love was such that they died together.'

Raskapoor's heart was deeply touched, and wiping her tears, she asked the reason for the death of the two divine lovers. Rudra had not asked the priest that question. He said, 'Every time I tell you such stories, you cry. They died some forty years ago, so no one talks about how or why they died. You should instead feel happy that they died together, or the one left behind would have been miserable.'

On that day, Raskapoor prayed to die with her husband like Mahananda and Bani Thani.

Soon after Basant Panchami, Raskapoor's music and dance lessons resumed. Nargis could not believe how the girl had transformed in just ten days. She smiled at Chaand. 'My friend, it seems spring has indeed arrived at the glass palace. Your bud has turned into a fragrant flower. Wait and watch, her fragrance will soon drift to the palace!'

Chaand, who knew the underlying thought behind those words of appreciation for her beautiful daughter, told Nargis, 'Keep your bumblebees far away. Both you and I know what transpires in the palace, so do not joke about it. You told the Maharaja she was my daughter, but why could you not introduce her father, who was right there?' Clever Nargis chose to simply smile instead of arguing and resumed the lessons, calling the rest of her team upstairs. She was well aware of the fact that Chaand was very upset with her ever since the day she took Raskapoor to the palace.

Days passed by in rigorous music and dance sessions. Chaand did manage to get Rudra and Raskapoor to meet as often as she could. Maha Shivratri, a festival that celebrates the day Shiva married Goddess Parvati, was the next big event for Raskapoor. She had informed her mother that she would observe a fast, go to the temple and break the fast in the evening, just like Rudra did. Her mother invited Rudra to break his fast with her daughter. Rudra, who was longing to spend more time with Ras, proposed to perform 'Rudrabhisheka', the very special Hindu ritual, in their courtyard, instead of them coming to the temple. As the mother and daughter looked startled, he explained that the ritual invoked Shiva's blessings to fulfil wishes and rectify the evil environment.

'So, Ammi, he wishes us to worship him—that is why he calls it Rudrabhisheka,' Raskapoor laughed. Her mother immediately asked her not to laugh as Rudra, being a Brahmin, would not joke about a ritual. Chaand, a practising Muslim, was not hesitant in performing any ritual to get her daughter married before she could be trapped in the world of nautch girls. She welcomed the idea but told him that they did not have any phallic statues. He advised them not to be anxious as he would make it with clay as well as bring all the ingredients. The next afternoon, when he walked in with the priest of the temple, Chaand could not believe her eyes—a Hindu priest in a Muslim home!

The enlightened priest, observing her amazement at his arrival, spoke with a smile, 'I am here to perform Rudrabhisheka for Shiva's devotee, your daughter.' Rudra had requested him to do this, and he accepted it as he could see Rudra's growing love for Raskapoor. Deep inside him, he felt that he could not change their destinies, but he could at least pray for that divine girl. Lasting over a few hours, the ritual ended with the offering of camphor. The priest blessed Ras. 'Your name means the essence of camphor. Ras, my daughter, camphor is a purifier—remember that. Remember if your soul is purified, you can come clean out of the sludge, like a lotus.'

The priest then hurried off for the next ceremony while Rudra and Raskapoor indulged in an intense conversation about Shiva, Parvati and the rituals. Suddenly, Rudra asked her, 'Do you know why the green leaves or bel patra are offered?' She nodded in affirmation and answered, 'Because that is the ritual.'

Rudra then explained to her the significance of symbolism in Hinduism. 'The trifoliate leaves of the golden apple tree offered to Shiva, bel patra, represents Goddess Parvati, as the tree is supposed to have grown from droplets of her sweat. We celebrate their marriage as we offer the leaves to unite Shiva and Parvati. Ras, you know, the leaf also represents the holy trinity of Hindus.' After breaking their fasts, when Rudra left, Chaand and Raskapoor talked for a few hours about how Rudra created such a spiritual experience at the glass palace.

For a few weeks, life remained uneventful till the day her two teachers returned from Varanasi. When they saw Raskapoor, they could not help but express their amazement to Chaand. 'In just a few months, your daughter has grown up so much!'

Chaand, who knew her daughter could outdo any princess or much-sought-after tawaif with her beauty and talent, brushed aside their comment. She said, 'She is still a growing child.'

The two teachers handed over two brocade veil cloths to Raskapoor. 'We got these from a weaver in Varanasi. Wear them when you go for your first performance.'

Before Chaand could snub them, Raskapoor replied, 'I perform every day before Natraj, and I will wear them today itself.'

Watching her perform, they both marvelled at the work their two assistants had done in teaching Ras very intricate segments as well as inculcating tremendous grace in her. Her footwork and her hundred and one spins left the teachers wonderstruck.

Mystic Love

Ever since Rudra had told Raskapoor the story of Bani Thani and the King, who thought themselves to be divine lovers like Lord Krishna and Radha, she started wondering if she could be as fortunate as Bani Thani. Spring had kindled a different emotion in her. Now, her dream woman Mahananda often dissolved first into Bani Thani and then into Radha dressed in the yellow outfit. She could not understand what was changing within her heart, but sometimes she asked herself if she could be the incarnation of Bani Thani. She could not share her thoughts with anybody without the fear of being considered crazy or possessed by an evil spirit and then taken to an exorcist either at a mosque or the Balaji Temple.

Indeed, the change in her emotions was reflected in her performance of gat, portraying Krishna and Radha at the same time taking a half turn. Both her teachers were amazed to see her divine expressions as she emoted the feelings of Krishna and the lovelorn Radha. Pundit Kundanlalji one day told her, 'Raskapoor, you have changed so much. Earlier, you were merely dancing, but now you are feeling the dance. Your face glows with mystic love.' Her music teacher, Ustad Hafiz Khan, explained to her that the emotion of mystic love liberates the soul. Seeing that she could not grasp what he was talking about, he simplified it, saying, 'Mystic love is no ordinary love between a man and a woman, it is the divine love between god and his devotee. The complete devotion to the almighty is expressed in two distinctive styles of music, 'Bhakti Sangit' among Hindus, focusing mainly on Radha and Krishna, and the 'Qawwali' of the Sufis. Very interestingly, in this season of Basant, that mystic love blossoms all around and is celebrated with devotional music both in the Hindu temples and the Sufi shrine of Hazrat Nizamuddin Aulia.'

Raskapoor wished to know whom the Muslims sang to as they had no Krishna and Radha. Hafiz Khan smilingly told her, for them Allah was their Krishna and all devotees represented his Radha.

And then, the inquisitive Raskapoor wanted to know who Nizamuddin Aulia was. Hafiz Khan told her about the Sufi saint, as well as about his ardent disciple Amir Khosrow whom the Ustad felt she must know about. Credited for his immense contribution to Hindustani music, Khosrow was a prolific Sufi poet and was supposed to have created not only different musical styles like qawwali, tarana and khayal, but had also evolved the sitar and the tabla by breaking the traditional temple percussion pakhavaj into two.

She also learnt that both her teachers had been frequenting Nizamuddin's shrine in springtime when the atmosphere was charged with the poetry of Khosrow sung by the Qawwals. Like in the temples of Krishna, in the shrine the devotees played with the colours and the petals of the spring. The inner soul of the seeker was submerged in the intensity of mystic love, yearning to unite with the divine lover. Mesmerized, Raskapoor asked the Ustad if he could sing a Sufi verse for her. He readily agreed. He sang, with the accompaniment of his musicians and the dance teacher, the captivating qawwali he had heard a few weeks ago when he had gone to offer a floral covering at the shrine:

'Today there is a special celebration, a celebration of radiant colours. Mother, my beloved's courtyard is filled with the colours.

Colours are splashed at the home of Nizamuddin Aulia, mother, I was madly searching the mystic colours here and there.

But my body and soul seek only one shade—the tone of my mentor Nizamuddin.

Mother, that colour is all around me. That colour is within me.

No spectacle is more colourful than the one at his home, mother.

All other colours wash away, the colour of the mystic love remains forever, mother.

On the wedding night, I sleep with my beloved, I lie awake all night.

My body is dyed in the mystic love, my soul is dyed in the mystic love, I am united with my divine beloved.'

In the end, as Ustad sang to the rising pace of the percussionist and the other musicians clapping along, the resounding mysticism overpowered Raskapoor. She suddenly got up and swirled around, emoting every word of the great poet Khosrow. Both the musicians and the dancer appeared to be intoxicated with divine love. While the amazed musicians were sweating, their dancer was radiating divinity. Images of Mahananda, Radha and Bani Thani were dancing in her eyes. She seemed to be in another world, united with the divine beloved . . . Shiva, Krishna and the king. Finally, when the tired musicians gave up, Raskapoor slid to the ground, and her anxious mother helped her to the bed inside. She opened her eyes only the next morning.

Seeking the Divine

It was not just Raskapoor, but also all the rulers of her land, who prayed to the divine to protect the devotee from all hazards.

Like his grandfather Sawai Jai Singh II, Sawai Pratap Singh too was an ardent devotee of Govind Dev, the presiding deity of Jai Nagar. The palace looked directly towards the temple so that the ruler could bow before him as soon as he woke up. When Emperor Aurangzeb issued orders to demolish all the temples of Brij Bhoomi covering Mathura and Vrindavan, the main statues were moved to other places. Govind Dev ji was brought first to Amber, and then Jai Singh moved the statue to his newly founded city.

While scholarly Jai Singh connected with the deity on an intellectual level, his poet and music-loving grandson developed a strong emotional connection with the deity. He dreamt of Govind Devji every night and sought the divine each time he faced a crisis of any kind. With his special deity in mind, Pratap indulged in writing devotional poetry, as well as music. Throughout his life, he was entangled in war, betrayals and women; yet he wrote some 1400 poems under the pen name Brijnidhi, the treasure of Brij. Of the six Krishna temples and one Shiva temple built by him, the most significant was of 'Brijnidhi'. A highly emotional man, Pratap went a step ahead of his father in expressing his admiration for Radha. He highlighted the significance of worshipping Radha in Lord Krishna's invocation when he wrote, 'Bless me, the queen of Vrindavan'. Pratap Singh even conducted Krishna and Radha's marriage in the temple. While Pratap Singh arrived with fanfare accompanying the bridegroom Lord Krishna, his minister Daulatram Haldiya gave away the bride Radha in the wedding ritual. The bridegroom's party was treated to a royal feast, the bride was given a full trousseau, and then the couple was happily housed in the sanctum sanctorum.

With the grand celebrations at Hawa Mahal, no one could envisage the fresh gush of turbulence right at the beginning of the 19th century. The battles fought far away left the city unscathed, while the autumn full moon celebrations had rejuvenated the spirit of its inhabitants. Pratap Singh was the only Maharaja since the time of his grandfather who had added a jewel in the crown. He kept a close watch on the perfect completion of the facade flanking the main artery of the city. All looked well, but Sawai Pratap Singh chose to benefit from the civil war situation in the Scindia camp, rejecting all the clauses finalized earlier to meet the financial demands of Scindia. He plunged into a war undermining the resources of the enemy, who had the much more experienced commanders to lead the brigades. His plans were dashed with the strategic response from the opposite camp. Finally, he was forced to bring down his elephant and retreat on horseback while all his camp, baggage and guns were captured. Pratap Singh could never recover from the pain of that humiliation.

Pandit Shiv Narain had noticed the first signs of Pratap Singh's failing health. For some time, he had been observing the decreasing energy levels in a man who was just in his thirties. Gradually, Pratap Singh started spending most of his time either in the ladies' quarters or in the temples.

One day when Pandit Shiv Narain came to the glass palace, he shared the news of the fast-deteriorating health of the ruler. He told Chaand, 'I think something terrible is going to hit our city. Several experts on Ayurveda have been coming to treat the Maharaja. I hear no medicine is working on him. No one talks about his illness, but rumours are floating about. Some say it's a blood disorder, while others say it's leprosy.'

Although Chaand felt sorry for him, she could not restrain herself from commenting, 'I can tell you the cause of it.'

Shiv Narain was shocked to hear her and immediately asked who had told her the well-kept secret.

She smiled and said, 'Panditji, you are a learned man. How could you not know the cause of it? Our Maharaja is an incorrigible addict of women and wine. If you are not on the right path, no amount of prayers can help.'

He was dumbfounded for a few minutes trying to interpret her comment, which almost seemed a warning to himself. He then decided to leave, giving a firm direction to her. 'Do not think like a tawaif,' he said. 'You uttered these words to me but now never utter them again, at least for the safety of our daughter.'

A few weeks after this conversation, the news came that the Maharaja had retreated to the basement of Brijnidhi temple. The healers, too, stopped coming. Inside the palace, prayers were being conducted and the Brahmins, like Chaand's lover, were summoned daily. When the news reached her ears, she had a gut feeling that the Maharaja would not be able to witness the full autumn moon of the year 1803. She wondered if the Maharaja had been isolated because of his disease being infectious; or whether those who claimed to be close to him did not want to be near him to comfort him? Did his god only decide to give refuge to his devotee in his final journey? As she was pondering over Pratap Singh's end, she was hit by his reckless act of exposing his young son to the world of wine and women. Taking him along to such celebrations, like the one at Hawa Mahal, seemed a highly irresponsible act on the part of any father.

The ground under her feet seemed to shake. Chaand shuddered with the thought of the demise of the Maharaja, knowing well that in such an eventuality, the prince would be the next successor. Reputed to be a wayward adolescent, he was also rumoured to have a roving eye. Being a sensitive and protective mother, she had already gauged the plans Panditji and Nargis had laid to unveil her precious jewel Raskapoor in the palace. What could she do but pray to the almighty for her daughter's well-being? That seemed to be the only option left with the doomed mother! She was indebted to her paramour for not only liberating her from the infamous quarters, but also giving her the lavish home. In her earlier residence, she could have been entertaining more than one client night after night with the operator of the nautch house earning on her behalf. There, Mishraji would have indeed not spent the kind of time he was spending with his daughter in Kaanch Mahal. Ras would have been subjected to a dreadful upbringing, growing up in the world of tawaifs. Chaand was at the mercy of Mishraji and could not dare to confront him. Often, she cried at her incapacity to flee to a different world where she could ensure the future of her daughter.

On 1 August 1803, the expected news of the death of their ailing Maharaja hit the state. Even though they knew his end was near, they mourned his demise. His subjects saw him as a very kind-hearted man. After a benevolent Maharaja, they were sceptical about his successor, who they considered unfit to take charge of their state at that point in time. The general feeling was that their god-fearing Maharaja was let down time and again by his clan, or else the state would not have been in such a mess. They failed him each time he was attacked and plundered by the Marathas and Pindaris. So much so that even Jean Pillet, the French Captain who was serving in Jaipur, was deeply sympathetic towards Pratap Singh. He tried his best to forge an alliance between the Maharaja and the East India Company. The coalition was envisaged to not only extend the much-required support to the Maharaja but also to uphold British interests. He advocated an alliance of mutual benefit, calling Pratap Singh an 'Upright Prince'. The pact, however, did not materialize as the Company limited itself only to the affairs of the state of Oudh.

People talked about the kindness Pratap Singh showed in extending refuge to the dethroned Prince Wazir Ali who had murdered Mr Cherry, a resident in Banaras, and was on the run.

Their ruler had adhered to the age-old tradition of giving refuge to any asylum seeker without fearing the Company. Not just that, when the Company mounted pressure on him to surrender the murderer, he yielded only after obtaining the undertaking that they would not give a death penalty to Wazir Ali. Such was the stance of Pratap Singh, that the British Governor-General gifted him Rs 3 lakh.

A Whirlwind of Changes

The day Raskapoor swirled in a frenzy to the lyrics of the Sufi poet, her thoughts churned along. The following morning, she woke up feeling a profound difference inside her, starting to make sense of her reality and emerging from the world of her childish fantasies. She knew that she would always be a tawaif's child and never the daughter of a highly respected Brahmin. She smiled at the hypocrisy of the world around her in which neither Pratap Singh nor Pandit Shiv Narain could muster up the courage to own their children born out of wedlock. That day, she decided not to have a child out of wedlock. Her worried mother, who had been awake all night, was taken aback to see a different Raskapoor standing in the courtyard the following morning. She looked beautiful but older than her age. After that, Chaand marked the change every day, for alarmingly, her teenage daughter was growing up very fast.

While her mother was getting worried, Rudra was becoming more and more convinced that he wanted to marry that divine beauty. He dreaded the day of her first performance, which appeared to be fast approaching as he observed his beloved turning into a full-grown woman. Her delicate features, her long neck, and well-rounded figure with its slim waistline often reminded him of the painting of Bani Thani. Both enjoyed each other's company and spent as much time together as Chaand could duly plan for them. The idea of marriage did lure Ras when she witnessed the spectacular Gangaur procession with elephants, camels, chariots, and musicians. That day Rudra had gifted her clay images of the divine couple Issar and Gaur. Raskapoor gradually began to feel Rudra's emotions and soon realized that he was in love with her. She, too, was getting emotionally attached, but wisdom cautioned her. How could she harm her best friend knowing the wrath he would have to face from one and all if they discovered his love for her.

Soon after the death rituals of Pratap Singh, the crowning ceremony of his successor Jagat Singh took place. Jagat Singh's succession was not challenged as he was the only legitimate inheritor. He was a seventeen-year-old young man who already had many wives and concubines. That the young prince loved to indulge in the world of wine and women were the only facts known to the people of the city. They were apprehensive about the changes he would make after taking over the administration. His kind father was not there to guide the young man.

Before he died, Sawai Pratap Singh was about to sign the much-awaited treaty with the British upon the arrival of Marquess Wellesley as the new Governor-General of India. This was a time when across the world, the British and the French were at loggerheads. In India, the French were well aligned with the growing power of the Marathas. Wellesley arrived with the intention to forge alliances with the princely states ravaged by the Marathas. After months of deliberation, just as a treaty of offensive and defensive friendship was to be signed, Pratap Singh passed away. The first thing that Jagat Singh wanted was to live a peaceful life, not be overloaded with responsibility or subjected to extractions and threats. He hastened to sign the first alliance with the British and concluded it on 13 December that very year. In the new year, Jagat Singh had to support the British forces against the Maratha advancement as per the clauses of the alliance.

The newly appointed Maharaja was unable to celebrate his coronation in the befitting style that he yearned for. One day, he summoned Nargis to express his heartfelt desire to hear a new voice, a wave of fresh air to soothe his nerves. She smiled to herself, knowing his longing for a new companion despite having a fleet of women in the zenani deorhi. Nargis could not tell him straight away that she had an untouched jewel, which he would not be able to part with. Any such news could trash her dreams, as the man in front of her would have insisted on possessing the new find then and there. Time was needed to work out a fool-proof plan.

Raskapoor had once told Nargis about her pledge that the first time she would sing and dance outside of the glass palace would only be in a temple. Jagat Singh, however, was not devout like his father.

In fact, after the conversation with Nargis, Jagat Singh continued with his all-night parties, moving not one but several steps ahead of Pratap Singh. The palace condoned his over-indulgence because of him being a teenager who they believed would soon outgrow such addictions.

Finally, after a few months, Nargis hatched a plan with the very smart Pandit Shiv Narain. Both were eager to bring the extraordinary Raskapoor before the Maharaja in a subtle manner before Chaand got any inclination of their wicked plan. They shortlisted Brijnidhi temple as the venue and the Radhashtami, the birth anniversary of Radha, as the occasion. Nargis went to Jagat Singh to unfold her plan, 'Hukum, your highness, I have discovered not just the voice that will refresh your senses, but a beauty who will mesmerize you as never before. She will remind you of Bani Thani of Kishangarh.' Jagat Singh handed over a pouch of gold coins to her and insisted she brought the girl straightaway.

'We have planned to bring her to the temple, not the palace. The girl is too young. She has taken a pledge to perform only at a temple the first time she performs outside of her home. Above all, she is a devotee like your father who will go to a temple but not to your palace. Accordingly, after considerable thought, I have chosen Radha's birthday for you to get a glimpse of her. In fact, that day, you should be seated in such a manner that you can see her, but she cannot see you,' Nargis explained.

The mysterious plan ignited his curiosity. He could not wait for the day to arrive, which was still weeks away. Jagat Singh was not his usual self despite being in the company of women every single night. His thoughts wandered around the unseen beauty on whom Nargis had showered all those superlatives. Her words were still echoing in his mind: 'If the Moghul Emperor Shah Jahan had Mumtaz Mahal to build the Taj Mahal for, and the Kishangarh Maharaja had Bani Thani to be immortalized in a painting to be remembered for generations, the new girl will also create a history of sorts for her beauty and brains.'

No amount of persuasion of the young Maharaja could get Nargis to agree to bring the girl before the planned day. She rejoiced in his increasing interest in the girl and wondered what would happen to him the day the aura of Raskapoor filled the Brijnidhi temple. She had suggested to the Maharaja to brief the priest at the temple for the unique offering he was going to make with devotional music and dance to celebrate the birthday of Radha. On that day, an exclusive seating arrangement had to be prepared for the Maharaja so that the artists only addressed Radha and Lord Krishna, not their Maharaja. Jagat Singh did as she suggested, and the unsuspecting priest was thrilled, thinking that the new Maharaja was going to be an ardent devotee like his father.

Nargis was also preparing Chaand and Raskapoor for the exciting celebrations at the temple. One afternoon, after the sessions, on the advice of Nargis, the two Gurus blessed Raskapoor. They said, 'You have proved to be a remarkable disciple who has very quickly become an accomplished singer and dancer. A true artist is not only supposed to have great skills and a captivating presence but wisdom too. Raskapoor, dear daughter, you are a god-gifted artist. As you had desired to sing and dance in a temple, we have chosen the right place and the occasion for you.'

Humbled, Raskapoor touched the feet of the great masters as well as all present there—the musicians, Nargis and her mother—adhering to the Hindu tradition to express her gratitude. She then asked her teachers, 'Have you really planned a performance in a temple?' They both nodded. Ustad Hafiz Khan replied, 'Yes, we have, but dear child, we call it a musical and rhythmic invocation of the divine, not a performance. We have decided to celebrate Radha's birthday at the Brijnidhi temple.'

Raskapoor was thrilled at her teacher's words. 'Ammi, what a beautiful idea it is to call it a divine invocation! Don't you think the idea of the two Gurus is so nice?' she addressed her mother.

'Indeed, it is! You are a devotee of theirs right from your childhood, so Radha and Krishna will be very pleased with your invocation. They will shower all their blessings on you. I am sure my Radha will also soon find her Krishna,' said the unsuspecting mother, giving her consent. The priest of the temple could not see the hidden agenda behind the proposal and excitedly went about the preparations for that day. Nargis was congratulating herself to see her plan to go her way but mumbled under her breath, 'In the name of the divine, the gullible devotees get cheated.' They all parted happily. On their way back, the two teachers asked Nargis, 'Did we do our job of convincing the mother and the daughter well?' Nargis gave a sarcastic reply, 'Well, you are not just music and dance teachers but great actors. Look at you two teachers, one Muslim and one Hindu, coming together in the name of your gods Allah and Bhagwan when it comes to deceiving someone to earn money. Anyway, may the almighty pardon all of us as he knows we had to do it to survive.'

Raskapoor began to excitedly dream of the divine invocation. She started preparing the dances and the songs that would please Lord Krishna and Radha. She heard verses of various devotional poets but decided to choose the poems of Soordas and Meera Bai on Rudra's suggestion. Time and again, she tried to interpret those verses in her dance movements and sought his approval.

Meera Bai's story had fascinated Raskapoor ever since the day she first heard it from Rudra. Meera Bai, the princess of Merta, was an ardent devotee of Lord Krishna right from her childhood. She felt that she was betrothed to Lord Krishna for centuries. Such was her belief that the worried parents got their young daughter married to the ruler of Mewar. Meera did not give up her conviction despite all persuasion. Finally, she was sent a cup of poison by the ruler to either give up her belief or drink the poison to leave the world, and she opted to drink the poison. One of the first songs selected was:

'What all should I tell you my Girdhari, my dark-complexioned handsome Krishna.

All I can say to you is our love is eternal. It carries through the cycle of births. It will never vanish.

My dark-complexioned Girdhari, everyone will be spellbound with your captivating appearance.

Come to my courtyard of the palace. Everyone will sing welcome songs.

I will decorate the floor with ceremonial patterns, I will offer myself together with my soul. Take me in your shelter. I, Meera, have served you in all previous births, I will remain only yours in the next births too.'

Rudra could not believe his eyes when he saw her transforming into three legendary women. Radha, Meera Bai and Bani Thani came alive through her phenomenal dancing and singing skills. Raskapoor had told him explicitly that his participation in her rehearsals was going to be as a stand-in for Lord Krishna. All he was supposed to do was smile like Krishna each time she performed. He wanted to say to her that he could do that all his life if the two were united. In all forms, she appeared to be one with her divine lover. After standing in for the lord for weeks together, he started seeing himself as her divine lover. But his dream crashed each time she finished the rehearsal. She joked with him, 'Now you are no more my lord.'

Chaand loved the rehearsals and prayed for Rudra and Raskapoor to be married, and that he should flee with her princess. She was convinced that if her daughter wore a sky-blue outfit and Rudra wore a glowing yellow outfit, the couple would remind one and all of Radha and Krishna. Chaand had asked Rudra one day, 'My son, you know all about the Hindu gods and Goddesses. Can you tell me what was Radha's favourite colour?' Rudra had told her she loved Neelambri, the colour of the blue sky, and then talked about Pitambari, the glowing golden yellow colour, being the favourite of Lord Krishna. He further explained their reasons for choosing those colours. 'Krishna wanted to reflect the glowing love of Radha for him as if to say he adorned Radha only. Radha wished to appear one with her divine lover whose complexion was dark. Hindu women do not wear black when they get married, so Radha found the blue-sky colour apt to immortalize their divine love. The couple represents one another as their souls are united.' Chaand was deeply impressed with his profound knowledge, and if she had her way, would have first sowed the yellow attire for Rudra. It took her almost two weeks to painstakingly hand-stitch a fantastic sky-blue ensemble for Ras. She wanted her daughter to try it on before Rudra came for the last rehearsal a day before the temple celebration. Deep down in her heart, she longed for Rudra to be the first one to see Raskapoor as Radha. She had even given her the jewellery as well as a mukut, the divine crown, and a flute. Raskapoor came out after putting on her elaborate attire, holding the bamboo flute. Chaand was wonderstruck to see the incarnation of Radha before her eyes. As luck would have it, Rudra walked in too. Raskapoor stood smiling in the arched doorway, still holding the flute.

Rudra's heart pulsated, and he had a tremendous urge to take her in his arms and say, 'See Radha! Your Krishna has come to your palace courtyard!' He restrained himself and commented, 'Radha Rani of the temple will be surprised to see this Radha from Kaanch Mahal.'

Raskapoor burst out laughing and told him to get ready to be her Krishna as she would start the rehearsal after changing her clothes. Chaand had advised Nargis to conduct the formal rehearsal in the latter part of the day, planning for Rudra and Raskapoor to have their last session. After finishing the last rehearsal, Raskapoor as usual teased him, but this time she said, 'Now you are free from being my lord!' Rudra took note of it, and that comment haunted him as he left the glass palace. He lay awake all night.

Early in the morning, he got ready and decided to chant the hymns of Lord Shiva to collect himself as he had to fulfil his promise to Raskapoor. She had pleaded with him to come early in the morning to recite all seventeen hymns of Shiva Strota together as she wanted to seek the blessings of Natraj for the offering at the temple. The glass palace reverberated with the holy chants.

Raskapoor was ready to sing and dance in reverence of Krishna and Radha. But she was unable to comprehend the reason for her best friend's point-blank refusal to accompany her to the temple. What bothered her the most was that all her requests were falling on deaf ears, the ears of someone who was always so willing to fulfil her every wish at any cost. She had known that her mother would not be present inside the temple being a Muslim. But a devout Hindu like Rudra refusing to go to a temple baffled her.

Raskapoor tried one more time that morning, 'You have been my Krishna all these days, and now you do not agree to be there in Krishna's temple. I am requesting you one last time and will not request you again. If you still decline, then I am sure Krishna will be angry with you.' He still declined, but then Raskapoor insisted on knowing the reason for his choosing to do so. 'Raskapoor, you know I am a poor Brahmin who keeps away from the palace, and the temple is within the palace. Besides, you are going with Nargis Bibi, and I would rather be not seen in her company.'

As Raskapoor's eyes filled with stunned tears, Rudra realized that he had upset her with his reply. He immediately tried to rectify the situation in a comforting tone. He said, 'Don't be upset. I will be here with your Ammi Jaan and wait for you till you come back. We have already prayed to Natraj, and now I will go and pray for you at the temple. Now smile.' He walked out before the commotion of the preparation of her visit to the temple hit the glass palace.

The divine invocation was planned at dusk. All those who had to go for it assembled in the courtyard of the glass palace. Her two teachers were resetting their instruments and replaying the rhythmic cycles on the percussion instrument. Inside, Chaand and Nargis dressed up Raskapoor. Pandit Shiv Narain arrived in his curtained buggy, which was going to take Raskapoor to the temple. When Raskapoor came out, Pandit Shiv Narain's heart swelled with pride. He credited himself for producing such divine beauty. He immediately handed out yet another pair of anklets, the same as the ones he had given her earlier. Nargis put them on Raskapoor's feet, which were adorned with alta, the lac dye. When she stamped her feet to try the anklets and make sure not to lose one like the last time, Pandit Shiv Narain admired her incredibly beautiful feet and could foresee all men falling at them.

Finally, when the time of departure came, Raskapoor touched the feet of her parents. For the first time, Pandit Shiv Narain had tears in his eyes, as deep inside, he felt guilty that he was not man enough to declare openly that she was his daughter. Chaand hugged her daughter and cried; she felt as if she was giving her daughter away. Raskapoor was seated in the buggy, which slowly rolled out into the diffusing sunrays. The courtyard was still, the silence haunting. Chaand cried her heart out, dreading the eventual parting from her daughter. Rudra knew precisely what her state of mind was and came inside to be with her. She wiped her tears, and Rudra roped her into his engaging conversation, even though the absence of Raskapoor was hitting him equally hard.

The Radhashtami preparation had started days earlier. As their Maharaja had desired to witness the divine invocation while remaining invisible to the artists, the priest prepared a plan for the approval of Jagat Singh. He approved it but with some additions. For nights together, he pondered over how he could remain invisible and yet be able to get the full view of the fabled beauty as well as see her performance. Finally, he decided he would see her enter the courtyard from the top balcony, which faced the entrance, and as the artists settled in, he would make his way down for a closer view. He chose to sit with the priests on the veranda just outside the main altar. Accordingly, he instructed them to cover all the arches over the courtyard of the temple and the two arches of that veranda. To ensure that no one got suspicious about the special arrangements, he further instructed the priest to also provide a covered corridor in the courtyard and on the top of the terrace.

Suddenly he hit upon a clever idea of camouflaging himself. He expressed his desire to wear a shawl and headgear exactly like the priests. The surprised priest admired the enthusiasm with which Jagat Singh was planning to celebrate the birthday of Krishna's Radha Rani. It was the first time that Jagat Singh was visiting the temple after becoming the Maharaja. Nargis, too, decided not to be seen anywhere near the temple that day. Jagat Singh had already been informed of this as had the girl's father and the musicians.

She had arranged for a group of Hindu ladies from her end to be at the venue. They were briefed to first help Raskapoor dismount from the buggy, give her the silver plate with the lighted earthen lamps and lead her into the temple.

On the day of the celebration, not just the Brijnidhi temple, but the way leading to the temple also wore a festive look, festooned with flowers and the leaves of saraca asoca, considered to be the 'sorrowless' tree by Hindus. Intricate patterns were painted with lime and ochre. Jagat Singh, as planned, came well in advance to make his special offering to Radha before his esteemed guest could sense his presence, walked through the covered passage to the terrace and sat in the curtained balcony. Raskapoor was dreaming of her Krishna and Radha all along the way and came out of her dreams when the buggy halted at the temple. The group of women-in-waiting helped her dismount. Before they could hand over the plate with the lighted lamps, Raskapoor gave them the red packet in her hand.

'This is for Radha Rani,' she said. 'I have to put it at her feet.' It was the attire that her mother had made to offer to Radha Rani on her birthday. The woman who took it assured her. 'Very nice. I will carry this and walk with you.' Raskapoor was deeply touched by the warmth in her words, and then suddenly, she was struck by the absence of her Nargis Mausi. Curious, Raskapoor looked all around to see if she could spot her, but the women affectionately said, 'Let's move inside and place the lamps at your Radha Rani's feet before they extinguish.' They helped her in manoeuvring the way up by holding her dress so that she did not trip.

Nagara, the double drum, and shehnai, the ceremonial pipe, were playing outside while inside the sound of the double-barrel percussion pakhavaj and the manjeera, the clash cymbals, resounded. Jagat Singh's heartbeats were increasing in tempo. He put his right palm on his chest to feel the beat, wondering what was wrong, for this was not the first time in his life that he was seeing a beautiful girl. He eagerly awaited her entry and moved forward to peep through the garlands of marigold. He was taken aback to see her right foot first as she stepped in. He had not seen such beautiful feet before, as white as marble, painted with red motifs and adorned by dangling anklets. Jagat Singh had heard it from connoisseurs of beautiful women that the small and delicate feet of a woman were a confirmation of her ravishingly beautiful face. His heart pulsated in expectation as his eager eyes moved upwards, scanning the figure of the lady with lamps coming closer. The moment he had the first glimpse of her face, he was stunned. Her face was not just extraordinarily beautiful, it radiated divinity in the light of the lamps.

With the two ladies holding her dress on either side, a tray of lamps in her hand and the divine crown, she reminded Jagat Singh of a bride entering the home of her in-laws after the wedding ceremony; but there was never one as beautiful as her. When she came closer, and he saw the expression in her eyes and the slight smile on her face, he felt as if Radha Rani had arrived in person on this earth. He wondered who was more beautiful—Bani Thani or the girl who was walking before him. He suddenly realized he did not even know her name. The girl then entered the covered courtyard moving out of his sight. He could not wait to see her again. Impatient Jagat rushed down and joined the group of priests. The priests themselves were so mesmerized to see the extraordinary devotee walking in that they did not even notice him there. Without blinking, Jagat Singh watched her complete the ritual.

Raskapoor was one with Krishna and did not feel the presence of anyone else till she finished. As advised by the lady-in-waiting, she handed over Radha Rani's dress to the priest and touched the feet of the group without looking up. Jagat Singh, too, was in that group. He had not expected to feel her first touch, and his inner soul vibrated. Raskapoor walked to the courtyard and bowed before her teachers and all the musicians. She picked up her tanpura, the string instrument that gives a continuous harmonic drone supporting the melody, and sat down on the velvet carpet. The first note of her voice, like her first step in the courtyard and her first touch, overpowered Jagat Singh's senses—and she was yet to dance. Her song was filled with emotions that could move even Krishna's heart:

'Oh, my friend, a bow has hit my eye. My mind revolves around that loving face.

His divine figure now stands in my heart. I stand in the balcony of my palace, wait endlessly.

How do I live without my beloved? I, Meera, am already sold to Girdhar (Krishna). And people call me characterless.'

Her song moved the group of priests and Jagat Singh. She then got up, handed over her tanpura to one of the musicians and sat down to tie on her dancing bells as her teachers tuned their instruments. She took her stance to begin with '*thatt*', the overture to the dance form, Kathak. As the music began, she moved her eyebrows, neck, shoulders and her hands in subtle ways, casting her spell. She folded her hands in the namaskar gesture and bowed in respect, first towards the deities, then towards the accompanists, seeking their blessings for her performance. She then exited, and her teacher recited the words of *amad*, the introductory piece. In her second entry, she performed the intricate patterns termed *toda* with a hundred spins. Loud cheers filled the temple. Her dance transported everyone into another world, and they felt that even the sky was dancing along with her. Her teachers set the mood for *gat bhav*, singing the beautiful melody, which the dancer had to emote. It was carefully selected by none other than Nargis to entice the Maharaja with Raskapoor's expressions. The lyrics were playful, depicting the yearning of Lord Krishna and Radha for each other:

I, Radha, was going to graze her cows with her other friends.
On the way in the middle of the path Krishna was standing, smiling and holding his magical flute.
He blocked my way, held my wrist. All my friends were laughing, I was embarrassed, I was shy.
I then decided to teach him a lesson, snatched away his flute, showed him the flute as a stick.
Oh, Radha, give me my flute back, your Girdhari pleads with you.

She was Radha one moment, and Krishna the next. It was like divine magic for the onlookers. She sang while dancing, just as she had rehearsed with Rudra. For the first time, she saw someone else before her eyes other than Krishna and Radha, and that was Rudra. Her audience was overwhelmed because her performance made them feel the deep love that Meera had for Krishna, and they had tears in their eyes. How the dancer so easily traversed through the whirlpool of varying emotions was beyond their comprehension as Raskapoor ushered in the festive spirit with the Brij Holi. Nargis had instructed the ladies-in-waiting to shower petals on her as she spun, which added to the effect. Everyone started chanting 'Bolo Radhe Govind' at an increasing pace, the musicians played the drums and cymbals joined in, and the dancer spun round and round. She seemed to be unstoppable, and the accompanists were dripping with sweat. Finally, they chose to bring her to 'Sam', the culmination point, and the percussionists threw their arms up in the air. Raskapoor, as a well-trained disciple, anticipated the moment as the percussionists played 'Tihai', the three same rhythmic patterns, that concluded the composition. She finished precisely at that point, and the loud tap of her foot resonated with the syllables of the beat 'Ta Tirkit Dha'. Standing still in the graceful posture with a side glance, she looked at her musicians flashing a naughty smile.

When she bowed to the deities and completed her chanting of 'Jai Shri Radhe', Jagat Singh returned to the real world. He had carried pouches of gold coins for all the musicians and a special necklace to give to the girl if she turned out to be what Nargis had made him imagine her to be. Now, that necklace seemed insignificant to honour that divine beauty whom god had made with such precision. If he had his way, he would have bestowed his empire on her that evening. He handed over the pouches for the musicians first and a special red pouch for the star of the evening to the priest, who was advised to give the pouches as if they were from him without any mention of the Maharaja.

The priest did exactly that and then put his hand on the dancer's head, saying, 'You are a goddess yourself. Today, we all felt as if we were seeing Radha Rani dancing in devotion before our eyes.' On her return journey, she was ecstatic with her songs and dances, which made her feel one with the supreme power. She longed to meet her mother and Rudra to share her joy with them, not caring to look inside the pouch to see what the priest had given her.

At the glass palace, Chaand was standing in anticipation of her daughter's arrival. As the buggy stopped, Raskapoor hurriedly moved the curtain aside and seeing her mother, couldn't hold back. 'Oh Ammi, I have never felt so happy as I did while singing and dancing in the temple!' Her mother asked her to first get down from the buggy and that they would talk once they were upstairs.

Raskapoor handed over the pouch to her mother. 'The priest was so happy with my performance this evening, he presented me with this. You know Ammi, he called me a goddess, a Devi.' Her mother smiled and helped her dismount. Feeling like a free bird, she held up her skirt with both her hands and hurriedly climbed up the steps. She was surprised to see Rudra standing in the courtyard.

'You poor Brahmin, why didn't you come—there were so many Brahmins there who admired my song and dances. Nargis Mausi wasn't there either,' she said, sounding puzzled. 'But I saw you there, standing behind Krishna and Radha when I sang and danced to the lyrics I practised with you.' Raskapoor smiled. Rudra did not tell her that while he was talking to her mother, all he could see was her face before his eyes.

Raskapoor rushed to her room to change out of her festive attire and then came out to share her divine experience. However, Chaand asked her to wait till next morning. Right now, they were to eat dinner, as Rudra too had to go home. Raskapoor accepted the idea. She appreciated Rudra's considerate thought of not leaving her mother alone.

In her heart, Chaand was very happy to hear her daughter's first reaction. She had an inkling that Raskapoor was going to dazzle all who were there, including the priest. Before Raskapoor had left, she had stood before her mother. At that time, Chaand had asked her to turn around. She pretended to adjust the veil from behind but what Raskapoor did not realize was that her mother had taken a bit of Kajal on her ring finger and put a black dot behind her daughter's ear to ward off the evil eye. Being overtaken with anxiety and nervousness, Chaand had decided to let her daughter go only after putting the *nazar ka teeka*.

After dinner, Rudra left, and Chaand told her daughter, 'I knew that you would captivate all hearts, including those of Lord Krishna and Radha. I thank god for giving me a daughter like you. Sleep well, and dream of all your gods and goddesses.' The two then hugged each other and went to sleep.

Back in the palace, Jagat Singh lay wide awake awaiting sunrise. He wanted to summon Nargis at the crack of the dawn to tell him all the details about the girl who had taken his sleep away. Her magic had made Jagat Singh chant 'Bolo Radhe Govind' while meandering through the secret passage back to Chandra Mahal, and her face was dancing before his eyes. At the palace entrance, his retinue of staff, hearing the filtering chant, could sense their master's enchantment. When he emerged into the courtyard of his palace, he asked them to chant with him and they were wonderstruck with this change in him and overjoyed to see their Maharaja turning into a devotee like his father.

Away from the City Palace and the glass palace, Nargis and Pandit Shiv Narain, as planned, met with the women-in-waiting to get a first-hand account of the evening, right from Raskapoor's arrival at the temple, till the time she left after casting her enchantment on all those present. Their elaborate account made the two conspirators feel the impact Raskapoor must have had on Jagat Singh, and they already expected Nargis to be called by him the following morning.

Nargis, that shrewd professional, said, 'Panditji, let's not be in a hurry. Let his yearning increase. I will not respond to any communication sent by the palace by pretending I have a high fever.'

Mishraji conceded to her plan, as he knew how difficult it would be to get Raskapoor away from her protective mother who would turn into a protective tigress if she suspected any harm coming to her cub. The morning after the temple celebrations, Chaand looked inside the pouch given by the priest to her daughter. She wondered anxiously how the priest could have given Raskapoor such an expensive gift. It was a necklace with seven pearl strings, a *satladha*, and a pendant of emeralds and rubies on each string. She suspected the presence of the Maharaja at the temple, kept secret from her.

She rushed to her daughter's room to ask, but she was still fast asleep. Lovingly, she brushed her fingers through her hair to check if the black dot was still there. It was, and she felt relieved that at least no one could cast an evil eye on her.

Feeling the warmth of her mother's fingers, Ras held her hand, turned around, and said affectionately, 'Oh! My dearest Ammi, all my life, I want to wake up with the touch of your hand.'

Her amused mother replied, 'My dearest Ras, that can happen only till the day you get married. Anyway, first tell me, who else was there at the temple other than the priests, musicians, some women and your father?' Raskapoor wondered why her mother was asking that question first thing in the morning, but suddenly remembered. 'Ammi, father was not there. I only saw Krishna and Radha Rani. Really Ammi, you will not believe me, but I could feel that they were all around me!'

Her mother was struck by the absence of the father, but brushed aside her suspicions. She thought perhaps he was among the group of priests and Ras, overtaken by her devotional fervour, just didn't notice him. She then dangled the necklace before her daughter's eyes.

Shocked, Raskapoor asked, 'Ammi, who gave you such an expensive necklace?' Chaand realized that her daughter had not cared to see what was in the pouch presented to her by the priest. She diverted her attention with a completely different story, telling her that it was kept in her custody by an old friend, and that morning she was returning it to her. Raskapoor never showed any interest in what the priest had gifted her that evening or where the gift had really come from till the day she left the glass palace.

An Autumn Full Moon with a Difference

No one could have ever imagined that the autumn full moon would be so different that year that it would raise the curtains on a drama in the real life of the city, which would only end with the demise of Jagat Singh. Nargis, just as she had planned, was summoned the very next morning after the celebrations at the temple. Because she did not go for a few days feigning illness, the impatient Maharaja showered present after present on the ailing patient. Nargis enjoyed being pampered as she and Raskapoor's father decided on their strategy before she met the Maharaja.

Finally, after a week, she responded. The restless Maharaja, whose thoughts were revolving only around the divine dancer, urgently wished to know her whereabouts and how she could be with him. For the first time in his life, he felt he was in love!

He confided his emotions in Nargis, going a step further, saying, 'Nargis if she comes into my life, I am sure no one will ever be able to take me away from her. She is the girl whom my soul was in search of. You know I saw myself as Krishna and her as my Radha.'

Nargis told him she knew that he would be a different man once he saw her and her performance. She advised him to follow her plan without being jumpy as she had to take care of the girl's mother, who was bound to resist. Nargis still did not tell him about the father of the girl, or else he would have pressurized Mishraji to act immediately.

Pandit Shiv Narain listened carefully as Nargis described her meeting with the Maharaja. He began to put his plan into action, and Nargis left that to him as she had to take care of her end of it at the City Palace. Mishraji appeared at the glass palace with ecstasy writ large on his face and bags full of presents for both Chaand and Raskapoor.

'Chaand my dear, have you heard how our beautiful daughter won the hearts of the priests? The head priest of Brijnidhi temple talked endlessly about the beauty and talent of the dancer who danced like Radha.' The alert mother knew then that he was not in the group of the priests present at the celebrations. Her suspicion turned into a confirmation that there was a secret plan afoot. She dreaded that plan, but before she could ask any questions, he called out for his daughter. He blessed Raskapoor, handed over some gifts and asked her all about the evening at the temple. They ate dinner together, then Mishraji left. Chaand did not get a chance to ask him why he was not there at the temple.

Raskapoor and Rudra continued to meet as usual. He had heard all the praises for her, which had reached even the ears of the priest of the Gupteshwar temple. The priest never asked who that dancer could be, knowing it could not be anyone other than Raskapoor. As her well-wisher and a father figure, he did not want to play any part in the situation, which he believed was not as straightforward as described. He knew the idea of special celebrations at Brijnidhi temple could not have been the brainchild of a Maharaja like Jagat Singh, who was known more for his worldly pleasures than his spiritual bent.

Raskapoor observed that Rudra had started expressing his deep love for her in many ways. So, she knew she had to stop him, not to break his heart, but for his well-being. New wisdom had dawned upon her ever since the evening when she identified herself with Radha. Like Radha, she could only be a lover, never a wife. Even the all-powerful Krishna could not marry Radha, as he in his real life was a prince and Radha was but a milkmaiden. In her case, she was only a tawaif's daughter whose Brahmin father chose not to be seen anywhere near her, not even at the temple. Besides, this meant that she could marry only a tawaif's son or else just be someone's mistress. And only the rich and powerful could afford a mistress, not a poor Brahmin like her trusted soul mate. All this was exactly what she told Rudra when finally, one day, he proposed to her.

He was amazed to see the transformation in Raskapoor since her divine invocation. Her face had the radiance of wisdom adding to her beauty. He told his love that he would marry her and take her away from the world of tawaifs. He did not want this extraordinary soul to end up being condemned to live the life of a nautch girl, sought by many, respected by none and abandoned by all at the end. Rudra was an earnest man, and unlike her father, he would go any distance to marry her, but Raskapoor was determined that she wanted to nurture their friendship as a tree of protection where they would be there for each other if needed.

About a week before the autumn full moon, Pandit Shiv Narain turned up at the glass palace and sat the mother and daughter down. He said, 'Now the time has come to explain to you two that a tawaif's daughter is ordained to live a life not just to entertain one but many men of all kinds. Not all will be as concerned as I have been for Chaand. I will be there for you all my life, but what will happen to Raskapoor? When I was called by the Maharaja and told that he wants to make Raskapoor a part of his life, I felt that it would be the best for my daughter. Raskapoor will not end up at a nautch house as you did Chaand. She will live a much better life, and I will be there to ensure her well-being.'

Chaand was startled to see the ease with which the father spoke these words and asked him, 'Was the Maharaja not at the temple? Was the plan of the celebrations not masterminded by Nargis and you?' Mishraji was well prepared to reply to all her questions in an earnest manner. He said, 'Yes, with only one intention in mind, that if Raskapoor won his heart, she would lead the life of a Queen.' Knowing he was sweet-talking them, only to realize his nefarious intentions to climb up the political ladder and be the most powerful man in the royal court, Chaand, who was intensely irritated and frustrated with his ways, chose to confront him exposing his game plan in front of his daughter. 'Oh really, do you see your daughter like a queen or yourself as the prime minister of the Maharaja?' she asked with a sarcastic smile. She told him that she was grateful to him for the life he had given to her but not at the cost of her daughter's future only to fulfil his ambitions.

Chaand, feeling cheated and miserable, reminded him of the day she had told him that her only aim in life was to see her daughter married. Mishraji told her to face the reality of her life that the marriage could only be possible with another tawaif's son, resulting in a deplorable life. All through the conversation between her parents, Raskapoor was wondering where the Maharaja was that evening and how she did not see him. While her parents indulged in an intense conversation, she prayed to Shiva, Parvati, Krishna and Radha seeking their blessings, and asking them to show her the right path.

At the end of the turbulent conversation, Panditji addressed Raskapoor, 'My dear daughter, I have paid special attention to giving you deep insights into mythology, history as well as life in the palace to prepare you for the day you will enter it. You are better armed to rule the heart and mind of Jagat Singh than all those wives of his. There is an age-old saying, "Only that one is the queen whom the king loves". I am more than sure that not only your beauty, but the wisdom, the knowledge of mythology, and the deep devotion for the Hindu gods Shiva and Krishna you possess will make you an integral part of his life. It is very rare to have a charismatic personality like yours. A man like him or myself may stray for a while but will always come back to his real love, irrespective of other women or marriage alliances. Don't I come back to your mother? I can tell you to take my word for it, for she is that love for me.'

Streams of tears were rolling down Chaand and Raskapoor's eyes, and silence prevailed for the next few minutes. The learned Brahmin had expected those tears and let them flow. They needed to deal with the blow he had struck. After some time, he took both of them in his arms and hugged them, extending comfort and warmth. For a few moments, the father in him felt the surge of emotions for his daughter, who not only loved him but looked up to him, and he was letting her down. He was wracked with a terrible sense of guilt, but then the worldly-wise Brahmin collected himself to safeguard his dreams and dignity. Quickly internalizing that he was not the only one to have a love affair with a nautch girl and father a child illegitimately, he freed Chaand and Ras pulling himself back. Sailing out of that passing storm, he convinced himself that respectable men with power had been doing so for time immemorial and would continue to do so.

When they were all done, he seated them to unfold the plan for Raskapoor's upcoming journey. Maintaining a comforting note, Mishraji informed them, 'The royal entourage will come to take Ras to Amber Palace for the autumn full moon celebration the Maharaja will be having that night only with our Raskapoor. No one else will be there. Start preparing. I will return in a day or two to see your smiling faces.'

He left, and both Chaand and Raskapoor went to their rooms. It was as if lightning had struck the glass palace. Their dreams and aspirations shattered. As she stepped into her room, the disoriented Raskapoor sat down, burying her head in her palm. Overlapping words uttered by her parents rattled in her mind. She did not know whether she was coming or going. Unwittingly, her parents had opened the Pandora's box before her, and she was at an utter loss to figure out what would be suitable for her. For the first time, the traumatized girl experienced a sudden headache, forcing her to lie down to rest her head on the pillow. Sleep was miles away from her. She saw myriad of images floating on the ceiling—the temples of Krishna and Shiva, the face of the priest, the wedding of Tulsi, Krishna's birth celebrations, evenings on the terrace with Rudra, the dance rehearsals with him posing as Krishna, her mother dressing her up for the invocational performance at the temple, and of course, the visit to the palace. The images spun at a fast pace. Feeling giddy, she closed her eyes. In the other room, hapless

Chaand could only curse her destiny lying in bed wide awake. It was a long and dark night for both.

As the first temple bells echoed in the early hours of morning, Raskapoor opened her eyes. She could not comprehend whether she had fallen unconscious or asleep. With the first glimpse of the divine statue, she hurriedly got out of bed. Settling her hair, she stood in front of the deity. She folded her hands as a devotee seeking solace. Looking into the eyes of Lord Natraj, she poured her heart out, 'God, I only seek your protection. Protect me like you protected Mahananda. It is because of your blessings only that I have not been doomed to entertain many men as Mahananda had to. Now, like Radha, I pray only to belong to one man, seeking his love, and above all, his respect. Please bless me.' Raskapoor was filled with anxiety. She then decided to chant to Shiva. After reciting the invocational hymn for an hour, she opened her eyes with a realization that being a tawaif's daughter, it did not matter who her father was. The devotee expressed her dismay in that heart-to-heart conversation. She could not justify the humiliation of the children born out of wedlock. She smiled at the way her father, in a bid to convince her mother, called her their child and then a few minutes later, described Raskapoor as a tawaif's daughter who could only marry a tawaif's son! In that one fateful night, she had lived many years. She sought refuge in Shiva to face her destiny as a retribution for her past Karma, and to pray to change her fate at least in her next birth. Finishing her prayer, Raskapoor uttered the last wish aloud: 'I am bearing the fruit of my past life actions, urging you Shiva to accept my one plea. Please ensure that children not be shamed, owing to the status of their parents.'

After leaving the glass palace, Pandit Shiv Narain decided to seek a private meeting with Jagat Singh, which was granted without any delay. As they sat together, seeing his expression, the Maharaja asked him to spell out the reason for that particular meeting.

Pandit Shiv Narain Mishra began on a serious note, 'Your Majesty, I believe you have invited that dancer again for a private celebration at Amber on the full moon night. Do you know who that girl is?' Jagat Singh gave a straightforward reply. 'I do not know, and I do not care. Panditji, she is not like any girl that I have been in the company of. None of my ranis are like her. She is a divine beauty who is adorned by wisdom and grace. Not only that, but she is also a gifted singer and a dancer as well. My heart yearns for her, and her face remains before my eyes. So, with all due respect to you, Brahmin Maharaj, I will not change my decision.' Pandit Shiv Narain, having assessed his feelings, smiled and said, 'It is heartening to know your feelings for the girl. Now I can tell you that she is none other than my daughter, Raskapoor. She is my child with Chaand, and that is the reason for this meeting—to ensure her well-being.'

Jagat Singh was amazed to hear that and held the priest with both his hands. 'This is wonderful news for me. I give you my word that she will be the queen of my heart. I would like to marry her like the Maharaja of Kishangarh who married Vishnu Priya, Bani Thani.'

Pandit Shiv Narain was content that he had fulfilled his duty as a father but remarked, 'Hope you can muster that courage!' As he was leaving, Jagat Singh asked him to wait for a minute. He then handed a pouch of gold coins to him and told him that after the full moon night, he would become a special aide of the Maharaja with much higher perks. Mishraji patted himself for accomplishing the goal to absolve himself from the guilt that he felt at the Kaanch Mahal. That night, he had meditated to ride over emotions to achieve the mission, a lesson that he used to teach his disciples, all the while ignoring the basic principle of the selflessness of the purpose. He laughed as that thought struck him, remembering how often the spiritual leaders set different rules for themselves. Betraying his daughter's trust and respect did not seem to bother him anymore. Imagining the rise in his stature, he looked forward to seeing the reaction of his arched opponents. The triumphant man headed back home in self-admiration.

At the Kaanch Mahal, the following morning after Mishraji left, Chaand was stunned to see Raskapoor's calm face, almost as if she had already overcome the hard blow. Was she fascinated with the prospect of life in the royal world? If so, she wondered if her daughter could even visualize the difficulties and challenges lying ahead. She saw Raskapoor turning into a spider weaving a cobweb of fantasies and dying in it, not finding her way out.

'How are you, my lovely daughter?'

Raskapoor smiled and asked her mother, 'You tell me, how are you? Mother, I first prayed to Natraj, and then I chanted to Shiva early this morning for an hour. Now I know that what my father has offered is the best option for me in this life, being the daughter of a tawaif. If you feel the splendour of the palace lures me, you are wrong. I know you want me to marry Rudra, whom I, too, consider to be the best man on this earth, but for sure, we do not want to ruin his life. He is a poor Brahmin who will not be able to fight this world, and your daughter will be dragged into a swamp. Remember what the learned Brahmin, who happens to be my father, also said: the only option for a tawaif's daughter was to marry the son of a tawaif. When we cannot change our Karma, we leave ourselves in the hands of god, who is always there for his true devotees. We will both prepare for my next journey and smile when my father comes back.' Chaand was aghast to notice the way she repeatedly called herself a tawaif's daughter and the scornful expression while calling her father 'a learned Brahmin'. The girl standing before her did not appear to be her daughter.

She was speechless to hear this discourse from her daughter, who seemed to have turned into a saint overnight. She collected herself to explain to her daughter the difference between philosophy and reality, but in vain. The young girl did not change her stand and remained resolute in facing her destiny. They even discussed the matter with Rudra, who was amazed at the reasoning power of a girl of Raskapoor's age. He tried to reason with her and also proposed to marry her. His proposal included the great escape beyond the borders of the state before the full moon. For the first time, the lover in Rudra chose to be expressive. Holding her hand affectionately, he said, 'Ras, I love you deeply, and I can tell you that life of girls like you always ends up on a sad note.'

'You mean the life of a tawaif's daughter, no?' She interrupted him with teary eyes, but smilingly she said, 'I will not mind if you even called me that, for you truly love me.' She chose to share how

her father had called her a tawaif's daughter, not forgetting to add
'the learned Brahmin'. Extremely upset, Rudra could not believe
the insensitivity of her father. Reading his expression, she chose
to divert his attention. Mischievously she asked him what he was
suggesting as his action plan. He reiterated the idea of marrying
her and escaping to a safer place where they could live together
happily. Trying to address her self-esteem, he added, 'You know,
when you and I will be married, I will call you Brahmini Ji, for
a Brahmin's wife is called a Brahmini. I will not let anyone refer
to you as a tawaif's daughter as your father did. With me, even
your father will not dare to do that.' Visibly upset, Rudra, who
could not recall the last time he cried, had tears rolling down in
sympathy for the heartbroken girl. Holding hands of his love, he
told her that he felt the pain of the wound inflicted on her soul
by her father. According to him, intelligence, wisdom and wealth
without compassion were unworthy of any respect.

Those tears overwhelmed Ras, but then she wiped his tears
with her scarf and laughed, saying, 'Escape—you are such an
intelligent man and came up with such a simple idea. Escape—
then be killed by the men sent by the king and my father!' She
explained to Rudra that if he was killed, she could even land up in
a dingy brothel. Even though he was devastated by Raskapoor's
decision, her last argument finally made him realize that he was
pitched against the powerful. He admired her commitment to
saving his life with no sign of anxiety about her own. His respect
for her grew many folds with that argument. He was struck by her
ability to handle her emotions, while despite all his spirituality, he
was sinking.

Raskapoor held his hand, sharing her love and respect for him
and letting him know that had the circumstances been different,
he would have been the only man she would have loved to marry.
Continuing to hold his hands, she disclosed that he was the only
person she trusted completely. She even shared with him the
unpleasant conversation between her parents and her private
ordeal that night. Profoundly feeling the compassion for his love,
he took her in his arms. She too clung to him for some time. With

that hug, they silently shared their feelings for each other. For the first time, he kissed her on her head and whispered into her ear, 'You will be my only love, and remember, I will be there for you in your hour of need. If you are not in my life, I will rather die for you than live alone. Now, my life will be only to ensure your well-being.' Moving the head buried in his chest, she looked into his eyes, holding back her tears, and smiled with an expression of gratitude.

After a while, Raskapoor, taking his arms away, asked him for a favour to bring her mother to let her go. Together, Raskapoor and Rudra convinced Chaand to accept the situation and prepare for the inevitable day. Rudra assured her mother that he would be there any time Raskapoor needed him. He told Raskapoor that he would go to the Gupteshwar temple every single day to pray for her as long as he lived, and she could send him a message via the priest or her mother. His concern made Raskapoor emotional, and she smiled at him with her teary eyes.

Two days later, Pandit Shiv Narain entered the glass palace, speculating all along the way as to how he would manipulate the second round of intense conversation and deal with the emotional turmoil of his daughter. To his utmost surprise, he saw Raskapoor smilingly greet him and ask him how he was. The father felt that he should have been the one to ask her that question. Her striking composure rattled his mind, and he couldn't even give a simple reply.

Seeing her father lost in deep thought, she asked him, 'Are you well? Are you worried about my mother and me?' Her shocked father tried to cover his embarrassment. 'No . . . no, my dear daughter. I am well; I was just thinking about the two of you.'

She handed him a glass of water, 'Do not think about her as she is not thinking about you at this time. Her thoughts are around my journey to the palace, and mine is around my mother. Please know the tawaif and her daughter have shared a special cord. You know, Guruji, as a learned Brahmin, what Ammi taught me in her simple way, you could not, despite all your knowledge. She told me about Naal, the cord that binds the baby with her mother. That cord can invisibly stretch in any direction, and that cord will not let the two of us separate in this lifetime even if we are not together.'

The learned Brahmin could not even dream of a statement like that coming from her. Instead of feeling thrilled with the news about the ongoing preparation for her journey, he was standing before his daughter as a defenceless guilty party. Her smile said it all. She seemed to have distanced herself from her biological father. Her comfort in talking about herself as a tawaif's daughter caused a sudden pain in the heart. He was feeling the loss of his only daughter in her new avatar, confidently referring to herself as a tawaif's daughter. Just an adolescent, the girl had acquired an edge over him by speaking those words so stoically. He could not figure out what was going on in her mind. He was shaken up with the thought that she was trying to tell him that she had no father, or subtly announcing his death. He held his head in both his hands, dying a thousand deaths. Ras went inside to call her mother. Mishraji lifted his face to see her go inside without asking about his predicament? Did he have a headache? His daughter would have certainly done that, he knew that very well and felt a profound loss at the sudden change at Kaanch Mahal. He was amazed at the turbulence within the man who was already on the way to accomplishing his long-cherished ambition. Running his fingers through his hair, he mocked himself for allowing to be pulled back by those fatherly emotions, having known that the children born out of wedlock were never meant to be owned up by respectable men who fathered them.

A couple of minutes later, Chaand walked into the courtyard holding the new light-pink outfit, which she was stitching for her beloved daughter. She greeted him with a respectful smile but with visible sarcasm, 'Pranam Panditji. Did you get the alms?' Nonplussed, Mishraji immediately asked, 'Which alms are you referring to?' Chaand smilingly said, 'The acceptance of your proposal as Raskapoor already told you. I heard as I stood near the door.'

He was disarmed entirely to meet the peaceful attack launched by the mother and daughter. He felt a chill running down his spine and wanted to leave immediately but could not, as he had to talk to

them about the day of Raskapoor's departure. In a bid to ride over
the unnerving situation, he sheepishly initiated the dialogue, 'I am
so delighted to see that both of you have been able to see the reason
behind my bringing that proposal. It is a miracle, as I had thought
that we would enter into yet another discussion,' Mishraji said.

'Indeed, for me too, it was a miracle, and the magician was
none other than your daughter, who reasoned it out with me.
I trust only her, and she trusts the almighty,' Chaand solemnly
responded to him. 'What she told me will put any father to shame.
Her words pierced my heart, "Ammi, I am happy to be only your
daughter. I do not want a father who will not be my father out of
this place. Your Mishraji will undoubtedly remain my respectable
teacher, but I cannot now accept him as my father. Will you please
tell that man only to be my teacher or Guruji as he liked me to
call him? Now I understand why he never asked me to call him
Pitaji as the other Hindu children call their fathers. I do know
that since he is not a Muslim, he cannot be addressed as Abba."'
Those repeated words were hammering in his head. Mishraji did
not know how to react, for just a few minutes ago, he had brushed
aside his fatherly emotions.

Always on guard, Mishraji did not allow himself to either
respond with words or any facial expression. His rational mind,
instead, offered the opportunity to clear his position as well as play
the next move. Accordingly, they were apprised of the conversation
he had with Jagat Singh revealing the fact that Raskapoor was his
daughter, which he felt would in some way retrieve a little share
of his daughter's love that he seemed to rejoice in over the years.
The plan for the day of the departure was then detailed out. 'At
the early dawn, I will come in my buggy and take Raskapoor. The
royal entourage will be there in the 'pigeon courtyard' between the
Udai Pol and Dundhbhi Pol. My buggy will join there. When the
elephants manoeuvre the square Martin ka Chowk, the tail end
of the procession will come to a standstill, and those women-in-
waiting you met at the temple will help dismount Raskapoor and
seat her in one of the ceremonial palanquins. The operation will be
so swift that no one will even be able to take a note of it.'

As he finished, he realized that Chaand and Raskapoor were not even listening to him and he asked his daughter, 'Do you know where you will get into a palanquin?' She smiled and replied with indifference, 'Wherever I will be asked to.'

'At Martin Ka Chowk.'

To draw her attention, he tried manipulating her with a bit of history, a subject that she jumped to with an unusual eagerness. 'Let me tell you about the man after whom the square is made. Martin de Silva was a hakim, a physician, from Portugal, who became an associate of Sawai Jai Singh in astronomical pursuits.' For the first time, he noticed that his daughter did not even care for his knowledge. Realizing that his words were landing on deaf ears, embarrassed, Pandit Shiv Narain decided to leave, 'So, you two prepare for the day and I will come to escort you. You will be the queen of hearts!'

As he was going down the steps, Chaand called after him, 'Please tell Nargis and party not to come as Raskapoor has decided to spend the next few days just with her mother.'

The only other person the two wanted to have around them at this time was Rudra, who despite being heartbroken, stood like a rock by the side of his love, saluting her grit. Raskapoor showed unfathomable courage once she accepted the situation. Any other girl in her place would have resisted, crying her heart out, unless she was tricked into being delivered at the destination or was lured by the glamour of the royal life. Raskapoor, on the contrary, showed incredible resolve to face the consequences. Together, Rudra and Ras lent all their support to Chaand to come to terms with the situation. Those last few days filled the glass palace with total bliss as the three put all their efforts into the preparation for the full autumn moon.

On the eve of her departure, Raskapoor said, 'Ammi and Rudra, I know my absence will haunt you both. You are my life, Ammi. Rudra, as Parvati, I will find you as my Shiva in my next life. Ammi, can I hold Rudra's hand for one last time? From tomorrow I will turn into another Radha belonging to only one man, and hopefully, I can turn the Maharaja into a Krishna.'

Both her mother and Rudra were stunned by her statement,
oozing faith and conviction. They could not question an ardent
believer's faith in a bid to make one last attempt to change her
decision, having given her all possible grim details of a ruler's
wayward lifestyle and the tragic end of girls like her. Their long
conversations reinforced one fact that Raskapoor was no ordinary
girl who was either naïve or eager to live in a palace. Her prayers
and her spiritual bent of mind had, perhaps, readied her to go
with the flow. As a firm believer of destiny and Karma, she seemed
all set to meet her destiny and accept what was ordained. After
a couple of minutes of seeing her mother lost in her world, Ras
laughed and repeated her question, 'Ammi, am I getting your
permission to hold Rudra's hand one last time?' Returning from
her thoughts, Chaand responded with a burst of laughter, 'Ras,
you surprise me. One minute, you are a spiritual master, and the
next moment, a naughty child! Why do you ask me for permission
to hold his hand? I honour your attachment to each other. For the
first time, the glass palace will have an overnight male guest other
than your father, and it will be Rudra. You can hold hands and
pour out your hearts to each other, but Ras, you must sleep early,
for you start at dawn tomorrow. Rudra will see you off from the
courtyard, and I will walk you down when your father arrives.'

She left the two alone, and after an hour, Raskapoor retired
to her room. Chaand had made arrangements for Rudra to sleep
in the living room. All three of them remained awake through the
night. In the morning, Rudra and Chaand placed Raskapoor's
bags in the courtyard below, well before Mishraji arrived, to see
her off properly and not rush the last minute. Chaand held her
daughter close, to look at her face minutely one last time, put the
black dot under her ear and then gave her a tight hug. Raskapoor
walked towards Rudra and hugged him. That was going to be the
last time he would feel her that close. And he saw it as her parting
gift to him to cherish all his life. They heard a buggy rolling in.
Chaand asked Raskapoor to hurry. 'One moment, Ammi!' Chaand
wondered what she wanted to do in that last minute. Raskapoor
turned around and, like Mahananda before leaping into the fire,

she set her parrot and rooster free to find their freedom even if she could not.

Down below, while Mishraji smiled, Chaand and Raskapoor hugged each other once again, making their way towards the buggy. Chaand helped her daughter get in. Neither of them had shed any tears. Mishraji wondered where they got that courage from, forgetting the fact that emotionally, a woman was much stronger than a man. The buggy rolled out, and Chaand went back into the courtyard. She clung to Rudra and wept to her heart's content. She requested him to keep praying for Raskapoor's well-being.

Part Two

Camphor Lighted

Amid the Aravallis

As tradition had it, the queens of the Maharaja were addressed not by their names but by their clans. And when a king was going to be away from the palace, the first to know of his movements was the Chief Queen in the ladies' quarters. Accordingly, Jagat Singh informed 'Bikawatji', his Chief Queen, about his desire to go for a shikar to hunt big game in the jungle around Nahargarh and Amber and halt at Amber on the full moon night. She did not find any reason to be suspicious about this, knowing her husband's love for hunting. As it was, the head priest of the Brijnidhi temple had briefed her a few days ago about the recent change in his behaviour. According to him, the king was turning into an ardent devotee like his father. He advised her not to interfere too much with her husband's life to prevent him from falling back into his old habits. In any case, the priest reminded her that her keeping an eye on him like a hawk had already created a chasm between them as a couple. He convinced her that at least the wayward Maharaja was trying to take some time off for different activities other than mere worldly pleasures.

Jagat Singh left a few days in advance for Amber to oversee all the arrangements to welcome his much-awaited guest. The especially deputed staff there was given a different story. They were told that all those elaborate arrangements were for the autumn full moon celebration. Jagat Singh's hunting team was asked to proceed as planned, but without their Maharaja who was suddenly compelled to stay back to take care of some urgent matters. Knowing his impulsive behaviour, they too did not find the abrupt change in his programme suspicious. There was only one person who was taken into confidence and instructed to receive his special guest.

Gulab, his trusted concubine, had pledged to be loyal to Jagat Singh because he had showered love and affection on her in abundance, something she had never dreamt possible in her life, especially from a ruler. Because of just a few blissful weeks, Gulab became indebted to the Maharaja for a lifetime. She was summoned from time to time for a couple of nights. Those nights catered to her womanly desires as well as left her with expensive gifts. The king loved her tactful ways to quench his constant thirst for physical pleasure, and within no time, she became his confidante. Knowing his nature well, she knew that the special guest was going to be there for a short spell, as had been the case with others like her who had been brought to Amber. They exited from his life once he did not desire their company anymore. No one knew how or where they disappeared. She was grateful to him for not sending her away, ensuring her well-being, and giving her a place in Amber.

The palanquin bearers, taking their wobbly steps, moved at a slow pace. Raskapoor was nearly asleep. She had not slept a wink through the night. Unable to resist, she gave in and slept like a baby in a cradle the entire way. It was only when the palanquin tilted up that she realized that the bearers were ascending and were about to reach the palace. She quickly fixed her hair and dress. Around dusk, the palanquin reached the courtyard of the palace. The bearers put it down on a carpet where Gulab and her fleet had lined up to receive their esteemed guest. The women who had walked along the palanquin surrounded it, and the bearers moved away. Through the sheer curtain of the palanquin, Gulab was stunned to get her first glimpse of the face inside. She quickly moved the curtain aside. She had never seen such an extraordinarily beautiful girl.

'No wonder such elaborate arrangements were made to welcome her,' it occurred to Gulab. She helped her guest alight from the palanquin. Raskapoor herself was dazed to see lamps lit along the steps going up. Before she could even glance around, the women on the steps started showering petals on her. She climbed the steps to the sound of ceremonial music, which reminded her of the evening at the temple. In her heart, she prayed to Shila Devi, whose temple was just next to the steps. If she had her way, she would have visited the temple first.

As instructed, Gulab led her to the ladies' chamber through the secret passage while Jagat Singh saw her arrive from the far end of the third courtyard. Gulab suggested that she first get ready to meet the Maharaja. Raskapoor handed her the jewellery box and the pale pink ensemble. The attendants helped her get ready. When Gulab took out the seven-string necklace, Raskapoor realized that her mother had not even kept the necklace for herself.

When she was ready, Gulab looked at her carefully and could not take her eyes off of her. 'You are a celestial princess!' she complimented her beautiful guest. 'Let me put a black dot to keep away the evil eye,' she said and put a little kohl under her ear. Gulab showered her with such warmth that Raskapoor was immediately reminded of her mother and yearned to be with her.

Gulab could read her thoughts and held her soft hand, saying, 'I know you are missing your mother just as I did once. But now it is time to appear before the Maharaja who is eagerly waiting to see you.' With a few other girls, she led her to Jai Mandir. Jagat Singh was waiting there, all set to receive Raskapoor. He held her hand, advising his staff to hand over the tray with pouches of gold coins.

He said, 'Gulab, these are for all of you. Now you all are free till I call for you.' Gulab could now, after seeing his guest, fully appreciate why the king was so generous. She left.

Jagat Singh could not stop looking at Raskapoor. She, in turn, had a soft smile on her face as tutored. A few days before leaving her home, her mother gave her a few tips for the first time when she was presented before the Maharaja. Chaand had advised her to maintain a subtle smile and let him strike the first chord. Ammi appeared to be well experienced in casting an everlasting impact in a dignified manner when she said, 'Ras, the sound of the first chord sets the mood for the melodious notes ahead.' Walking towards him, she had mixed emotions. Amber fort's high walls and secret passages, manoeuvred just a while ago, had already freaked her. It was much different than Jai Niwas, she felt, for that palace did not have that unsettling eeriness. The realization that she did not have any known person around her was making her heart palpitate. At Hawa Mahal, at least Nargis Mausi was with her, and at the temple, her teachers were right there. She was feeling nervous when she came closer to the Maharaja. She remembered her mother's advice and decided to hide the nervousness, masking it with her magical smile.

When she looked up and had the first glimpse of Jagat Singh, all her apprehensions could not stop her from registering his imposing personality. Through her prayers, she had learnt not to fear the unknown, but standing before him, she went blank.

After a few moments, he spoke, 'I have two moons before my eyes. One in the sky and one before me; I am at a loss to decide which one is more beautiful!' Then he turned Raskapoor around swiftly. 'Look up, Ras. How beautiful is that moon!'

Both looked towards the moon, and he sought her permission to talk to the moon. For a second, she wondered if he was intoxicated or crazy. He read her expression, and in a loud voice, addressed the moon, 'See another beautiful moon on this earth. Are you not as surprised as I was with the first glimpse of this moon?' He took her face in both his palms. 'He cannot answer, for he is too surprised to see you. He is speechless!'

She could not control her laughter, and Jagat Singh told her, 'You look even more beautiful when you laugh. I do not want you to fear me, Raskapoor. That day at the temple, when I felt your divine touch, I knew you were not an ordinary girl. Then when you sang, I felt I could see Meera Bai and finally when you danced, I could feel the presence of Radha Rani.'

Raskapoor immediately knew that the Maharaja had stood among the priests. He was the one who had gifted the necklace, and not a priest as she had been told. At that very moment, she realized that the elaborate plan was hatched cleverly by two people she once had so much faith in, Nargis Mausi and her so-called father. She was not at all surprised why; always apprehensive of those two, her mother could not see through the plan of the invocational performance. Not just that, even her respected teachers and the

Maharaja had played their role to perfection, Ras concluded. She was not angry but amused by the idea of turning a Maharaja into a priest.

She spoke for the first time, 'You turned into a priest and then sent me this necklace. Am I right?' Her intelligent question posed with a naughty expression in her eyes stole his heart. They strolled on the terrace, hand in hand, under the full moonlight for a while. He even talked about what her father had told him, and then walked her down to Jai Mandir. Embellished with mirror work all over the ceiling and the walls, it glittered as the lamps flickered. Raskapoor was spellbound, and the Maharaja asked her to look up, 'See, just as your face reflects all around at this moment, after seeing you at the temple, your face was all around me.' He took something out from his pocket and asked her, 'Tell me, Raskapoor, what is in my fist?' She could not guess at all and requested him to show her what was there. He naughtily dangled an anklet close to her eyes, asking her if she had seen that anklet before. 'That is the one I lost when I came to the autumn celebrations of the full moon at Hawa Mahal,' she said, not believing that he was the one who found it. She asked him how he knew that it belonged to her.

He smiled and said that he did not know it till the day he saw her feet at the temple. 'You were wearing anklets like this one. For days together, I felt I had seen such an anklet somewhere else. One night, however, while I was thinking of you, I was suddenly reminded of the anklet I had found at Hawa Mahal after that function. Looking at the size of the anklet at that time, I could feel the sadness of the little girl who lost it. I kept it in a pouch just in case that girl ever turned up in search of it, but then after a few days, I forgot all about it. When I was reminded of the anklet, I wanted to present it to its owner on the very first occasion I ever met her. Are you not intrigued to find today what you lost in a palace so many years ago? Is it not strange to get the lost anklet back in yet another palace?'

'Girls grow so fast. That child who I did not take any notice of, turned into such an extraordinary young girl that I have now stopped noticing anyone else.' He then seated her next to him for dinner, offering her the first bite with his hand. After that, they again walked in the moonlight, feeling each other's warmth.

Raskapoor took notice of his impressive personality. Jagat Singh, with broad shoulders, a prominent head, a well-groomed beard, an erect posture, and mannerisms to match, was undoubtedly a lady's man. He had a charismatic aura. She noticed the one big difference between him and Rudra, whose intellectual and slightly aloof attitude needed some time to take the plunge into any relationship. He certainly would not have moved so fast to come close to any girl even if it was she herself, the love of his life. Whereas Jagat Singh was not to let any moment go in coming close to his lady, as became evident when he compared her to the moon in their very first meeting. Walking on that full moon night, side by side with Jagat Singh, her emotions were swaying like the tidal effect of the full moon.

He, on the other hand, knew that Raskapoor was an untouched jewel and needed to be made comfortable. The conversation with her father made him realize that she was not merely a concubine's daughter. She also had the genes of the learned Brahmin, and that piece of information evoked respect for Raskapoor in his heart.

He indulged her in a conversation around Krishna and Radha, and that all in his clan were ardent worshippers of Krishna. 'I remember the devotional song of Meera Bai you rendered at the temple. I must tell you that the moving lyrics and your voice almost brought me to tears. I will take you to the Jagat Shiromani temple dedicated to Meera Bai, Krishna and Vishnu,' Jagat Singh said, kindling her interest.

As expected, his generous offer drew her appreciation. 'How nice of you to think of taking me to that temple. Is it very far?' Jagat Singh pointed in the direction of the temple. 'It is down below. It was built in memory of my namesake.'

Curiously, Raskapoor asked him, 'Do you mean another Jagat Singh? Who was he?' Jagat Singh laughed. 'It feels good to hear my name in your voice. Kunwar Jagat Singh was the son of my great ancestor Man Singh I. He died at a young age. After the death of the son, his mother Kanakwati had it constructed almost

200 years ago. The small statue of Krishna is not of Radha's Krishna but Meera's Krishna.' Raskapoor was overwhelmed with the thought of being able to touch the feet of that statute, which ignited the mystic bond between Krishna and Meera.

He walked her towards the specially laid out bedroom in Jai Mandir. The intoxicating aroma of rose and jasmine welcomed the couple. Raskapoor, who had been lost in her thoughts of Meera's Krishna, came out of her dream world the moment she spotted the two velvet pillows on the big bed and dangling garlands all around to herald their union. Her heart palpitated with the idea of spending the night with a man, a total stranger, for the first time in her life.

She thought of Rudra in place of the king and felt how different that would have been; not filled with apprehensions but with the ease that she was yearning for at this crucial time. Her mother had briefed her on what to expect. The farsighted Chaand could envision the discomfort her daughter was going to feel when the ruler took her to bed. A few days before her departure from the glass palace, while combing her daughter's hair, she chose to explain to her that even much-married brides, including queens, more often than not, did not see their bridegrooms before marriage. To prepare her daughter for that fateful night, she advised her, 'Ras, you have shown such confidence in going ahead with the proposal brought by your father. Now, do not be nervous or afraid when the king comes close to you. Be like a coy bride.' Remembering her mother's words, Raskapoor pulled herself together and transformed into a newly married bride. She slipped into the arms of Jagat Singh thinking of Radha and Mahananda, who like her were not married to their partners, but their bond was immortalized in mythology. She was determined to play the role of a coy bride with full honesty, moving along the designs of her destiny. Her much-experienced partner admired her beauty, grace and spontaneous responses, noting with pleasure that Raskapoor had not been exposed to the world of tawaifs.

Jagat Singh got up early and was amused to see Raskapoor in deep sleep with her head on his arm. He gently pulled his arm out, placing her head back on the pillow. As he moved away, the sunrays stroked her face, and he was mesmerized to see his sleeping beauty. After admiring her chiselled figure, he pulled the veil cloth over her bare body. The first night he spent with her had cast a spell forever.

Feeling the light on her face, she hurriedly got up and fixed her hair and her clothes. She looked a bit embarrassed, and he asked her, 'How did my queen sleep?' Raskapoor smiled and replied, 'You may call me your queen, but I know I am not one and will never be one.'

Jagat Singh was taken aback to hear that and questioned her further, 'Will you not like to be my queen?' Raskapoor again smiled. She said, 'It is not about my liking it. But will you be able to show courage the way the Maharaja of Kishangarh did, when he married Bani Thani?' Jagat Singh was stunned at her clear-headedness. He could see that none of his queens could match her personality. 'I will show that courage one day, Ras, let the time come. First, tell me how would you like to start the day? Gulab will come to take you to the Man Singh Mahal and get you ready.' Raskapoor expressed her desire to visit Shila Devi's temple. She knew the Mother Goddess alone could give her the strength to make herself comfortable in the company of a strange man in an equally strange environment. In a few moments, Gulab came. Jagat Singh asked her to pick up the new clothes, which he had brought for Raskapoor, as well as a jewellery box placed next to them. Gulab realized that the Maharaja was pampering his new companion more lavishly than his earlier companions.

On the way, she could not resist the temptation of asking Raskapoor how the night was. 'As any bride's first night.' Raskapoor's reply amazed Gulab.

'You are not his bride. He has not married you,' said Gulab trying to bring her back to reality. 'I know that, but for me, we were married as Krishna and Radha were, for we spent the night together. Do you know what Krishna had told Radha after being in bed with her? He told Radha that the two of them were already married in the "Gandharva tradition" as they became one

Amber, the territory awarded to Raskapoor with the title of 'the Half Empress'

The latticed arches of Amber

Amber, main entrance

Man Singh Palace in the Zenani Deohri, Amber

Kanch Mahal, where Raskapoor was born

Hawamahal

Zenani Deohri, or the ladies' apartments, City Palace

Brij Bihari Temple, which Sawai Jagat Singh II got constructed

Ras Vilas, the double-storey structure added by Jagat Singh

Nahargarh, or Sudarshangarh, where Raskapoor's name echoes

The city of Jaipur viewed from Nahargarh

Gaitore, where the last rites of the Jaipur maharajas were
performed and cenotaphs were built, but none of this
was done for Sawai Jagat Singh II

The arched pavilion leading to the painting room at Pundrik Ji Ki Haveli

Barahdari, the pleasure pavilion with twelve arches in the centre of the ladies' apartments at Amber

Jagat Shiromani temple at the foot of the palace

Krishna and Radha in the Sheesh Mahal, Amber, ignited the deep love between Jagat Singh and Raskapoor

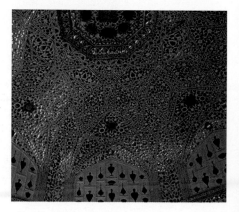

Sheesh Mahal, Amber, where the two lovers wove many dreams as the oil lamps created a galaxy of stars

Painting by Gulab Chandra

Painting by Shakir Ali

The two lovers, Jagat Singh and Raskapoor, depicted in a painting at
Pundrik Ji Ki Haveli

Jagat Singh II with his father, Maharaja Sawai Pratap Singh, and courtiers;
a painting inside Pundrik Ji Ki Haveli

in their physical union.' Raskapoor's reply was beyond Gulab's comprehension. She ushered her inside to get her ready.

Jagat Singh had brought a beautiful Rani Poshak, the pink attire endorsed by the queens of the Rajput princely states. Her jewellery had a rakhadi and a nose ring, as worn by a Rajput bride. Gulab, who was aware of the traditions, was surprised to see even a chura, the set of ivory bangles, which was supposed to be worn by a Rajput bride. Sometimes the privilege to wear those bangles was accorded to chosen concubines, but for that, a special ceremony in the zenani deorhi was a must. She knew Jagat Singh had not bestowed that honour to any woman so far.

'What magic have you done on our king?' Gulab asked Raskapoor, who had no idea about the significance of those bangles. She was unable to comprehend the meaning of the question. With so many bangles on her arms and forehands, she started feeling strange. All those accessories gave her a sense of loss of freedom and the question hit her, 'Was she taken as a prisoner?' Overriding her apprehension, she chose to respond to Gulab's weird question, 'I am a devotee of Shiva, Radha and Krishna, and do not believe in any tricks or magic.'

Gulab silently walked her back to the Sheesh Mahal, where the Maharaja was standing in his ceremonial attire, waiting for Raskapoor to arrive. She looked ravishing, dressed almost like a bride, and he held Raskapoor's hand, asking Gulab, 'Does she not look like a queen?' Gulab wholeheartedly agreed but had serious concerns about the impact that this newly forged bond would have on the palace. Jagat Singh seemed to be totally smitten with Raskapoor, unlike the other women before her, and according to the palace grapevine, there was an extraordinary change in his behaviour ever since the temple visit.

While Raskapoor went to the Man Singh Mahal to get ready, he had summoned the head priest of the Shila Devi temple, informing him about the special guest's visit to the temple. The priest, who had already heard about the arrival of this guest the previous night, could appreciate how important she was, as the ruler himself was going to accompany her, which he had never done before. As desired by Jagat Singh, the priest was ready to receive them and make a special offering with the lamp to the resounding sound of the big silver drum.

Jagat Singh walked her down the steps descending into the courtyard leading to the temple. Raskapoor stood in front of the black rock image with folded hands, greeting the goddess. She chanted some hymns, invoking Mother Goddess' blessings. The priest was wonderstruck by the divinity on her face. Her flawless diction and the chanting rhythm made him certain that she was raised by a Brahmin. He vaguely remembered the alliance of Pandit Shiv Narain and Noormahal, but he was not sure if they had a child together.

On the direction of Jagat Singh, he began the ritual and offered the deity the sweets and liquor already sent to him by the ruler. As tradition had it, Rajputs offered alcohol and sacrificed a goat to make an offering to Kali Mata, the goddess, who in her fierce incarnation battled with demons and defeated them. Her worship was of considerable significance to the warrior clan. After the ritual, the holy water of the Ganges was poured in the right palm of the devotees to drink. Captivated by the power of the statue, Raskapoor was in a deep trance, so when the priest brought the second jar to pour the second offering, Raskapoor drank it without moving her eyes away from the goddess. Raskapoor tasted liquor for the first time. The bitter taste hit her head, and she turned towards Jagat Singh with a questioning look to ask what it was. The priest quickly offered the sweets.

On finishing the ritual, Jagat Singh led her back to the hall of mirrors, narrating the story of the deity who was brought all the way from Jessore in East Bengal by Maharaja Man Singh. 'The image belonged to the kingdom of Pratapaditya. He was leading the campaign on behalf of the Moghul Emperor. A great warrior like him first faced defeat at the hands of King Kedar and felt humiliated and disgraced. He prayed day in and day out to Goddess Kali to empower him to avenge that defeat. She appeared in his dream asking him to establish her shrine in Amber after the victory. He won and then installed this image, which he recovered in the form of a black slab from the ocean. It was washed away into the ocean, and the image reappeared from that slab,' Jagat Singh said.

'Oh! Now I understand why the goddess is called Shila Devi, because shila means stone,' Raskapoor responded spontaneously. 'You are a very intelligent girl, my love,' complimented Jagat Singh, impressed.

Entering the room, Raskapoor was surprised to see her tanpura and the two strings of dancing bells or ghunghroos. 'You brought these from the glass palace? But when?' He smiled and told her that just after the day she left the glass palace, another carriage carried them on his instructions. She silently admired his smart planning. The ruler told her to pick them up as and when she wished to sing or dance, as he was determined to make her comfortable. 'I fell in love with you as you sang and danced. It was mystical, as I had never felt that kind of love for any of the women in my life. I told myself, "Jagat, this is the last and final call of love."' He assured her of his infinite love for her and that there would be no other woman in his life after her.

> Raskapoor laughed and recited a verse to make him appreciate that the path of love was not easy:
> Love, love, everybody says, but no one knows what it truly means. Why would the world cry as the loved one dies?
> Love is immortal and infinite. It is like an ocean, and you must drown in it.
> No one can return. Like Varun who drank the wine of love, he became the god of water. Lord Shiva is worshipped because he drank poison out of love.

Her philosophical recitation made him wonder if it was a verse composed by her, but she explained, 'No. The great mystic poet Raskhan, a Muslim, but an ardent devotee of Lord Krishna, wrote those words for us to understand what real love is all about'.

He wanted to know if her father had taught her that verse. 'No, it was Rudra, who taught me a lot about mythology and the poetic verses. He taught me this one after I was mesmerized by his recitation and explanation of its deep meaning. Each time I recite this verse, his recitation echoes in my mind,' she informed him with a dreamy smile.

That reply inspired yet another question, 'Who is Rudra, is he a priest?' Raskapoor, without any hesitation, talked to Jagat Singh about her childhood friend, and Jagat Singh appreciated her earnestness. He was relieved to see that his beloved had a true friend in Rudra, and not a lover. He became curious to know what her childhood was like and asked, 'You sound like a wise teacher of Hindu philosophy. Did you only indulge in such discourses? Did you ever play games like other children?' Raskapoor smiled and told him, 'I only played Chaupad and Shatranj with my father and Rudra. There was no other child of my age there, and I loved to hear stories. Mythology and history have such wonderful stories and not many children are fortunate enough to hear them. My first playmates at home were a parrot and rooster, and together we chanted the hymns of Shiva.'

Jagat Singh burst out into laughter. '. . . a parrot . . . a rooster as playmates!' He thought, a prince like myself was deprived of those childhood stories, which gave Raskapoor an edge over him. He asked her, 'Would you like to play a game with me? It is going to be a competition. Are you willing to accept defeat?' With a naughty expression, she asked him, 'What makes you so sure that you will win? Do not challenge a Brahmin and that too a girl!' Jagat Singh summoned Gulab to bring a big heap of cotton and milk in a big silver bowl. Gulab, in her wildest dreams could not imagine what the king was going to do with cotton and that silver bowl. When she returned, he told Gulab, 'You will be the referee of the competition between the queen of my heart and me. First, you will make many pieces of that cotton, then throw them in the air, and the two of us will collect them. The one who collects more will be the winner. The second competition will be to retrieve the ring from the silver bowl, and the finder will be the winner.'

Gulab was shocked. 'You mean the games of gamble that the bride and the bridegroom are made to play?' Jagat Singh told her, 'Yes, you are right. So, let's begin.'

Raskapoor competed with the resolve to defeat the king as she ran, ducked and jumped to get hold of the pieces of cotton. She was declared the winner of the first game.

Jagat Singh was delighted to see a childlike side to Raskapoor, but teased her, 'That was an easy game. You surely are going to lose the second one.' Raskapoor with her big and vigilant eyes kept a tight watch over both him and Gulab and grabbed the ring the moment it was dropped.

Raskapoor said, 'Now it is my turn to suggest a game. It is a mind game. I am going to ask you a riddle posed by the Sufi poet, Amir Khosrow. I will give you a few moments to think and reply.'

Jagat Singh who had never indulged in solving a riddle, pleaded with Gulab to team up with him. Raskapoor accepted the idea and posed the riddle:

'One female lives in a well, its water flows in the field. Whoever tastes its water, then does not aspire for life.'

Both Jagat Singh and Gulab looked confused and asked her to repeat it. She repeated it not once but quite a few times, and even extended the time limit. She gave them a clue too. She said, 'She has been your companion in good times and bad times.'

Jagat Singh recalled the names of his several companions and finally asked her to tell him the answer.

Raskapoor teased him, 'Concede your defeat first!'

Jagat Singh folded his hands and said, 'Devi Raskapoor, I accept my defeat.' Raskapoor laughed and said, 'How strange that two of you could not tell me the simple answer, which is—a sword. Now think again—she lives in a well, which is her sheath; the blood flows like water when it is used; one who is attacked with it, cannot survive.' Jagat Singh conceded defeat, not for that moment but for his lifetime, thought Gulab. Music, mythology, history, love and laughter echoed in Amber palace and time flew by. A week had passed, and with no news of his return, his anxious and trusted advisers decided to pay him a visit. They advised him in all sincerity to take charge of the administration. There were serious concerns about the mounting threats of the ruler of Jodhpur, as well as Marathas, not to forget the intrigues of his own feudal vassals.

However, Jagat Singh was in no mood to awake from his dream world and responded with full respect, 'You are my trusted advisers. You have more experience of royal administration. I was not even ready to take charge, but for the untimely demise of my father. With you being there, my presence is not required. When you need my signature or consent, then come to me here. I will stay for a few more weeks.'

They were somewhat surprised to hear this, wondering whether the Maharaja was going to be back at the City Palace to celebrate the festival of Diwali, which was just a week away. One of the advisers dared to remind him about the festival for which his presence was mandatory.

Jagat Singh shocked them with his reply, 'I think, after years, I feel like celebrating Diwali in our old capital. You can apprise the palace of my decision, asking everyone back at the palace to celebrate the festival with the usual fanfare.'

The ease with which he communicated his decision startled the advisers, and they pleaded to him to be there for at least the festival and then return to Amber again, but Jagat Singh rejected their proposition. He was not ready to return to Jai Nagar. Their Maharaja, known for his roving eye, always in search of a new companion even while in the company of another, stood before them a changed man. He was radiating a divine satisfaction. The two advisers were slightly alarmed to see the visible difference that his newly forged relationship had brought in him in just a few days. They could feel that the new link was going to impact the history of their state. Returning to Jai Nagar, they felt an urgency to take up the matter with the council of ministers and the feudal lords before it was too late.

Standing behind the door, Raskapoor could hear their conversation. As a girl conversant with the intrigues of the princely states cited by her father several times, she decided to advise her lover to take charge of his administration. She wanted to be his strength, like Radha, who ensured that Krishna took charge of his kingdom and not his weakness.

After seeing the two advisers off, he returned to the room and saw Raskapoor pensively gazing into the void. He lovingly took her hand in his hands, asking, 'What are you thinking about, my love?' Raskapoor smiled, 'I think it is time for you to return to the palace and get back to work. Also, it is an absolute must for you to be there for the festival.' Jagat Singh realized she had heard the conversation between him and the advisers and reassured her, 'Ras, I know I must get back to the palace but where is the hurry? I want to be here in Amber with you for a few more days, celebrate the festival with you, and arrange for you to return with me. I am certainly not going to go back alone.'

Raskapoor tried to tell him that she would be fine to stay in Amber, but he put his finger on her lips. They spent hours in each other's arms and the day dissolved into dusk. It was time for Gulab to set up the arena for the ruler to be served his preferred beverages. Raskapoor alerted Jagat Singh to get ready and headed to change into yet another outfit brought by her lover.

Dressed in turquoise blue, Raskapoor coyly walked towards her prince charming. Jagat Singh couldn't tear his gaze away from the pristine beauty. He stood up and sat her next to him. Looking at the two lovers, Gulab too could feel their deep connection and spontaneously prayed to the Mother Goddess to bless the couple and left.

Jagat Singh held on to Raskapoor's delicate hand tenderly, and with each passing moment, he felt intoxicated as never before. He had not touched the liquor served by Gulab in the silver goblet. After some time, he proposed a walk on the top terrace of the palace. Knowing her master well, Gulab had set up velvet mattresses and bolsters at each level for the couple to sail on the love boat in the isolated valley commanded by the Aravalli range.

They strolled for hours together, enjoying each other's warmth, and finally, Jagat Singh suggested spending the night on the terrace, leading her to the spot where under a canopy, a special arrangement had been made for them. Raskapoor was reminded of the night that Radha and Krishna had spent together in their favourite corner of Madhuban, near the Yamuna River.

'Do you know Radha and Krishna united in body and soul in an open arena like this and Krishna called it a "Gandharva" marriage?' she asked Jagat.

'No, my love, I do not know that, but this is the perfect moment for you to tell me that beautiful story,' the Maharaja put his head in her lap.

Stroking his hair, she started narrating the story, 'Radha and Krishna disappeared in Madhuban one night. They were together like us in one corner, away from the eyes of the world. As Krishna took Radha in his arms, she asked him if he would always be there for her and continue to extend the same love to her. Krishna reassured her with the analogy of the sun and the moon. "As long as those two are there, our love will blossom," he told her with a smile. His words liberated Radha from the cobweb of her doubts. Krishna then held her in a tight hug and kissed her on her head. The night was getting cold. They clung to each other to share their warmth, which resulted in uniting their bodies and souls.

Returning to the real world, Radha asked him if they would be together, even after he got married. Krishna smiled once again, and told her that he had already married her in the Gandharva tradition. On noticing the confusion in his beloved's mind, he explained to her that sexual intercourse among a consenting couple denoted marriage if the male was of royal lineage. Radha, who was unaware of Krishna being a descendant of a royal family, told him point-blank that he was only a cowherd boy. Krishna then revealed everything to her about his birth but reassured her that she would be the queen by his side. Surprised by the revelation, Radha told him that she could not be his queen, as she would not be able to deal with the intrigues of royal life. Nor would he be the Krishna she got to know in Vrindavan. Instead of being a queen, she would rather see him reflecting in the waters of Yamuna or amidst the trees of Madhuban.'

Jagat Singh pulled her close to him, 'Ras, unlike Radha you already knew I am of a royal lineage and we are already united in body and soul. You are my queen, and I reiterate that as we unite at this moment like Radha and Krishna in Madhuban.' The night was rather cold, and they clung to each other. At dawn, Jagat woke up, and as he lovingly touched her forehead, he panicked. She was burning. He tried to wake her up, but she did not open her eyes.

Jagat Singh lifted her in his arms and rushed down to put her in the bed. He pulled his own quilt over her. He then summoned Gulab to come with a bowl of cold water and a muslin cloth. Within minutes, Gulab arrived, and the Maharaja hurriedly put the wet cloth on Raskapoor's forehead to administer the cold compress. Worried, Jagat Singh asked Gulab to get the Raj Vaidya, the indigenous physician of the royal family, to Amber as quickly as possible. Gulab sent the royal messenger with two horse riders of the royal cavalcade to bring back the physician without any delay. Jagat Singh did not leave Raskapoor's side, cursing himself for making her spend the whole night on the terrace. Intermittently, he placed the cold muslin cloth, calling her name out, and even praying to all the deities that his lady love believed in.

After some hours, her fever came down, but she neither opened her eyes nor responded to his calls. At about dusk, when the royal physician was ushered in, Jagat was chanting Radhe Krishna . . . Radhe Krishna . . . with his eyes closed. The physician was struck by the beauty of his patient, who was lying still like a delicately carved marble statue.

'Khamagani, Annadata,' he greeted Jagat Singh, drawing his attention. The Maharaja urged the physician to do everything possible to return her to a state of consciousness. The physician asked the Maharaja to calm down and took the wrist of his patient in his hand. He read her pulse, examined her eyes, and informed him that the patient had developed excessive Kaph due to exposure to cold.

'She has a very mild fever. All she needs is to be kept warm. I am going to give her a special herbal potion to reduce the excessive Kaph, and I am more than sure she would be fine by the morning,' the physician smiled. The anxious Jagat Singh smiled for the first time since morning.

'You lift her head a bit,' the physician advised Gulab as he took out the bottle of the special potion. Slowly, he poured it in her mouth and was mesmerized to see it trickle down her throat through the glass-like skin on her long neck. Magically, Raskapoor opened her eyes. 'How are you, my child? Do you feel better?'

the physician asked her, looking into her almond-shaped eyes. He put his hand on her head and gently told her how worried the Maharaja was about her. She looked weak and frail but smiled and nodded her head in gratitude towards the royal physician and the Maharaja. Her gentle expression touched the heart of the elderly physician, who was already over-awed by her beauty. Jagat Singh requested the royal physician to stay overnight at the palace so he could see his patient once again in the morning. He gave special instructions that the much-venerated physician be well looked after.

When they were alone, he turned towards Raskapoor and took her hand in his, saying, 'Ras, I never knew that I could be so nervous. You were lying unconscious, and I was cursing myself for making you spend the night in the open without realizing that it was so cold. I earnestly beg your pardon.' Raskapoor was shocked to see the all-powerful king pleading guilty before a girl of her background. She said, 'Please do not say that. You have showered me with so much love and respect. We are one in body and mind. Why then must the Maharaja beg his love to pardon him! With your tender care and the magical potion given by the royal physician, I will be fine by dawn.'

He put his hand on her eyes, and she fell asleep. Not once, but many times he got up to check on her. He was pleased to see her fast asleep. At sunrise, she got up early feeling rejuvenated with the herbal potion. She left the bed and as she stood in the arch praying to the sun, Jagat Singh too woke up. He said, 'You should not be standing there after being so unwell.'

Raskapoor smiled and in her inimitable way, teased him, 'Why? Are you too tired from looking after me?' He got out of his bed and hugged her, saying, 'I will never be tired of looking after you, but I want to confess that I know one thing now—if ever something happened to you, I too will not be able to live.'

Raskapoor smiled and suggested that it was time for both of them to get ready before the royal physician came to see her. Gulab came in to help Raskapoor, and while she combed her hair, she gave her a full account of how the Maharaja looked after her while she lay unconscious. 'He did not leave your side all day and did not touch even a morsel of food. He himself was putting the cold compress on your forehead. You certainly have stolen our Maharaja's heart, as I have never seen him care that much for any woman in his life,' said Gulab.

Her account made Raskapoor express her gratitude towards him. After she was ready, Gulab put a dot of kohl under her ear as her mother did, and teary Raskapoor thanked Gulab too for taking such good care of her. Gulab realized that Raskapoor possessed an extraordinary demeanour, which could win the admiration of even her arch opponents. She ushered Raskapoor to where the Maharaja was waiting for her to have breakfast.

'Hazoor, look at her! Who could say she was so unwell yesterday?' Jagat Singh smiled. 'Yes, Gulab; you are so right. I think she was not ill but was only testing my love for her without realizing that if she prolonged her act, I could have been dead! Come on Ras, before you decide to fall ill again, sip this saffron milk.' Jagat Singh brought the silver glass close to her lips. Just then, the royal physician walked in to check on his patient but witnessing that scene from a short distance, he knew she was well. From that spot, he could also read the pulse of his ruler, who had definitely developed a high degree of love that was going to raise alarm bells in the palace. However, his heart was filled with emotions seeing the happy couple.

Gulab announced the arrival of the physician and Raskapoor and Jagat Singh greeted him.

'You look not only well but so beautiful, my daughter. I cannot imagine you are the same girl who I saw as my patient yesterday,' he said, as he read Raskapoor's pulse.

'It is the magic of your medicine. I am indeed grateful to you for coming here,' said Raskapoor.

Jagat Singh gave him a velvet purse with gold coins, and the physician blessed the couple before leaving the palace.

'Can I ask you for a special gift this day?' Raskapoor asked Jagat Singh, who readily committed to giving her what she desired. He did not imagine that the gift would be Raskapoor asking him to celebrate Diwali in Jai Nagar. He knew that there was no way out for him, and he had to plan for his return. However, he decided that he was not going to go back alone. He was sure he wanted to take his love along with him, but even he knew that he could not directly send her to the zenani deorhi, where she was bound to be subjected to harsh treatment. He wanted her to be accorded full respect, and after thinking over his idea to take her along with him, he decided to summon his advisers that very day.

They arrived in the evening, and Jagat Singh informed them, 'As you wanted me to return to the palace at least for the festival, I am going to come but not alone. What I need you two to do is to organize a well-provided apartment just adjacent to my private apartment. You have about five days to get the Ras Vilas for my new queen Raskapoor.' They were shell-shocked with that most unexpected condition laid by their Maharaja, who had even chosen the name for her abode. Their look was immediately picked up by the Maharaja, who suggested them the way out to accomplish that task in such a short time. Jagat Singh laughed aloud and then told them that they should not dread the deadline set by him, for they did not have to raise her residence from the ground level brick by brick. He made it sound rather simple, asking them to convert the beautiful three-arched pavilion between his palace and Madho Niwas, the residence of the Chief Queen. The plan was drawn with precision, leaving no room for his advisers to request him to postpone the project to move his lover to Jai Niwas for a later date. Jagat Singh described in detail how the masons could enclose the pavilion from all sides. The carpenters and the tailoring unit of the palace could get the furnishings ready while his favourite miniature artist could embellish the interiors. His words left the two advisers dumbfounded, but they knew the adamant nature of their ruler too well to reason with him. They headed back to Jai Nagar wondering how they were going to execute this impossible mission. Their Maharaja had certainly grown crazy in the company of his new lover if he was thinking them to be magicians with a magic wand or Aladdin's lamp.

A Commotion in Jai Niwas

Ever since Jagat Singh left for his sudden hunting expedition in the Aravalli range, the atmosphere within the palace had become unusually different. Life seemed to be in a flux. Some attributed it to the sudden change in weather, while others felt that it was the effect of the major preparations for Diwali. Whispers about the new love of the Maharaja were getting louder, but no one, not even his nineteen wives, seemed to pay much heed to them knowing the Maharaja well. They were getting their own apartments lavishly replenished and indulging in their own beautification, vying with each other to be the lucky one to spend the festival night with the missing Maharaja.

It was the chief guard of the ladies' quarters, Nadir Mohan Ram, a clever eunuch, who noticed the double story apartment coming up overnight between the Madhav Vilas, the apartment for the Chief Queen, and Chandra Mahal. When he saw the two advisers of the Maharaja supervising the new construction the following morning, he decided to apprise the Chief Queen of the Maharaja. She brushed aside the information given by Mohan Ram knowing what a gossipmonger he was. Mohan Ram himself was convinced that there was something fishy behind the construction of the new apartment. He decided to keep a close eye on the construction, which was going on round the clock. When he saw a miniature artist embellishing the apartment, he decided to take a peek at the interiors when the advisers were not about. He sweet-talked one of the handsome artists into giving him some more information by complimenting him on his talent and looks, and gifting him a silver coin.

'This new apartment is being readied as desired by the Maharaja to welcome a very special guest on Diwali. It is named 'Ras Vilas' by none other than the Maharaja himself,' said the artist, revealing the information that Mohan Ram was looking for. Firstly, the Maharaja was missing for days together, and then he was getting a new apartment made overnight. This made Mohan Ram more than sure that the Maharaja was bringing in a new companion. What was unusual, though, was that a special dwelling place was being made for a concubine in the palace itself for the first time.

Mohan Ram knew that no unmarried lover of the Maharaja could be housed anywhere near the zenani deorhi without the knowledge of the Chief Queen. The unmarried women, whom the king took a fancy to, were grouped according to their status as *pardayat*, *paswans*, *paturs*, etc. Of these, the pardayats were of higher status than the others, and they underwent the choora ceremony even though no marriage ceremony was performed. How could the Chief Queen not smell the dust storm building up around the palace, wondered the shrewd eunuch. As a loyal servant of the palace, he decided to alert her. The second time round, the Queen could feel the ground beneath her feet shake. She immediately summoned the other wives of Jagat Singh.

The sudden call from the Chief Queen surprised all other queens, as they gathered collectively only on ceremonial occasions, or when special guests were invited. On those occasions too, they merely exchanged pleasantries, as all of them indulged in politicking to gather more power and outsmart one another. Basically, their relationship was wrapped in suspicion and mistrust, duly garnished by their fleets of personal staff.

'I have called you all to unite in facing a crisis never witnessed by this palace before,' the anxious Chief Queen said. Her tone worried the other queens, and they asked her what had happened. The Chief Queen expressed her concerns over the behaviour of the Maharaja, which started from the day of the celebration at the temple in honour of Radha—him going on a sudden hunting expedition and not being back till a day before the Diwali festival.

'Do you all know that he has even ordered the construction of a special apartment next to mine, which he has named Ras Vilas?' They all expressed their ignorance.

She further asked them, 'Do you have any idea of the purpose behind the building of this apartment? Had it not been for the loyal Nadir Mohan Ramji even I would have been as ignorant as you are. We, as his wives, know that he is always looking for a new lady and I am sure that now he has found one. We have learnt to deal with his new finds, off and on, but what is worrying me is this new feature of making an apartment for his new lover. He has never accorded so much importance to any woman.' For the first time, they were all on the same wavelength, as they shared their apprehensions and pledged to unite in dealing with the crisis.

The following morning, the palace witnessed two dramatic acts—one within the ladies' quarters and the other in the office of the Council of Ministers. The royal physician was summoned to the apartment of the Chief Queen, who had developed an unbearable headache. He read her pulse, diagnosing hypertension. After giving her the requisite medicine, he suggested to her that she should calm down.

He said, 'You seemed to be in the grip of worry and anxiety, which can result in many ailments. I fail to understand why people like you, with all the comforts in the world, worry so much, and the poor take their problems in stride. Has the Maharaja Sahib returned from Amber?' Wondering how the royal physician knew about the Maharaja being at Amber, she replied, 'Not yet. He is expected back by tomorrow, but who informed you that he was in Amber?' He smiled, telling her how he was rushed to Amber to treat the Maharaja's lady guest. The royal physician was so much in awe of his extraordinarily beautiful patient that without any ulterior motive, he described the beauty and grace of the young girl he had treated at Amber. His narrative worked faster than his medicine, as the Chief Queen rose from her bed to see the physician off and sent her trusted maid to call Nadir Mohan Ram.

Inside the office, where the select group of ministers and influential feudal lords were summoned, the meeting was surprisingly being chaired by the former prime minister known for his total commitment to the Kachchwaha dynasty, Dinaram Bohra. The confidant of the royal family specially summoned to hold the meeting, the matter seemed to be serious.

He started his address on a sombre note, 'This is not a formal gathering to take a decision on an administrative point, but is a gathering to collectively gauge the implications of the new love of the Maharaja.'

At his words, the laughter of the feudal lords of Samode, Chomu and Dooni echoed. There was nothing unusual in their Maharaja finding yet another lady love. They viewed it to be the privilege of the ruler and wished to close the meeting.

'Respected Bohraji, you made us come all this way for this trivial matter. Do not worry. These kinds of relationships are short lived and do not warrant such high-level consultation. Let us all go back home and celebrate Diwali.' The veteran politician asked them to be seated, and spoke again, 'It is not as light a matter as you think. In fact, if you do not pay attention, I can see it having serious implications for the state. This is not an ordinary relationship that your Maharaja is indulging in. I am fully aware of the developments since the celebrations at the temple. He has been away from the palace for so many days so that he can be in company of his love. Above all, I have seen both the Maharaja and the young girl together at Amber, and he has got a new apartment constructed right under your noses for her. Let me inform you that he will be coming for Diwali only with her.'

His words made them all curious to know who the girl was. As they raised questions about her background, he said, 'She is an extraordinary girl bestowed with divine beauty and grace. Her wisdom and knowledge radiate through her persona. Don't take her to be merely a dancing woman's daughter. As a Brahmin, I can say that she also has Brahmin blood in her.' As he subtly talked about her lineage, he made eye contact with Pandit Shiv Narain for a fraction of a moment. Hearing the alarming words of Dina

Ramji, all those present started discussing the best way to get rid of the girl. While some proposed finding him another beautiful courtesan, others proposed another marriage alliance knowing marriage customs would compel the Maharaja to be away from his dangerous liaison for some time.

After consideration, the Thakur of Geejgarh came up with the name of the granddaughter of his elder brother, the Thakur of Pokhran. Everybody present readily agreed to the proposition, completely overlooking Jagat Singh's nineteen marriages that did not keep him from finding new partners. The power wielding feudal lords took it upon themselves to get the marriage ceremony concluded soon after the proposal was received. With that well-placed decision, the fear of the mysterious lady love's influence on their wayward Maharaja vanished, and they happily dispersed to celebrate Diwali. Away from the politics, Jagat Singh was excited about taking Raskapoor to the palace despite being aware of the tough resistance he was going to meet from all sides. Instead of being worried, he was amused to visualize his other wives coming together to hatch all sorts of plans to remove Raskapoor from his life, underestimating his resolve to protect his love from those evil heads. He could also foresee his vassals, some of them related to his wives, coming up with what they considered to be the best way out, which was bound to be yet another marriage alliance.

'Ras, I am so excited to take you with me to the palace. But you do know that will not be easy. You will meet many hurdles. My nineteen wives will stand as a united force against you, while my ministers will try their best to remove you from my life,' said Jagat Singh, trying to prepare Raskapoor for her turbulent landing in the palace as they strolled hand in hand on the terrace. Raskapoor showed no signs of apprehension.

'I fear nothing in life, for your love will enable me cross all the hurdles,' she said.

Jagat Singh then naughtily quizzed her, 'What would you do if they fix another marriage for me?' Raskapoor replied confidently, without panic, 'I will see you off like all your other wives, pray for your safe return, and welcome you with your new bride. I am

inspired by Goddess Parvati and Radha. Remember, Parvati took
many births to finally marry Lord Shiva while Radha, after the
Gandharva marriage with Krishna, did not worry about his two
marriages with Rukmini and Satyabhama.'

Jagat Singh was amazed to hear her words, marvelling at the
girl standing before him. 'Ras, there was no woman like you, there
is no one like you, and I am sure there will be no one like you. No
one can ever replace you in my life. Perhaps only one or two of my
wives would find mention in the history of my empire but nothing
about me would be recorded without your mention.' Raskapoor
smiled, and he gave her a tight hug. In that moment of passion,
with her teary eyes, Raskapoor made him promise his complete
trust in her. 'You already have so many wives and you may even
have more but remember, for me you are my only life partner.
Right from my childhood, I pledged to be a one-man woman. Like
Radha and Krishna's eternal bond, even though they never met
again after he left Mathura, I will hold our alliance close to my
heart till I breathe my last. Please promise me that you will never
heed to false rumours and suspect my integrity.'

Picking up her tear on his index finger, Jagat Singh gave his
word, 'This is not just a tear but a pearl of wisdom. I give you
my word, knowing fully well that the day I go back on it, I will
be doomed, for my life will be filled only with repentance. If I
cannot trust you, then I will never be able to trust anyone else.' On
the day before Diwali, the Maharaja's advisers informed him that
Ras Vilas was complete. With lavish interiors and silk curtains,
the new apartment was all set to usher in his love. The Maharaja
explained his plan to Gulab. She would accompany Raskapoor to
the Govind Dev temple around dusk. He would be there to receive
her. Right before sunrise, Jagat Singh set off with his entourage
for Jai Nagar. His advisers were already there to greet him at
the palace as ceremonial music heralded his return. It was about
midday, and the palace was abuzz with festive excitement.

Inside the zenani deorhi, when the queens were informed about
the return of the Maharaja, they were eager to know if he had come
with his new companion. Always on alert, their informer Nadir

Mohan Ram brought the heartening news to the Chief Queen, 'Prepare for a grand celebration in the evening. Our Maharaja has arrived without the much talked about lady.' He was duly rewarded by her and she sent messages to all the other queens to be ready in their finery to welcome him back and celebrate the festival together. As Jagat Singh walked into Preetam Chowk, he asked his advisers to first show him Ras Vilas. He inspected the new apartment minutely, visualizing the first reaction of his lady love, who must have started her journey towards Jai Niwas. Complimenting the advisers, he made his way to Shobha Niwas to see where he would seat Raskapoor when he would introduce her to his wives. No one could sense what he was planning.

He informed the Chief Queen of his brief appearance in the main courtyard of the zenani deorhi for the ritual, after which they were all going to be on the terrace of Shobha Niwas to witness the fireworks display. While all the queens were excited about his arrival, he himself longed for the arrival of Raskapoor. Close to the fixed hour of her arrival, he strolled in the sprawling garden, making his way to the temple. When a group of female devotees landed in the temple courtyard offering their prayers to the deity, only the Maharaja standing under a tree at the far end knew Raskapoor was standing amidst them. The firecrackers were keeping all eyes riveted towards the sky and no one knew when the group of women was led away. There was so much excitement in the ladies' quarters for the special ritual for Goddess Laxmi that a kind of lull prevailed around Ras Vilas, which facilitated the easy entry of Raskapoor into the new apartment.

Jagat Singh whispered into her ear, 'Thanks to Goddess Laxmi, finally my real queen is with me.'

He showed her the door that led to his private apartment as well as briefed her about the plan for the rest of the evening. He directed Gulab to dress Raskapoor in the beautiful kajalia, a black attire embellished with gold embroidery traditionally worn for Diwali. He had already got the altar of Goddess Laxmi placed in the apartment and informed Raskapoor, 'Before going to the ladies' quarters, I will come here, and together we will invoke her blessings. Gulab will then lead you to Shobha Niwas and I will be there soon after I finish the other ritual.'

Raskapoor, who had submitted herself to the will of Lord Govind Devji before entering the main arena, merely swayed with the directions of Jagat Singh.

The Maharaja knew he had created history as he was the only Maharaja of Jai Nagar who had added an abode in Jai Niwas for his lover. Relating with the ecstasy of the Moghul emperor Shah Jahan, who had built the Taj Mahal for Mumtaz Mahal, made Jagat Singh even more proud of himself. But he omitted the fact that Mumtaz was the lawful wife of the emperor while Raskapoor was not.

Jagat Singh got ready for the rituals, sporting his ceremonial attire, the royal barber set his beard and moustache, and his aide carefully tied his headgear. He wanted to see his reflection in the eyes of his beloved and made his way straight to Ras Vilas. As Gulab ushered him in, his own eyes were blinded by the dazzling beauty of Raskapoor, who stood in the centre in the exquisite black outfit. As he stood still in admiration, she took a bit of kohl from her right eye and put a dot behind the ear of her beloved. In her subtle manner, she conveyed to him how handsome he looked that evening. Together they prayed to Goddess Laxmi, and he asked Gulab to bring his Diwali gift for Raskapoor. He himself put the bajuband, the two armlets embellished with precious stones, around her delicate arms.

When his entry was announced in the zenani deorhi, all his wives came out with trays of lamps to greet him. Oblivious to the coming of Raskapoor, they delighted in pampering him. While the Chief Queen sat next to him, she made his other wives sit around as the group of priests conducted the ritual. Jagat Singh had carried special gifts for all his wives and their staff in a bid to please them before they tackled him for finding yet another love. He asked all his wives to come to the terrace of Shobha Niwas and quickly headed there himself.

Raskapoor was already seated on the velvet mattress when Jagat Singh arrived there. He said, 'Your aura makes this palace look even more beautiful.'

From the garden below, the fireworks specialists started the
display again, and all his wives arrived on the terrace. He surprised
them by greeting each one of them by name. They indulged in light-
hearted conversation till one of them candidly joked, 'Where is the
priceless jewel?' He gave them a shock as he moved the silk curtain
of Shobha Niwas, saying, 'The jewel is right here. Raskapoor is the
jewel in my crown. Let me assure you all that your position and
respect will remain intact. I will always honour you all, provided
you all take a pledge to accord the same respect to Raskapoor.
Like Krishna and Radha, we are a married couple. We became one
with the blessings of the Mother Goddess in Amber adhering to the
tradition of Gandharva marriage.' Raskapoor, with her eyes cast
down like a new bride, was asked by Jagat Singh to greet all his
wives. She got up and respectfully bowed before each one of them
in the traditional way as taught to her by Gulab. The Maharaja
knew he had exploded a powerful bomb after which a fraught
silence prevailed in Shobha Niwas. When Raskapoor finished
greeting each one of them, they headed back for the zenani deorhi
without a word.

Jagat Singh could read their thoughts and knew well that
they would spend hours, first in putting all the blame on the poor
innocent girl standing before him for the act that he alone was
responsible for, and then come up with designs to remove his love
from his life. All his marriages took place only as tactical moves
to make the state more powerful, and none of his wives had been
chosen by him. Besides, he failed to understand why they rejoiced
in manipulation, deceit and intrigues, which distanced him further
from the environs of the zenani deorhi. His connection with his
wives was occasional, and more on a physical rather than an
emotional level.

He wished he could have married Raskapoor before marrying
all of them. If he had, his life would not have been entangled in
such distasteful environs. Raskapoor observed that the Maharaja
was lost in deep thought and offered to retreat to Ras Vilas if he
had to be in the zenani deorhi. Jagat Singh held her hand. 'I have
not brought you here only to let you go back there. I am going to
spend this festive night with you in Shobha Niwas.'

The couple spent a blissful night, waking up with the sound of the divine bells of the Govind Dev temple where the deity was offered the first prayer before sunrise.

On the other side, in the female quarters, all hell had broken loose. His furious wives spent a sleepless night. They could not imagine that the Maharaja would defy all royal norms so blatantly, shaming the state. Hailing from the powerful clan of Rathores, the Chief Queen Bikawatji blew the bugle of revolt.

She proclaimed, 'Look at his audacity, asking us to extend full respect to her. Indeed, I have never ever seen such a beautiful girl and even if she belonged to an ordinary Rajput family, we would have let him marry her. But we all come from well-known warrior clans and cannot allow the Maharaja to bring a tawaif to rule over us. I am going to summon all the feudal lords closely related to us to deal with the matter before the situation gets out of hand.' All the other queens agreed with her and decided to send messages to their parents.

Early in the morning, when the feudal lords of Chomu, Samode, Geejgarh and Dooni received the message from Bikawatji to meet her in Preetam Niwas, they thought it to be the customary gathering for Diwali. Before meeting her, they decided to offer nazrana, the coins of goodwill presented to the Maharaja on festive occasions. They were seated in the Saravatobhadra, the hall of special audience, expecting to be called by the Maharaja. They were, however, taken aback to see the Maharaja walking towards them holding the hand of his much talked about love. When they offered the goodwill coins, he directed them to offer them first to Raskapoor.

While the other three followed his direction, Chaand Singh, the Thakur of Dooni defied him and decided not to hand over the coin to anyone else but the Maharaja. Clever Raskapoor realized that very moment that she would meet tough opposition from his end. Jagat Singh could not care less and introduced Raskapoor to them. 'She is the queen of my heart. To make it clearer, she is my Ardhangini, or better half, according to the Hindu tradition. Last night, I requested all the queens to accord full respect to her, and now I am requesting you all to do so. Ras, these are all my senior family members.' Raskapoor, with her gaze on the ground, bowed down before each one of them. Much as they were shocked and furious, they were all over-awed by her beauty and her respectful way of greeting them. Jagat Singh's defiant stance made them totally mute and they begged his leave and headed to meet Bikawatji. After the exchange of formal greetings, she raised the topic of Raskapoor, requesting them to intervene and remove her from Jagat Singh's life by hook or crook.

'I do not mind even getting another marriage organized for him. In the hustle-bustle of the marriage, you all can ensure her disappearance,' Bikawatji came up with her wicked proposition. Geejgarh Thakur told her about his idea of getting a proposal for the granddaughter of Pokhran Thakur. 'She is a member of my clan, so I too will talk to my family. In fact, that will also strengthen the bond of Kachchwahas and Rathores,' he said. Bikawatji conveyed her consent promptly. Raskapoor's presence was a nightmare for both, but they knew that it would take months to materialize the dream wedding, first in getting the proposal through, considering the reputation of their candidate, and then getting him to agree to yet another marriage, for his disenchantment with political wedding alliances was well known. Raskapoor's arrival was like a devastating earthquake, of which she was the epicentre, resulting in the tsunami of plans to distance the Maharaja from her. No one could see that her entry in the life of the Maharaja was going to result in the aftershocks throughout his reign irrespective of her being in the palace or not.

Spring Showers Love, Celebrations and Royal Honour

Life in Ras Vilas and Shobha Niwas exuded love and mutual respect. With each passing day, Jagat Singh was getting more and more impressed with Raskapoor's wisdom and insights as he discussed matters with her related to governance. She seemed to have an inherent knowledge of statecraft as she led him to weigh the pros and cons of each decision he made, reining in his whimsicality swiftly. With nothing at stake, she was always objective, unlike all his queens who only wished to be more powerful and win his proximity. Her reasoning to help him shed his prejudices, see through the intentions of vassals playing against one another and take a keen interest in strengthening his position within a short spell at the palace often made him wonder whether she was an empress in her previous life. Sometimes he felt that he and his landlords put together would not be able to match her administrative skills if she held the reins of his state.

His respect and love for her gradually made Raskapoor totally comfortable but she often missed her mother and her best friend Rudra, whom she had not seen since the day she left the glass palace for Amber. She had seen her father Pandit Shiv Narain a few times, but as expected he chose to maintain a safe distance from her. Initially, she did not appreciate this, yearning to talk to him if only to enquire about her mother and Rudra. One day, when

164

Jagat Singh was missing his own father, he decided to arrange for Raskapoor to meet hers, summoning him to Shobha Niwas.

When Pandit Shiv Narain came and wished to know the reason for the sudden call, Jagat Singh laughed and said, 'To let the father and daughter talk in peace.'

Raskapoor was overwhelmed by such a thoughtful gesture from the Maharaja who was known to be a self-centred and inconsiderate human being. Jagat Singh left the two alone to talk.

Forgetting all her anger, Raskapoor, who was longing to be with her family, first hugged the father and then cried to her heart's content. Her father tried to calm her down, 'I know you are missing your mother as much as she misses you, but I keep her updated about your well-being. Ras, I know I have wronged you beyond repairs and even god will not pardon me for the sin I have committed. Seeking punishment for myself each day, I pray for you every night. I may not meet you, but I am keeping an eye on you because I know that given the opportunity, everyone would want you removed from the life of the Maharaja. You are lucky to win his genuine love and respect as I have not seen him express to any of his wives or lovers. I can only give you one piece of sincere advice: do not trust anyone in the palace, however sweet they may be to you. The palace has a cobweb of informers and mis-informers, so be careful choosing your words.'

Raskapoor felt a sudden rush of emotions for her father. He was trying to ensure her well-being, despite being in a situation of not being able to acknowledge her as his daughter publicly. Wiping her tears, he informed her about Rudra's regular visits to the glass palace, and how he enquired about her each time they met. He drew his daughter close to him, giving her one last hug as he heard the footsteps and the voice of the Maharaja in the courtyard. Overwhelming feelings rolled out through their tears.

When Jagat Singh entered the chamber, he playfully teased Raskapoor, 'Panditji, look at your daughter who is so much in love with me that she does not want to meet you or her mother, and not even her best friend, Rudra!' Feeling even more confident in the presence of her father, Raskapoor responded, 'Look at your Maharaja who brings your innocent daughter to the palace and does not let her meet her mother. How can I go out of the palace till the Maharaja facilitates it?' Immediately, Jagat Singh asked Pandit Shiv Narain Mishra to inform her mother as well as Rudra that Raskapoor would be meeting them a week later.

On the given day, Raskapoor did not know whether she was going to the glass palace or her mother was going to visit her with Rudra. After the two were ready, Jagat Singh informed Raskapoor that he would walk down the secret passage to Brijnidhi temple, which he had last walked the day he saw her at the temple. She was delighted but a bit disappointed to hear no mention of meeting her mother.

Jagat Singh led her to the shrine of Radha-Krishna, and together they bowed before the deities. He walked her down the basement, opening a door on the other side, where a group of maids were waiting with four palanquin bearers.

To her utmost surprise, Raskapoor discovered that Jagat Singh had ordered the construction of a tunnel on the other side too, opening straight into the courtyard of the glass palace. He needed that last week to complete the project. Immensely grateful, Raskapoor, committed to herself once again to remain loyal to Jagat Singh in good times and bad. She knew now that even in times of adversity she would not give up on him, as she had never ever dreamt of the kind of love that he had showered on her. Deep within her, she knew his world was a make believe one, for which she had no leaning, and that her reality was far away from his. Besides this, much as she was indebted and loyal to Jagat Singh, given the choice in her next life, she would still choose someone like Rudra who enriched her intellectually.

Jagat Singh fixed the time for her return, telling her that he would be waiting at the same door to receive her. Promising her besotted lover that she would be back on time, she looked forward to meeting her mother and Rudra so she could pour her heart out. While the palanquin manoeuvred through the tunnel, Raskapoor saw herself emerging out of a fantasy. She saw her Ammi, Rudra and her father at the opening of the tunnel.

When the palanquin was put on the ground, she took no time in getting out to hug her Ammi. 'Even in a palace, a daughter will always yearn for her mother. You know Ammi, not a single day passed without me thinking of my real home. You have no idea how much I have missed you.' Raskapoor sobbed inconsolably, resting her head on her mother's shoulder. 'You have made two wise Brahmins also cry. Look at Rudra.' Wiping his tears, Pandit Shiv Narain drew her attention towards Rudra, who was wiping his tears too. Raskapoor smiled.

She rushed into her room and changed into one of the dresses that she used to wear before she left for Amber, as her royal attire and expensive jewellery made her feel strange in her own environs. 'Ammi, now I feel like myself,' she said, making herself totally comfortable on the mattress on the floor.

'Yes, now you appear to be the real Raskapoor,' Rudra spoke for the first time since her arrival. He was aloof but reflected his innate love for her subtly, unlike the Maharaja, who was rather over-expressive with his passionate feelings. That detached stance of Rudra always drew Raskapoor.

As usual, she teased him, 'So you have been missing the real Raskapoor?' Rudra too tried to tease her, 'Yes! You looked so artificial in that fancy attire.' Raskapoor, who was visibly irked with his remark, asked him if he was jealous of the Maharaja who had whisked away his real Raskapoor. Unruffled with her stark comment, Rudra responded, 'Why would I be jealous of the Maharaja being a lover of natural beauty? My Raskapoor is a real one while he has a copy and that too so made-up!'

Seeing the two friends arguing just as they always did, Chaand advised them to sit on the terrace while she prepared the meal.

Moving to the terrace, Raskapoor candidly asked him, 'Rudra, you may not admit it, but were you not over-awed to see me in that royal attire?' Rudra was unable to hold back his feelings and was pushed to accept the fact. 'Ras, indeed I was over-awed to see you appear like a queen. In fact, I wondered if any of his other queens has such an impressive persona as yours. You must, however, appreciate the fact that I am not a Maharaja and I would feel your presence only when you appear like this, in your normal way. If you are dressed in that royal attire, there will always be a distance between you and me.'

Their conversation spanned various subjects, including the Maharaja's love and respect. Before going down for their meal, Rudra told her to not be swayed by all the love and respect, but also to always be vigilant, for he had known of once-intensely loved women of rulers, disappearing without a trace. No one knew if they were dead or alive. 'I will continue to pray for your well-being and his unending love for you. God forbid, should you be in any crisis, you can always send me a message. I will always be there for you,' Rudra assured her earnestly.

Raskapoor was deeply touched. They all enjoyed their meal together and then it was time for Raskapoor to head back to the palace. Chaand took her daughter inside to help her change back into her royal attire and have a one-on-one conversation. She alerted her young daughter of the ever-present danger in the palace. She tried to explain to Raskapoor that despite what the Maharaja felt for her, she would always be perceived only as a concubine. Raskapoor knew her mother's apprehensions were right, but she again told her, 'It does not matter to me how the palace today or history tomorrow perceives me. If it did not bother Radha, why should it bother me? Ammi, our truth is ours, not what the world proclaims.' Chaand was amazed to see the wisdom and confidence of her daughter. Pandit Shiv Narain, Rudra and her mother saw her off, waiting till her palanquin disappeared into the darkness of the tunnel.

As arranged, Jagat Singh was waiting to receive his beloved. Raskapoor felt fortunate to have two special men of her life, one on either side of the tunnel. The Maharaja helped her dismount from the palanquin. As he walked back to the palace holding her hand, Raskapoor expressed her gratitude to him for what he had done that day.

'You have no idea what you have done to me, Ras, and you cannot imagine what I am going to do for you. Had it not been for you, I would have never found my real self. I was not born a womanizer or a wayward man. The more I spend time with you, the more I am convinced about the role of the environs in which a child is raised irrespective of the status of the family he or she is born in. I was lured into the world of women and wine as a young boy, and my marriages were planned for me as per whims and fancies of the intriguers, who continue to be all over the palace even now,' Jagat Singh said, opening his heart to her for the first time.

Deeply moved, Raskapoor told him, 'Remember Prince Siddharth? He indulged in every act, which was quintessential for a king, from worldly pleasure to killings, but the world today reveres him as Buddha.'

After the intense conversation, when they reached Shobha Niwas, he asked her, 'Ras, my love, were you happy to see your mother? Did Pandit Shiv Narain invite Rudra to your place as advised?' Raskapoor was astonished to know that the Maharaja had arranged for Rudra to be there, wondering if he was trying to test her feelings for her old friend. 'I am wondering how many surprises you planned for me. It was indeed so thoughtful of you to have suggested that and I must tell you Rudra was very happy to hear of your immense love and respect for me. You are indeed a special person to not to have an iota of doubt about my meeting a man whom you are yet to meet.'

Jagat Singh hugged her tightly. 'I have met you and that is enough for me. You will be happy to know that even in my absence, you can meet him here as well as at the glass palace. I know you have no friends here, and I will not even advise you to cultivate any friendship here, as it is bound to betray you.' Ever since the celebration of Diwali, Jagat Singh showed hardly any inclination to visit the zenani deorhi. His queens knew that they were at the mercy of Raskapoor, as the Maharaja never forgot to tell them that Raskapoor was the one who reminded him constantly to visit them. His obsession with his lover was making the queens restless, and their worries increased. Some prayed, some consulted astrologers, while others conspired.

At the moment, they were anxious to know whether he was going to hold the special celebration on the fifth day of Basant as per the palace tradition. Their anger knew no bounds when they heard that Jagat was going to celebrate, but only with Raskapoor, for whom he had ordered not one, but two of the special yellow ensembles from the family rangrez who was dyeing them in saffron.

Raskapoor wanted to celebrate Raag Basant from dawn through the night. Shobha Niwas was decorated with seasonal flowers, and a special menu was given to the royal kitchen. Jagat Singh was ecstatic to know that Raskapoor had herself chosen to sing and dance for the first time since she became a part of his life. He saw it as a divine coincidence. The last time he saw her sing and dance was at the temple; and now the next time was going to be when, on one hand the goddess of art and wisdom was being worshipped, and on the other hand the forty-day *phag* celebration began in Brij, the territory of Radha and Krishna. His beloved had requested him to invite her masters and accompanists when she sang and danced for him.

As the golden yellow sun rays touched the courtyard, Jagat Singh spotted Raskapoor glittering in the yellow attire, offering water to the sun, and then turning towards the temple of Govind Dev ji. She bowed in reverence and prayed to the deity with her eyes closed. After finishing her prayer, as she opened her eyes, she was pleasantly surprised to see the Maharaja standing next to her dressed in a new regal attire in a similar yellow shade. He led her to Shobha Niwas and Raskapoor saw her teachers and accompanists welcoming the couple. She moved forward and touched the feet of her teachers.

Jagat Singh then drew her attention towards the marble statue of Goddess Sarasvati, which he had asked the master marble carver of Jai Nagar to make to celebrate this special day of his life. Handing over a garland to Raskapoor to invoke the blessings of the goddess, he said, 'Raskapoor, you have made it possible for this palace to get the first statute of the Goddess of Wisdom and after today you will be her custodian, taking her to Ras Vilas.'

Raskapoor could not control the stream of tears flowing down her eyes as she remembered the day she was given the statue of Natraj by the priest of the Shiva temple. Overcome with respect and gratitude, Raskapoor bent down to touch the feet of Jagat Singh, but he did not let her and instead wiped her tears with his palms. Raskapoor joined her teachers and accompanists, and seeking the permission of all, picked up her tanpura.

Raskapoor said, 'I decided to celebrate Raag Basant, which evokes the romance in the air when the exuberance of fragrant flowers fills life with love as never before. Raag Basant is usually sung at night till midnight, but during this season it can be sung at any hour. I am going to sing a classical composition in Raag Basant Mukhari. It is not an easy melody and I have not done any practice, but I hope I have blessings of Goddess Saraswati, Radha and Krishna, my teachers and the honourable Maharaja to render it without making any mistakes.' Her teachers were amazed to see the choice of her melody, but her first note was enough to win their admiration for their amazingly gifted pupil. Shobha Niwas echoed with her melodious and powerful voice . . . 'The fair milk maiden left to fetch water from the river Yamuna, suddenly she was intercepted by a man who went on teasing her. I, Radha, the innocent one, could not read his thoughts. He dragged me with my arm to the woods, he hugged me with such devotion, I spontaneously fell in love with the teaser—one and only Krishna.'

Raskapoor embellished the composition with intricate notes and such finesse that it resulted in resounding applause and a standing ovation from the Maharaja. The teachers were startled to see that she had surpassed their training.

Away from Shobha Niwas, when one of the maids of the Chief Queen heard Raskapoor sing, she rushed to inform her. She, in turn, quickly summoned all the other queens. They all placed their ears against the nearest wall to hear the drifting notes; and much as they disliked her, conceded that they had never ever heard such a magical voice like Raskapoor's. The celebrations in Shobha Niwas reached their zenith at night when Raskapoor danced to phag set in Raag Kaafi, yet another melody for the season. She was dressed in a dazzling yellow outfit and danced as she sang, 'Splash colours, splash colours, splash the colours on the son of Nand. I will turn his dark complexion into red. Rubbing the red colour on both cheeks, I will turn him into a woman and make him dance like a woman, to the beat of drums. Do not be scared my friends, just grab him for me to put the red dots on his cheeks.'

Much amused, Jagat Singh asked her to repeat the line about turning Krishna into a woman. As she started again, he grabbed her veil cloth, covered his head with it and they danced in gay abandon. It was a historic moment for the teachers. While the accompanists raised the pace of the beat, her music teacher joined in the song. The sound from Shobha Niwas in the quiet of midnight pierced the ears of all the queens who were appalled at how their husband was celebrating while they lay abandoned in their respective residences. They summoned Nadir Mohan Ram to find out exactly what was happening in the out-of-bounds Shobha Niwas. He placed himself at the exit gate of the palace so that he could meet the group of musicians as they made their way out. Sensing their delight over the day-long celebrations, Mohan Ram said, 'You should not be surprised to see me here at this hour. The sound of your beautiful music has kept the dancer in me awake, hoping to meet you and request you to take me as your disciple. I can assure you I will prove to be better than her.'

Filled with the excitement of the unimaginable reward they had received, they suggested that he follow the tune of their gifted disciple, which made the Maharaja dance till the moment he ran out of breath. Mohan Ram could not believe what he had heard and ran to the Chief Queen, who was sitting with the other queens. 'Can you imagine, she made our Maharaja dance! He danced with her—the teacher himself told me.' They were aghast to hear that.

Jagat Singh was thrilled with the celebration of Raag Basant in his palace and wanted to honour Raskapoor in a befitting manner. He eagerly waited for the celebration of the festival of colours, Holi, to make it as special for Raskapoor as she had made Basant Panchami for him. He had ordered a special costume for the day of the festival, a phagunia—white and red attire with rich gold embroidery. Following family tradition, Jagat Singh was to go in a ceremonial procession out of the Tripolia Gate to play Holi with his subjects. All arrangements were made outside, and the Maharaja was awaited eagerly by his feudal lords. Inside, he insisted that Raskapoor dress in phagunia and walk with him to the point where the procession was lined up.

Raskapoor tried to make him understand that her walking along with him would raise a hue and cry in the palace and pleaded with him to let her stay back at Ras Vilas. Jagat Singh did not yield to her request, leaving her no option but to follow him. At the far end, when the feudal lords saw a lady walking in a phagunia alongside their Maharaja, they thought that he was bringing the Chief Queen along to see the procession off, which in itself tantamounted to breaking the tradition as only men were allowed there. When Jagat Singh ordered the elephant to sit on the floor, everyone was dumbfounded, including Raskapoor who could not envisage his next move. He led her to the silver ladder and asked her to get on the elephant. She was made comfortable on the back seat of the silver and gold howdah while he sat on the front seat and signalled his staff to start the procession.

The feudal lords were shocked to see how defiant their ruler had become. Of course, they attributed it to Raskapoor, who herself was ignorant about what Jagat Singh's plans were. But the people were delighted. For the first time, a lady was coming out on the royal elephant in a ceremonial procession seated with the Maharaja. They had neither seen the queen nor Raskapoor before. They were overjoyed to see who they thought was their queen and her extraordinary beauty for the first time. Many were reminded of the Moghul Emperor's beloved wife empress Noor Jahan who was the only lady known to ride an elephant with the ruler on a hunting spree.

Jagat Singh excitedly splashed colours on his people who were hailing him, sometimes intentionally throwing a fistful at Raskapoor and enticing her to splash some colour towards him. As the cloud of colours of love appeared over the Maharaja and his beloved, the image of Krishna and Radha riding on the elephant floated before Raskapoor's eyes. It was not merely the excitement of an elephant ride for her, as she was living that moment on a different plane. She could not but be grateful to the deities for granting her that blissful moment, as well as sought the blessings for the man in her life, Jagat Singh. He had defied all norms, elevating her life to a level beyond the imagination of any girl of her background. She could die at that moment as she did not yearn for anything more in life.

After spending couple of hours amidst his people, giving them a glimpse of the queen of his heart, Jagat Singh returned to the palace. His vassals were very upset to see him display utmost caution in helping his lover to dismount the elephant and they just wanted to leave the scene. Jagat Singh was well aware of what was going in the heads of his feudal lords whom he had shocked with the move of taking a lady into the ceremonial procession, especially one who was merely a nautch girl's daughter. He sensed the stance they would take in the festive Durbar after Holi when they would come to offer their customary gratification, leaving no stone unturned in belittling his love and ridiculing his act.

The queens too were furious after the ceremonial procession. They considered that the Maharaja had once again shamed not just his state, but the states to which they belonged too, by his actions. Strangely, they somehow adhered to the age-old perception of holding the lady-lover responsible and absolving the husband for straying. They were eagerly awaiting his arrival to spring him out of the trap of the wicked Raskapoor.

Jagat Singh was well aware of the smouldering fire in the female quarters, but decided to go ahead with his plan to defend Raskapoor and safeguard her from the wrath of these people. The plan was already in place. It was a well-kept secret that only few who were executing it knew, and that also in bits and pieces. The Maharaja had assigned roles to his team without revealing the full script. On the day of the Durbar, Jagat Singh decided to seat Raskapoor on the silver throne on his left side, the customary seat for the wedded wife, outraging the feudal lords and vassals.

Once again, he asked them to hand over the silver coins they were offering him to Raskapoor instead. After the Diwali shock, all of them had already decided not to do so if he ever came up with that directive undermining their stature. It was the unanimous view that the gratification meant for the king in no way could be offered to a concubine. Offended vassals did not mince any words to defend their dignity. They not only raised the issue of her being of low status but even called her an illegitimate child.

As decided, Pandit Shiv Narain Mishra made the first surprising announcement, 'No child is illegitimate. Birth is a legitimate act of Mother Nature and that profound truth must be perceived. I am a Brahmin, and I will not let any girl be ridiculed for her birth. Before you gentlemen, I adopt her as my godchild. You all know that adoption can change the fate of a child, even elevating them to the position of a ruler.' The court was shocked to hear the announcement of the learned Brahmin. Raskapoor had tears in her eyes, for finally, she had a father!

Before they could deal with that shock, yet another one came from the Maharaja himself. 'You are all upset about her not being from a royal family. Today before all of you, I hand over this stamp paper to Raskapoor, who on receiving this, will be known as Ardha Rajan or the Half Empress, ruling over Amber.'

He turned towards Raskapoor, who stood up in utter disbelief. 'Raskapoor, I bestow the territory of Amber upon you in appreciation of your infinite wisdom. I hand the stamp paper to you in this Durbar. Also, to honour you for being a part of my life, I issue this special silver coin in your name.'

The dumfounded Raskapoor received the stamp paper and a big velvet bag with the special silver coins to give away to all those present in the Durbar. A mournful silence took over the festive celebrations, and after all the formalities, the feudal lords dispersed as if they had attended a death ritual. Within no time, the news reached the Chief Queen, who hurriedly called all the queens, 'Here we have just started the worship of Gangaur to seek the blessings of our revered Mother Goddess for sixteen days to ensure a blissful married life; and there our Maharaja has gifted his beloved concubine a part of his empire, bestowing the title of Ardha Rajan on her! Imagine a concubine becoming the reigning queen of Amber, which had such prestigious rulers like great Sawai Jai Singh and Raja Man Singh!'

In utter disbelief they asked her if this was just gossip to shatter the festive fervour for the festival in a bid to get the complete hold of the Maharaja. 'What complete hold are you talking about? Your great Maharaja himself is falling at her feet,' she said. 'I have never ever seen him display his love so blatantly. He is so much in awe of her that he has no qualms in proclaiming her the queen of Amber, as well as issuing a silver coin to mark the occasion. Now, I think we must pray to the Mother Goddess to remove her from his life at any cost. To tell you the truth, I see no reason in women praying for their husbands when they use them for satisfying their desires and shower love on other women, including concubines.'

Her words made them all think about the futility of adhering to age-old traditions. They sat in silence for some time like women mourning the demise of someone. The Bhatiyani queen from the desert kingdom of Jaisalmer spoke, 'You are right. Let us abandon the sixteen days of ritual and send out the palanquin in his procession without the image of 'Gaur Mata'. That will be the best way to avenge the insult he has subjected us to. All of Jai Nagar will mock him.'

The Chief Queen tried to calm the wives. She said, 'Do you realize such an action can cost us our lives? His anger will not let him pardon us. This is the time to hasten her exit without offending him, or else let us be prepared for his marriage with that wicked concubine.' Medtani Rani, who hailed from the land of the mystic poetess Meera, could appreciate the deep-rooted relationship of Raskapoor and Jagat Singh as Meera's with Krishna. She spoke up for Raskapoor, 'Why call her wicked? Why hold her responsible for all his acts instead of holding him accountable? As I am told, it was our husband, the man we are praying for, who lost his heart to her. She had not even seen him till he manoeuvred her way to Amber. We must display collective wisdom to bring back our husband to his senses instead of being after her life. Remember, she is a woman like us, not a witch. Let us request Geejgarh Thakur Sahib to bring the proposal of Chaand Kanwar for our Maharaja at the earliest possible.' Deep inside their hearts, they all seemed to have the same feeling for Raskapoor and voiced their agreement to go ahead with what the Medtani Rani had proposed. Raskapoor had not anticipated the sudden change in her status with a godfather and the title 'Queen of half the empire'. While being accepted by her father filled her heart with ecstasy, the title enclosed her in the grip of anxiety and fear. It was going to be a crown of thorns and she had never even aspired for it. She was happy with the love and respect she evoked in the heart of the ruler.

Soon after reaching Shobha Niwas with Jagat Singh, she requested him to revoke his order. 'Maharajadhiraj, I have no words to express my gratitude for laying your confidence in my ability to share your political burden, but you have no idea what difficulties your actions today will pose for us. All the maharanis and the courtiers must already be fuming with anger and blaming me for your drastic moves. I am grateful to you for getting my real father to publicly adopt me, but I beseech you to take back the award of the title and the empire. You cannot visualize the dire consequences these announcements will result in. I am happy to rule your heart.'

Jagat Singh's love for her was touching new heights. 'That goes without saying. You already rule my heart, and you are the only woman to do so. However, I cannot see the queen of my heart being belittled by my people, and so I beg your pardon for not granting your wish to revoke my order. We united at Amber, and I am sure you will take the reins of Amber with full responsibility and make me proud. The maharaja of Jai Nagar would like to request the queen of Amber to join him for dinner.'

After dinner, as they walked on the terrace, Jagat Singh shared the current scenario that his empire had to deal with. He apprised her of the constant threats from the Marathas with the decline of the Moghul empire. His father Pratap Singh had tried to forge an alliance with the British in view of the alliance of the Marathas with the French. The British were trying to restrict the growing power of the French and were looking for the states that had suffered at the hands of the Marathas. Pratap's attempts succeeded after his death when the newly appointed Governor-General Lord Wellesley made a treaty of alliance in 1803 with the ruler. Intently listening to Jagat Singh, Raskapoor wished to know what that treaty entailed. He informed her, 'This is a treaty of offensive and defensive alliance. With this treaty, the future of Jai Nagar looks more secure.'

Raskapoor quickly questioned him, 'Does the treaty guarantee security of your empire against all external threats?' Jagat Singh, happy to see her keen interest said, 'Yes, my love, it does. The honourable Company has guaranteed security of this empire against all external enemies. Just before our encounter at the temple, the Governor-General wrote to the Secret Committee of Directors that I was "permanently relieved from the payment of the accustomed tribute extracted by Daulat Rao Scindia". The arrangement made by the Governor-General also took care of the constant threats of encroachment by the chieftains and other states. In fact, you came into my life to celebrate liberation from all these troubles and a secure future for this state.'

Having heard everything, she warned the Maharaja, 'Remember, a ruler can never be relieved forever by such treaties, which are forged according to the convenience of the one in command. The treaties can always be revoked arbitrarily. Also, a ruler has to forever be on alert, even in times of celebration.'

Jagat Singh marvelled at her deep insights. He said, 'I am surprised to hear your words of caution, which have never been uttered by even my vassals.' Raskapoor was able to see the plight of the all-powerful ruler standing before her, who was merely a puppet on several strings manipulated not by one but many. He was destined to live in an environment submerged in intrigues, distrust politicking, constant threats and warfare.

She felt sad thinking about his life as an innocent child living in such environs, realizing how fortunate she was to have a simple childhood with enriching experiences. Her heart reached out to that young man. A question loomed large in her heart. Was she falling in love? It was a strange feeling that inspired her to be by the side of the man, who in a way, was marooned on an isolated island. Yet the feeling was not the same that intertwined her soul with Rudra. With these entangling thoughts came the realization of the many facets of the elusive emotion called love. She was not deceitful to either of the two men. She suddenly saw herself as two different people—one at the glass palace, deeply in love with Rudra who would have never ever deserted her and the other one, at the palace who was gradually falling in love with Jagat Singh knowing fully well that it could land her in a dungeon to die alone. Could a person be born twice in one life with such contrasting emotions and lifestyles?

As expected, the feudal lords were duly outraged by the actions of their Maharaja. Some even considered him to be a complete misfit to occupy the throne but could not figure out how to dislodge him. Chomu Thakur went to the extent of saying, 'It would have been better if the late Maharaja did not have a son. That would have likely made him adopt an heir from the Chomu family, which was next in line. I would have not behaved like this Maharaja of ours.'

The Thakur of Geejgarh laughed. 'Well, we all know how your family aspires to come to the throne of Jaipur! You certainly would have done well if you had not come across a beauty like Raskapoor. Don't we all know what a bigtime womanizer you are? We might all condemn it, but our Maharaja for once has been earnest as well as respectful towards the woman he is in love with.'

Dooni Thakur intercepted him, 'Instead of admiring this fatal attraction you call love, immediately follow up the proposal from Pokhran. I have already been summoned by the Chief Queen to get you to expedite this proposal before our insane Maharaja hands over the reins of the whole state to his lover.' Geejgarh Thakur assured them that he would head for Pokhran after the Gangaur festival.

With that news, the queens continued with their daily rituals of offering prayers to the Mother Goddess. On the final day, they all got together to worship and send off the bejewelled image of Gangaur in a grand procession, for which the people of Jai Nagar thronged the terraces on the either side of the road. Raskapoor could hear the hustle and bustle of the festival. She yearned to pray to the family deity for a long and peaceful life for the Maharaja, but knowing it was not possible, chose to offer her prayers to the image, which Gulab made with ashes picked up from the pyre of the Holi festival.

Shortly before the procession moved out of the palace, Jagat Singh arrived with a red outfit for her, 'This is for you, my Gangaur. You know when a woman is beautifully dressed, adorned with all her jewellery, and called 'Gangaur', it denotes that her beauty is beyond words. Gulab told me about your prayers for my well-being and setting up an image here. Now, quickly get ready. I will take you to Shikar Oudi, the pavilion, which was once used for hunting and which is now meant for the ruler to witness the Gangaur procession.'

Raskapoor, in all her wisdom, refused to go along with him to avoid more trouble for him. However, as always, he was stubborn and she had no option but to dress in red and go along. His feudal lords had no choice but to stand and usher in the two of them.

Furious, Dooni Thakur whispered in the ear of the Geejgarh Thakur, 'We cannot let Raskapoor trample all over us, and trash our status and dignity. Now you have no option but to leave for Pokhran at sunrise tomorrow morning.'

Raskapoor had seen the two in whispered conversation. Despite her not being able to hear a word, her sharp eyes read the expression on their faces, sensing a conspiracy being hatched. After witnessing the procession, when the Maharaja was heading back for Shobha Niwas, Geejgarh Thakur walked towards him to excuse himself from the council's meeting the following day, as he had to leave for Pokhran to visit his elder brother for some urgent family matter. Jagat Singh wished to know what the matter was. Ummaid Singh told him to wait till his return when he would share all the details.

The next morning, Raskapoor decided to share her gut feeling with Jagat Singh. 'Hukum, I think I know the mission for which Ummaid Singh had to suddenly rush to Pokhran early in the morning after my appearance with you at the pavilion. I also know who rushed him.'

Jagat Singh was totally rattled to hear that from her and asked her how she knew the details of his trip.

Raskapoor spoke with a smile on her face, saying, 'Remember I had told you that a ruler always has to keep his eyes wide open and be on alert? Now that you have allocated a ruler's role to me, I have to play it well. But even if you had not allocated that role, as your partner I have been vigilant all along. May I now congratulate you?' Utterly confused, Jagat Singh asked, 'Congratulate me for what? Do not talk in riddles. Please tell me what you are talking about.'

His eagerness made Raskapoor talk in a straightforward manner, 'I know all of them are upset with the honour and respect you have accorded to me, which they cannot tolerate any more. Both, your wives and the feudal lords, have united to uproot me from your life without confronting you. They have decided that to divert your attention from me, there is no other way but to arrange a wedding alliance for you with a beautiful girl of an appropriate lineage. The girl in question is the granddaughter of Geejgarh Thakur's brother, the Thakur of Pokhran.'

Listening to her every word intently, without blinking an eye, he asked her, 'And who do you think is the one who has rushed Ummaid Singh to Pokhran?' Raskapoor, with a firm note divulged the name. 'Dooni Thakur, who has been openly showing his displeasure at my presence each time we have appeared together. Last evening, I saw him whisper something to Geejgarh Thakur and immediately after that, you were asked to give permission for the trip.'

Jagat Singh realized what she said was true, and also that being close to his Chief Queen, Chaand Singh would definitely have come up with this idea in league with her. Jai Nagar had never forged any alliance in the past with the Pokhran family and the selection of the state was made cleverly. The time it would take to travel to the isolated state in western Rajasthan confirmed Jagat Singh's suspicions. Knowingly pitched against such tough resistance, he still pledged to foil their plan. Turning serious, he told Raskapoor, 'You, at least, do not congratulate me, knowing my disenchantment with these manipulated wedding alliances that serve an ulterior motive. Let them come up with their idea and then I will shock them with my idea.' Raskapoor reassured him of her love and loyalty even in the eventuality of such a marriage alliance against which she would not pose any resistance, as she had informed him earlier too.

Wedding Alliances and Growing Troubles

Despite an alliance with the Governor-General, Jaswant Rao Holkar once again chose to defy the British government. He collected a force of thugs and plunderers to amass a fortune via princely Rajputana, raiding the new territories under British protection. Already posted with his Bombay Division in Rampura to safeguard the region, Major General Jones was then advised to tackle Holkar's force in Jai Nagar. As an ally of the British, the Kachchwaha ruler was asked to back the campaign with his army. Jagat Singh was already managing his army to deal with the crisis of yet another marriage with Princess Krishna Kumari of Udaipur. Being an ally, he had to put aside that plan and extend all desired assistance to the British. But the situation was going to get worse for Jagat Singh.

While the foreigners acknowledged his invaluable support, Jagat was stunned when he got the news that Wellesley's plan of expansion was being replaced with the policy of non-intervention. This would lead to the dissolution of all alliances with the princely states. This was because England had become involved in a war with Napoleon and could not grant the demand made by Wellesley to raise European troops in India. Back home in London, his government chose to limit its engagement with their newfound allies in India.

Soon Wellesley was removed, and Lord Cornwallis was sent as his replacement. Lord Cornwallis joined his new assignment on 30 July 1805, and on 3 August itself, he sent out Lord Lake to direct Major General Jones not to extend any aid to Jai Nagar in the future.

Jagat Singh shared the news with Raskapoor. 'You were so right. I am now convinced that so-called allies can betray you at any point, given their selfish interest, leaving you in the lurch. However, Ras, if Lord Lake is on my side, I am sure he will try to convince the new lord to extend their support because of my unquestionable loyalty, having fulfilled all the conditions of the alliance.'

Raskapoor could see the inherent uncertainty in alliances of convenience. The Maharaja seemed rather anxious about the onslaught of the Marathas. Raskapoor tried to comfort him in that dire state of affairs. 'If you have so much faith in Lord Lake, I am sure he will protect your interest in view of all the support you have given in containing Holkar. So, keep your patience and wait for his response. If Lord Lake turns around the decision in your favour, he too could be recalled like Lord Wellesley. Basically, I feel you cannot take any such arrangements for granted in the current scenario.'

No sooner had the Gangaur festival celebrations ceased than Jagat Singh's life was inundated with a number of different problems. He was caught up on both fronts, the political as well as personal. Often, he wished to escape with Raskapoor to a faraway place where he did not have to face any of these problems. He missed his late father, who died so early, not allowing him enough time to learn the nuances of politics and diplomacy, rather throwing him straight into the deep end where he had to learn a new move every day. What an unfortunate year that was, when not one death, but two deaths dragged him into the deep sea of troubles from the pleasure-filled life that he was leading.

In 1803, when his father passed away, the ruler of Jodhpur, Maharaja Bhim Singh also died. The death of the Jodhpur ruler posed a severe crisis for both the Sisodias of Udaipur as well as the Kachchwahas of Jai Nagar. No one could ever envisage that the crisis would take such an unfortunate dimension. At the time of his death, the Maharaja of Jodhpur was betrothed to Krishna Kumari, the princess of Udaipur. This had happened in 1799 when she was just five years old. After the demise of Maharaja Bhim Singh, his cousin Man Singh came to the throne.

Jagat Singh was utterly at a loss to figure out how the proposal of Princess Krishna Kumari was finally diverted to Jai Nagar. Some courtiers informed him that after the demise of Bhim Singh, the feudal lord of Mewar requested Maharaja Man Singh to honour the betrothal. They expected him to marry their princess, which he turned down, finding it an inappropriate idea to marry the fiancé of the late Maharaja, saying, 'I am like the son of Maharaja Bhim Singh, and I consider this match objectionable.' He went ahead in advising those courtiers to marry Princess Krishna Kumari wherever they could find the befitting match. As against the refusal by the Maharaja Man Singh of Jodhpur, many others saw it as the outcome of his wicked ways; he had attacked the vassal of Ghanerao despite knowing that the vassal was a close kin of the Mewar ruler. The prospective son-in-law had annoyed with his outrageous act. His misadventure resulted in the annulment of the engagement of his daughter. Maharana Bhim Singh chose not only to withdraw the proposal but send it to Jaipur's ruler.

Jagat Singh, however, did not attempt to find out the real reason behind the proposal of the Mewar princess being sent for him. Of course, he knew the intention of the anti-Raskapoor brigade in bringing up the proposal of the granddaughter of Pokhran via the Geejgarh Thakur. Both the proposals, in any case, did not lure him, for he had found his sweetheart. With Raskapoor by his side, he did not wish to let any other girl enter his life. All his courtiers pursued the proposal of Pokhran, and to his utmost surprise, even Raskapoor told him to go ahead with it saying, 'Why do you want to annoy your feudal lords and wives further? As you and I followed the footsteps of Krishna and Radha, we know our truth—our 'Gandharva marriage' at Amber. Once again, I say, as it did not matter to Radha that Krishna married Satyabhama and Rukmini, it will not matter to me. Our relationship will be eternal. Remember Krishna and

Radha never saw each other again after he left for his kingdom.' Jagat Singh felt extremely fortunate and proud to have found Raskapoor. On a playful note, he told her, 'Unlike Krishna, we are going to not only see each other but be together; and only when you promise me that will I accept the proposal received from Pokhran.'

As he hugged her tenderly, she promised him and asked him, 'When will you head for Pokhran?' He laughed, 'I am not going anywhere. Pokhran will come to Jai Nagar. First, let me give my acceptance tomorrow morning, then I will give you all the details.'

The following morning, all the Thakurs gathered in the office of the Maharaja. They were all ready to formally apprise him of the proposal received from Thakur Sawai Singh for his granddaughter. Soon the waiting period ended as Jagat Singh entered. While taking his seat, the Maharaja spotted the thakur of Geejgarh and quickly asked him, 'Thakur Sahib did you go to your residence first or have come here straight from Pokhran? So first, acquaint me on the urgent matter that rushed you to Pokhran, of which I am pretty sure all your good friends present here are already aware. When a meeting is solicited collectively, it means the subject has already been discussed amongst the meeting seekers. Am I right or not, Dooni Thakur Sahib?' His opening remark was laced with sarcasm. Geejgarh Thakur smiled, 'I was summoned by my brother to settle an urgent issue, and with your blessings, I have been able to discuss it in detail. In fact, it will be finally settled this morning with your agreement.'

Jagat Singh knew very well what they wanted him to agree to. Excited, Ummaid Singh of Geejgarh took no time in divulging his mission, which he had accomplished. 'I have some good news for you. My brother was getting very anxious about the marriage of his beautiful granddaughter, asking me to look for a suitable young man from a royal family. I could not think of anyone more suitable than you, so I instantly brought up your name, and he readily accepted the idea. He took no time in asking me to take the formal proposal as the uncle of the girl, as well as fix the date for the day as early as possible. He wishes to make grand arrangements for the wedding party for a month-long stay.'

Jagat Singh took a few minutes to respond to the proposal, keeping them guessing. Dooni Thakur was all ready to argue with him on the merit of the proposal as well as push him to agree. To their utmost surprise, Jagat Singh not only willingly agreed to the proposal but thanked Geejgarh Thakur for bringing up his name to marry the niece. He was particularly generous in expressing his gratitude.

'You certainly are magnanimous in proposing the name of a much-married Maharaja for your niece—a beautiful young girl. I am delighted to agree to the proposal and ready to give you an early date as well but only on one condition.' Not giving him any time to reconsider the proposal, a beaming Dooni Thakur responded, 'We are all so happy to have your response to this proposal. This group will honour any condition of yours. Just let us know now itself, so we can announce this great news to all.'

Jagat Singh, without any hesitation, addressed Geejgarh Thakur, 'As the uncle of the girl you brought the proposal, and I would like the uncle to have the honour of hosting the celebrations at his haveli here. This would not take very long to arrange and be more convenient for the bride's family too.'

Jagat Singh's condition shocked everyone, as their conspiracy to keep him away from Raskapoor for weeks together was being foiled. They tried to argue with him, but he remained firm. How could he be far away from his love for weeks together when he only yearned for her company! Having conveyed his acceptance, he quickly got up, seeking their blessings and not forgetting to take the last dig at them, 'I know you must be keen to share the news of the dream wedding with the Chief Queen, while I too wish to rush to share the proceedings of this morning with the queen of half our empire. In fact, you will all be delighted to know that the proposal has been agreed upon with her blessings only. She is the one who convinced me. She is an extremely farsighted young woman and saw this proposal coming much before you all brought it up, but the only thing that she could not foresee was my plan to have a wedding here in the Geejgarh Haveli! Now I must hurry to give her this surprise.'

With those words, he quickly made his way to Shobha Niwas, leaving the conniving vassals dumbfounded. They seemed to be paralyzed for a few minutes being unable to get out of their bewilderment till finally, Dooni Thakur asked Geejgarh Thakur to come along with him to meet the Chief Queen.

Raskapoor was in deep meditation, reaching out to the almighty to bestow her with the courage of Radha and Parvati, who were blessed with true love beyond the understanding of ignorant minds who only saw it come after a wedding knot was tied. She knew that life for her in the royal arena was ridden with obstacles that she alone had to face; for in that problematic world, she could not take the love and protection extended to her by her lover for granted. Much as he reassured her, she was aware of the vulnerability of a man in his position who could finally be led astray with rumours and conspiracies.

Time and again, she remembered Rudra, who believed in the strength of one's faith in the almighty to deal with the worst crises. He puzzled her each time when he talked about the unbelievable power of human beings, which could be discovered only in times of fearsome calamity.

Jagat Singh, standing at the entrance to the room, was captivated with the divine tranquillity on her face. He sat down not far away from her, waiting for her to open her eyes. Almost an hour passed by before Raskapoor opened her eyes and chanted the hymn for peace thrice. She was surprised to see Jagat Singh sitting there and asked, 'When is the wedding party taking off from Jai Nagar?' He smiled and reminded her of what he had said about Pokhran coming to Jai Nagar. 'I was certain I did not want to be gone for weeks together and be far away from you. I accepted their proposal wholeheartedly on your advice but only on one condition—the marriage would take place at Geejgarh Haveli. Now her uncle, who brought the proposal, will have to arrange it at his place. You know, Ras, though they were visibly shocked, they had no way out but to accept my condition.'

Raskapoor herself was visibly shocked, for his move was beyond her imagination. The lover in him had invoked smart and sharp thinking, Raskapoor observed, amused. For the first time, she was vocal in her admiration of his plans. Then she asked him, 'What will you do when it comes to Krishna Kumari? I can foresee that proposal will not only be an easy one to accomplish but will spring up dire consequences.'

Jagat Singh noticed Raskapoor looking a bit worried. 'Why do you worry about that one? All the people around me will be submerged in preparation for the Pokhran wedding. I have only been sent the proposal because of Man Singh turning it down. I have not even thought about it.'

Raskapoor's thoughts wandered around the fate of the young princess of Mewar, which swung like a pendulum from Marwar to Jai Nagar. When she was still young enough to be playing with dolls, the royals were busy playing with her life. The child had no clue who she was going to be married to. Raskapoor's heart reached out to the princess who was sure to think that her wedding was going to be a fairy-tale affair.

'If you have not thought about it yet, then you should think about it now. I feel you should convey your acceptance and marry her at the appropriate time. First, the death of the Maharaja she was engaged to, then his successor's point-blank refusal could dent the life of the innocent princess through no fault of hers,' advised an emotionally charged Raskapoor.

Jagat Singh was so taken aback with her words that he wanted to shake up his love to wake her and think about her fate and how she was threatened from all sides. He put his arms around her instead and asked her, 'Do you ever think about yourself and your fate?' Raskapoor told him that she did not have to worry about anything. Having received the treasure of his love and given over the reins of her fate into the hand of the almighty before entering the palace, there was nothing she feared any more.

At Pokhran, when Jagat Singh's condition was revealed to the bride's father, he was first saddened that he would not experience the cherished moment of seeing his daughter's palanquin take off from his home; but then gave in after the Thakur of Geejgarh convinced him otherwise. The news reached Man Singh who was very annoyed to see his important feudal lord not holding the ceremony at his own fort, and instead taking his daughter to the bridegroom's territory before the marriage.

He reprimanded the Thakur, 'How can you dishonour us by taking the girl there? Such an act will never be undertaken even by an ordinary Rathore, for he too will consider it to be beneath his dignity, while you are an important vassal of Marwar. How can you forget that for the Rathores of Marwar, the Maharaja of Jai Nagar is no big deal, especially if marrying their daughter to the Maharaja means undermining our dignity and honour?' The Thakur of Pokhran, whose heart was swelling with pride at the thought of having his daughter married to a Maharaja, and such an important one, at that, saw the questions raised by Man Singh as an unbearable insult.

He took no time in hurling back the insult, breaking his self-esteem into pieces, 'What honour is the Jodhpur Maharaja talking about when it is he who has dishonoured this great land? Soon the girl, who would have been the Maharani of Jodhpur, will be the Maharani of Jai Nagar. Do you realize how small the Rathores will be in the eyes of Kachchwahas?' Outraged by such a belittling response from the Pokhran Thakur, Man Singh immediately decided to marry the princess of Udaipur asking both the Maharana of Udaipur and the Maharaja of Jai Nagar to not to go ahead with the wedding and cancel the planned alliance.

Not caring for what Man Singh had said, the Pokhran Thakur, on the other hand, went ahead with planning the wedding of Chaand Kanwar at Geejgarh Haveli. Her uncle was also excited because his haveli was to be the venue for the Jai Nagar Maharaja's wedding. He could see the line-up of royals at his haveli. A few weeks later, the Thakur of Pokhran arrived with all the paraphernalia to arrange the lavish wedding, which would become the talking point for years to come. It was also his intention to disregard Man Singh's opinion completely. As was expected, Man Singh chose not to attend the wedding, although it was the norm for Maharajas of princely states to be present for marriages in the families of their feudal lords. Months were spent in strategically planning the campaign against Raskapoor in the zenani deorhi, but in the meanwhile, the scene changed dramatically at the behest of Maharaja Man Singh of Jodhpur. The Pokhran wedding took a backseat as the wedding proposal of Krishna Kumari became a big bone of contention among the important princely states of Rajputana.

War Bugles Resonate across Rajputana

Man Singh's grandfather had created a history of sorts when it came to love affairs with concubines, a common pursuit of royals across the world. Bijay Singh lived and died for a concubine named Gulab Rai. Their romance went many steps ahead of other such liaisons. It is said that they even had a son, but his untimely death turned the vivacious Gulab Rai into a statue. She neither cried nor talked for weeks. Her grief was felt by her lover, who too had lost a son, yet he knew he had his other children while she had none. He then decided to help her ride over her immense loss and grief by putting his grandson in her lap. 'Here is your child whom you will adopt and raise. I declare your son Man Singh to be my successor. Gulab Rai, the mother of Man Singh, is also awarded a big estate.'

The concubine was ecstatic; this sort of generosity was never usually displayed by Maharajas. To legitimize that adoption, he ordered all his chieftains to greet his successor. But they refused to extend that honour to the adopted son of a concubine. They did not care even though he belonged to the royal family. Once a child was adopted, he would only be recognized as the child of the family taking him. They were furious, seeing it as an act undermining the status of the honourable vassals. Bijay Singh was forced to go for a second adoption of Man Singh by his son Sher Singh. However, even though Man Singh was declared as his grandfather's successor, his uncle, Bhim not only manipulated his succession but also eliminated all the uncles and cousins seen as possible threats except for Man Singh, who was growing up in Jalore. Bhim Singh did not sit quietly, writing off the child in Jalore, who he felt could always come back one day and claim his right to the throne. He tried to secure the Jalore Fort, but that long-drawn operation failed.

On the other hand, growing up hearing the stories about being declared as the successor of Bijay Singh and the hurt of being given for adoption to a concubine fanned the burning aspirations of Man Singh. He longed to dispel the shadow of the concubine and sit on the throne of Jodhpur as the Maharaja. His only mission in life was to see the very vassals who had declined to recognize him as the real successor, line up to do so. The long siege of the Jalore Fort had cost both sides a lot. Running out of food supplies just as Man Singh's surrender became imminent, the news of Bhim Singh's death came in, ending the eleven years of resistance for Man Singh. The gates of Jalore were opened for him, and he lost no time heading to Jodhpur. In his great hurry to mount the throne, Man Singh did not even wait for the customary presence of the most important vassal of Pokhran.

The seeds of revenge long sown in the heart of Sawai Singh, given the murders of his ancestors at the hands of Bijay Singh, sprouted with the insult thrown at him by his chosen successor Man Singh when he did not wait for him before ascending the throne. In the meanwhile, the vassal got to know of the most unexpected news of the pregnancy of Maharaja Bhim Singh's wife. He collected all the fiefs to sign the resolution that if the late Bhim Singh was blessed with a posthumous son, he would be crowned, and Man Singh would have to step down in his favour. After signing the resolution, they all made Man Singh sign it. Sawai Singh ensured a well-protected hideout for the pregnant queen, who as destiny would have it, gave birth to a son. But knowing the intense desire of Man Singh to be the Maharaja of Jodhpur, she secretly sent her son in a basket to the master planner Sawai Singh. The child was named Dhonkal, which uncannily meant 'uproar'! Both Man Singh and Sawai Singh were at daggers drawn from the word go and could not see eye to eye on any matter.

No one could have ever envisaged that the conversation between Man Singh and Thakur Sawai Singh would break into a long-drawn battle. The spat between the two bruised Man Singh's ego immeasurably. On realizing that the Thakur had ignored his advice of not going to Jai Nagar for the wedding, he raised the famous ongoing affair of the bridegroom with a concubine. He taunted the Pokhran Thakur, 'I hear Jagat Singh has been dragged into accepting the hand of your beloved granddaughter in a bid to get rid of the legendary concubine Raskapoor. You are priding yourself in forging a wedding alliance with the Maharaja who treats a concubine as the queen of his heart. He has been living with her in the palace right under the nose of his queens. Your daughter will only be an addition to that fleet! Man Singh's remarks were filled with contempt for Sawai Singh, who in return threw back a hard-hitting reminder that Man Singh himself was adopted and raised by a concubine, despite being the grandson of Maharaja Bijay Singh of Jodhpur.

When Sawai Singh was preparing for his granddaughter's grand wedding, Man Singh was planning his wedding alliance with Krishna Kumari. It had become a prestige issue for him. He issued letters both to the Maharana of Udaipur and Jagat Singh to apprise them of his decision to marry Krishna Kumari. Because of that decision, they were further advised not to go ahead with the proposed wedding of Krishna Kumari with Jagat Singh. His letter outraged the Maharana of Udaipur to no end, and he quickly advised Jagat Singh not to yield to Man Singh's advice. 'We are no vassals of Man Singh and are not bound to act on his whims and fancies. I am soon going to send you the nuptial gifts to perform the first formal ceremony of tika. You should, however, be in readiness to send your contingent, as I foresee Man Singh going in for an armed attack.' Jagat Singh, who was not in any case too keen to have yet another wedding after being induced into accepting the one in the offing with Pokhran, got upset with the content of Man Singh's letter but did not mind withdrawing.

Just then Sawai Singh intervened, provoking him that his withdrawal would be an irretrievable humiliation for his clan, which was held in such high esteem by the Moghuls as well as the

British. Jagat Singh saw merit in his words but still went to his trusted counsellor Raskapoor. 'What do you suggest should be my reaction after this letter, my beloved?' he asked. Raskapoor silently heard the contents as well as the viewpoint of Sawai Singh, and on a firm note responded, 'You should send the advance team with the presents for the wedding ceremony at the earliest possible time and go ahead with the wedding as fixed by the Maharana of Udaipur.' Jagat Singh adhered to her advice and sent a lavish spread of gifts guarded by 4000 men.

On the other side, the crafty man that he was, Sawai Singh once again reminded Maharaja Man Singh of how he was going to disgrace his state for posterity as Krishna Kumari was betrothed to the Maharaja of Jodhpur, not the man. He shared all the details about the contingent of Jagat Singh heading towards Mewar saying, 'As a vassal of Marwar, my loyalty lies with the land of Rathore rulers, and I will fail in my duty in not updating you on this matter. It will be a sad day for me to see Krishna Kumari marry anyone else other than the Maharaja of Jodhpur.' He was killing two birds with one stone dethroning Man Singh and eliminating Raskapoor while Jagat Singh was long gone, using Krishna Kumari as the stone. Man Singh, already determined to marry Krishna Kumari, did not even bother to question the advice or read the mind of a man who was never in his favour.

Overcome by anger, he hastened to block Jagat Singh's contingent as well as the secured party of the Maharana with his 3000 horses. He ordered his forces on 19 January 1806 to shatter the dreams of Jagat Singh and the Maharana of Mewar midway. Man Singh succeeded in his mission, and the men of Jai Nagar and Mewar could not deliver the wedding gifts. Although he was advised by his military commander Inder Raj Singhvi not to lead the campaign, he mustered all the vassals of Marwar to raise a force three times bigger than the combined army of Mewar and Jai Nagar.

Seeing the large-scale force of Man Singh, the contingent with the wedding gifts had to seek shelter with the vassal of Shahpura. The commander of the Mewar contingent gave consent to the vassal of Shahpura to provide a written assurance that the wedding gifts would be sent back. Man Singh, on the other hand, had sought the help of the Gwalior ruler Daulat Rao Scindia. He advised Jagat Singh not to launch an attack on Jodhpur, and himself proceeded with his forces to mount pressure on the Maharana of Udaipur to not move with the wedding of his daughter with Jagat Singh.

The East India Company, having opted to keep away from the infights, instead of forging a truce between the Rajput states, was monitoring the Krishna Kumari episode with keen interest. Just around the time the forces of Jagat Singh and Man Singh came into direct conflict in March 1806, the Company's Accountant-General Henry St George Tucker wrote to George Robinson, the British Colonial Administrator. He viewed the situation as an interesting development that could help their cause. While describing the brewing conflict between the two prominent Rajput states, he felt that they were ready to 'take up arms for the purpose of deciding their claims to the fair hand of the princess'. Tucker, who could see the Rajput conflict involving Scindia and Holkar, too felt that would 'make a desirable diversion' favouring the Company.

Scindia was biding his time to realize his long-cherished dream to marry the beautiful princess of the powerful clan of Mewar, the Sisodias. He was trying to influence the two suitors to give up the idea of such a marriage, which would lead them to the battlefield, but he failed to do so. On the mediation of the other Maratha ruler, Jaswant Rao Holkar, vassals of both sides decided to resolve the issue in a manner that was honourable for all. After prolonged deliberations, the best way out was seen as going for two marriage alliances between Marwar and Jai Nagar and forgoing the agreement with Mewar. The truce forged on 18 July 1806 was to turn foes into relatives, with Jagat Singh marrying Man Singh's daughter and Man Singh marrying Jagat Singh's sister. Holkar was trying to be friendly with both parties to increase his fortunes. In the monsoon season of 1806, the nuptial gifts were exchanged with the tika ceremony. The vassals on either side agreed that the two weddings were to be performed after the impending Pokhran marriage.

A Time to Celebrate

Within the female quarters at the palace, the queens got the news of Jagat Singh's condition to go ahead with the wedding only if it was arranged at the nearby Geejgarh Haveli. Being sharp women, they guessed the reason behind it. The Chief Queen was the first to voice her opinion, 'Our Maharaja has most certainly outwitted us. He knows that this wedding proposal has not only been brought up but expedited to keep him away from his love. Do not worry. Together, we will all brief the bride on how to conduct herself when he is with her. We alone will dress her each day in such a beautiful and attractive manner that our Maharaja will forget all about Raskapoor. I am more than sure that he will be smitten by his new bride and will not leave her for weeks together. In that time, Raskapoor will be dealt with by the Thakurs as they have assured us.'

Medtani rani, who could not withhold her response to the plan and the intentions of the Chief Queen, enquired, 'What do you mean? Would she be killed? Does that not amount to committing a crime?' After hurling those questions, she added a crucial thought, 'Also, may I tell you that if souls connect, then even a separation cannot break the relationship. In fact, it can strengthen it, lest you forget the relationship of Radha and Meera.'

The other queens, who were visibly irked, brushed aside her comment in view of her leanings towards mysticism and mystic poetry. She was one, rallied against the rest of them, who were convinced that Jagat Singh marrying Chaand Kanwar would end the abhorred episode of Raskapoor. They all considered the retreat to Amber as the last one for Jagat Singh and his beloved.

Jagat Singh returned just a few days before the wedding. He had spent a blissful time with Raskapoor reliving the time when they first met at Amber. Raskapoor sang not once but many times for him. She chose songs of love, longing and even separation. Jagat Singh felt that it was her love circulating in his veins instead of blood, and the day that love would be taken away he was going to be left at the point of no return. After the retreat at Amber, he saw his forthcoming wedding as a routine event, for which he felt no excitement. Each time he was summoned for some wedding ritual, he was with Raskapoor either in Ras Vilas or Shobha Niwas. No amount of pressure from his wives, to be away from her at least after a divine ritual, changed his behaviour. They could not keep him away from her.

On the contrary, after every ritual, he hastened back to give her a first-hand account. Jagat Singh seemed to be her reporter on the location, rather than the bridegroom. Thrilled with himself for bringing all the details before anyone else could give her a version that was untrue or served their own purpose, he marvelled at the ease with which she heard his descriptions. At times she sought more information about the rituals and the royal customs that she was not familiar with.

When he described how his wives and other female relatives had applied kesar *ubtan* (saffron beauty pack) on him, she burst into laughter. 'Now I know you have turned into such a handsome man only as of the result of your many marriages.'

Slightly embarrassed, the Maharaja reached out for her hand. 'They all think I am looking handsome as never before after our retreat to Amber. Shall I tell them what your company does to me?' Knowing his rebellious nature, she warned him against uttering any sentence to that effect, asking him if she would have the chance to see him dressed as the bridegroom.

'What made you ask me that question? How could you imagine that I would head for marriage without seeing my real queen? You know, Raskapoor, I will dress in my best to first appear before you, as your bridegroom, but will you dress as a bride?' Raskapoor wondered what he meant as he left. She saw him whispering something to Gulab as he walked out of Ras Vilas.

On the day of the much-awaited wedding, the palace was reverberating with ceremonial sounds. A grand procession was lined up, with the elephant bearing the flag, and all the vassals stood in their noble attire awaiting the bridegroom. Inside the female quarters, all the wives bedecked themselves as if they were going to be the brides that day. All the excitement was driven by their perceived triumph over their common enemy, Raskapoor. They were convinced that she would vanish from the palace after the Pokhran wedding. The royal bridegroom was eagerly awaited. He was taking rather long in getting ready. Raskapoor remained in Ras Vilas imagining the scene outside, as she dressed in the bridal outfit Jagat Singh had chosen for her. She had mentally prepared herself to not feel hurt if Jagat Singh did not show up that evening, appreciating how difficult it would be for the bridegroom to disappear like that just before his wedding ceremony.

As she was going to sit down before the altar to pray for the wedding to have no obstacles, she was surprised to see Gulab hang a decorative piece just above her apartment door. She questioned Gulab about putting it up at an hour when the wedding party was about to leave.

Before Gulab could answer her, Jagat Singh appeared as if out of thin air and spoke up, 'Because I have asked her to do so. It is a toran, which is put at the entrance of the bride's home. The bridegroom touches it with his sword, assuring her of his protection before he enters her home.' He reached the toran with his sword and came in, 'Did I not tell you that I would come as your bridegroom?' She could not believe what he had done. It was an overwhelming moment for her. Still, she hurriedly wiped her tears and reached out for the tiny box of kohl and put a dot on him to ward off the evil eye. She said, 'Grateful as I am for this honour, now the royal bridegroom must leave, for the wedding procession has to depart at the auspicious hour.'

When Jagat Singh reached the zenani deorhi, everyone was in awe of the handsome bridegroom who exchanged pleasantries with each of his wives before being sent off to mount the royal elephant.

At Geejgarh Haveli, all the preparations had been made to welcome the bridegroom's party with much fanfare. The vassal's idea was that the bridegroom's thoughts should not drift even for a moment to his lover back in the palace. The haveli was lavishly decorated. Royal tents were pitched all around. The bride's father had brought along a big group of Langas and Mangniyars—the folk musicians of the desert. Nautch girls were invited from as far as Lucknow, and the best liquor was arranged, with some imported brands courtesy of the British.

When the sound of the bridegroom's party drifted to the haveli, all the women rushed to greet the bridegroom, and the haveli resonated with songs and drums. As the bridegroom dismounted, the sky was illuminated with the most spectacular fireworks. The bride's mother was holding a big silver plate on which the traditional stand with several oil lamps was placed to welcome him, according to the tradition.

Dholans, the group of women singers attached to the Pokhran Thakur's family for generations, started singing the traditional song as the bridegroom's elephant approached the main entrance of the haveli to strike the toran hung down from the terrace above the door with his sword. Jagat remembered the ceremony he had performed at his beloved's abode, and the image of her beautiful face and the divine demure floated in his eyes. He completed the ritual mechanically and dismounted, making way for the welcome ceremony. He smiled deep in his heart, taking note of the words of the song rendered by the Dholans:

'Our handsome bridegroom, like a saffron colour marigold flower, so handsome he looks that he can attract an evil eye.'

The bridegroom was confident that no one could cast an evil eye on him because of Raskapoor's dot of protection. The bride, who had just bathed and was dressed in simple attire, stood on the balcony with many dreams in her eyes. She had to throw sweetmeats on the bridegroom, perhaps a custom to seek the bridegroom's attention amidst the hustle-bustle. He was so lost in Raskapoor's thoughts that he did not even take notice of what his new bride was doing.

She then went inside to change into her ceremonial attire sent by the bridegroom's family for the *phera*, a wedding ritual. The time for the wedding ceremony was chosen according to the auspicious times, early in the morning under the star-studded sky, taking the horoscopes of both the bride and the bridegroom into account. To pamper him till then, the bridegroom was taken to the royal tent. There, a stage was set for a late-night feast. An entourage of liveried staff was lined up to serve the bridegroom and hundreds of his guests.

As he was seated, the folk musicians began with their repertoire of songs, from welcome songs to songs of bravery, romance and hunting—catering to all the noble pursuits. While the Langas sang to the sound of their string instrument, the Sindhi Sarangi, the Mangniyars sang to the resounding sound of their native instrument, kamayacha. As they finished, the well-known court singer, Jameela Bai, sang to entice the Maharaja to drink more and rejoice in those beautiful moments. 'The barmaid has brought the goblet filled to the brim. Drink . . . drink prince, fill the environs with the colours of celebration, the one who is drinking is the man worth millions.

The barmaid . . .'

Her powerful voice struck a chord in the bridegroom's heart, and he wished he could run and take Raskapoor in his arms. The sharp eye of Dooni Thakur caught a glimpse of the lost look on the bridegroom's face, and he immediately advised that the nautch girls be brought in. Hailing from the region of Lucknow and Varanasi, these gorgeous and talented girls were all set to capture the heart of the Maharaja. They relived the romance of the Moghul Darbar, weaving intricate patterns of rhythm, accentuating sensuous expressions and movements. Being an art lover, he did appreciate their art, honouring them with gold coins, but he wanted Raskapoor to be by his side to really enjoy it.

Finally, he was summoned inside for the wedding ceremony. The priests chanted holy hymns, the tired bride was almost

falling asleep, and the bridegroom saw the meaninglessness of
the auspicious time fixed for the ritual. Each time his wedding
ceremony was set the same way, yet not one could result in the
kind of bond that he and Raskapoor had been able to forge.
Raskapoor's company was stimulating in all respects. More than
often, he wondered as to how one woman could play so many
different roles with so much ease and honesty. She was his lover,
his spiritual teacher and a political adviser. He found a true
companion in her who could talk on so many different subjects.
While Raskapoor had already committed herself to be loyal to
the man in her life, she was also gradually drawn towards him
emotionally, as he showered not only love but dared to defy royal
norms to add dignity and honour to her life.

After the wedding ceremonies were concluded, the wedding
party made its way back to Jai Nagar. Like Geejgarh Haveli, the
palace was all set to receive them. No effort was spared in giving a
grand welcome to the bride. His wives inside saw her entry as the
stepping-stones for the departure of their arch-rival, Raskapoor.
The royal couple was also made to play the traditional games.
Jagat Singh's heart was filled with the memory of the excitement
and ecstasy he had experienced in playing those games with
Raskapoor!

After all the rituals, they were led to the apartment area
allocated for the new bride, which was rather lavish, Jagat Singh
noted. If he had his way, he would have escaped to Ras Vilas,
but he was trapped in the royal customs like a bird in a cage.
Feeling much relieved, all the queens retreated to their apartments,
contemptuously visualizing the loneliness of Raskapoor. The bird
in the cage found his moment to escape once everyone was fast
asleep. He glanced at the face of his new bride, who he felt sorry
for. She was in deep slumber, which was justified after the tiring
series of rituals at her home as well as the palace. He quickly
disappeared into the tunnel connecting this apartment to Shobha
Mahal. There, as had been arranged, Raskapoor was waiting for
him. The bridegroom spent the rest of the night with his lover.
Interestingly, the couple spent those hours in conversation that
had become an integral part of their lives in the few months

they had spent together. The days of the wedding created an intense longing to talk to each other. Jagat Singh took no time in asking Raskapoor, 'Did you miss me as much as I did you? I was physically present there, but mentally I was with you. I just wanted the ceremony to be over, for I had left my heart here.'

Raskapoor herself was unable to deal with the void his absence had created. They had never been separated since the day they came together. When she sat down to pray and chant to be with her deities so she could overcome the longing for his company, she was surprised to see her thoughts being distracted and wandering to him. She even sought their forgiveness and begged them to help her get over her lack of concentration. Having experienced such emotions for the first time in her life, how could she not be but truthful to the Maharaja. She did not hesitate and confessed her feelings for the first time, not adhering to her usual subtle ways, and that was rather pleasing for the Maharaja. As the bells echoed at the Govind Dev temple for the early morning prayer much before sunrise, Raskapoor asked him to make his way back to the zenani deorhi before anyone got to know about his great escape.

'You are unnecessarily getting so worried. Let me be here with you for some more time,' Jagat Singh pleaded like a child.

Raskapoor did not give in, and the reluctant lover had to get back to his new bride. He slipped into the bed by her side while she lay asleep and planned his next escape from what felt like a dungeon to him. The next morning when the newly married couple came out, all the wives of Jagat Singh felt much relieved. After all, to them, it was his first night away from Raskapoor! Jagat Singh continued with his escape night after night without anyone finding out. All the women in the life of Jagat Singh were happy with the new schedule of the Maharaja. Only Raskapoor was on tenterhooks. She was apprehensive that the reckless Maharaja would be spotted by one of queens' confidants. Her fears came true as the wicked eunuch Mohan Ram finally caught a glimpse of the Maharaja hurriedly making his way back to the apartment of his new bride at the crack of dawn. Mohan Ram had gone to the Govind Dev temple to pray for a raise in his salary. He could not believe that god was going to grant him his wish so soon! The eunuch hurriedly made his way to the zenani deorhi with the alarming news to broadcast to the Chief Queen, who, as he knew, was bound to reward him with exclusive perks. He took no time in breaking the news to her. The story, as expected, was shared then and there with all other queens, barring the new bride. They all decided to initiate her into how to get her husband to be all over her. They could not reprimand the Maharaja but saw the castle they had built in the air come crashing down. They began convening meeting after meeting, with one vassal or the other, to find a way to uproot Raskapoor.

Reopening War Fronts

When all seemed settled, the wicked mind of Sawai Singh was at play. He did not much appreciate the idea of a truce that would create a stronger bond between the two rulers, Jagat Singh and Man Singh. He worried that his beautiful granddaughter would not receive the same treatment if her husband contracted yet another marriage, especially with a princess. That alliance could not be too far, and once it was forged, his dream to dislodge Man Singh would never come true. Man Singh had left no space to bring Sawai Singh on his right side, having chosen to stay away from the wedding of his granddaughter. With all these thoughts, he once again brought up the subject of the return of the nuptial gifts of Krishna Kumari before Jagat Singh. With brewing malice in his heart against Man Singh, the conniving vassal strategically planned to instigate Jagat Singh to avenge his humiliation when the royal party was forced to return.

Choosing his words carefully, he told Jagat Singh, 'Much as I am delighted with the wedding of my granddaughter, I am reminded of how your honour was shattered, making the contingent turn back. Your humiliation has created an upheaval deep inside my heart. How will you be able to accept your fiancé's marriage to someone else? Such an acceptance will be undermining the prestige of your state. I, as your well-wisher even at the risk of my granddaughter's future, would advise you not to fall in Man

Singh's trap. He could always withdraw from the truce and resend his proposal for Krishna Kumari. After all, he backed off from a signed treaty to vacate the throne in favour of the posthumous son of the late Maharaja of Jodhpur. If you wage war against the unpredictable Man Singh, we will bring to Marwar its legitimate ruler. And you would be able to protect your honour by marrying Krishna Kumari.'

Sawai Singh was successful in drilling his words deep into Jagat Singh's mind. Those wickedly chosen words stayed with him. He finally made up his mind to deal with Man Singh once and for all. But he still chose to turn to Raskapoor before going ahead with such a drastic action. He knew that they both wanted Jai Nagar to blossom in peace and harmony, having been dragged into constant unrest—the plunder by the Marathas and the uncertainty of the protection assured by the British. Raskapoor was herself taking stock of the emerging turmoil and dreaded the long-drawn civil war among the princely states of Rajputana with the three major stakeholders Jagat Singh, Man Singh and Maharana Bhim Singh of Mewar. Princess Krishna Kumari's wedding meant putting at stake the honour of the three significant regions—Dhundhar, Marwar and Mewar ruled by the three rulers, respectively. Raskapoor did pray for a peaceful solution to the problem. She realized the gravity of the problem, which was going to result in significant losses for all three, making them vulnerable to manipulation by outside powers. She yearned for the advice of her soulmate Rudra, who she thought was the only one to play the role of a truce maker without any vested interest, but a secret meeting with him was impossible as she knew she was under surveillance round the clock.

After seeking divine blessings one last time, she responded to Jagat Singh on raising arms against Man Singh. She said, 'Much against my belief in a peaceful solution, I would advise you to go ahead with the action planned against your brethren as Lord Krishna did while advising the Pandava brothers in the Mahabharata. There is one thing I would like you to remember, this is not a battle for territory or power, but to retain the prestige of a girl to ensure her betrothal. I am told Man Singh had initiated his action only on the information given by Thakur Sawai Singh on the movement of your contingent. I am at a loss to see what kind of a grandfather he is. You have just married his granddaughter and he is not worried about his son-in-law. It is not a playground but a battlefield where anyone could be killed,' Raskapoor concluded with a pensive look in her eyes. Jagat Singh was taken aback by Raskapoor's observation about his grandfather-in-law and even considered it to be valid. But he had no way to detract.

The situation was already getting alarming for Jagat Singh with the death of Lord Cornwallis, the one man who was favourably disposed towards him. Sir George Barlow, who came in his place, had already upheld the policy of 'non-intervention', and on 3 December 1805, all the British treaties with the Rajput states were nullified. Another treaty set Scindia and Holkar free to deal with the princely states of Rajputana as they deemed fit, which meant they were free to plunder them as in the past. His friend Lord Lake did represent in favour of Jai Nagar, but failed. Jagat Singh also conveyed his state's disenchantment explicitly to the British government via his emissaries.

One of the principal agents of the Rajah of Jaipur, in a conference with Lord Lake at Delhi, had the boldness to observe that this was the first time since the establishment of the British government in India 'that it had been known to make its faith subservient to its convenience', recorded Major General John Malcolm in his book *The Political History of India*. The abrupt snapping of the treaty was even condemned by the impartial British historian Horace Hayman Wilson. While arguing in favour of the Jaipur ruler, he wrote in his book *The History of British India*, 'His abandonment was wholly indefensible.'

With British support gone, Man Singh's humiliating action, and the free hand given to the plunderers, Jagat Singh was witnessing threats from all sides. To a Rajput, his honour came first, especially when it was on account of a woman. And so, Jagat Singh focused on Man Singh first. At the same time, Sawai Singh had given him yet another reason to wage war against Man Singh:

to dislodge him once and for all and bring in the lawful claimant to the throne of Marwar.

'His Highness Dhonkal Singh is alive only because I ensured that he was smuggled out of the area under Man Singh's command. He is growing up under the protection of the vassal of Khetri. If you can dislodge this mad ruler Man Singh, illegally ruling as the Maharaja of Jodhpur, and are able to get the rightful heir, young Dhonkal Singh on the throne, we will all be there to witness your wedding ceremony with Princess Krishna Kumari. Once you wage war at the eleventh hour, we will betray Man Singh and join you on the battlefield for the decisive strike to accomplish this mission. We all then will head for Udaipur together,' said Sawai Singh. Raskapoor was all for Jagat Singh's wedding with Princess Krishna Kumari. She had two reasons for this: securing Jagat Singh's honour as well as the honour of the princess who was subjected to such an ordeal, which belittled the dignity of women overall. She wondered why on earth no one thought about the emotions of that young girl, putting their honour before hers.

From the beginning of the plan of attack on Marwar, she was not convinced about Jagat Singh being entangled in the succession dispute of Marwar, which she thought was Sawai Singh's only mission. She wanted Jagat Singh to explicitly convey a firm message to Man Singh to back off from Krishna Kumar's wedding proposal. But she wanted him to let the internal matter of succession of Marwar be resolved internally. She chalked out as well as discussed all the details of Jagat Singh's campaign against Man Singh from beginning to end and shared this with Jagat Singh in front of her father, Pandit Shiv Narain, who was astonished at the military genius of his daughter.

He could not hold himself back from asking her, 'Ras, where have you got such insight from?' Amused, Raskapoor reminded her father of Shatranj, the chess games that they played together where the teacher was often surprised to be defeated by his pupil. Jagat Singh, on getting the approval of the learned Brahmin, decided to follow her plan without even sharing it with Sawai Singh. Raskapoor was rather worried and anxious about Jagat

Singh's campaign and well-being. She consulted several astrologers
with the help of her father for the auspicious day to launch the
campaign. Her father and the raj guru, the royal priest, consulted
several eminent astrologers. Finally, the day chosen was Makar
Sankranti, the 14th day of the dark half of the month of Magh
according to the lunar calendar, a very auspicious day for the
Hindus. Raskapoor saw it as a perfect beginning for a victorious
campaign, but it came with a rider. Pandit Shiv Narain informed
both Jagat Singh and Raskapoor that the astrologers believed
that if the Maharaja returned by the festival of Gangaur without
venturing further to get the control of Mehrangarh Fort of Jodhpur,
he would win; or else he would fail in accomplishing his mission.
His failure would be an outcome of the long-drawn engagement
with the forces of Marwar, as well as lead to dire circumstances
and a tragic end of the saga of Krishna Kumari, which would run
down all honour seekers.

Jagat Singh was even more convinced by this to let Sawai Singh
deal with the matter of Dhonkal Singh while he would usher him
in the territory of Marwar if all went as planned and go ahead with
his marriage to Krishna Kumari. On the night before his departure
with his army, he discussed with Raskapoor the pros and cons of
his long absence from the palace, knowing that it could lead to
conspiracies against her.

'I will go on this mission with a heavy heart, anxious about
your well-being. You will have to be on alert round the clock. Do
not venture to the female quarters to befriend any of my wives,
and remember, no one is your friend. When you are lonely, you
can connect with the priest of Brijnidhi temple and go to the
glass palace where you can meet your Ammi as well as your best
friend, Rudra. You have met them only once since arriving here.
Raskapoor, my love, I do not know how I will fight the enemy, as
your face will be before my eyes.'

Raskapoor, herself holding back her tears, saw the lovelorn
eyes of the ruler heading for the battlefield and was suddenly
reminded of the story of Hadi Rani narrated by her father not
once but many times on her request. When the husband of Hadi

Rani was summoned to the battlefield, he showed reluctance, not being able to take his eyes off the beautiful face of his bride, whom he had married only a week before. When he relented and went on to battle, he sent a messenger to bring a memento from her so he could feel her presence by his side. Hailing from the warrior clan of Rajputs, she felt that her beautiful face would distract him on the battlefield. She took the sword of the messenger, telling him to take the memento given by her under cover. Without blinking an eye, she slit her neck in one blow, cutting off her head. Even though he was shattered to see the souvenir sent by her, he fought bravely, with her head tied around his neck.

Seeing Jagat Singh stand before her that night like Hadi Rani's husband, she smilingly asked him for his sword. Jagat Singh was clueless about her intention, and handed her his sword.

Taking it out of the sheath, she asked him, 'Would you like me to give you my head as Hadi Rani did? I may not be a Rajput, but remember, I am a woman.' Jagat Singh did not wait for a moment to get his sword back knowing the strong will and courage behind the grace and beauty of Raskapoor. Before making his way out, Jagat Singh gave her the list of his trusted messengers who would ferry their letters. Dreading the long parting, the two lovers assured each other they would exchange messages regularly, keeping in mind the travel time the messengers needed.

His queens gave Jagat Singh a formal send-off, and he mounted the elephant. It was not long ago that Jagat Singh was given a similar send-off, but the mission was the Pokhran wedding, not a war. Raskapoor was not there to bid him farewell but as in the past, he went to her before he went to the zenani deorhi. She prayed for his victory and safe return and as usual, put a black dot behind his ear to ward off all threats.

In Search of Allies

Jagat Singh was at a loss for allies after being abandoned by the British. The war between Jai Nagar and Jodhpur made both sides seek the support of the plunderers who were not bound by the British treaties any longer. All the foes of the past—Scindias, Holkars, Pindaris and Amir Khan Pathan, who became the first Nawab of Tonk—saw this as a god-sent opportunity to make their fortunes. All they were interested in was to drain the two revenue-yielding states of their resources. They could change colours like chameleons! Their intentions made both Man Singh and Jagat Singh suspicious. Man Singh was not happy with Holkar's mediation and chose to seek the support of Scindia. This alerted Holkar as he could see his arch-rival Scindia's entry into Marwar. He moved a step further in backstabbing Jai Nagar by tempting the British to seize Jai Nagar as it yielded a revenue of over Rs 1 lakh annually. He proposed to share the booty with them. Holkar did not waste time asking the British Government to provide two battalions of their troops for the success of the proposed plan. He was smart enough not to annoy the British after the Anglo–Holkar pact and specified that he would not do anything without the consent of the British government. Nothing came out of that proposal as the British adhered to their policy of non-interference at that time. The East India Company was monitoring the dispute over the princess of Mewar, sitting far away instead of lending help in resolving the issue.

Jagat Singh knew the contacted wagon of allies could not be trusted partners and would betray him in favour of the highest bidder. He was reminded of the day Raskapoor had so explicitly described treaties and alliances to be a matter of convenience that could not be taken for granted. She even advocated seeking the help and support of forces who had wronged him in the past. 'Your state treasury should dole out money to buy the support of those who are ready to auction it. If you do not bid for their support, they will go with Man Singh. In times like this, you should not let your ego come in the way. It will be important to approach the British as well to see their stand, as I am quite sure Man Singh too will request their support.' Jagat Singh was inexperienced and young, and the diwan of his state realized that he was an unwilling fighter. Accordingly, he negotiated support from all corners of the country. A statesman of the highest order, Jagat Singh's diwan, Rao Chaand, was able to bring Meer Makhdoom of Hyderabad, Wazid Khan, Khuda Baksh, Meer Sadruddin of Sarangpur, Meer Mardan Ali and the Nawab Khan Jahan under Jagat Singh's banner. Amir Khan's loyalty was also ensured by paying a heavy price with perks. Jagat Singh did not mind opening up his treasury to buy support to finish the Man Singh story as early as possible and go back to Raskapoor.

Well-directed by Sawai Singh, Jagat Singh initiated the attack on Marwar, heading towards Parbatsar, the boundary between the two territories, and taking a detour around Shekhawati. Together with Sawai Singh, unimaginable support was received from Maharaja Sujan Singh of Bikaner, who had been convinced to help Jagat Singh bring Dhonkal Singh to the throne. While Jai Nagar's diwan's strategy was to attack Jodhpur from the rear and cut off supplies, Sawai Singh's aim was only to manipulate the threads of the puppet—Dhonkal Singh.

Delighted with the bribe paid to win his support, Amir Khan, who commanded the territory of Tonk, was all ready to move straight to the salt city of Sambhar with his forces, including a fleet of Pindaris. From there, he headed to Danta Ramgarh to join Jagat Singh's contingent. To add to the significant number, Jagat Singh's planners also bought a division of Bala Rao Scindia. When the considerable force assembled under Jai Nagar's banner along with a formidable section of artillery, they did not delay their march towards Parbatsar.

Man Singh, on the other hand, found the time to be right for Jaswant Rao Holkar to repay him for providing shelter to Holkar's family while he was entangled in warfare with the East India Company. In the first phase, all looked well to Man Singh, who was soon to be joined by Holkar and his contingent near Ajmer when he set off for the encounter at Parbatsar with his 60,000 horses. He, however, was in for a rude shock—deserted at the last minute by Holkar, who had been compromised with a considerable bribe to withdraw in favour of Jagat Singh. Half the bribe amount was to be paid when he backed off and reached the southern city of Kota.

Seeing themselves outnumbered by Jagat Singh's contingent and the sudden firing from all around, Sawai Singh, as planned, broke away from the unit of Marwar. He had already discussed with his team of vassals that the first phase of the campaign was to get Man Singh out and bring Dhonkal Singh in. As Sawai Singh defected, so did his vassals. Only four chiefs of Kuchaman, Ahor, Jalore and Nimaj were left with Man Singh. Such was the pitiable condition of Man Singh that he did not care to plunge into battle head-on. As a Rathore, he preferred to die rather than retreat.

When his four chiefs restrained him from going ahead with his plan, he even tried to take his own life, but once again, his four loyal chiefs did not let him succeed. Thakur Sheonath Singh of Kuchaman said to Man Singh, while helping him dismount from his elephant, 'A ruler has to use his wisdom, which is not in committing suicide. Have you forgotten the story of Maharaja Ishwari Singh of Jai Nagar, who had committed suicide in a situation like this, fearing his fall? He was not even given a place for his last rites at Gaitor, the royal crematorium. You can avenge today's defeat and betrayal as well as punish the betrayers only when you are alive. Retreating at this hour and emerging a victorious ruler later will add pride to the annals of Marwar and Rathores.'

Man Singh acceded to the advice given to him, and mounted a horse and fled. As the cannons raised a thick cloud of smoke and sand, no one could see him escape. He reached the city of Merta, but knowing that he was not safe there, he decided to make his way back to a safer place. Man Singh's deserted camp was plundered for war booty. Scindia's commander took eighteen guns, and Amir Khan took charge of the elephants and decided to go on a looting spree in and around Parbatsar.

The encounter of Parbatsar took place nearly two months after setting off from Jai Nagar. Jagat Singh was victorious in Parbatsar, making Man Singh retreat. When Jagat Singh and his allies reached Merta and got the news of Man Singh heading back towards Jodhpur, he longed to celebrate his victory with Raskapoor. Still, in a bid to be done with the wedding at Udaipur, he chose not to go back to Jai Nagar and apprised Sawai Singh of his decision.

Man Singh's retreat had baffled Sawai Singh, for he had not anticipated him fleeing from the battlefield, disregarding his self-pride. He guessed that the move was to prepare himself for a full-fledged attack on Jai Nagar, which in turn would result in Pokhran's fall. He was not going to let Jagat Singh leave him to face the wrath of Man Singh as it would result in failure of bringing the rightful claimant to the throne of Marwar. The shrewd old man told Jagat Singh, 'An accomplished hunter never leaves a wounded tiger to charge back at him with full force. Man Singh should not be allowed to muster his troops to attack again. He is already a defeated man, and we should see his complete demolition now itself. It will not take us long with all the support we have. After capturing Mehrangarh Fort and handing it over to Dhonkal Singh, we can all proceed peacefully for the wedding.'

Jagat Singh fell for his sweet talk without judging the merit of the move suggested, which was bound to have far-reaching consequences.

Venturing Beyond the Line of Defence

Both lovers had drawn a line of defence, beyond which they were bound to be endangered. Jagat Singh had warned Raskapoor not to enter the zenani deorhi knowing the queens were gunning for her life. She had given him the time limit as cautioned by the team of astrologers, who had also warned against getting anywhere close to the impregnable Mehrangarh Fort.

In a way, both were swayed by the victory at Parbatsar. Jagat Singh had rushed a special messenger soon after Man Singh's retreat from the battleground to give Raskapoor the news of his success. He wanted her to hear the news first, before the others. He was also keen to let her know of his early return to kick off the preparations for his wedding. But he then decided to head directly from Merta to Udaipur.

Raskapoor's excitement knew no limits on getting the news of her paramour's victory, and she hastily got ready in some of her most beautiful clothes to break the news to patrani, the Chief Queen. As she rushed towards the zenani deorhi, Gulab tried to call her back, but Raskapoor did not pay any heed to her calls and hastened to make her way to the forbidden quarters of the palace. Gulab ran after her through the secret passage, but before she could catch up, Raskapoor had entered the zenani deorhi. Gulab could foresee the turbulence and misfortune befalling Raskapoor. Shell-shocked and sad with Raskapoor's move, Gulab slowly made her way back to Ras Vilas, anxiously awaiting her return. Gulab was aware of the cunning mind of the Chief Queen who ruled the intricate world of zenani deorhi. Raskapoor's entry stunned the patrani, who was sitting in the pavilion of the central courtyard under a brocaded canopy on a velvet mattress with four maids waving brocade fans. 'I am Raskapoor. I beg your pardon for coming here without your consent, but how could I not rush to share the news of our Maharaja's victory with his Chief Queen!' Raskapoor said.

The Chief Queen, who was spellbound to see the beauty of her news reporter, took a few moments to collect her thoughts to respond to the surprise sprung on her. Much as she detested her husband's lover, she could not restrain herself from admiring the divine beauty and confidence with which she stood before her. To her, she was an epitome of elegance fit to be a queen. If it were not for her lineage.

However, the queen chose to adopt a stern stance with Raskapoor. She was questioned on the source of the news as well as her challenging entry. 'So, you are the concubine who is using her beauty to play with the dignity of Jai Nagar. The concubine who manipulated the Maharaja to make her the queen of half of his empire! Let me tell you, a concubine can never rule. How dare you come to give me the news, breaking the protocol of the palace! You dared today but never cross your limits again. Remember, no concubine or lover of the Maharaja stays in his life for long,' she warned Raskapoor in a bid to break her spirit.

Raskapoor's entry made all the other queens dash to the courtyard to have a glimpse of her much talked about beauty. They were stunned by her beauty and the belittling words of the Chief Queen.

Deeply hurt, Raskspoor tried to maintain composure to deal with the unbearable pain caused to her. She knew that she would not be welcomed there, but did not expect that a woman of the Queen's stature would bring herself down to that level. Raskapoor looked around, greeted all the queens and finally addressed the Chief Queen.

'We perceive someone in the light of our feelings. Remember the words of the epic writer Tulsi Das who wrote *Ram Charit Manas*, your highness. His words define the role of feelings in our perception . . . "As he feels, so he forms the image of his god." All human beings are perceived in different ways. To you, that man is a Maharaja and a husband, but to me, he is a man deeply in love like Krishna. I do know I am a concubine, but for him, I am his Radha, and for me, His Highness is Krishna. Like Radha's sakhis or friends, I had come here to meet my friends. Now, respecting your direction, I leave from here, giving you my word never to enter this area on my own. I will play the role assigned to me by my Krishna, your husband, and take charge of state matters. It is wisdom, not lineage that rules. I still seek blessings from you all,' she said with dignity and hastened back to Ras Vilas just as she had done on her way to zenani deorhi. Despite the response of the patrani, Raskapoor returned not as a depressed woman but as the daughter of a learned priest determined to take charge as the queen of half the empire bestowed upon her. Gulab could not speak to Raskapoor, who headed straight towards her prayer altar. She sat before her deities, a stream of tears flowing down her eyes for some time, and after that, she chanted hymns and lit the lamp seeking the blessings of god almighty.

The glow of the fire reflected on her face, and she addressed Gulab, 'I know you want to know what happened in the zenani deorhi that has made me shed tears as never before. The tears before my gods came as their blessings to relieve me of the pain and start again with a new resolve. Gulab, tears are not always a sign of weakness but a way to share your emotions, be it sorrow or happiness. As far as the first encounter with the beautiful royal ladies is concerned, I can sum up with the proverb used by mother: "A gold vessel filled with venom!" Gulab, I pray for their happiness. Now let's get going with the celebrations for the return of the victorious Maharaja of Jai Nagar Sawai Jagat Singh!'

Raskapoor, as well as all the queens of Jagat Singh, planned for victory celebrations and awaited the news of his arrival. He, however, had changed his plans after being convinced by Sawai Singh, and sent another set of messengers to inform the palace accordingly. The change in his itinerary was heartening for the queens who saw it as an excellent way to keep him away from Raskapoor for a more extended period. Raskapoor, on the contrary, was alarmed, fearing the consequences of a long-drawn battle.

The summer season was getting harsher by the day. Man Singh's territory, known as the parched land, was hit by a series of sand storms, not at all conducive for the Jai Nagar men to venture to. This was undoubtedly going to be a misadventure, reasoned the queen of half of Jagat Singh's empire. She quickly scribbled a message for the Maharaja to send back with his messengers. She defined his victory at Parbatsar as a divine accolade and pleaded with him not to be swayed by the tempting propositions of Sawai Singh. The message ended with a sentimental appeal, 'Radha is lonesome in the royal jungle and yearns for her Krishna's company to shower his love as never before.' She sealed it in a silver container and handed it over to one of the messengers sent by Jagat Singh.

In his camp, Jagat Singh was eagerly awaiting the return of his messengers, wondering why his beloved could not send him a message with the help of the fleet of messengers deputed at her command. He was penetrating the territory of Man Singh, successfully pushing him further back. Man Singh first contemplated moving to Jalore, where he was raised. He had made his way from there to the Marwar throne and so considered Jalore as his lucky charm to retain his crown. His vassals advised him against it, convincing him not to leave the Mehrangarh Fort, which would become an easy target for the enemy's forces in the absence of the Maharaja himself. While planning his next move, Jagat Singh received the silver container sent by Raskapoor. He hurriedly opened it and read the message. Sawai Singh, who at that time was in a meeting with Jagat Singh, saw the change of expression on his face. He asked him, 'What are you thinking about? We have to head in the direction of Phalodi without any delay.'

Jagat Singh asked Sawai Singh if it wasn't enough to cast a spell of fear on Man Singh to stop him from obstructing the path to the wedding altar. He tried to reason with the unreasonable Sawai Singh that because he had been humiliated and pushed back, it was the right time to negotiate with Man Singh to ensure the ascendancy of Dhonkal Singh as the Maharaja of Marwar and Man Singh's relocation to Jalore.

Sawai Singh was petrified to see the possibility of Jagat Singh crashing his mission at the last hour with the sudden change in his stance after reading the message, which he knew was from none other than Jagat's wise string-holder, Raskapoor. Sawai Singh, in his heart of hearts, knew that her advice would favour Jagat Singh's cause, but then his own mission was going to fall apart. He resolved to stop the message service between the two lovers. He also convinced Jagat Singh to maintain patience as the victory over the Jodhpur Fort was not too far away. Withdrawal at the last minute would give a wrong signal to Man Singh, who would think that the Maharaja of Jai Nagar had run out of his resources to retaliate with full vigour. Jagat Singh trusted Sawai Singh, as he was the man of the region putting him in a better position to assess the situation, and decided to move forward.

Raskapoor, who was monitoring the campaign, found out about the fall of Phalodi and it being given as war booty to the Maharaja of Bikaner. Gulab at the same time found out about the celebrations arranged by the Chief Queen, who hailed from the Bikaner family. Raskapoor saw the fall of Phalodi as the fall of the Jai Nagar forces, who would be forced to retreat and not succeed in capturing the fort. She decided to send a messenger of her team, writing a few lines of a song about kurjan, the migratory demoiselle crane that visited the small village Kheechan in Phalodi every winter and flew back to Eurasia after the festival of Holi in March. That bird was considered the messenger bird in the desert land. The lines scribbled by her reflected her state of mind at not being able to stop her beloved from moving ahead:

I was sleeping in the palace. In my sleep, I leapt up because of turmoil. Our parting has been too long. At least my dreams should unite us.

You, kurjan, carry my message. Get the lovelorn lady to meet her long-lost lover. Get him to come back home. Oh! Kurjan, I urge you to give my message!

That was the last message from Raskapoor to reach Jagat Singh. His heart was torn apart. If he had wings, he could have flown back to her. Sawai Singh was rather anxious to see the messenger arrive at Phalodi as well, while he had already blocked the one leaving from their end who never reached Raskapoor and never came back. He immediately took up the issue of the messenger service with vassals like Chaand Singh Dooni who wanted to get rid of Raskapoor. Finally, both ends were tied up, and the messengers sent by the two lovers had actually disappeared from their way and were never seen by their intended recipients, which the two never got any indication of. Raskapoor attributed the gap in communication to the distance and the conflict, while Jagat Singh was given indirect news about her, which the different men got on different occasions sent by his vassals stationed at Jai Nagar. As was evident, all the news relayed about Raskapoor was spiked in a bid to tarnish her character.

On 30 March, the forces of Jai Nagar laid the siege around Jodhpur, and soon Jagat Singh moved in a procession to the camp to hold a Durbar. He was joined by his diwan as well as Amir Khan. After plundering Peepar and Bisalpur, Jagat Singh had already got hold of twenty-two guns of Marwar. Soon the decision was taken to proclaim victory. Accordingly, on 16 April 1807, the triumph over Jodhpur was announced in the name of Maharaja Dhonkal Singh. What was left next was to capture the fort, take possession of Mehrangarh and bring Dhonkal Singh to the throne in a formal ceremony. No one expected the siege to prolong for months. The victory, which appeared as if it was coming soon to Sawai Singh, became elusive each passing day. Both sides were working on their strategies. But, away from the scene, worried and anxious, Raskapoor was working on hers.

Holkar being already compromised, Man Singh decided to approach Scindia. Knowing full well that Scindia, too, was paid a hefty bribe by Jagat Singh, he chose to send Kalyanmal Lodha to work on the inherent greed of the Marathas. The offer being more lucrative than Jagat Singh's and the desire to restrict the growing influence of Holkar and Amir Khan, Scindia readily accepted, to the utter surprise of Lodha. He had worked long to navigate the negotiations, but the more than willing Scindia made his task simple. Scindia not only ordered his army to move in support of Man Singh, but also dispatched his three highly experienced commanders Ambaji Ingle, Bapuji Scindia and Jean Baptiste to lead the operation.

How easily the Marathas could be swayed was very much known to both Jagat Singh and Sawai Singh. Lodha was taken aback to see how swiftly the three men sent by Scindia had already crossed over to the enemy's camp. Singh's envoys outsmarted the Jodhpur camp. They welcomed the three commanders in a lavish manner, giving them a much better offer from Jagat Singh before they could reach the Maharaja at whose request they had been dispatched. All said and done, Rajputs did not back off from their word so readily, and that was just the right reason for them to consider Marathas inferior to their clan, the disgusted Lodha concluded. The three commanders sent by Scindia started participating in the councils of Jagat Singh to confer on the strategic moves. Yet none of them could foresee that the siege would continue for five and a half months.

Raskapoor took over the administrative matters of Amber. She had no one else without any personal stake to turn to for consultation except Rudra. She preferred him over her father, who would not take a minute to cross over while making a choice between his daughter, that too out of wedlock, and rising in the corridors of power. After all, wasn't he the one who had taught her by telling her stories from history that the power-hungry can swallow anything, putting integrity aside easily?

It was not easy for her to get Rudra to enter her glittery yet dark arena. He was unwilling, but after many messages from Raskapoor, he decided to extend the much-needed support, as he had promised when Raskapoor was leaving Kaanch Mahal. Raskapoor reminded him of that promise, pleading that in the complicated situation where her survival in the palace was threatened, he was the only man she could trust, not even her father.

Raskapoor herself headed to Amber, letting the Chief Queen know via her messenger of her departure to take charge there. She ensured that her message reached the Chief Queen only after her arrival at Amber.

Holding Raskapoor's letter in hand, the Queen questioned the messenger, 'When is she leaving? Does she not know in the absence of the Maharaja Hazoor, a concubine should seek my permission? Anyway, now that she has chosen to defy me, you may inform her that I forbid her from stepping out of the Ras Vilas.'

The stunned messenger mustered the courage to inform her that the queen of the half empire had already left the previous day. According to him, she was in a great hurry.

'What was the rush? Could she not wait for my response?' reprimanded the Queen. The messenger tremblingly told the Queen that Raskapoor was scheduled to have a meeting on matters of state while he was to deliver this message to her. Raskapoor was determined to run her down, the shocked Chief Queen realized. She felt the urgency to clip the upstart's wings, leaving her wounded to bleed to death! How was that concubine going to deal with intricate state matters, for she neither had the experience nor a fleet of vassals and councillors to advise her?

A close watch had to be kept on the activities at Amber, but the Chief Queen herself needed a trusted informer. Finally, she chose the eunuch Mohan Lal, who could be silenced with payments for exceptional espionage service. Nadir Mohan Lal deputed a fleet of other eunuchs located within and outside Amber Palace in confidence. He bought the loyalty of some of the concubines too by working with the one in charge at the Zenana Mahal of Amber. It was not a difficult task to manipulate the ones who had fallen out of favour with the Maharaja, doomed to live a life of non-existence. For those women, the role of a spy was a step up. Promised fortunes for their service, they promised to keep an eye on Raskapoor round the clock.

Raskapoor, being away from Jai Nagar, did not suspect the conspiracy hatched by the Chief Queen and the eunuch, and focused on her first meeting with Rudra in the Sheesh Mahal at Amber. Her Ammi had arranged for Rudra's arrival at Amber. Another person who knew about the meeting was the priest of the Gupteshwar Mandir. In fact, he was the one who had convinced Rudra to help Raskapoor as she had messaged the priest too. Making his way up the steps, Rudra was intrigued, wondering if

they were going to lead him to the end of his life. He did not fear
death, and if he was meant to die for his soul mate, it would be his
nirvana, he believed.

Raskapoor was eagerly awaiting his arrival in Diwan-e-Khas,
the hall of private audience. She had directed Gulab to receive her
esteemed guest, usher him in for the secret meeting with her and
then take him to the apartment, which was ready to host the guest.
Raskapoor had described the wisdom and personality of her guest
in great detail to Gulab, who was experienced enough to know the
emotional bond the two shared. From the extended conversations
she had with Ras while Jagat Singh was gone for months together,
and the eagerness with which the queen of Amber was awaiting
her guest, Gulab knew that if the Maharaja had not surfaced in her
life, Raskapoor would have been with the much-respected guest.
She could see the admiration for the man sparkle in her eyes each
time she talked about him.

Raskapoor had requested her father to send a carriage for
Rudra—that was the least he, as her father, could do. She had told
Pandit Shiv Narain that she needed someone as her adviser in the
absence of the Maharaja to take care of Amber. She said, 'You
would have been the best person in this situation to be with me,
but you have to be at Jai Nagar.' She had very subtly appeased
her father, who would certainly not have appreciated her selection
undermining his wisdom and insight. The carriage, too, was
chosen to throw a cloak of secrecy over the movement of Rudra
towards Amber. It was directed to leave well before dawn. Gulab
was taken aback with his graceful persona as he dismounted from
the covered horse carriage at the foot of the fort, from where she
had to lead him to the venue of the first meeting.

When Rudra came in front of Raskapoor, he was surprised
to see her regal stance, befitting a queen. He greeted her with
respect and Raskapoor asked him to be seated, signalling Gulab
to go out. All seemed very official till Gulab left, and she then
addressed Rudra, 'I am very angry with you. You have come after
my sending you so many messages and Ammi's mediation. You
have changed! Remember the time that you used to long to meet

me!' Rudra, maintaining his usual serious tone, replied, 'I have not changed and will never change in this life, but you are well aware of changed circumstances, which make you vulnerable. I have to take care of your well-being. How much ever the Maharaja may be in love with you, and how much ever you may be sure of his trust in you, it will take no time at all to burn all those emotions to the ground the moment the forces envious of your position ignite the fire of suspicion. Don't take his love and trust for granted. Remember, you are one against so many who would like you to disappear into thin air. The rich and the famous, as well as the ones in power, can get away with anything while an ordinary woman like you would be disgraced and maligned irrespective of your good intentions. Mark my words—from this moment, your way ahead will be ridden with thorns. Now let me know why Her Majesty, the queen of Amber, has summoned this poor Brahmin.'

They both burst out into laughter that resounded across the courtyard, and the first alert knocked on the mind of the eunuch guarding Man Mahal. He knew the time had come to launch his espionage mission.

The secret meeting went on for hours as Raskapoor ran through all the events and intrigues and the Jodhpur campaign, consequences of which she feared were going to be disastrous for her beloved Maharaja. Rudra could not but admire her loyalty and concern for the man in her life, as well as the trust she had placed in him to play the crucial role of her adviser. While Raskapoor was narrating all the details, Rudra was carefully screening every word uttered by her.

Finally, when she finished, he came up with his first tip, advising her to be vigilant as never before. He then instructed her specifically not to lend her ears to anyone claiming to bring specific information and not to share her strategies with anyone. He advised her to take charge of the army allocated for Amber and recruit men suitable for the job—not on the basis of their clans. He was reminded of their archery competitions in the backyard of the glass palace, where she defeated him many times, with her perfect aim. He reminded Raskapoor of the game and then directed her to polish that skill.

She laughed, 'That was just a game, and I loved to defeat you. How can that victory over you lead me to face the crisis now? Stop treating me like a child at this hour!'

Rudra assuaged her anxiety and laughed, telling her that he had made a serious mistake forgetting that he was standing before Her Highness, the Queen of Amber! Their laughter once again filled the silent corridors of Amber, convincing the eunuch that the meeting was for their playful romance in the absence of the Maharaja!

After taking a breath, Rudra, on a serious note, cited the example of Ahliya Bai Holkar, who not many years ago had shown her courage and grit wielding arms on the battlefield. He warned Raskapoor that she should be in readiness for the battlefield and not get accustomed to the luxuries of royal life. Since the Maharaja was far away, his state could fall prey to any attack. Rudra had gathered from their long conversation that Jagat Singh's team of vassals left behind nurtured their own ambitions and could not be trusted. He could also foresee betrayal by the likes of Amir Khan, who could defect easily and not hesitate for a moment to look for better gains in the long-drawn siege in the dreadful heat.

He talked about all those apprehensions in detail with Raskapoor, inspiring her to take on the role of the legendary Ahliya Bai, who sat on an elephant with four bows and the arrows fitted on four corners and killed several men of the enemy's forces to defend her empire. Rudra reiterated his belief in her innate wisdom, resolve and skills, as he marvelled at her commitment to her lover.

Both were delighted with their long deliberations and came out as the sun was setting. Rudra desired to take her leave before it got too dark, expressing his fear of the tigers and leopards in the valley.

Raskapoor smiled, 'Rudra, how can you leave me alone in the wilderness where even more dreadful beasts can attack me within the four walls of this palace as well as in Jai Nagar? I can only be safe when my Maharaja is back!' Rudra interrupted her, 'Do not tell me that you want me to be here till his return. How could you even think of that when this day alone can lead to your ouster from his life? For god's sake, have mercy on yourself.'

Raskapoor asked him to have no fears, laying her full faith in Jagat Singh's love. 'Rudra, Maharaja knows my loyalty and integrity too well. I have already made arrangements for you in the apartment at the other end of the palace.'

Rudra prayed to Shiva to uphold her conviction. He headed towards the apartment with Gulab, who was summoned by Raskapoor after the meeting. They met again for dinner and walked on the terrace, reminiscing about their childhood.

Rudra stayed at Amber for weeks together, being compelled by Raskapoor. He observed that she was alarmingly getting submerged in a whirlpool of apprehensions with no message from Jagat Singh, while her fleet of trusted messengers was evaporating as the men never returned. She had sent messages expressing her concern, relaying wishes, reassuring him of her love, updating him of all the developments back at home, even about taking on Rudra as her trusted consultant till he returned. She still managed to keep an eye on the siege of the Mehrangarh, and spent hours conducting the exercise of her army and practising her archery skills from different angles sitting on an elephant. In between her hectic schedule, she held discussions with Rudra, and finally, at dusk, they sat together to chant hymns as they used to do while she was at the glass palace. Nadir Mohan Ram's men were monitoring their liaison but found nothing romantic about it despite sending two veiled eunuchs on the rampart to check if Raskapoor and Rudra were walking hand in hand when they went for a walk post-dinner. They even joined the alms seekers at the temple to keep an eye on the two. They wondered if Rudra was her spiritual guru and if Mohan Lal was unnecessarily trying to implicate them in an illicit affair. They decided to let Mohan Lal know all the details about the activities of Raskapoor and her guest, whom she never called by name in front of anyone else, so they chose to name him Guruji.

The wicked Mohan Lal decided to add a twist in the tale, which in truth had no potential to insinuate suspicion in the mind of Raskapoor's ardent lover, the Maharaja. He worked out a fictitious story around the facts to suit the intentions of the Chief Queen. After running the story several times in his mind, he headed to meet the Chief Queen.

'That concubine has fooled our innocent Maharaja. She viciously lured him into showering all his love on her and even bestowing upon her half his empire. The greedy woman is planning to dislodge the Maharaja to take reins of the whole empire. She is conducting a military exercise, inducting hundreds of fighters while she rides an elephant and practices archery. My men are very impressed to see her successfully hitting targets at a great height and distance. She is certainly preparing for a battle to capture our territory while Maharaja Hukum is away. Can you imagine, doing all this, she has even hired an adviser whose company I am informed our lady loves to be in at night!' he rattled off his concocted story in one go.

Before he could go on constructing that juicy story further, taken aback with the daring manoeuvre of Raskapoor, the Queen interrupted him, 'I should have certainly not underestimated the self-esteem and intelligence of that concubine. She has outwitted not just me, but the Maharaja's men left here to command the situation on the ground in his absence. All these vassals have only been making their fortune at the cost of the state. They are considering this time to be a long holiday when Jai Nagar is in a difficult phase of the war. Who is her adviser? Is he one of the vassals who were eyeing her beauty? Can you believe even the vassals of Chomu, Samode as well as her arch opponent, Thakur of Dooni, were smitten with her beauty to the extent that they would lap up any opportunity to be in her company? The long absence of the Maharaja and his impeded return present the golden chance for any of these men who have been envying my husband. Mohan Ram, I could have handed her over to any of the contenders, but why is that man with her at Amber fanning her dreams to be the queen of our empire? In any case, the Maharaja has to be apprised of her agenda but one must first play on her affair with the man. He trusts her blindly, and will not believe the story of her political attack against him, and consider it to be our farfetched idea. It is her romantic adventure with any man other than himself, which would break his rock-solid belief in her love and loyalty for him. Just give me the name of the man, and then I will send my messenger to him before she proceeds with her designs.'

Mohan Lal was happy with himself for putting fuel into the fire burning in the heart of the Chief Queen, flames of which were bound to reach Raskapoor. He was unable to give the name of the man, telling the Queen that Raskapoor never called him by name in front of others and he was referred to by the secret service as Panditji or Guruji. Mohan Lal was rewarded richly for the story, which was further spiced up by the Chief Queen to narrate to Jagat Singh.

Raising the Siege

Months had passed, but Man Singh, who had experience managing the long siege of Jalore Fort, which lasted for years, was able to resist this one, despite running out of resources. The garrison was formed of 5000 of the most dependable men. They were also accustomed to dealing with harsh weather and juggling the draining resources, having lived in the arid terrain. Man Singh knew how an entangled kite could be cut by giving a long rope, which was locally referred to as 'sheh' and 'maat', or that defeat would lie with the opponent. He had used the two terms while playing and winning the game of chess. The heat and dust did not bother him unlike it did his opponent Jagat Singh. Above all, unlike Man Singh, Jagat Singh was not fighting the war on his home ground. He was not prepared for the long siege and was getting worried about exhausting all supplies, and the coffers getting nearly empty.

Another major fear was also clouding his mind and dampening his spirit to bring the battle to the intended conclusion. He was far away from his territory and was getting worried about its vulnerability. With each passing day, he was getting increasingly apprehensive about his princely state falling prey to the attackers in his absence. Man Singh wished to prolong the siege to cause impatience in his opponents through an endless wait with no result in sight. It was certainly not easy for him either, as his Maratha support had crossed over to Jagat Singh's camp, that too after reaching his territory. He began reminding his vassals how they were letting their land get dishonoured, which was against the essential trait of the Rathore clan. On the other side, after their arrival in June, the Generals of Scindia started participating in policy decisions, which undermined Amir Khan's importance. Daulat Rao Scindia became anxious seeing the growing importance of Amir Khan in Jagat Singh's territory. Amir Khan had forged a pact with yet another rival of his, Holkar. He had discussed the matter with his general, Ambaji Ingle, who had assured him he would dilute Amir Khan's position while in Jodhpur.

Ingle did not delay raising the subject with the two trusted advisers of Jagat Singh, his diwan, and Thakur Sawai Singh of Pokhran. He warned the two of the possibilities of Amir Khan's defection the moment he was given a more significant piece of the loaf, for he had deep designs to grab the two princely states.

Ingle, over a few meetings, convinced Jagat Singh to clip the wings of Amir Khan, who was getting too big for his boots. He described Amir Khan as a petty man with a mission to rip his ally of wealth and power. The Marathas had known Amir Khan's character. From his humble beginnings belonging to the Pashtun sub-tribe, he had become a Nawab by acquiring land. He emerged as the founder of the Principality of Tonk. Amir Khan was Holkar's General, and Holkar got him the title of Nawab.

With the constant interference of the three generals, the Jai Nagar camp developed groupism and infights. Jagat Singh started keeping Amir Khan at a distance, which made him contemplate crossing over to Man Singh's camp. The final blow came when Jagat Singh stopped the payment of the daily allowance of Rs 5000 to Amir Khan to belittle him on Ingle's advice.

Feeling deeply insulted, he deserted Jagat Singh and took charge as Man Singh's general. It turned into a battle of the old rivals Holkar and Scindia. Amir Khan was Holkar's confidant, who was holding the command of Man Singh's forces and making strategies solely to wipe out Scindia's men commanding Jagat Singh's forces. He discussed matters in detail with Man Singh,

fixed the reward for his services, and decided to march towards
the territory Jagat Singh had acquired while making his way to
Jodhpur. In between, he got the vital news that one of the three
generals of Scindia Sirje Rao Ghatge had had a major fall out with
Ambaji Ingle, and he decided to first move to Bisalpur to bring him
on his side. From there, he gathered the support of the disgruntled
general and advanced further.

Jagat Singh was distraught on all accounts. Victory was
slipping away, and he felt he was paying for not heeding the advice
given by Raskapoor to not venture near Jodhpur. Disillusioned
with the betrayals and uncertainty, he yearned for a place to
find solace, which he knew was in the arms of Raskapoor. Jagat
Singh had not received any message from her for a long time, and
the signals received from Jai Nagar were filled with insinuating
remarks on her fidelity. While highlighting her romantic links, the
strong possibility of her launching an attack on Jai Nagar was also
underlined.

He was not prepared to believe any word against Raskapoor,
but the seed of doubt was sown. He was restless, wanting to
confront her as early as possible. Just as he was trying to figure out
a plan to head for Jai Nagar, he came to know that Amir Khan had
reached Peepar and plundered it ruthlessly. After that, Amir Khan
tried to lure Bapu Rao Scindia to defect from Jagat Singh's camp,
but he did not succeed. He found it to be the opportune moment
to attack Jai Nagar itself in the absence of Jagat Singh. On getting
the information about Amir Khan's men marching towards his
empire, Jagat Singh alerted Bukshi Sheolal to pre-empt his entry
and launch the attack first.

On the 3 August 1807, Amir Khan was forced to have his first
encounter with Jagat Singh's men. Sheolal's forces appeared all
of a sudden near Kishangarh and, to the utmost surprise of Amir
Khan, even managed to defeat him. Amir Khan, like a wounded
tiger, charged back just as Jai Nagar was elated over their victory
in the absence of their Maharaja. While Sheolal and his men
celebrated, Amir Khan planned to launch an attack to avenge his
unexpected and annoying defeat. A fortnight later, Amir Khan's

forces launched their attack, and on 18 August, defeated Sheolal's contingent. Amir Khan chased them back to Jai Nagar as they fled the battleground. His arrival near Jai Nagar created utter chaos and the fear of his taking over the city itself in the absence of their ruler became a near possibility.

The news of Amir Khan camping on the outskirts of Jai Nagar and the defeat of Bukshi Sheolal reached the Queen of Jagat Singh's half empire too. She knew if Amir Khan was all out to take hold of the territory of Dhundhar, commanded by the Kachchwaha ruler, he would not spare even the region of Amber. She discussed her apprehensions with Rudra.

'I fear that the man whose mission is to see the downfall of my Maharaja could even attack Amber. I feel it will be important to open a dialogue with him, as well as summon the Maharaja back to take charge of his territory. There should be an effort to bring a halt to ongoing warfare, which is not in the interest of anyone. Two men are ruining the happiness of all princely states— one, the born villain and traitor, Amir Khan, and the other, the egotist and selfish vassal of Marwar Sawai Singh. My messages remain unanswered, and my messengers do not return. I am at a loss about what my plan of action should be. Rudra, we cannot be silent spectators in the ruination of our empire.'

He could see the merit in her idea of opening up a dialogue, not just with Amir Khan alone but also with the other princely states as well. Rudra contemplated on her thoughts and responded, 'If all princely states could come together, they could be a force to reckon with for any of these invaders or intruders from foreign lands. Because of their lack of unity and tendency to fall prey to the bait offered, the foreign handlers succeed in playing them against each other. If these different parties put their ambitions ahead of their sacred land, it will be subjected to bloodshed and unrest for centuries. I appreciate that a person of humble origin like you is so anxious to protect our land, but Raskapoor, we have to wait for the return of the Maharaja.'

His words made Raskapoor come up with another suggestion, surprising Rudra. She said, 'I think you are the best man to go and meet the Maharaja and convince him to return before it is too late.'

Taken aback, he responded after remaining quiet for some time, 'Ras, my dear friend, when I came here, I prepared myself to die for your cause. I am ready to go, but will I be able to reach him? Even if I reach him, will I be able to come back to you? If you still wish me to go ahead to accomplish your task, I will leave today itself.'

Raskapoor was left with no choice. As the sun sank behind the Aravalli range, Rudra set off for Marwar. His parting words were, 'Raskapoor, you are the woman I loved, and you are the woman I will die for. You left the glass palace but lived in my heart. Till my last breath, I will pray for your well-being for you are like a spider caught in the royal web.'

Raskapoor, herself traumatized by the idea of not being able to see him ever again, confessed her feelings in a choked voice. 'If I were not born out of a concubine's womb, my fate would not have led me here. You are my true love for births to come. Do I need to say more?' Raskapoor cried endlessly, watching Rudra disappear in the eerie darkness. Like the other messengers sent before him, Rudra too never came back.

Back in Jodhpur at his camp, Jagat Singh decided to return to Jaipur in view of the growing threat to his empire. He discussed it with Sawai Singh and Ambaji Ingle, but they still argued in favour of his continuing the siege, declaring that victory would finally be his. However, Jagat Singh's patience had run out after the months-long siege, and the news from Jai Nagar was alarming. He was standing at a juncture where victory was nowhere in sight while the loss of his empire was closing in. He had to make a decision. He chose not to give in to the arguments of the men whom he had trusted so far. He advised Sawai Singh and Ambaji to move with Dhonkal Singh to Nagaur for his safety in the changed circumstances and decided to lift the siege. Forty canons with a lot of wealth acquired from Marwar were sent with the advance party. A huge amount of protection money, amounting to £120,000, was paid to the Marathas to escort him back safely to Jai Nagar.

He did not even care about paying a bribe secretly to the man who not only betrayed him but posed a threat to his very own state. Amir Khan was assured payment of £90,000 not to block Jagat Singh's entry back into Jai Nagar. Amir Khan agreed as he was always ready to give his services to his rivals, as long as they filled his coffer in return.

Having tied up all the loose ends, he raised the siege on 14 September and started the journey back home. When all seemed settled, Jagat Singh was surprised to meet resistance by the vassals who had defected from Man Singh and were on his side till recently. Their conscience had been kindled by the call in the name of the honour of Marwar's belongings being taken out of their land. Under the commandership of Induraj Singh, once a diwan of Marwar, the vassals gathered their resources and launched such a powerful attack that Jagat Singh's forces had to leave behind all the spoils, including the forty guns. Much excited, Man Singh celebrated Jagat Singh's defeat to the extent that he even raised the status of Amir Khan, who took all the credit for that moment of triumph. Man Singh got the massive Jai Pol constructed to commemorate the victory over Jai Nagar.

For the defeated Jagat Singh, the saving grace was that Amir Khan was not allowed to enter Jai Nagar, forcing him to change his plan. Amir Khan did not waste any more time in getting back to Marwar, where he feared the problem of ascendancy could bounce back with full might. Maratha forces were there with their generals, siding with Sawai Singh to get Dhonkal Singh to the throne, and Amir Khan was determined to not only break their alliance but silence them once for all. This was not due to any loyalty he felt for Man Singh; it was a service he was going to render only after ensuring a more significant payment. He already was given a residence in the fort along with the honour of being seated by the side of the Maharaja.

On his arrival in Marwar, he was given a grand welcome by Man Singh. He discussed the imminent threat of ascendancy and negotiated the price to plan and execute wiping out that threat forever. Man Singh was delighted to hear his plan and even paid an advance of £30,000. Amir Khan headed towards Nagaur to hold two separate meetings, one with Bapuji and the other with Sawai Singh, with countering messages, to create an irreparable rift between the Marathas and Sawai Singh.

He first met Bapuji and convinced him about Sawai Singh's strategic planning for his devastation as he had done in the case of Jagat Singh. He advised him to compromise his alliance with Man Singh and leave Marwar. Bapuji Scindia, being another extractor, wished to know the price for the compromise. Amir Khan offered to share 50 per cent of his gain in striking the settlement, but Bapuji became greedy and sought more.

Then the shrewd player took the Afghans in Scindia's forces aside. He provoked them into demanding their long-due payment for their services, knowing that Scindia had not been paid by Jagat Singh and would not be able to pay such a significant amount. He asked the Afghans to create mayhem in the camp and hurl insults disgracing Scindia. Scindia was held captive, and he finally bent down, pleading for Amir's intervention to set him free. Imploring him for mercy, Scindia was forced to accept the condition to leave Marwar and never to return, without seeking a penny. Scindia had no choice, and as he was set free, he marched straight towards Jai Nagar without looking back even once. Thus, in February 1808, Amir Khan successfully managed to clear Marwar of the Marathas siding with Sawai Singh.

After packing the Marathas off, he moved to the man who alone was responsible for triggering the dispute over Princess Krishna Kumari's marriage, with the sole mission of engaging Man Singh and Jagat Singh to manoeuvre the enthronement of Dhonkal Singh and to hold the reins himself. Amir Khan was camping at Mundawa near Nagaur. He came up with a special plan for the man for whom he had no mercy. He was not going to spare Sawai Singh. Because of him, he was disgraced in Jagat Singh's camp. After thinking it over, he, like a shrewd politician, decided to play the religion card. He sent a messenger to get permission to offer prayers at the holy shrine of Peer Tarkin. His message was cleverly worded. It said, 'A devotee will be granted permission by another devotee who has ardent faith in almighty god.'

Sawai Singh, who knew very well that Amir Khan's words always had a hidden agenda, took it as a divine call and granted permission then and there. Amir Khan offered his prayer the very next morning and made it a point to thank Sawai Singh as per his plan. Again, he chose his words cleverly, 'I have come to express my gratitude and respect to you for granting my request. The much-needed solace came after I offered my prayers there. I have been feeling distressed to not be rewarded as assured after defeating Jagat Singh in such a humiliating manner. Man Singh is not the right man to be Maharaja of the glorious land of Marwar.'

Amir Khan had spoken the last sentence to lure Sawai Singh to ask for his favour. As expected, Sawai Singh immediately offered to pay him £200,000 on the day Dhonkal Singh was seated on the throne. Amir Khan accepted his offer readily, going a step further to make sure that Sawai Singh had no iota of doubt in his mind. He pledged on the holy book that he was carrying, more for the meeting than for the prayer, offering to even lay down his life for the coronation of Dhonkal Singh. Both of them hugged each other like long-lost friends.

At the request of Amir Khan, Sawai Singh introduced him to Dhonkal Singh. Amir Khan greeted the young man as he used to greet the Maharajas. Sawai Singh apprised Dhonkal Singh of the agreement they had struck. Amir Khan invited the two to celebrate their coming together at his camp the following night. He made lavish arrangements for his guests of honour. A special royal tent was pitched to seat over 500 guests, as Amir Khan had made it a point to invite all the chieftains of Sawai Singh together with his followers. The guests were welcomed with the loud sounds of the drum, the ceremonial wind instrument surnai and the welcome drink of saffron kesar kasturi spiked with opium to give a high. They were then seated for the musical extravaganza. Drinks flowed like a river, not leaving any goblet empty even for a moment. First, the ensemble of Langas and Mangniyars entertained everyone with their repertoire of songs and then came in Bano Begum, the legendary tawaif and voluptuous beauty.

With years of experience in seducing the royals with her mujra, Bano was a recognized institution to initiate the young elite

from across North India into the world of etiquette, similar to
the Japanese geisha girls. It was about midnight when she sang, 'I
forgot my two anklets on your bed, now I fear the whole world
will know where I spent the night . . .'

The guests showered money on her, and both Sawai Singh and
Dhonkal Singh promised to give her not just anklets but a box
filled with jewellery if she chose to spend a few nights at their fort
in Nagaur. Bano Begum then sang yet another song, 'Now I am
not letting you return home, my love. I have been so lonely and
miserable, the queens have your kingdom, but my only treasure
is you, my prince.' As she finished and made her way out, Amir
Khan too went out to get dinner served. Just then, the royal tent
collapsed, falling on the guests. It came as such a surprise that
in their inebriated state, most of them could not even attempt to
escape. It was not a natural calamity but a planned massacre by
Amir Khan, who had pitched the tents in sections and had gone out
only to signal his men to pull out the posts of the section towards
the side of the guests.

Sawai Singh, breathing his last under the debris of the camp
décor, could hear the faint lyrics of Bano's song '. . . I will not let
you return home . . .'

Amir Khan moved to his camp along with Bano Begum to
celebrate the success of his plan that he had worked out in
consultation with her. He came out late in the morning to identify
Sawai Singh's body, who was his main target. He did not worry
about Dhonkal Singh, who had somehow succeeded in getting
out of Nagaur and reached Bikaner beyond the reach of the
nasty conspirator. Amir Khan, who had rooted out the problem
of succession, made his way to Jodhpur to recover the reward
money from Man Singh. He was rewarded with the control of
the sub-divisions of Parbatsar, Makrana, Sambhar, and was given
the two towns Mundiawar and Kuchilawas as a gift with a sum
of £100,000.

Life Was Never the Same Again

Defeated with such humiliation and returning empty-handed, Jagat Singh arrived at his palace where months of absence had brought drastic changes. One such change was the absence of his lover, whom he was longing to see first. He had sent a message to her to come to Ras Vilas from Amber. Jagat Singh had expected to see her delighted with his return. He was confident that she would extend a warm welcome to him despite the disappointing outcome of the long and futile engagement in Marwar. As his real well-wisher, he imagined that his loss of face would already have her thinking about a future course to help him regain the prestige of his empire. He also planned to ask her about the army exercise at Amber, only to reaffirm his faith in her loyalty and not to investigate.

Although his wives greeted him without showing any remorse over his defeat, he knew that there was something deeper in their warmth. He asked the Chief Queen about Raskapoor, but she responded sarcastically, 'You thought that ambitious concubine would have been here to welcome you? In fact, she left for Amber without informing anyone in the palace, secretly planning to be with her handsome lover. She has been training to wage war to upgrade herself from being the queen of half the empire to taking over your whole empire. I am sure she is the one who instigated Amir Khan to desert you in Jodhpur and rewarded him with her

love once you were defeated. I am told that she had spent quite a
few nights with him too after dispatching her lover to some distant
place. Now I hear that unfortunate lover is nowhere to be found.
Who knows, she might have dispensed with him, too. Concubines
don't really love anyone for them; it is just a game to gain power.'

She hoped her words would provoke him to initiate drastic
measures against her. Jagat Singh decided to bring Raskapoor to
Jai Nagar and sent a message to her to come without any delay.
Raskapoor, who had been so badly insulted by the Chief Queen
forcing her to move away to Amber, refused to come to Jai Nagar.
She was both sad and delighted at the same time—sad because of
Jagat Singh's defeat, but delighted that she would see him soon
after such a long separation.

Her self-respect prevailed over her heart as she worded her
reply, 'The queen of the half empire needs to attend to some urgent
matters at Amber. She would be pleased to take the Maharaja to
the Shila Devi temple for blessings to protect his empire. When
you did not send me any messages, when you did not choose to
reply to any of my messages, when messengers sent to you never
returned, which includes the only man who I could rely upon in
your absence, how do I know it is you sending me the message
to return and not the Chief Queen or anyone who wants me to
disappear from your life?'

Raskapoor's reply and the stories of her preparation for a
military coup were rattling the defeated man. His biggest loss was
the loss of trust, as he could not decide whom to trust and what
to trust. To bring his mind to rest, he decided to head for Amber.

Raskapoor knew that the Maharaja would not wait long to
see her once he entered his territory. She was eagerly awaiting his
arrival in Amber, ready to receive him warmly. She knew that the
Maharaja had undergone much turmoil in the past few months.
Victory had many parents, but defeat was always an orphan and
her man at that moment was just like an orphan who needed
tender care to make a way forward.

When she received the news of his arrival at Amber, the sun
had already set. She lit thousands of oil lamps and fire torches

to welcome him. Her heart was pounding at a fast pace with the excitement of being with her lover and ending their long separation. She wanted to pamper him with all her love after such stressful months. Inside the palace, all the courtyards were richly decorated. Jagat Singh observed the difference in his welcome to Amber and Jai Nagar. He marked the sensitivity of Raskapoor, which set her apart from all the women in his life. When the two came face to face, Raskapoor welcomed him traditionally, putting a red tilak on his forehead and a floral garland around his neck. Neither of them spoke until they were alone.

Raskapoor's eyes were filled with tears of happiness, and she led him to his room. Jagat Singh spoke first. 'Ras, my love, your reply intrigued me as I could see that our messages disappeared somewhere on the way, leaving us doubting our love. But not a single day passed without me thinking about you. I cannot tell you how much I regretted not following your advice and moving towards Marwar. When I was in the thick of the crisis there, I got the news of your military training and recruitment.'

He was interrupted by her, 'Surely you were also told about my planning to attack Jai Nagar. Am I right?'

He acknowledged that she was right about that piece of information, but told her that he did not believe it.

'I want you to rest assured from my end and let our coming together after so long not be lost in questions and answers. You made me the queen of half your empire, and I wished to play that role with all sincerity and shoulder my responsibility. The Amber army is now ready to march along with you. Now, do not regret the past, but look forward. I must tell you I am happy that you have returned, for I feared for your life and prayed for your well-being!' She hugged him, showering him with her affection.

It became clear to Jagat Singh that there was more than one person who had conspired to block the message service between Raskapoor and him, and that group had to be put under a scanner. He admired her resilience not just to survive but also to be able to give him a backup with her well-trained army. His heart was filled with love for her, and the two lovers rose at dawn, reliving the first night they had spent together. Sun rays were kissing her smiling face, and Jagat Singh held her close to his chest, rebuking himself for getting anxious about the tales contrived to disgrace her.

Pulling herself away from him, she revealed the programme for the day. 'We have to get ready and first seek the blessings of Shila Mata. Then you have to inspect your Amber army to plan your future strategies. You are only defeated, not dead. You will experience victory. You will certainly be able to ride over these difficult circumstances.'

They went to the temple first and then to see the military exercise. She made it a point to introduce the recruits to their Maharaja. He was surprised to see her calling each one by his name. On their way back, he complimented her wholeheartedly for undertaking such a remarkable mission. He commended her on knowing the names of each recruit.

She continued smiling, looking straight into his eyes for a few minutes. 'You have to reach out to the people who work for you and give them a sense of belonging. Being a woman, that too a concubine—as the Chief Queen likes to address me—I had to work relentlessly to earn their respect and faith. Now the half queen is ready to hand over her territory with her army,' she responded with a sense of accomplishment.

They spent some blissful days together, and then Raskapoor reminded him that he had to get back to Jai Nagar to resume his work and take charge of the administration, which needed his vigilance and actions. She even told him that all could not be taken for granted in Marwar. She guessed what had happened after Jagat Singh and the Jai Nagar forces returned empty-handed. She knew Amir Khan was bound to go all out to erase the threat of succession of Dhonkal Singh, dealing with his supporters, the Marathas and the Pokhran Thakur. In her opinion, once Amir Khan accomplished this last mission, he would strengthen his resources with the grant of land and the substantial reward money to again target Jagat Singh's territory.

He was surprised to see her asking him to go alone. 'Ras, my love, I cannot be there without you. If I leave you here, my mind will be here. You have to come with me. Ras Vilas is waiting for you. You are my queen, and you have to be by my side. I will not live without you.'

Raskapoor did not give in to his earnest request, which almost sounded like a supplication. She was, however, not willing to be belittled by anyone anymore, not in the least by the Chief Queen, for she was a woman of substance, not merely an illegitimate child of a concubine. She had narrated to Jagat Singh the circumstances which had compelled her to take on the role of queen assigned by him and play it fully. She promised him that she would return with him the next time he came. But she had one condition—she needed him to find the whereabouts of the man who had guided her in his absence and was her trusted counsellor.

It was then that he asked her for the name of the man who everyone was talking about. Without hesitating for a minute, she revealed Rudra's name underlining the feeling that he should have known instead of asking her. 'They were not just talking about him but alleging an affair between him and me in a bid to tarnish my character. I could feel that in the last few days, they had probably even sown a seed of doubt in your mind . . . you have to acknowledge that fact. If you had not entered my life, I would not have just had an affair with that incredible man but would have married him. He put his life in danger to help you, respecting my earnest wish to save your life. No one else would have put his life at stake as he did without any fear. Rudra is one of his kind . . . or was one of his kind. I don't even know if he is alive or dead. He was the last messenger I sent to you to convince you to return and not continue with the mission to Mehrangarh.' She wiped her tears. Jagat Singh could not argue with her, empathizing with her anxiety over Rudra's well-being. He made his way back with a heavy heart, having asked her the question that had raised suspicion on her character. Feeling a bit embarrassed and guilty, he respected her inner strength to say what she said while revealing Rudra's name without any hesitation.

When he returned alone, those opposed to Raskapoor were delighted, for they believed that their mission of distancing him from her was accomplished. The news created ripples of excitement among the vassals led by Chaand Singh of Dooni as well as in the zenani deorhi. Each one of them was taking the credit for the disenchantment of Jagat Singh with Raskapoor, an apparent result of their juicy and false stories of her affairs and scheme to take over Jai Nagar. Dooni Thakur was the one who ran to the Chief Queen to announce Jagat Singh's return without Raskapoor.

'Maharani Sahiba, I have got great news for you of our victory!' She was surprised, for after that disgraceful defeat, the thought of any victory so soon was unimaginable for her. She took no time in mocking him as she asked, 'Thakur Sahib, how much did you drink last night? Were you trying to get over your defeat in the terrible showdown by the Jodhpur forces? Did your beloved Roopa, your new concubine, pamper you by filling your goblet all night, leaving you to imagine your victory?'

He would have given a befitting reply to all her questions as he was not a man like her husband to forget his duty and be overpowered by a beautiful lady's love. Instead, he announced the victory over Raskapoor. Their resounding claps and laughter reached the ears of the Maharaja, who was making his way to Shobha Niwas. That sound of jubilation made him guess who had conspired to get his lover out of the palace, and who ensured the disappearance of the messengers sent by her. While the vassals wished to know what action was being proposed against Raskapoor, Jagat Singh was figuring out a plan to locate Rudra and to bring Raskapoor back to the palace.

Before he could know Rudra's whereabouts, he received two pieces of alarming news from Marwar. The first was the detachment of Bapuji from Dhonkal Singh and him being expatriated from Marwar. Before the announcement of that unforeseen development could sink in, the big news of Sawai Singh's murder came in, and gloom hit the palace, as he was Jagat Singh's grandfather-in-law. His new wife remained inconsolable for weeks together while all other queens tried to console her. The plot executed ruthlessly had been a big blow for even Jagat Singh.

Both reminded him of what Raskapoor had said about Amir Khan's mission of erasing the threat of ascendancy in Marwar. He could not but once again feel that she was the perfect fit to rule a princely state with such farsightedness. He wanted to be by her side but was still unable to get any news about Rudra. As if that was not enough, all the concerned parties were pushing for action against Raskapoor. She could again present a threat to his empire, they feared.

Finally, one day he summoned Chaand Singh to remove his apprehensions once and for all and help other team members of his in the zenani deorhi too. He informed Chaand Singh about how Raskapoor had made him inspect the army cultivated by her and introduced the Maharaja as their chief. Chaand Singh, with deeper designs, tried to convince the Maharaja not to believe what she said, as the concubine could once again be laying a honey trap for him to defend herself from any drastic measures against her. On that argument, Jagat Singh told him to trace her adviser who could testify to clear his doubts for even a murderer had the right to defend himself. He cleverly underlined that the culprit could also go scot-free without a testimony.

'Thakur Sahib, produce that man before me, anyhow,' Jagat Singh ordered the man who he believed had a hand in the disappearance of his messengers.

Before Jagat Singh could undertake the investigation of the allegations against his lover, Bapuji Rao Scindia appeared to collect the money promised to him before launching the campaign against Man Singh more than a year back. Jagat Singh had also struck a similar agreement with Holkar at that time. Bapuji wanted to redeem his lost prestige after his unceremonious expatriation. When Amir Khan was too far away and involved with other matters to intervene, Bapuji saw it as the right time to get his due. He first tried to recover the promised number of Rs 40 lakh via negotiations but seeing his weak position after losing face in Marwar, Jagat Singh point-blank refused to pay him a penny.

Unable to bear a defeated man defying him, Bapuji attacked Jai Nagar in June 1808. He captured the forts of Lunera, Beejwada, Nawai, and threatened to destroy the fortress of Tordi if Jagat Singh did not pay the assured sum. Finding no way out, the helpless ruler had to resort to seeking the help of the man behind his defeat.

He connected with Amir Khan to strike a compromise with Man Singh. Jagat Singh even tried to get the help of the British, despite knowing that they had adopted the policy of non-intervention. It did not bring the desired results. He decided to appease Holkar too by appointing his trusted man Chaturbhuj as his prime minister and getting another confidant of his, Bal Mukund, as their joint legal representative with the resident in Delhi.

None of his efforts to get help seemed to go right. In those difficult circumstances, the one person he wanted with him was Raskapoor, who could help him pull through the rising crisis cleverly, but she would not come till Rudra's whereabouts were found, and the man in charge to do that kept deferring on account of Bapuji's pressure, which needed his attention first. He only gave one assurance that his men were at it, and according to him, the search operation might take them months. There was apprehension about Rudra escaping to one of the four principal holy places of Hindus.

Jagat Singh's frustration was growing as he could see no easy solution to settle the matter with Scindia and to bring his lover back to the palace. His increasing restlessness led him to take Chaand Singh, along with his trusted vassals, for the negotiations with Scindia, and he decided to visit Raskapoor, whose absence was not letting him think clearly.

They were meeting after months. Jagat Singh hurriedly climbed up the steps to the palace, not wanting to lose even a minute to see his lover. On the way leading to the hall of mirrors, he acknowledged the greetings of the attendants without stopping even for a moment. Gulab observed the unusual hurry with which the Maharaja came in from Suhag Mandir above the Ganesh Pol. She admired the unique power Raskapoor had over him. Raskapoor, who was awaiting his arrival, was standing like a bedecked bride to welcome her man. The moment he saw her, he threw out his arms to reach out to her and embraced her, pouring his heart out.

'I am like a dead man without you. I cannot tell you how difficult and painful the last few months have been. I have put none other than Thakur Chaand Singh to trace your friend Rudra. He has been at it and is even considering extending his search operation to the four holy shrines, knowing the spiritual leanings of your friend. Now you have to return with me. We will together monitor the search operation. I am under so much pressure from every side. You were absolutely right about Amir Khan acting to erase the succession problem. He has made Scindia leave Marwar, who is now plundering my territory and twisting my arm for payment. Ras, you have to be with me now.' Raskapoor looked into his eyes, which were seeking her reply, and responded to him, 'I may not be there physically, but I am with you mentally all the time, like Radha. Remember her saga after Lord Krishna left the territory of Brij and never saw him again until the fag end of her life.

Radha having fulfilled all her worldly duties, decided to go to Dwarka, where Krishna had settled down after killing his demon-like uncle Kansa. Krishna, appreciating his lover's wish, brought her to the palace and respecting her wish to maintain her anonymity, employed her as a maid. After a few days, she realized that the real pleasure was not in physical proximity but in spiritual closeness. Radha left the palace one day, wandered for days together on the streets of Dwarka, till her frail body could not move. Tired and weak, Radha fainted in a dark, winding lane. After some moments, she slowly regained her consciousness as the faint and distant sound of the flute became louder and came close. When she slowly opened her eyes, there he was . . . her Krishna, playing the flute. It was the same melody that he played in Vrindavan.

Radha was thrilled to see Krishna. She knew the time was fast approaching for her soul to leave her body, and she expressed her desire to die listening to his flute. Krishna composed a melody to soothe her soul for a swift release. Radha was sinking in the deep ocean, her soul uniting with Krishna, as he played the last loud note, and felt their souls had mingled to become one. Krishna broke the flute into two halves to be consigned with her mortal remains.'

As Raskapoor finished this heart rendering story, she noticed the tears rolling down Jagat Singh's eyes. She wiped his tears with her veil cloth. She smiled and hugged him, saying, 'We have to celebrate their spiritual love. I want my soul to be assimilated with yours to annihilate my birth Karma, and free my soul from the cycle of birth and death. Should I be born again, I will like to be born free without the baggage of my lineage, which has brought us to the present situation. As I have recounted Radha's story today, I can foresee many tales around my life and death like her, but those will be narrated to accuse me, for I am the offspring of a concubine. However, now we are together, let us celebrate the days of Krishna and Radha in Vrindavan!'

They laughed as never before, and the two lonesome lovers spent weeks of bliss. Finally, on the eve of his departure, designated by Raskapoor, Jagat Singh asked her to be ready to move back to Ras Vilas. Raskapoor surprised him with her reply as she informed him that she was already set to go along with him, for she had decided to keep a close watch on the search for Rudra. The opposite camp was more than sure that the Maharaja would have grilled Raskapoor thoroughly on the allegations made by them and awarded the punishment leading to her exile in a dungeon. Her days to rule as a queen were over, was the collective belief. They were all ready to celebrate the news, neither concerned with the Maharaja's defeat in Marwar, nor Bapuji, who had captured a few forts and had laid a long siege around the fortress of Tordi. They were not bothered about Jagat Singh's nearly empty coffers and Bapuji's pressure to settle the payment, because they were busy dreaming of the jubilation they would feel on the removal of Raskapoor from their lives.

When the Maharaja entered the palace hand in hand with Raskapoor, their flight of dreams came crashing down. He walked straight to Ras Vilas. The stunned queens and vassals did not give up. They convened several meetings to work once again to strategize her ouster. They started justifying their husband's defeat as they felt defeated at the hand of a concubine. Lying awake for nights together at times, the Chief Queen even contemplated doing away with both of them if he did not dispense with Raskapoor. She cursed the Marwar Maharaja, who had not let the marriage of Jagat Singh and Princess Krishna Kumari materialize, which she was sure could have distanced the Maharaja from his lover. With the tension of Bapuji's demand and the siege, that marriage proposal too could not be brought up.

In such circumstances, the festive occasions at the palace were also lacklustre. They were celebrated as a routine to keep up with the aspirations of the city's citizens. The entourage of maids dressed the image of Gangaur as the queens appeared only to send her off. They came in only after several reminders by the handmaiden of the Chief Queen. She was taken aback to hear the patrani remark, 'What does it matter if we come or not, for technically the one we are supposed to pray for, does not belong to us. Is it not strange that when the procession moves with all the fanfare, the outside world will think that the royal ladies have made the offerings first, while that ritual today was undertaken by all of you? All these rituals become meaningless if we do not hold to what they stand for.' The baffled handmaiden managed to convince her to come with the rest of the queens to give a ceremonial send off to the deity, who ironically, ensured marital bliss.

Life for Raskapoor, too, was not easy. While she was filled with anxiety over the missing Rudra, Jagat Singh was often depressed over his defeat, as well as faced pressure to deal with the operations of Bapuji. Determined as she was to help her man, she advised him not to refrain from forging a friendship with old foes, which included Man Singh and Amir Khan. First, he resisted her suggestion, recalling the humiliation he had faced at their hands, but then sought time to mull over her advice.

In the meanwhile, Raskapoor was trying to move forward with her primary mission to find her missing friend. But each time, Chaand Singh Dooni dodged her, citing ongoing troubles and explaining that only after those were settled would the search operation be undertaken. Seeing Amir Khan's manoeuvre, she was forced to put the mission on the back burner till Jagat Singh's troubles were cleared.

Bapuji scaled up his pressure, leaving no other option for Jagat Singh but to accept Bapuji Scindia's final offer to sign an undertaking of the payment of tribute or khandani as the Marathas termed it. After receiving the duly signed and stamped khandani, Bapuji lifted the months-long siege of Tordi in May 1809, making his way to Nagpur.

Jagat Singh got some respite after his reconciliation with Scindia and decided to go ahead with Raskapoor's suggestions. Soon after, Amir Khan arrived in June to negotiate a peace process with Marwar but to their surprise, he aroused serious troubles for Jagat Singh.

After days of deliberations, it was concluded that Man Singh would extend his friendship on two conditions—appropriation of all the loot of the battle of Gingoli at Parbatsar and reimbursement of the negotiated amount to Amir Khan. After receiving his amount, he left.

Later in the year, they heard that the Holkar chief had gone insane. Amir Khan, as an old associate, went to take control of Holkar's affairs. He stayed away from princely Rajputana for a year, but continued to take care of Holkar's interest in the states to guard against the Scindias, for he knew that the sovereign states were the playground of these arch-rivals.

Despair in Mewar

The Scindia and Holkar dynasties, as expected, could not keep themselves away from either of the three states of Mewar, Marwar and Dhundhar. In August, Scindia approached both Marwar and Dhundhar, adopting the policy of 'conciliation', given Holkar's growing influence with Amir Khan backing him. Because a lot was happening on that front, Jai Nagar got some time to breathe. Raskapoor reminded Jagat Singh of his initial mission to contain Man Singh at Parbatsar. 'More than a year has gone by since you planned a campaign against the Jodhpur Maharaja to marry the princess of Mewar. I often think of her situation, being treated like a rope in a tug of war, pulled this side and that by the rulers of Marwar and Jai Nagar. Where does she stand, Maharajadhiraj? Have you for once thought about the plight of the young girl who is waiting endlessly for her prince charming, to be finally married? At times, I also wonder what kind of father the Maharana is who has landed her in this mess.'

Jagat Singh told her that he intended to marry the princess soon, as both Scindia and Amir Khan, having been paid such hefty amounts, were not likely to create hurdles. 'I have thought about her plight and wish that the proposal had never come for me. Believe me, Ras, after you, I have never longed for any woman however beautiful she might be. Now in this situation, I am compelled to marry the princess.'

However, destiny had something else in the store. Before Jagat Singh's plans could materialize, the forces of Scindia as well as Holkar reached Mewar, leaving the Maharana in no position to talk about the wedding of his daughter. It is believed that the Chief Queen, antagonized by Raskapoor's return, in a bid to give Jagat Singh a tough time, sent advance information of his plans to marry Krishna Kumari to his rival suitor Man Singh.

The latter was so enraged that he refused any reconciliation with Scindia or pay the tribute he was hoping to get. Scindia planned to teach Man Singh a lesson by waging a fight, but once again Amir Khan proved to be cleverer, having left behind a well-equipped army under Mohmmad Shah Khan for just such an eventuality. Scindia and Holkar almost came together to reduce Amir Khan's power. They had even agreed upon the terms of the alliance, but that failed in March 1810 when their rivalry resurfaced. Amir Khan also landed in Mewar upon receiving some intelligence— Holkar's representative Dharm Chela had a deep-seated desire to usurp Holkar's position. He was becoming more powerful, as Yashwant Rao Holkar's mental health was already beyond redemption. Amir Khan was alerted by Holkar's wife, Tulsi Bai. He decided to take Holkar's army under his wing and gathered them to deal with the Scindia threat, retrieving the khandani or the tribute he had extracted in Jai Nagar, as well as plundering the two sub-divisions of Kastor and Sadri in Mewar, which were under Scindia's control. Scindia could not face the challenge and was forced to turn towards Nathdwara.

Amir Khan twisted the arm of the Maharana of Mewar to sign an agreement to mortgage the whole of Mewar to Holkar for the meagre sum of Rs 13 lakh. Fifty percent of the mortgaged amount was paid in advance, and for the remaining amount, two hostages were handed over to Amir Khan. The agreement gave Holkar the upper hand and his position became strong.

Amir Khan turned his attention to the other unresolved matter at hand—the marriage of Princess Krishna Kumari, which had resulted in years of war, a tragic tale that has been woven into the legends of the Rajputs.

The Maharana of Mewar, eager to conclude the long-pending wedding of his beloved daughter, spoke to Amir Khan, 'Has Nawab Sahib been able to convince Maharaja Man Singh to let the wedding of Princess Krishna Kumari materialize with Maharaja Sawai Jagat Singh?' Amir Khan mocked his question. 'How could you think that Man Singh would let Jagat Singh take away the war trophy for which he has been fighting for so long? He would rather kill Jagat Singh or even your daughter than let the two marry. Look, Maharana Bhim Singh, you have only two options. Either you marry your daughter to Man Singh or sacrifice your daughter. She cannot be allowed to live and I will ravage your glorious Mewar if you do not marry her to Man Singh. I will trash the honour of Mewar. The recent mortgage agreement must be kept in mind while making your decision. We will meet tomorrow at sunset on the Pichola pal (the banks of Lake Pichola).'

The Maharana remained restless the whole night, weighing the pros and cons of the two unbearable options given to him. At dawn, after performing his prayers, he recalled the history of Mewar, which was replete with anecdotes of the honour of the land being saved. He was not going to marry a princess of Mewar to Man Singh, who had first turned her down, and was the man behind the actions of Amir Khan, who was now forcing him to go back on his word to Jagat Singh. Breaking the engagement on the persuasion of his enemy would certainly disgrace his land.

He discarded the first option. His heart ached to realize the only option, dreadful as it was, left for him. The beautiful face of his sixteen-year-old daughter loomed before his eyes. Shutting himself in his room, Bhim Singh did not eat or drink a drop of water the whole day. His thoughts revolved only around what he was going to have to do to his daughter. Finally, as the sun started going down, he prayed one last time. After the last prayer, he got ready, and proceeded to the banks of Pichola. He was surprised to see Amir Khan there before him, taking a leisurely walk. Before Amir Khan could ask him anything, Bhim Singh spoke, 'Mewar would sacrifice its daughter rather than sacrifice its honour at the wedding altar. You gave me only one option, knowing that

Man Singh would never be given the honour to be a son-in-law of Mewar. So, I have accepted to send my daughter into the lap of death.'

Amir Khan was stunned to see the Maharana turn into a stoic within twenty-four hours. Amir Khan asked, 'I can give you more time to reconsider that painful decision as well as advise you to go for the softer option of the wedding with Man Singh.'

The Maharana refused vehemently and informed Amir that the decision was made. Amir Khan pushed him further, giving him a week to take action on his decision. In the distance, the sun was sinking slowly in the valley behind the Aravalli range. Amir Khan left, but the Maharana watched the sunset, imagining the face of his princess dissolve into the horizon.

Bhim Singh knew that Krishna Kumari would meet her death in the female apartments with the help of her own family. The world would only hear stories of her end, not knowing which one was true. Bards would recite poetry, describing her as a martyr, preferring death over dishonour.

After consulting her mother, the Maharana gave the task to her younger brother. He was convinced to lift his sword to save the honour of the land. As he stood at his sister's door, and saw her innocent face greeting him, he could not dare to enter the room to behead his sister for no crime of hers. He not only turned back, but also went to his parents, threw the sword down and burst out crying. If he did the deed, he would never be the same person, considering himself guilty as long as he lived.

Krishna had seen the sword in her brother's hand and knew that her life was the root cause of Mewar's increasing troubles. As a little girl, Krishna fell asleep listening to the fairy-tale stories about the day she would get married to the Maharaja of Jodhpur. Often, she would play and arrange her marriage. The mock wedding would be joyful, with laughter, songs and dances performed by the little girls in the female apartments. Krishna's mother always dreamt of the day of the wedding between the royal houses of Mewar and Marwar. She never imagined the untimely demise of the prospective bridegroom. After mourning for a few months, when her husband received the acceptance of Maharaja Jagat Singh of Dhundhar to marry Krishna Kumari, the mother could not but think that her daughter was a fortunate girl! And now, instead of planning for her daughter's grand wedding, she would have to prepare for her discreet death so as to not to let anyone outside the family get a whiff of the dreadful plan. The mother in her cried for hours together. But her lineage made her go ahead with the task.

For Krishna, while she was growing up, references to marriage brought news of changes of the bridegroom, which made no difference to the girl who only longed for a fairy-tale wedding. Later, however, when the wedding plans were deferred time and again, she could sense her wedding would not be the fairy tale she had always dreamt of, but a strategic alliance. She pleaded with her father to drop the idea of marrying her to a maharaja altogether, as she did not care for it, having become aware of their lifestyle. All that fascination of being a queen dissolved gradually with the stories of the kings' many wives, concubines, their illegitimate children and the treacherous squabbles between territories. Reaching the age of sixteen, which she had been told was 'sweet', seemed far from it to her; instead, she felt things sour with each passing year, especially when questioned about her marriage by her friends and cousins. Girls of her age across the princely states were not just married but mothers of children. She was sick and tired of conversations beginning and ending with the talk of her wedding. Besides all this, constant warfare between the two suitors had put the peace and prosperity of her land at stake, and she wanted to escape from the situation.

When her brother failed, the brutal role of putting the dream bride to death was assigned to one of her aunts. After seeking the forgiveness of god almighty, the aunt prepared the opiated concoction Kusumba or the safflower. It was designed to make her sleep peacefully and depart from the world; a world which would make life impossible for her.

She gave Krishna the goblet of the potent poison, but it did not work. Then a second goblet was prepared, and Krishna gulped that down too, but surprisingly that too failed. Krishna did feel a bit uneasy knowing it was poison. Surprisingly, she was not afraid of death, being raised not only on fairy tales but also hearing the saga of Rani Padmini. Krishna idolized the queen who leapt into the fire rather than surrender her honour to the Muslim invader Allaudin Khilji, and Meera Bai who accepted poison to realize her spiritual love. She decided to celebrate her death, which was standing at the door where she had imagined her bridegroom would be. Taking the third serving from her aunt's hands, Krishna Kumari requested her to give her bridal clothes. She struggled to put them on in her state of giddiness but managed to dress up like a bride.

'Inform all that I left Mewar as a bride to meet my bridegroom in heaven like Meera Bai,' she said, and picked up the third goblet and drank the concoction in one breath. Both she and the cup lay on the floor within no time. The sound of the goblet clattering to the floor and rolling away from her, smothered the faint sound of her last breath. Her mortal remains were consigned to flames amidst resounding cheers of, 'Long live Princess Krishna Kumari . . . long live Krishna Kumari!'

Standing far away from her funeral pyre, a Sadhu proclaimed, 'Three rulers are responsible for this sinful murder of a harmless and innocent girl. All three of them will be punished in this very life, and death will not be as kind as she was to the princess. They will meet their fateful end in pain and anguish. An innocent girl is an incarnation of the Mother Goddess . . . You can overpower her body but not her soul, which will never let the culprit live peacefully however powerful they may be.'

Krishna Kumari died on 21 July. It was monsoon, and the parched land of Rajputana was soaked with sorrow. Her mother could not bear the sorrow of her untimely death of which she was equally culpable, not having put her foot down and saved the life of her daughter. Monsoon . . . when her daughter should have been celebrating the joyful festival of Kajali Teej, she was murdered by her own family. Her laughter haunted her mother. Often, she saw Krishna sitting on the swing rising high towards the horizon and gesturing her mother to join her. Even though she had given her consent in the name of honour, her mother was overcome by guilt, which extinguished her desire to live. Soon after Krishna Kumari's death, her mother too died.

No one could ever envisage such a tragic end of the princess. Her suitors too felt guilty. The main culprit Man Singh had made Amir Khan give the option of her death only to use as a tactic to get the Maharana to marry his daughter to him. He could not in his wildest dreams think of a father putting his daughter to death when he had the option of getting her married to save her life. Jagat Singh, on the other hand, felt upset with himself for giving precedence to the campaign in Marwar over the marriage, which would have saved her from such a tragic end.

The news of her unfortunate death reached the British government, and on 4 November 1810, the sad incident projected as a political necessity was recorded in the Asiatic Annual Register for 1810–11. The details shared in the account tormented people in London as well: 'The most important political event, which has occurred in Hindustan is the death of the princess of Udaipur by poison . . . The rivalry . . . of these two Rajahs (for her hand) produced a war . . . The poison was administered to the princess by her own aunt, and with the knowledge of her father . . .' The account termed her as the second Helen, as her story reminded the British of the Trojan war and Helen of Troy in many ways.

Imagining finding solace for Mewar in his daughter's death, Bhim Singh could not ensure peace after Krishna's death. Amir Khan left Mewar but stationed his man Jamshed Khan to take care of his interests there as well as recover the tribute. After leaving Mewar, Amir Khan made a move towards Jai Nagar.

Restlessness Prevails

The death of Krishna Kumari, the woman who had to marry the Maharaja, hit Jai Nagar hard. Jagat Singh himself was saddened by the tragic end of the innocent princess, who was also his fiancée. He was not drawn towards her, being genuinely in love with Raskapoor, but marrying the princess had become an inevitable part of his life. With that part being removed so abruptly, he did feel the anguish of the amputation. Krishna Kumari did not deserve to be murdered, and he had unwittingly played the role of one of the culprits in her death. Haunted by that thought, he wished he could share his mental state with his soulmate Raskapoor, but she was herself hit by the grief of that shocking death.

The day she got the news, Jagat Singh saw her wailing for the first time. For days together, she would suddenly burst into tears thinking about the murder. One evening she herself raised the subject of Krishna Kumari asking her lover, 'Why is it that only a woman is made to die in the name of honour?'

Gradually Jagat Singh got over the saga of Krishna Kumari, but Raskapoor did not. Each night she apologized to the princess on behalf of her lover, praying for his peace; and she continued this prayer till her demise. Often, Raskapoor wondered if she was better off being an offspring of a concubine than to be born as that unfortunate princess, who did not know the emotion of love that a girl always aspired for. She, on the contrary, was bestowed with that love by not one, but two men, Jagat Singh and Rudra. Raskapoor was so grief-stricken, that she did not think even once to review the search operation for Rudra for months together.

Jagat Singh was under pressure with the arrival of Amir Khan, the main culprit of Krishna Kumari's death. His arrival meant serious troubles for Jagat Singh. Amir Khan had come to extract money from Jagat Singh, and he made that clear as he started plundering the territory. Finally, the Maharaja was forced to sign an agreement with Amir Khan on 11 May 1811 to pay Rs 10 lakh to him and Rs 6 lakh to his commander Mohammad Shah Khan. The money was to be recovered from the vassals of Shekhawati. Amir Khan, like a chameleon, changed colours within seconds as per his designs with no respect for the agreements. During his negotiations, he realized that Jagat Singh was on a deserted island with no help around him. Amir Khan, taking advantage of the situation, raised his own amount to Rs 17 lakh and left the territory only after getting Jagat Singh to sign the agreement.

Since Jagat Singh had consented for Mohammad Shah Khan to exact the money assured to him from the vassals of Shekhawati, he started ravaging their territories. The forceful extraction of wealth was accompanied by other excesses, breaking the terms of the agreement. Holding the Maharaja responsible for their plight, the vassals of Shekhawati began to design plans to undertake operations to settle scores with Amir Khan as well as the Maharaja and his loyalist vassals, who had inflicted trauma of such magnitude upon them.

On the other side, Daulat Rao Scindia was working towards the revival of the old ascendancy issue, provoking Man Singh to besiege the throne from Jagat Singh. When Jagat Singh received this information from the espionage service, he shared it with Raskapoor. Raskapoor was shell-shocked. 'I could never imagine after all the agreements with Marwar that Man Singh would plan to take over your throne,' she said.

Raskapoor obviously did not know about the other Man Singh in Jagat Singh's life until that moment. She was then informed of the posthumous birth of his cousin. The cousin was the son of his father Pratap Singh's brother Prithvi Singh who died an untimely death due to a fall from horseback considered to be the design of Pratap's mother and her paramour Firoz Pheelwan, the elephant keeper. After this, Pratap Singh succeeded to the throne, while fifteen-year-old Prithvi Singh's second wife, the Princess of Kishangarh's pregnancy was kept under wraps. After the demise of her husband, she went to Kishangarh, where her son Man Singh was born. He was the legal successor of Jai Nagar, but the queen mother would not have let him live. For the safety of the boy, he was sent to Narwar under the watch of Scindia. Somehow, that threat was aborted with British intervention. It had put aside the claimant's plea on the ground of being away from the throne for thirty-four years. With the clear-cut directive to Scindia to not create any such upheaval in Jai Nagar, the plan was shelved, supposedly never to resurface again.

In Delhi, Metcalfe had taken over as the Resident on 25 February 1811. He was keeping a close watch over the Rajput states, as he was of the view that they should be taken into British protection and the policy of non-intervention be discontinued. He was appalled to see the oppression and devastation of the Rajput states by the Marathas as well as Amir Khan. Many of these states were eager to come under British protection. Metcalfe wrote to his government to abandon their policy, which could be of great advantage in the future to command this land. He highlighted the connection they would be able to establish between Bengal and Bombay as well as Gujarat and the northern states to contain the Maratha power, too. Despite arguing vehemently, he did not succeed in getting the much-desired change in policy.

Around the same time, Jai Nagar's territory came under threat from the vassal of Macheri. The enemy was closing in, and Jagat Singh, with his near drained treasury, had to face the wolf called Amir Khan, who was ready to fiercely charge at him as he was not able to fulfil his commitment. Raskapoor was dismayed to see the worried look of Jagat Singh night after night despite all her efforts to cheer him up.

'Ras, if you were not by my side, I would have long ago lost my territory as well as my life. You are my true well-wisher,' he remarked on one such night.

She then suggested two strategies to deal with his problems. 'I have been pondering over the complex situation and feel you should once again approach Metcalfe immediately to stop the Thakur of Macheri from entering Jai Nagar and return to his territory, as well as reshuffle your ministers.' Duly encouraged by Raskapoor, he sent his emissaries with a request to the Resident who averted that threat. But his difficulties were far from over as Amir Khan was pressurizing him to get the money agreed upon. Following Raskapoor's advice to keep offering small baits to arrest Amir Khan's hunger, he proposed to pay small instalments. But his prime minister Megh Singh Diggi wanted Jagat Singh to pay the whole amount once and for all which cost him his job. It was apparent that the prime minister was not acting in accordance with his master's plan.

An experienced and competent hand was needed to deal with the situation. Raskapoor chose Khushaliram Bohra, who had quit only a year ago due to the mistrust between him and the Maharaja. Initially, Jagat Singh was not keen to get him back but then gave in, and the ministry was reshuffled in July 1811. Bohra, who was an old hand, taking stock of the treasury, refused to pay any money. Again, a request was made to the Resident for protection but to no avail, despite Metcalfe's letter written on 23 July 1811 to apprise the Governor-General of the growing threat of the whole territory of Jagat Singh being plundered.

It was in the knowledge of the British Resident that Khan was all set to recover his dues by force and had requested Bapuji Scindia and his brother to join hands. Jagat Singh did send his emissaries to negotiate different options with the British Resident, of which one was to pay the British the tribute to be paid to the plunderers in return for their role in averting the threat posed by Amir Khan and his associates. But again, the British chose to be silent spectators

because of a possible French attack on India, for which they had
to have Marathas on their side. Maratha support implied support
from their allies and trusted men too, which included Amir Khan.
Jagat Singh was sinking in a whirlpool of conspiracies and threats,
despite Raskapoor trying her best to pull him out. She did not
want him to succumb to pressures like his ancestor Maharaja
Ishwari Singh who committed suicide. She proposed to him to
once again to discuss matters with the prime minister in view of
the most recent communication of Metcalf not succeeding, which
left only one option—negotiate with Amir Khan and decide on the
mode of payment.

Bohra yielded, but Amir Khan raised the amount as well as
changed the mode of payment, mounting further pressure. The
old and fragile Bohra abandoned all negotiations and was ready
to go to war against Amir. Jagat Singh was so exasperated with
the adamant attitude of his prime minister that one fine morning
he removed him from the post. Jagat Singh's decision surprised
all his vassals as no name was announced as Bohra's successor.
Raskapoor herself was startled to see such a decision taken without
naming a successor.

'I know the prime minister was too stiff and had to go, but
I cannot understand why you did not announce the name of his
successor at the same time. Don't you see that the empty chair will
be mounted by jealousy well before you find the successor?' she
said, expressing her anxiety over his hasty decision. Her questions
made Jagat Singh realize his mistake. He sat down to think as to
who the right person for the job could be, because nothing had
changed since the time Bohra was given the charge. In the absence
of a man with the calibre and trustworthiness the job required, he
once again ran through all the possible names. He had no choice
but to discard all. None of them could be trusted in view of their
internal conflict.

After sitting quietly for a few hours, he asked Raskapoor, 'You
alone can help me finalize the name of the man who could be
given the reins to successfully avert these threats amicably without
incurring the loss of our dignity. None of my vassals can be trusted
after Megh Singh Diggi crossed over to the other side and pursued

Amir Khan's unjust cause. It has to be someone other than these fiefs of mine.'

After a few minutes, she asked Jagat Singh, 'What about my father, Pandit Shiv Narain Mishra? He is a Brahmin with immense wisdom. He also does not have ambitions like your vassals to be more powerful and wealthy.'

Jagat Singh emerged from his confusion and wondered why that name had not struck him earlier. The pandit was certainly the best choice in the given circumstances. He admired Raskapoor's clear thinking. He got up and immediately hugged Raskapoor, saying, 'Thank you so much. I am going to summon the meeting to announce his name as the new prime minister.' His announcement shocked the vassals as many were lining up for the coveted job. Discontented aspirants saw the hand of the illegitimate daughter of the Brahmin who was ruling the heart as well as the mind of their Maharaja in his appointment. The whispers around Raskapoor being the daughter of Pandit Shiv Narain Mishra acquired a louder voice. What was initially a suspicion gradually turned into a firm belief first with Mishra declaring her as his godchild and then with his being given the key job undermining the aspirations of the vassals.

Jagat Singh's administration was witnessing factionalism and rising disenchantment, which posed a tough challenge before the new prime minister. The overbearing presence of Marathas and Pindaris led to many princely states seeking British protection, which the British Resident himself wished his government to take note of. The situation in Jagat Singh's territory was getting from bad to worse, leading him to describe the state of affairs there as 'ruinous' when he wrote to Edmonstone, the Chief Secretary to the British Government on 4 January 1812. He pleaded for British protection of 'Jypoor' in very strong words, which, according to him, could only be retrieved by British aid.

Despite expressing his deep concern for the marooned Jagat Singh and his devastated empire once again, the Resident could not succeed in altering the path of his government, which continued with the policy of non-intervention. Left with no option, the Maharaja of Jaipur subjected his people to heavy taxes to pay tribute to Amir Khan. Raskapoor did try to dissuade him from financially burdening the people who had already been hit by the constant conflicts that had drained the resources of the state.

'Maharajadhiraj has to open dialogue with Maharaja of Jodhpur to make the unreasonable Pathan appreciate the plight of the innocent people of your state being pushed to the wall with taxes imposed. History will not be kind to my love and blame all your failures on me,' Raskapoor implored him to resolve the crisis diplomatically, but to no avail.

She even met her father, trying to get him to muster his wisdom and use diplomacy effectively. Still, to her utmost surprise, he appeared to be losing ground, submerged as he was in the infighting among the vassals upset with his appointment in place of Bohra. She was stunned to see a very meek man standing before her, who was bound to lose the battle even before fighting it. Did she make a big mistake in suggesting his name as the new prime minister, she wondered night after night?

Amidst the uncertainty, Chaand Singh Dooni created another dramatic situation. Jagat Singh had imprisoned him for the disrespect shown towards his lady love publicly. But Chaand Singh attributed his imprisonment to Raskapoor. At that time, Megh Singh had freed him from Jaigarh Fort. He decided to exploit the absence of Amir Khan and avenge the Pathan's adventures in his territory where, of late, his General Raja Bahadur Lal Singh's brigade was attacking and looting the people. Rao Chaand Singh had already elected to act on his own without informing Jagat Singh. First, he chose to lay siege around the garden of Megh Singh Diggi just outside the walled city. It was a part of his weird plan to repay Megh Singh for freeing him from Jaigarh Fort. For some reason, he thought it wise to lay a siege and then grant a favour by setting Megh Singh free. The plan, however, failed as before he could set him free, Megh Singh managed to escape to his village to take refuge in his fort. Chaand Singh's plan added fire to the fumes as Megh Singh had already strayed away from Jagat Singh and joined the enemy's camp.

In mid-1812, Chaand Singh made up his mind to once and for all vanquish the problem called 'Amir Khan' from the princely states of the Rajputs. Already fed up with Jagat Singh's administration, where his mistress guided the ruler, he resolved to capture Tonk with the help of the disgruntled vassals of Shekhawati. He brought them around with the temptation of dividing the territory of Tonk under Amir Khan in proportion to their contribution in the ambitious campaign. While Amir Khan was in Marwar, his colleague Mookhtar-ood-Doula Mohummed Shah Khan was taking care of the Tonk region. He was not ready for Chaand Singh's sudden attack, which led to him seeking refuge in Amirgarh, the newly built fort of Amir Khan.

Chaand Singh was all out to clip the wings of Megh Singh Diggi, who was in league with Amir Khan, and accordingly, he laid the siege around the fort in Malpura where Megh Singh had taken refuge. Had there been no inner discord within the fleet of Chaand Singh, he probably would have been successful in his mission to get rid of Amir Khan. But with the useless and long siege of Malpura, resentment spread among the Shekhawati vassals who had come together with Chaand Singh only for containing Amir Khan and sharing his fortunes. They were not ready to stand together for too long and desired to abandon him. Megh Singh, on the other hand, sold off all his jewellery in a bid to pay tribute to Raja Bahadur Lal Singh and get the support of his troops to deal with the contingent of Chaand Singh.

Amir Khan too received the distress call from Mohammad Shah Khan, and he geared up all his resources, getting funds from Marwar to respond adequately. With Megh Singh Diggi already in action on the ground, Chaand Singh's men not only had to retreat but leave Jagat Singh's territory wide open for Amir Khan's tough counteraction. Some brigades reached Jobner, some Kalakh, while the fort of Beechun was seized. The year 1812 ended with mayhem in Jagat Singh's empire.

A Current of Change

The winter fog was dense that morning. Inside the palace, it was gloomy. Raskapoor, after contemplating the worries of her loved one, pulled him out to the terrace of Shobha Niwas. To cast away the gloom, she spontaneously announced, 'Maharajadhiraj, this change of the British calendar will certainly change the British attitude towards the princely states. Do you know the angrez sahibs changed their calendar only in the last century? My learned father had told me about it.' She burst out into echoing laughter as her lover wondered what was wrong with her.

Jagat Singh brushed aside her casual remark and shared his feelings indicative of his rather depressed state, 'Ras, I know you have been trying your best to keep me afloat while my empire is inundated with troubles. But I feel I am already in a sinking boat.'

Raskapoor smiled with an unusual calm on her face. 'First of all, the ruler of this empire has to rise above the negativity to look around and take note of what is happening elsewhere. A few months ago, the British signed a pact with the Prince of Baroda. I am sure Sahib Bahadur Minto's letters, as well as the news about the plunderers and continued campaigns, will force them to change their policy not only towards you but also Jodhpur and Udaipur. Who knows, they may even send a new Governor-General to introduce the new policy?' Raskapoor had changed from a seductive lover to a woman of substance, an astute ruler.

Jagat Singh was reminded of the rude comment of his vassals the time she rode with him on the elephant—'A concubine trying to be Empress Noor Jahan!' He imagined her as the incarnation of Noor Jahan—farsighted, fearless, forthright, and frank. Admiring her, he concluded—whether or not she was the incarnation of that powerful empress, he for sure was the incarnation of her doomed husband Emperor Jahangir!

Over a period of time, Raskapoor convinced him to yield to Amir Khan's terms to halt his frequent ravaging campaigns ever since the blunder committed by Chaand Singh in launching the attack on Tonk. She suggested this course of action when she saw the repeated requests for British support did not result in any deviation from the policy of non-interference. Knowing Amir Khan's unpredictable nature, she also brought up the subject of the two matrimonial alliances that were envisaged in order to find a truce with the ruler of Jodhpur, an ally of the predator Amir Khan.

Jagat Singh initiated the topic of the two marriages with Man Singh, according to which Jagat Singh's sister was to be married to Man Singh while Jagat Singh was to marry Man Singh's daughter. At his invitation, a high-level delegation arrived in Jai Nagar together with a priest in the summer of that year. The consensus was to arrange the two weddings without any gap because of the uncertainty all around. Both the priests and the vassals took considerable time in choosing the auspicious dates as well as the venues. All wished to avoid the month-long travel to and from Jodhpur. The weddings of the two Maharajas were bound to have much pomp and pageantry. Their being married many times before and also having several concubines did not seem to matter to both sides. Man Singh had thirteen queens and twelve concubines, but that did not bother the mother of the young princess. Similarly, Man Singh, the father of the girl who was to marry Jagat Singh, did not think twice, knowing fully well the overpowering presence of a concubine in Jagat's life, the queen of his half empire. Man Singh, to the contrary, was excited to think of the possibility the two weddings could extend to get a glimpse of the legendary Raskapoor.

The weddings were fixed for early September in the same year. As the auspicious dates necessitated, the weddings had to be solemnized back-to-back on 3 and 4 September. Accordingly, the two villages chosen for both the families to camp were at a short distance from each other. While the Jai Nagar entourage was to camp at Marwah, the Jodhpur contingent narrowed down on Roop Nagar. Man Singh was first to be married, followed by Jagat Singh's wedding on the very next day. The plan sent both the households into a tizzy. They had to quickly prepare for weddings, which were to be held away from their grand palaces.

Amir Khan came to know of the plan around the same time as he received a message from Jagat Singh to settle for peace. Among other conditions, Amir Khan asked for the removal of Chaand Singh from his post. Jagat Singh was reluctant, for his vassals were already resentful over the issue of appointments. Raskapoor noticed his dilemma over relieving the minister who caused such a devastating situation, that too acting on his own without the consent of the ruler himself. Finally, she convinced Jagat Singh to remove Chaand Singh for the time being, which would not only calm Amir down but also would be a strong lesson for him and the other vassals who chose to act against their Maharaja. He was removed from the job in July.

The news of the change in the British administration was also making waves, but the princely states of Rajputana remained more involved with the marriage of the two Maharajas. Raskapoor seemed to be the only one keen to remain informed about this. She indulged in conversations with her father occasionally to know the latest developments on that front as it impacted the fate of the struggling princely states. She was dismayed to hear the story of Lord Minto being recalled well before the date he had himself set, desiring to be discharged from his assignment in India. Back in London, the Prince Regent granted a special favour to his friend Lord Hastings to return to India, holding two positions—Governor-General and Commander-in-Chief. He was to arrive later in the year, but his appointment indicated change, and the alert Raskapoor caught it immediately.

Amidst preparations for the two grand marriages, Raskapoor often thought about the unfortunate princess of Mewar who could have been married to either of the two to-be-bridegrooms. She felt sad thinking about the tragic life of the princess, speculating whether her offenders even once thought of the girl who succumbed to death waiting for one of them to marry her. She wanted the marriage celebrations to be over quickly. Despite being asked by her lover to accompany him to Marwah, the venue for the Jai Nagar fleet, she opted out, for she knew the story of the ill-fated princess would haunt her. She saw Jagat Singh off with all her wishes to conclude the two marriages and return with positive energy.

As he was about to leave Ras Vilas, she took him by surprise. 'Don't you see changes coming in with the new Governor-General coming in earlier than the expected time?'

He hugged her. 'Ras, my love, I only thought of you when I first received that news, being reminded of our conversation on that winter morning when you talked about the change in the British policy and then about these weddings. I am going for this ritual only to fulfil your desire. All I need is you, Ras—I reiterate that fact once again.'

Pulling herself away from him, she advised him to only think of the weddings, clutching her veil to hide her tears. He saw Raskapoor attempting to hide her emotions. He stopped and said, 'Guess who is attending the two weddings? Your mission is accomplished so you can smile . . . Amir Khan will be attending both the weddings as the guest of the Maharaja of Jodhpur.' She flashed a big smile with the expression of a winner sparkling in her eyes. 'I knew that he would.'

Jagat Singh came back and hugged her again. 'I marvel at you for such insight into the complex politics of today. If I had my way, I would hand over my entire empire to you, and you could be a co-sovereign who I would have presented before the vassals; the very ones who announced, 'Here comes the Empress Noor Jahan of Jai Nagar!' They both chuckled, and Raskapoor turned him towards the door of Ras Vilas, saying, 'The to be son-in-law of the Jodhpur Maharaja must leave now.'

The Kachchwaha family left for Marwah in the last week of August, and so did the Rathore family, to reach Roop Nagar. Maharaja Man Singh, dressed as a bridegroom, arrived at Marwah in a grand procession. All the rituals were completed at a fast pace, as he was to be back for the wedding of his daughter the very next day. Man Singh was anxious, for one day he was the bridegroom and the very next day he had to welcome a bridegroom for his daughter!

Jagat Singh, on the other hand, was not anxious at all as he was not in the shoes of a father of the bride. He was a proud brother who was arranging the wedding of his sister with a Maharaja! When Jagat Singh sent Man Singh an invite to the exclusive mehfil, arranged only for his brother-in-law and Amir Khan, Man Singh was overcome with the idea of seeing the sensual beauty of Raskapoor, who had created a sensation across the land of Rajputana. He longed to get over with the wedding ritual so he could see and hear Raskapoor sing.

When the veiled singer entered and sat down, Man Singh's heart pounded, and he turned towards Jagat Singh. 'I was sure you would present your gem Raskapoor this evening. Shall I or will you request her to lift her veil?'

Jagat Singh surprised him with his reply, 'Never in my wildest dream would I present the queen of half of my empire in a mehfil. I have invited a beautiful tawaif Nawab Jaan from Oudh only for you and Janab Amir Khan, so you may ask her to lift the veil.'

Man Singh was stunned to hear the daring reply from the man who was going to marry his daughter in a few hours. It was too late for him to withdraw from that wedding alliance. With a heavy heart, the next day, he gave the hand of his daughter to the bridegroom Jagat Singh to complete the wedding ceremony.

Raskapoor restarted her search for her friend Rudra. With Chaand Singh being dislodged from his job, that too at her behest, she could not get him to even talk to her, forget about getting him to divulge any information of the search. Despite being neck-deep in the troubles of her lover, she worried about Rudra day in and day out. Raskapoor did not bring up the search operation with Jagat Singh, but that did not mean that she had abandoned her friend.

It was one of the days that she was returning after praying for the well-being of Rudra at the Govind Devji temple that she was stopped by Nadir Mohan Ram, the trusted eunuch and cunning detective of the zenani deorhi. He had seen her coming back to Ras Vilas from the terrace and hurried to strike up a conversation to share some juicy gossip, as he was feeling disenchanted at being left behind. He was quite excited to go for weddings, an exceptional time for eunuchs to receive lavish gifts. He was asked to stay back, especially to keep an eye on the movements of Raskapoor. He found nothing exciting in observing Ras Vilas as she remained indoors all through. Neither did she go out, nor did anyone come to visit her. That was the first time he saw her venturing out and decided to be respectful despite not considering her worthy of any respect.

He greeted her and asked, 'Has the Queen of Amber not been well? Today is the first day when I have seen you come out.' Raskapoor realized immediately that he had been left behind to spy on her. Mohan Ram did not let the opportunity for conversation slip away. He inquired about her mother as well as her friend Rudra. Raskapoor was amused to see that the eunuch even knew about Rudra.

'We knew how he helped you raise your army at Amber. Why does he not come here when you are alone and need company?'

Mohan Ram's question indicated that he did have some information on the missing Rudra, and the conversation was manipulated to share that information. Maintaining her calm, she told him that she had no news about her friend since she sent him with a message to Marwar.

Mohan Ram took a moment. 'Oh! That day he could not even cross the border of our territory.' Raskapoor was eager to know more, but Mohan Ram could only tell her that Chaand Singh Dooni and his men blocked her messenger service. Raskapoor wanted to know what happened to the messengers who never returned.

'Some were done to death while the others were tortured in hidden cells,' Mohan Ram replied. He could not tell her on which list Rudra was. Raskapoor was left with the dilemma over his being alive, dead or even half dead. Deeply pained, she made a promise to herself not to leave the world without knowing what happened to Rudra on that fateful day.

Mid-September, the wedding parties returned to their respective palaces. The big news to travel beyond Rajputana was the growing influence of Amir Khan, who was not only cordially invited to both the weddings but was even seated alongside the Maharaja Sawai Jagat Singh of Jai Nagar. The seating arrangement raised his status, being considered at par with the Maharaja. Bapuji Scindia, the arch-rival of Amir Khan was alerted by that news and decided not to leave the field open for him being a stakeholder himself. He chose to undertake an expedition to Jagat Singh's territory.

In early October, Lord Moira, later Marquess of Hastings, took charge in Bengal as the Governor-General and the Commander in Chief. Minto left for London, but the princely states felt that his repeated representations in favour of granting British protection to them, even though they did not succeed, had at least prepared the ground for the British to finally give up the policy of non-intervention. Lord Moira was new in the office, and he began to assess the chaotic situation all over the territory he had been given the charge of. In any case, he was never in favour of Wellesley's expansion plans forging alliances of protection. He had landed in India with the same view, not anticipating that it would be sooner rather than later that he would himself have to change his stance. Post the two weddings, and the appointment of the new Governor-General, one would have expected to diffuse the ever-present threat of the freebooters Scindia, Holkar, Pindari and the trickster Pathan.

On the other hand, Raskapoor expected the weddings would take away the focus of the zenani deorhi and the vassals from conspiring against her. The zenani deorhi, however, was hoping against hope to see the change in Jagat Singh's attitude and that he would overcome his obsession for Raskapoor after the significant wedding alliance that had recently taken place. All those women were proven wrong once again. When Jagat Singh hastened to Ras Vilas longing to see Raskapoor and visited his queens very rarely after that, they renewed their vow with a fresh determination to get rid of her.

Ambiguity All Around

If there was anything certain in Rajputana, it was the uncertainty. Things changed within minutes, and troubles could emerge from any side at any hour. No one knew who a friend was and who a foe was. It was not long ago when Jagat Singh thought that the two weddings would at least keep Amir Khan quiet, but again he started harassing Jagat Singh. Amir wanted him to pay a fixed amount early in the year 1814 to get his encroached territory back and see the military post removed. Jagat Singh was unable to hold the two ends of the long rope of troubles. While he was busy with Amir Khan, he completely overlooked the troubles coming from the Marathas.

Assessing, based on rumours that the British were inclined to offer protection to Jagat Singh, a letter was sent to Metcalfe by Bapuji Scindia warning against any treaty with Jagat Singh. The instigator of that letter was none other than Amir Khan. Bapuji Scindia ravaged Jai Nagar as well as levied a collection from the fort. Early that year, Lord Moira realized the inadequacy of the British policy of non-intervention as he recorded that the bands of Amir Khan were the special 'scourge of Rajpootana'. He even figured out that it was with the secret support of Scindias and Holkars that the Pindaris were becoming daredevils as they undertook their campaigns of dacoity.

271

In June, finally, the order was received in Calcutta advising Lord Moira to take Jagat Singh under British protection. Still, he was not willing to take the step in isolation, settling on one princely state only, given the requests received from other princely states too. He also knew that such an action would result in hostility from the Marathas, which would distract him from the campaign to contain the Gorkhas of Nepal who had encroached upon the territory of Oudh.

Mired in the uncertainty of British support, Jagat Singh was unable to keep an eye on what was transpiring between his queens and the vassals against Raskapoor. She herself was so overtaken by the twists and turns of the politics of the state that for the first time, she kept herself totally aloof from the intrigues of the ladies' chambers. She was more worried about the life of her lover than her own, which did not seem to matter to her at all in any case ever since she entered his life. She was aware of the omnipresent death threat in the palace environs, which were wrapped in intrigues and jealousy. The Chief Queen had conducted several rounds of meetings with the vassals already known to be anti-Raskapoor.

Dooni Thakur, who was once again feeling insulted at the behest of the concubine, together with the Thakurs of Samode, Chomu and Bagru, undertook the mission to bring other vassals on their side. Over the months, they were able to win over many other vassals like that of Jhilay, Achrol, Dudu and Neendad, to name a few. They then got hold of Megh Singh Diggi and convinced him that Raskapoor was the one who opposed his suggestion to pay Amir Khan in one instalment, which was what finally resulted in his dismissal. Megh Singh forgot his differences with the vassal of Dooni, who had laid the siege against him and joined hands to remove the concubine who they thought was determined to rip the vassals of their honour. They took a pledge to remove the lowly concubine who was behaving like Empress Noor Jahan and was even bestowed with the title of 'Ardharajan'—queen of half the empire. It disgusted them to see that Raskapoor was the only concubine in whose name a coin was struck, equating her with the Moghul Empress Noor Jahan, the only other woman to get that honour. They could not fathom the Maharaja's idea of bringing a concubine at par with the empress.

In their several meetings, another sinful idea reappeared—her alleged illicit relationships with many men, including Amir Khan, who was attacking time and again. One of the vassals tried to object to that idea as they had no evidence to prove that allegation. Chaand Singh silenced him. 'We can create not one but many pieces of evidence and also easily produce an eye-witness against a concubine, even when we know it is a false allegation.'

The whole of the year 1814 was spent coming up with a fool-proof conspiracy. The zenana was also successful in mustering the support of the much-respected Raja Khushaliram Bohra, who was replaced by Pandit Shiv Narain. Together they decided to launch a non-cooperation and disobedience movement against Prime Minister Mishra to make him redundant in the administration. This led to him losing all control over the administration, leading to a financial mess. He was a simple Brahmin, not a crook, and all his wisdom could not keep him away from the wicked plans of the crafty vassals. Many times he considered resigning, but his wisdom made him refrain from doing so, worried that it may somehow incriminate him as the guilty party, and the false allegations would be proven right.

But it came to be nonetheless. He was falsely implicated in glaring financial embezzlements by some of the officials. When Jagat Singh doubted his integrity, the self-respecting Brahmin chose to die rather than live a life of humiliation. On the night of 15 September 1815, Pandit Shiv Narain swallowed a lethal powder, which some ignorant vassals concluded to be a crushed diamond, not realizing that swallowing a diamond could not be fatal. Raskapoor was devasted to hear the news of the tragic demise of her father. She knew he was not guilty. How powerful and corrupt office bearers had proved an innocent person guilty so conveniently, nauseated her and she rushed to the terrace to throw up. She cried and felt guilty herself, for had she not proposed his name as Bohraji's successor, he would not have been subjected to such humiliation.

All said and done, she realized that his presence in the palace had lent her invisible protection. They hardly ever got to meet all through his tenure as the prime minister. Still, on those rare occasions when they met and had a conversation, he guided her with words of wisdom to survive in a world where everyone was hell-bent on eliminating her. Just a few days before committing suicide, he had chosen to visit her at Shobha Vilas, as Ras Vilas was out of bounds for any man other than Jagat himself. The meeting was granted on the pretext of the serious health condition of her mother, whom Raskapoor had not seen for a long time. In that last meeting, Pandit Shiv Narain asked her to be prepared for the worst kind of allegations, which could even lead to her character assassination, and cause a falling out of favour with her ardent lover, the Maharaja, as well as cost her life.

He was the messenger between her and the mother, who she hardly met despite the tunnel connecting her home with the palace. Raskapoor often did want to visit her mother but heeded the guidance sent by her. Chaand had advised Mishraji to convince her daughter that she must remain close to the Maharaja as a shadow and to nurture the bond with Jagat Singh by showering all her love and warmth. Raskapoor was reassured about one fact: that her mother would never be left alone by her lover, who had given her a word of honour even in the last conversation she had with him. Alerting his daughter on her vulnerability in the palace one last time before leaving, Mishraji repeated his commitment to look after her mother. His last words were haunting her, 'Ras, you do not worry about Ammi. I am there for her. When the situation is right, I will myself take you to Ammi.' That day never came.

While she had lost her father, her mother had lost the man of her life. She knew it well deep down that in their hearts was the love for each other, which could not be made public, in keeping with the norms and traditions. Mourning her father's sudden demise, she could feel the loss of her mother. With Mishraji gone, her mother would be devastated. She yearned to spend a couple of days with her heartbroken mother, but before she could plan to leave the palace, Jagat Singh relayed the news of the sudden death of her mother, conveyed to him by the priest of the Gupteshwar Temple. Chaand had not taken a drop of water ever since the news of her lover's suicide. Within five days of Mishraji's death, Chaand too left this world. Jagat Singh coordinated her visit to the glass palace with the group of priests who also performed the last rites of the mother. With tears in her eyes, she asked them, 'Can my mother now not be respected as a Sati who left this world soon after her lover's death? Will she still be rundown and called a "tawaif"?'

Ammi had chosen to leave this world the moment she got news of the demise of her soulmate, not taking a morsel of food and a drop of water. According to both their faiths, their souls were in transition to the other world at the same time even if they left their mortal remains on different days.' The priests were dumbfounded with those logical questions and unbelievable power of reasoning. While disappearing in the tunnel on her way back, she felt that with both her parents gone, the glass palace had come crumbling down. She could hear the echoing sound of breaking pieces in her brain, and to escape from that deafening noise, she sped up towards the palace, walking miles away from her home with the decision never to return.

For days together, Raskapoor speculated why a man with such wisdom, and who was innocent, could not defend himself. In her conversation with the Maharaja after the traumatic death of her father, she defended him, 'I will tell you that I can vouch for his honesty. He neither had a lust to defraud the state treasury nor any political aspirations like many of your vassals, who given an opportunity, could even take over your throne. You may not believe me today, but someday you will, when my prayers will be answered by the almighty to give you the power to see the truth.'

Raskapoor's words made Jagat Singh review the events of the past few days. He said, 'Ras, I am in a situation where I may even suspect my own shadow. I tried not to doubt Shiv Narain Ji initially, but not a single voice spoke in his favour. Believe me, his death deeply saddens me. In my wildest dreams, I could not imagine that he would commit suicide. Tell me what I can do now to pull you out from this agony?' Raskapoor, who was determined to settle scores with the treacherous fleet, which led to her father's death, did not take a minute to reply, 'Declare his son to be the next successor.' Her instant advice did not come out of any merit but sheer defiance against her father's adversaries, who led him to the path of suicide. She was burning with anger and pain, unable to figure out how a spiritual man of his calibre could decide to take his life. The daughter saw them as murderers who had ganged up, leaving no option for him. What made her blood boil was their insinuating theory of Mishraji being mentally ill of late. Their crocodile tears and meaningless words of mourning at the sudden and unthinkable demise could not absolve them of their collective crime. When Jagat Singh shared their grief with his lover, she wanted to argue with him that those who wished to eliminate her father succeeded in their conspiracy and must be celebrating instead. She knew it well the smart vassals had not killed him so could not be accused of any crime. The only way she saw to take her revenge was to block them with the appointment of the person they would not have dreamt of.

Jagat Singh was at first a bit surprised at her suggestion of bringing in an inexperienced young man for such an important job but then accepted her suggestion. Ganesh Narain's appointment put aside the claim of many powerful men, causing deep resentment in Jagat Singh's administration. But the crafty vassals believed that when the father could not stand their challenge, the son would not last long either.

Part Three

Camphor Extinguished

Treaty and Treachery

Amidst brewing tensions and conspiracies, Jagat Singh's territory was once again ravaged by the men of Amir Khan. He chose to remain in Jodhpur but sent his three armies to do the deed, as Resident Metcalfe reported on 15 October. Amir Khan had thrown away even the brotherly relationship with Man Singh, whom he had taken as his *pagadibadal bhai*, someone with whom he traditionally exchanged headgear in a sign denoting brotherhood. Jodhpur and Man Singh were also witnessing severe turbulence as the districts of Jagat Singh's empire were plundered. Vassals both in Jodhpur and Jaipur were conniving against their rulers. Man Singh's own queen was up in arms against him, together with their only son Chhatar Singh and the vassals antagonized by Man Singh's diwan Indraraj and his guru Deo Nath who were in control of the administration. Indebted for his throne to Ayas Deo Nath, Man Singh went to all lengths to express his gratitude to the spiritual master. The guru had advised Man Singh against leaving the Jalore Fort for a few more days, after which he would be led to the throne. The advice came true—the road to the throne became easy because of the sudden demise of Maharaja Bhim Singh, and Man Singh since remained in awe of the guru.

The spiritual master within no time owned more land than the vassals and turned into the 'sovereign's sovereign', provoking the ruler's family as well as the vassals. In the second half of 1815,

when Amir Khan arrived demanding that Man Singh pay the big
amount due after the war with Jaipur, Man Singh was unable to
meet it with the available resources. Amir Khan then pressurized
him for parts of the territory of Marwar. He was refused point-
blank by the arrogant Indraraj, the other man who commanded
the reins of the state along with the guru.

Seeing the internal disputes, Amir Khan chose to strike an
alliance with the rebellious queen. In return for a handsome
amount, Amir Khan got Man Singh's two trusted men, Indraraj
and the guru, murdered right under his nose in the fort. His
Afghan soldiers killed the two men just five days before Metcalf's
report on the three armies of Amir Khan holding Jagat Singh's
districts at ransom. Man Singh at that time was in Moti Mahal,
and was so outraged with the murder of his close associates that
he lifted his sword intending to charge at the murderers, but his
vassals stopped him, fearing for his life. The loss of his spiritual
master made Man Singh lose his mental control and he was unable
to continue administrating the affairs of the state. He could not
seem to focus on anything apart from talking about his guru. He
chose Gulraj, the brother of the slain prime minister, to be his
diwan. In Sawai Jaipur, too, the situation was turning from bad
to worse with violent dissent among the vassals who had initially
gathered to defend the territory of their ruler. Raskapoor knew
that the two-wedding alliance, which she had brought up again,
was not going to come to the rescue of Jagat Singh in view of
Man Singh's mental condition as well as the state of affairs in
Jodhpur. A question often haunted her. Was it divine justice that
the two states were being accorded, having brought such a tragic
end to Princess Krishna Kumari? She was at a loss as to why the
stars were not favouring any of her well-thought-out ideas like
pursuing the two weddings and the appointment of Pandit Shiv
Narain Mishra as the prime minister.

Amir Khan's recent actions in Jodhpur were enough to
conclude that man could never be trusted. Each time, the actor
in Amir Khan successfully manipulated the previously duped
support-seeker, dispelling all doubts and winning his full trust. He
was indeed the real 'Thug of Hindoostan' who could deceive the

sharpest of the sharp minds. The British saw him as a tool to deal with the princely states of Rajputana instead of ensuring peace in the region. Despite not being in support of British protection, Raskapoor started longing to salvage Sawai Jaipur from its present state, mulling over all the possibilities to strengthen the resources of the state. Raskapoor observed the situations and circumstances, both within the palace and all over his empire. She was able to feel the impact of the state of affairs, which was making her lover increasingly suspicious and irritable by the day. He was becoming vulnerable to conspiracies and deceit like the false allegations against the late prime minister, who unfortunately did not survive the dishonour. She thanked her gods each day for his love and respect towards her amidst such stressful environs. She knew that stress could make him turn his back on her. She was not worried about herself, but she was concerned about him, who was destined to be betrayed if she was not around. She had no other desire but the welfare of Sawai Jaipur and Jagat Singh. Wrapped in apprehensions about the future of the dream city of Sawai Jai Singh, Raskapoor persuaded her lover to come for a walk on the terrace of Shobha Niwas. They both witnessed a beautiful sunset.

Raskapoor lifted her index finger and asked him smilingly what it was.

'A finger,' he replied. Then she lifted her middle finger, then the ring finger, and then the small finger one by one asking the same question. Finally, she closed all the fingers together tightly and asked him the same question.

'A fist,' replied the intrigued ruler.

'So, tell me, will a finger have more power or a fist?' Raskapoor posed the question with a serious note.

'Obviously, Ras, the fist. You cannot ask a Rajput a question about physical power,' Jagat Singh replied with arrogance.

'Indeed! Then why can the rulers of the princely states and your fiefs not come together? Why do you Rajput men not see that you will emerge as a force to reckon with and free the land from the plunderers, without requiring British support? May I warn you that the day the princely states sign the treaty with the foreigners, they will lose their independence and one day may even cease to exist?' Raskapoor's response resonated with conviction, which Jagat Singh was unable to appreciate. He walked inside to sit for drinks. Outside, gazing at the silhouette of Sudarshangarh, she feared that Khan's aspirations to take over the princely states of Rajputana could materialize if he got a free hand.

Early in the year 1816, Jagat Singh renewed the solicitations for protection. The Earl of Moira could well appreciate the dire circumstances of Jagat Singh. That his state was on the verge of complete ruination became apparent, as the envoy sent by Jagat Singh to Metcalfe conveyed the willingness of his ruler to accede to any terms of the British in return for much-needed protection. He spelt out all possible options: offering the maximum tribute as per their resources—territorial rights anywhere in the empire, right to manage the entire territory, a free hand in appointing the ministers, total obedience as well as subservience of the court—all of which meant mortgaging the empire. The home government was already realizing the inadequacy of their policy of non-intervention ever since the publication of Malcolm's book *Sketch of the Political History of India*, but they were holding on to it with the fear of Napoleon's suspected intentions of entering India. In 1813, however, Napoleon was defeated by the coalition in the Battle of Leipzig, which gave some peace of mind to them to review the situation in India. Finally, when in June 1815, Napoleon's downfall came with the defeat in the Battle of Waterloo, the British were in a position to give up the policy of non-intervention pursued for a decade despite several requests made by various princely states.

Even then, the Earl of Moira waited to take up those requests as well as the advice received from London until the engagement with the Gorkhas of Nepal was over. In March, the Gorkha war got over, and Moira reviewed the request of Sawai Jaipur first as he was himself alarmed at the growing strength of Amir Khan. He realized he needed to keep him in check without any further delay. A treaty with Jagat Singh's state would give him the right to station his troops there. Lord Moira observed the quality of the army led by Amir Khan. He wrote that it was 'the best army in India next to our own'. He even feared that the army of Amir Khan would join Scindia, with whom the Pathan was bidding to establish a close relationship.

On 20 April 1816, three letters were issued, showing the importance of the treaty with Sawai Jaipur. The Governor-General wrote to the Governor of Bombay, 'The repeated solicitations of the Raja of Jyepur to be received under the protection of the British Government having recently been renewed with the augmented earnestness and the general situation of our affairs appearing to be favourable for carrying into effect the instructions, which this government has received from the Hon'ble secret committee for negotiating a treaty with the state of Jyepur, we have instructed the Resident of Delhi to commence negotiations with the Raja.' Resident Metcalfe was instructed on 20 April, and the same day Major General Ochterlony was advised to advance towards Jaipur with a clear-cut message for Amir Khan to withdraw from Jaipur peacefully or face the wrath of war. Alongside, the ruler of Jaipur was to be convinced that the British had come only to rescue him after his repeated requests. The treaty, as intended by the Governor-General, had to appear as an exceptional favour granted by the English to Jagat Singh. It could, however, not be concluded due to the delay on the part of Jagat Singh.

Terrible troubles once again hit Jaipur on the home front. Ganesh Narain, as expected by all except Raskapoor, was made to bow down amidst the severe opposition of all landlords barring Abhai Singh of Khetri. Humiliated, Ganesh Narain decided to group the men who had suffered similar treatment, which included Abhai Singh as well as Manjee Das Purohit, who was first moved out as diwan and then as the commander of the military. They decided to begin their aggression starting with the territory of Rao Raja Laxman Singh, who led the campaign against Abhai Singh. The territory of Sikar saw the wrath of the group of men enraged by their ruler. Such was the severity of the prolonged mayhem caused there that all the landlords gathered to collectively seek Jagat Singh's intervention and call for a special session of the royal court. Raskapoor's sixth sense alarmed her about the terrible consequences of the revolt led by Ganesh Narain that she would have to face if the court was held, being the one who nominated him as the successor.

On the designated day, all Thakurs in one voice solicited for an armed response to crush the violent raiders. Jagat Singh was compelled to give the go-ahead to take much-desired action under the command of Chaand Singh Dooni. Being dead set against the concubine, whom he held responsible for the unforgettable public insult he had undergone, he used the assigned responsibility to get revenge. He opined that such revolts, as well as the attacks of Amir Khan, were a part of a secret design of someone very close to the Maharaja who was aspiring to dethrone him. The team of landlords under Chaand Singh departed after this singular pronouncement, leaving Jagat Singh to worry about the insider who was planning to take the crown from him.

Often, he wondered if his empire would face troubles over ascendancy in the eventuality of the success of those designs. God blessed him with not one but three sons, but all three passed away as infants. He was totally devastated when his fourth son died during delivery. Jagat Singh's son, born of a concubine too, died early. The only surviving child was a daughter born of another concubine, but she could in no way become his successor. Raskapoor tried to give him solace each time when he despaired over the issue of his successor, 'Why do you worry? You are young, Maharajadhiraj, and life is not over for you. Your beautiful wives are young too, and capable of bearing a child. When I chose not to have a child of my own, I prayed for an heir apparent for you. That is the only boon I have been praying for every day. I am more than sure you will have your bloodline succeed even if you do not have the fortune to see him. Do not fear death, for who knows you may even be blessed with a posthumous son. No one can foretell what lies in store. I have heard of such instances from my father.'

Jagat Singh saw a ray of hope in her words and admired her selfless soul. He even questioned her about the insider who could be staging a coup, but Raskapoor chose to avoid answering those questions. She saw each day passing by as the grace of god, as she knew that her days were numbered in the palace. Raskapoor could foresee that sooner rather than later, she would be accused of being the mastermind behind all the troubles of the empire. Chaand Singh and company returned as the victorious fleet, having not only crushed the revolution but taking the main players as prisoners. The campaign to find the real culprit was taken up with all enthusiasm. Chaand Singh convened a private meeting with the vulnerable Jagat Singh to reveal the name of the mastermind. They sat over drinks in Shobha Niwas, and Chaand Singh divulged the name. Jagat Singh was stunned. 'Are you naming Raskapoor because you have been against her right from day one? I cannot believe this at all, for Ardhrajan, the queen of half my empire, has never expressed her desire to be a queen. If for once she desired it, I would be the first one to bestow that honour. I see her as the most capable person among all of us to take the reins of the empire in such difficult circumstances.'

Chaand Singh, maintaining his calm, smilingly responded, 'I knew you would never believe me, for you have loved that manipulating concubine with such honesty. If you set aside your love and see the real reason behind raising the army and review her so-called friendship with her lover Rudra, with whom she was seen till late at night many a time while you were away to Jodhpur, you will know that there is a hidden agenda. Now also reconsider the suggestion of the name of Shiv Narain to be the prime minister and then inexperienced young Ganesh Narain in the circumstances where one of us would have been the right choice. I have questioned my two prisoners Ganesh Narain and Manjee Das Purohit separately and they both informed me that they acted at the behest of Raskapoor. I also questioned Rodaram Khawas, the chief of the Amber army, who informed me that her plan behind raising the army was to attack Jaipur along with Amir Khan. Do remember that, like most concubines, she too has a mixed lineage, which encourages a different bond with Amir Khan. Finally, as we all know the life of an illegitimate girl child born of a concubine only shapes with the lust for power, be it men or money. These women maintain a highly deceptive appearance and can end up playing a wicked role, just like Raskapoor. If you do not wake up now, we will be forced to restore the prestige of our empire, which may even make you hand over the reins to one of us as a last resort.'

Chaand Singh had used a double edge sword to cut the roots of Raskapoor, deeply entrenched in Jagat Singh's life. He had wickedly sown the seeds of suspicion as well as threatened him with a bid to snatch the reins of power if he did not take action against his lover. As he was leaving the premises, he once again reminded the Maharaja to take up the impeachment of Raskapoor. He made it a point to initiate the proceedings without any delay as her activities were tantamount to treason, and she deserved to face trial as a traitor. Jagat Singh consented to start proceedings against her on the condition to produce Rudra in the court as well, as he was rather concerned about her illicit relationship. Chaand Singh sidelined that demand by questioning whether Jagat Singh's priority was his empire's safety or the loyalty of a concubine.

Having kindled the spark of patriotism, Chaand Singh smartly manoeuvred to first proceed with the charges of the treason, while the charge of infidelity could be withheld till the time Rudra was traced. He knew that the punishment for a traitor was a death sentence and in such an eventuality, it did not matter if the charge of infidelity was proven or not. He also knew full well that there was no way to produce Rudra alive or dead in the court. How could he confess that the mortal remains of Rudra were given to a sadhu leaving for Banaras to consign in the holy Ganges? How could he tell them that when he was on his way to Jodhpur with the message of Raskapoor for Jagat Singh they had taken Rudra into custody and locked him up in the basement of his own house? How could he tell him he and the Chief Queen tried for days to convince Rudra to acknowledge the illicit relationship with Raskapoor if he wanted to be set free? How could he tell him that after the idealist Brahmin turned down their offer, he succumbed to their torture tactics just a few months ago? Walking out of the palace, Rudra's last words echoed in his head, 'Yes, I have loved her deeply, and so did she; but she was taken away. She never looked back and remained committed to the Maharaja. We have a spiritual connection, and our relationship is beyond your understanding. I know my Ras, who longed to be with me just as much as I did, but she detests infidelity, which is very much an accepted feature of your lifestyle. I am happy to die protecting the honour of Raskapoor, who you may eliminate, but will not be able to erase from the history of your empire.'

Both Jagat Singh and Chaand Singh remained wide awake all night, filled with anxiety over the proceeding of impeachment and the treacherous plan respectively. On the following morning, when Raskapoor entered his chamber with divine offerings, without looking at her, he announced, 'Raskapoor, go back to Ras Vilas and appear in the royal court when you are summoned for the hearing on the case against you.'

Raskapoor turned back without questioning him on the proposed proceedings. The hours-long private conversation the Maharaja had with Chaand Singh indicated serious troubles ahead for her. From the beginning, he had resented her presence in the palace. Soon the proceedings began, and Raskapoor was made to stand in the dock. She was surprised first to hear the charges against her alleging a plan to dethrone her lover and become a ruler herself, and then on seeing the first witness.

It was Ganesh Narain Mishra, who was appointed as the successor of Pandit Shiv Narain on her recommendation. He did not have any consideration for the innocent woman standing in front of him as he stated, 'I was instigated to organize a revolt creating mayhem in Sikar by Ardhrajan Raskapoor. When she called me the first time to suggest such a plan, I tried to plead with her not to create unrest in the empire, which was already under attack from Amir Khan, another freebooter. She did not listen to me and instead lured me by assuring me of a lucrative assignment in her regime. She talked about the army raised under Rodaram Khawas to take over the empire. She even boasted of her close relationship with Amir Khan, but I dared not ask her what she meant by "close relationship".' He finished giving his testimony with a suggestive smile.

Raskapoor was asked if she had anything to say in her defence, but she declined. She was deeply hurt by her ardent lover asking her to stand in the dock instead of being her advocate. A fool-proof case was prepared with the definite intention to proclaim her guilty. Her self-esteem made her remain silent instead of being humiliated publicly. She knew it well that her rivals would leave no opportunity to mock her, twisting her words. Rodaram Khawas, Manjee Das Purohit and some others rounded up compromised witnesses who spoke against her at length on each day of the proceeding, and Raskapoor continued to decline to speak a word in her defence, not even asking anyone to defend her. Choosing to be absent while being present, the accused stood like a beautiful statue and the accusers could not help but be in awe of her beauty and graceful presence. Many of them, after the day-long hearing, wished the proceedings to continue longer to continue to get the pleasure of looking at her. Raskapoor's stance to not make any attempt to defend herself was taken advantage of by her adversaries led by Chaand Singh. When he sat with the ruler for drinks, he elaborated upon her treacherous crime, not giving him any space or time to suspend the trial against the concubine. Each day, he convinced him that despite being given the option to defend herself, an intelligent woman of her calibre was remaining tight-lipped only because there was no way out for her, having committed such a grave crime. Those late-night sessions ended with one closing statement, 'An innocent accused would leave no stone unturned in defending themselves!'

On the final day, the verdict was announced, declaring Raskapoor guilty. She was given a death sentence, which was converted to life imprisonment on account of her being a woman. She was ordered to be exiled in the prisoner's cell in Sudarshangarh, the fort overlooking the city. As decided, the guards came to take her to her cell before sunrise the following morning. She chose to dress in a saffron robe, which she had got for the occasion during the days of the proceedings. All she packed were three sets of this attire and the statues of all her gods and goddesses, including the ones she had carried from the Kaanch Mahal, her late mother's home. Raskapoor spent all night carefully displaying all the jewellery and the vibrant clothes presented by her lover. She put a big lock on Ras Vilas, handing over the key to her trusted maid to give to the Maharaja well after daybreak. As there was no other way to reach the destination, she was sent in a palanquin. Crossing the thick forest, she reflected on her journey from Kaanch Mahal to Sudarshangarh. Strangely enough, she had no hatred for her lover who fell for the baseless allegations; instead, she felt sorry for the mental state that led him to prosecute her and then award such a punishment. She did not grieve over her unjust conviction and smiled inwardly, recounting the moments of ecstasy he showered only on her and not on any of his queens. She reflected on his survival amidst the exceptional political circumstances. She worried about him, for, with her out of his life, he had lost not only a selfless lover but a true friend. Her heart went out to the man who would one day hold himself guilty for the unjust conviction of a woman who had nothing to take but only love to give. She prayed to the almighty to protect the ruler and his empire. Jagat Singh, after announcing the verdict, locked himself up in Shobha Niwas, not willing to see his love leaving the palace as a betrayer. He drank and drank till the goblet fell out of his hand, and he gradually slid onto the mattress in an inebriated state.

When the sound of the city echoed in Jagat Singh's ears, he woke up to a different morning, unable to forget the stoic expression of his love in the dock. He was at a loss as to why she chose to not defend herself. Her silence had driven him so crazy that he wanted to shake her and force her to speak up at least one last time. He hurriedly summoned the maid to ask if the lady had already left.

'Not only has she left, but she has left this key for you after locking Ras Vilas,' the maid said, handing over the key with a smile. Jagat Singh took the key and quickly rushed towards the apartment he had built for the only love of his life. As he opened the door, he was hit by the glare of all those precious ornaments he had bestowed upon her. He glanced around carefully and realized that she had left everything behind, save for the statues of her gods and goddesses. Jagat Singh broke down into tears, for somewhere deep down in his heart, he felt that he had inflicted a great injustice on an innocent woman. But it was too late for him to undo what was done. With all his vassals on one side, he could not dare to defy them and overturn the verdict. While the conviction of Raskapoor was celebrated in the zenani deorhi all the way to the havelis of the Thakurs, there were many among the subjects of Jagat Singh who were saddened by the verdict. They could see what their ruler could not—the truth! The wickedness of the Thakurs and the role of the witnesses who gave false statements under oath remained a talking point for weeks together.

Life after the Impeachment

Just after Raskapoor's conviction, Amir Khan launched a fierce attack on Sawai Jaipur. Manjee Das was rewarded with the position of diwan after the proceedings against Raskapoor, but Ganesh Narain was not as lucky. He was not rewarded for playing a key role in making the false allegations; instead, he was punished. Amir Khan had closed in till Jagatpura, forcing Diwan Manjee Das Purohit to gather Jaipur's forces under the protection of the Moti Doongri fort. The unrelenting Pathan mounted pressure to reclaim his pending amount. Focusing on the administration of his empire, Jagat Singh refused to pay off Amir Khan. Once again, he renewed talks with the British for the alliance. He sent Purohit to negotiate with the Resident in Delhi.

The news of the favourable attitude of the British towards Jagat Singh had reached even Amir Khan, and he feared the arrival of the British army to drive him out. In the meanwhile, Amir Khan received a very emotional plea from none other than Man Singh's daughter Sireh Kanwar. She addressed him as her uncle, for he had forged a brotherly relationship with her father by exchanging turbans with him. He was already contemplating lifting the siege because the forces of Jaipur foiled his every attack, and her message made him take the decision. Amir Khan was frustrated not to see the envisaged outcome of his fierce campaign and chose to step back in July 1816. Interestingly, the Jaipur camp considered his decision to be their victory.

As the siege was lifted, the momentum for striking an alliance with the British declined. Moira, too, chose not to pursue the negotiations seeing no imminent danger to the Jaipur empire combined with the indifference shown by Jagat Singh towards the negotiations. However, much as everyone was thrilled with the deemed victory, Prime Minister Manjee Das remained worried about Amir Khan's attacks, which continued off and on. He suggested to the Wakils to convince Metcalfe to send an 'English Gentleman' to Sawai Jaipur to show the seriousness of the British intent in extending the much-deferred protection. Metcalfe, who was a supporter of the treaty of protection, did not concede to the suggestion, which according to him, was also proposed as a measure to keep Amir Khan away from the Jaipur empire. He saw it as just another bid to keep the British in the loop without being committed to negotiating the treaty, as indicated by the indifference shown towards British overtures.

Manjee Das decided to send the reliable banker of the empire, Shankar Das, to start the talk of an alliance with the resident in Delhi. Metcalfe spelt out the terms of the tribute and compensation to the British for all the arrangements. They asked for an exorbitant sum of Rs 25 lakh initially, which was negotiated for days together. In the end, Metcalfe proposed Rs 10 lakh, but the negotiating team from Jaipur asked for the restoration of Tonk and Rampura, which at that time were with Amir Khan, courtesy of Yashwant Rao Holkar. The British refusal led to yet another breakdown in negotiations.

After the retreat of Amir Khan, Jagat Singh regained some degree of confidence in his team and let them deal with the negotiations with the British as well as take care of the day-to-day administration. He did take an interest in the administration more than before because Raskapoor had pleaded with him to do so. But nothing seemed to hold his interest or give him a purpose in his life. He was not at peace with himself since the conviction of

Raskapoor. He was lonely and restless. Not a single day passed without him feeling the urge to bring her back into his life, even if it meant a review trial where he would stand up in her defence. The void left behind by her was getting deeper and deeper, and inwardly he was drowning in it.

He was on the terrace at dawn and dusk, gazing at Sudarshangarh Fort, knowing that her cell in the basement did not even have a window to be able to see him yearning for her. Had it not been for the stern warning from the group of his vassals to dislodge him if he kept in touch with Raskapoor, he would have surely made not one but several trips there. He was not even allowed to venture into the forest under the pretext of his favourite sport, hunting. Fearing the lure of the concubine, Chaand Singh Dooni had kept strict vigilance over his daily routine. To keep him engaged in sensual pleasures, he even went to the extent of inviting some well-known nautch girls, but none could win over Jagat Singh. Lonesome as he was, he decided to serve Lord Krishna and his lover Radha following the footsteps of Raskapoor as he embellished the temple of Brij Bihariji, the only building he had got constructed in his lifetime. He went there every day, yet could not find the solace that he was in search of. It intrigued him how his lover showed no fear of death facing the trial, remaining stoic all through the bitter proceedings while he, the ruler of the big empire hailing from a warrior clan, was overtaken by the fear of his death. Fear struck Jagat Singh in his heart, and he could not sleep soundly since her conviction, often waking up at even the slightest sound. Lying awake in his bed, he longed for that deep and tranquil sleep, which he rejoiced in with the warmth of her arms around him. There was unrest both within himself and in his empire.

Knowing that Manjee Das was following up on the negotiations for British protection, Amir Khan saw the possibility of a treaty in near sight. He chose to once again advance towards Jaipur. On the other side, petty jealousies among the feudal lords reared their ugly heads once again—there were those within Jagat Singh's administration who were actively conspiring to remove Manjee Das himself. Some vassals were all ready to approach the British to remove not only Purohit but also place a new team as they suggested, which in turn would help them to take over command from Jagat Singh. There was desperation all around, leading to entangling and contradictory moves, evoking more suspicion. So much so, that the British forces began suspecting that the Jaipur court was negotiating with the perpetrator Amir Khan while being in talks with the Resident in Delhi. But Metcalfe was not interested in getting involved with the infights of the Jaipur court. In February 1817, the Earl of Moira was upgraded to the position of the Marquess of Hastings. Encouraged by his success in Nepal and being rewarded for it, Hastings decided to develop a comprehensive policy for the reconstruction of Central India. He worked out the new plan with the mission to keep the natives from uniting as a force against the British. He saw the larger picture, rather than dealing with the experimental approach of Jagat Singh towards the treaty. The news from Jodhpur, too, was not encouraging for a possible pact that would allow the Rajput states to stand united in averting any threats for either of them.

On 4 April, Man Singh's appointee, Gulraj Diwan, was murdered. On the advice of yet another guru from the Nath sect, Man Singh had to give the charge to his only son, Prince Chhatar Singh, against his will. The prince was not only too young to undertake such a responsible job but was also already seduced by the world of addiction and nautch girls. Jodhpur was in a vulnerable situation. Further, Manjee Das Purohit was sacked and imprisoned at the Amber fort.

Later, during the summer of that year, Resident Metcalfe was informed about the incompetence of Purohit and his colleagues and the utter mismanagement of Jaipur. Around the same time, Hastings got wind of the Maratha leaders forging a pact to join hands against the British. He chose to distance Scindia and Holkar, going in for separate deals with both of them. It took months to strike the deals, resulting in more delays in negotiations with the princely states of Rajputana. Amidst all that chaos, Raja Bahadur Singh of Lawa initiated action to put an end to Amir Khan's attacks and demands, which led to a nearly year-long entanglement at Madhorajpura wherein the family members of Amir Khan were held. In a retaliatory move, Amir Khan laid siege around the fort, bidding to break the impregnable ramparts of the fort itself. Yet another year ended in despair with no respite for Jagat Singh.

On Reaching Sudarshangarh

Raskapoor had always admired the commanding position of the fort. As the rays of the morning sun stretched over the ramparts, it glowed like a crown on the city. She visualized the dreamlike view of the town from there at sunset. She had hoped to witness that breath-taking spectacle from there with her lover, who had once even told her he would gift that fort to her someday. She remembered that day she had laughed at the idea of being gifted a fort! She did not desire that gift, but she had not ever thought she would land up there as a convict! At the fort, it was not unusual to receive convicts, but her arrival excited the guards as well as the chief of the cells. They lined up well before her convoy reached as if standing to give her a guard of honour. When she emerged out of her palanquin, they were spellbound by her serene beauty. Dressed in saffron attire, Raskapoor smilingly greeted them, leaving them smitten with her poise and ease. To them she appeared like a divine beauty, not a convict, evoking reverence, not contempt. Moving in the direction of her cell, she never looked back even once. It was a small cell with no window, just a slit in the wall to let the convict breathe. The prison head observed the new prisoner making space to set up an altar, on which she placed her gods and goddesses. She folded her hands and closed her eyes and, after seeking their divine blessings, she turned towards the old man to thank him for bringing her to the cell. He was surprised, for never before had any prisoner thanked him.

Seeing her offer the prayer first and then the respect shown towards him convinced the prison head of the spirituality she possessed, separate from the allegations made against her.

He asked her, 'Is there something that you would like before I put the lock on the door?' Her reply haunted him for hours together. Raskapoor had declined his offer, and said, 'With my god and goddess around me, I do not need anything. Give me only what you give to other prisoners, but if you do want to provide me with something special, then please give me your blessings to uphold my integrity.'

His years of experience in dealing with the convicts told him that the lady was someone special, even if proven guilty. Did he not know that in this vindictive world, the proven guilty also at times were not guilty? As per the code and conduct of the prison, the doors of the cells opened only at a given time, but the prison head took it upon himself to bring in her food so he could strike up conversations with her. He was surprised not to hear a word against the ruler, whom he felt had badly let her down. She did discuss the troubles of the empire and seemed eager to hear updates on the campaigns of Amir Khan and the treaty with the British. Sometimes their conversation revolved around history, and it was one of those conversations in which she, like a little girl, wished to know why Sudarshangarh was also called Nahargarh. The prison chief narrated the fascinating story of Sudarshangarh, or the fort with the beautiful view, turning into Nahargarh, or the Tiger Fort. It was not as simple a reason as that the hill's shape was like that of a tiger or that the environs were the hunting ground for tigers. Raskapoor intently listened to the story narrated by the old man, which reminded her of her childhood days when her father Shiv Narain used to tell her such stories.

Jai Singh built the fort as a part of the defence system for his new town. One wall of the fort kept falling down, even if it was rebuilt several times, and this perplexed him. Concluding it to be the mischief of some miscreants, he decided to get his soldiers to deal with them. Their report was even more troubling, as they informed him that they had seen one figure breaking down the whole wall, but that figure did not have a head. Jai Singh summoned the tantric master, the royal priest, Ratnakar Pundrik to solve the mystery. The master, through a special ritual, resolved the mystery as he discovered that the site was the dwelling place of the spirit of Rathore Nahar Singh Bhomiya, who would not let anyone infringe upon his dwelling space. On the festival of Rakhi, the priest managed to subdue the soul of Nahar Singh. It agreed to leave the place on two conditions—the king must build a temple with four canopies within twenty-four hours and rename Sudarshangarh Nahargarh, after him. Raskapoor loved such stories, and he, in turn, loved her childlike persuasion to hear his stories. Amidst those story sessions, they forged a unique bond. She saw her father in him, and he saw a daughter who he longed for all his life.

Raskapoor appeared to be at ease in her new environs despite living in a deplorable condition, compared to what she was used to in Ras Vilas. She neither complained, nor asked for anything, remaining totally content with whatever was provided. As the days went by, her devotion inspired the old man to let her offer prayers at the Shiva temple within the fort premises. Her in-depth knowledge of mythology intrigued him, till finally, one day, he asked her, 'Raskapoor, you are a nautch girl's daughter brought up in environs, which dealt mainly with sensual pleasures—how is it then that you were able to assimilate so much knowledge and wisdom too?' Raskapoor told him about her two esteemed teachers—Pandit Shiv Narain Mishra and Rudra. 'Oh! So, both your spiritual teachers are no more,' sighed the old man.

Raskapoor was flabbergasted. 'How do you know Rudra and that he is no more?' He took a few minutes to respond, 'I am sorry to be the first one to share this news. I know it because Thakur Chaand Singh, who had captured Rudra, had summoned some of the hard taskmasters considered experts in getting the truth out of hardcore criminals in this prison. Rudra's confinement was a well-kept secret, just as the Thakur Sahib wished. He was arrested because of his planned coup against our empire. I knew nothing about him till recently when one of the torturers sat before me and cried while breaking the news. "He was only a devotee of Shiva true to his name Rudra—he was not a criminal. Today he bled to death after undergoing months of torture. I am one of his killers. Please relieve me immediately as I cannot live in this world of sinners like the capturer of that harmless devotee."'

The pensive old man then concluded his story. 'Raskapoor, as he cried and pleaded, I let him leave, knowing his guilt and repentance will either transform him or not let him live for long. Between you and me, the actual culprit was that ruthless vassal, and the others used in executing the plan, were merely his puppets.'

As tears cascaded down her cheeks, he let her mourn the heart-rending news of the demise of her soulmate alone, locking the cell as he left. At dawn the next morning, when he opened the lock, she greeted him with swollen lids that could hardly open. She had cried till her tears dried out; he knew. 'Come with me. We will go to the temple,' he said. He knew that only with divine intervention she would be able to bear the deep pain she was feeling.

Life was never the same for Raskapoor after that day, as each day she apologized to Rudra for the torture he had undergone just because of her. She knew that only death could relieve her of that guilt. Why could she not be united with her two men in life or death?

The Year That Was

1818! No one could ever imagine this year would have so much historical significance except for the British, who were working on a strategy to establish the sovereignty of the East India Company over most of Hindoostan. They had set off their campaign firmly towards the end of 1817. They began with the separation of the two strong forces of the Marathas—Scindia and Holkar. Alongside this, they made a move to detach Amir Khan from the Holkar Shahi Pindaris, the plunderers in the Holkar camp—a move to dilute the power of both. However, Holkar's resistance led to the third Anglo–Maratha war, resulting in the final blow to Maratha power in the country.

As the new year began, the process to sign the treaties with Holkar and the princely states of Rajputana sped up. On 6 January, the treaty of Mandsore was signed with the Holkar clan, and the treaty with the princely state of Kota was ratified. On the very same day, a treaty was concluded with the state of Jodhpur, which was ratified on 16 January, with which the hold of Amir Khan over Sambhar and a few other spots in Marwar ended. The treaty with Udaipur was concluded on 13 January and ratified on 22 January. The treaty with the Holkar family provided for restoring the territory held by them to the states of Kota and Bundi. To negotiate the terms of the treaty, the company sent James Tod, who arrived in Bundi on 8 February.

The British, however, were still not able to get closer to finalizing a treaty with the empire of Jagat Singh, despite the ruler himself initiating the negotiations as early as January. Knowing that their king was not fit to be on the throne in the first place, and the leadership qualities shown were only because of the company of the real brain, Raskapoor, the vassals found it an opportune moment to take advantage of him with her being gone. They were not only resisting the terms of the alliance but were busy encroaching upon high-yielding land. With great difficulty, Jagat Singh's chief negotiator, Baisisal, the vassal of Samode, concluded the treaty with Metcalf on 2 April, which was finally ratified on 15 April. However, the unruly vassals, like those from Uniara and Khetri, were bent upon defying it. Bharat Singh Narooka refused to move out of Madhorajpura fort because of which the Resident was forced to exercise pressure. He sent Ochterlony with his armed men in June. By the second half of the year, the British were successfully stretching their wings over the mighty princely states. They had mortgaged their independence to the foreigners with the terms of the treaties, not realizing they had sealed their fate forever. Jagat Singh, like all the other rulers, saw it as the end of the Maratha tyranny, but that in turn left very little for them to do. For every little action, they needed the approval of the British. They were also forced to pay the tributes to the British that they once paid to the Marathas and the Pathan.

Raskapoor's conviction was a uniting factor for the zenani deorhi, but after achieving it, they were once again divided into different groups, conspiring against each other to wield more power. Jagat Singh was marooned and longed to be with Raskapoor. Finding no escape from his peril, he took to alcohol as never before and chose to confine himself within the four walls of Shobha Niwas. He hardly ventured into the zenani deorhi, disgusted by its intrigues and conspiracies. None of the queens cared for him, except for the Bhatiyani queen. She started sympathizing with him only because of occasional conversations she had with Raskapoor in their chance encounters walking back from Govind Devji temple. Raskapoor talked about his emotional and artistic temperament and how he was being tricked and misled by his people. According to her, Jagat Singh needed only love and loyalty. Sometimes she even teased the Bhatiyani queen, 'You are so beautiful and gentle. I am sure you will be the one to give him the successor he longs for!' To that, Bhatiyani queen used to reply, pulling her leg, 'That can happen only when you are not with him!' She remembered Raskapoor as the only one to have given true love to Jagat Singh, a feeling that she shared with Medtani Rani, another sympathizer of Ras, who advised her to maintain silence for her own welfare. Often, she felt guilty of standing together with the other queens who got her falsely implicated and humiliated her in the public eye. Her heart reached out to her, imagining the ordeal that the innocent convict was undergoing, her only crime being her unconditional love for their husband.

She felt sorry for the Maharaja, seeing him on the night of the Diwali festival when he made a short appearance to perform the customary ritual. Jagat Singh was grieving the separation from his lover, looking frail and sad. After thinking over it for a few days, she went over to Shobha Niwas early in the evening. He had just then woken up from his afternoon siesta. She teased him, 'I know that you were dreaming of Raskapoor!'

He smiled and responded, pointing towards Nahargarh, 'She is there, and I can only see her in my dreams. Am I not the unfortunate one?' The Bhatiyani queen inspired him to pour his heart out and talk about their relationship. She realized that Raskapoor was a phenomenal woman endowed with beauty, brains and compassion. The Bhatiyani queen shared what Raskapoor used to say about his offspring. It was the first time that Jagat Singh spent a night with any woman after Raskapoor was sent to prison.

Winter was already setting in. The days were getting short and the nights longer. Jagat Singh began drinking soon after sunset, often looking towards the Nahargarh Fort. A couple of drinks down, he only saw the face of his lover. Remembering her eyes as she looked at him that one last time standing in the dock on the day of the judgement, the all-powerful ruler felt weak in the knees. He knew that she was not the betrayer but was the one betrayed—

not just by her adversaries but also by him, who had proclaimed his eternal love for her. With that thought, he condemned himself for hours together until the drinks overpowered all his senses.

It was during their drinking sessions in the days of the proceedings that Chaand Singh had revealed Rudra's death. He had given him the news hailing his achievement in averting his half queen's coup to take over his empire in league with her accomplice Rudra. Jagat Singh then realized how the trap was laid out to eliminate the woman Chaand Singh blamed for his humiliation. It was too late for Jagat Singh to undo what was done, and he sailed along the tide landing him in no-man's land. Each time he went down memory lane, he asked for another drink before finishing the one in hand.

On 21 December, as the sun was setting, Jagat Singh ordered his drinks. Just as he finished his first drink, he started sweating, and within a few minutes, the goblet fell out of his hand as he rolled onto the ground. The group of servers summoned the royal physician. There was a commotion in the palace as the queens and vassals rushed to Shobha Niwas. The royal physician came in, trying desperately to revive him. After receiving mouth-to-mouth resuscitation, he opened his eyes, looking in the direction of one of the servers and, murmuring a few words, he breathed his last.

His murmured last few words were taken as the announcement for his successor. The whole empire was hit by the sudden demise of the ruler, and the wailing sound from the city below pierced the walls of the Nahargarh Fort. Raskapoor suddenly woke up to the mournful cries and, dreading the sad news, she anxiously waited for the cell lock to be opened. Early in the morning, the prison chief made his way to the cell, holding a lantern in his hand. It was much earlier than the usual time for the cell to open. Their eyes met, and the tears in his eyes conveyed that there was some bad news for her. 'Why has the city been wailing for the last few hours, and why have you come so early? Am I being hung to death today or being buried alive?' Raskapoor hurled a series of questions at him. He regained his composure, and wiping his tears, he broke the news to her.

'Just a few hours ago, Maharaja Jagat Singh died. It was so sudden and quick that the royal physician could do very little to revive him.'

Raskapoor felt the ground slipping from under her feet. She was prepared for her death as she had already died not once but twice, first at the time of her false conviction and then when she received the news of Rudra's murder, but she was not prepared to receive the news of the death of her lover.

She said, 'You know, this death is not as sudden as you are being told. I always dreaded it coming while I was there, but once I left the palace, why did it come so fast? All of them had resented me and wanted to uproot me. Finally, when they had achieved their mission, why was no one there to take care of the Maharaja?

'I could see the threat of death looming large over him with the conspirators around him. I dreaded his sudden end, and that is the reason I always took a sip of his drink each time a new container was brought in. He often laughed at my insistence to follow the tradition of manuhar, offering me the first sip before having the first drink with each service. He teased me often, "My Ras loves the alcohol but does not want to admit it. She drinks it sip by sip. The Maharaja of Sawai Jaipur does not mind as with the touch of her lips the drink becomes even more intoxicating." I never liked the taste, but I tasted it every time to see that there was no poison in it. He never got to know the real reason behind my taking the first sip in each round of fresh drinks that crossed the maze of secret passages of the palace. If he died at night suddenly, was he poisoned? No one will ever know, for no one will even attempt to find out. Please, I beg you to let me know the plan for his arrival there,' she said requesting him for the funeral details, pointing towards the cenotaphs at Gaitor below.

The expression in the big eyes of the lugubrious Raskapoor choked his throat as she gazed at him without blinking. Controlling his own emotions, he nodded, heeding her request, and quickly locked the cell without looking up even once.

Jagat Singh's sudden demise completely shattered her, for she was convinced that it was not a natural death, having heard about the conflicting views on the issue of his successor. Raskapoor had tried her best to protect her beloved, but all her wisdom and farsightedness combined with her eternal vigilance were in vain. She had not yet come to terms with the news of her soulmate Rudra's death, and now she had to deal with a second hard blow. Both the men had died an unnatural death only because of her. The thought was tearing her soul apart. For the first time, she felt like an orphan. A void prevailed around her, for even though she and Jagat Singh were far away from each other, Raskapoor had a sense of belonging.

Immersed in a sea of emotions, she was sad and numb all day. Not even one tear rolled out from her eyes. As night set in, even in the closed cell, she could feel his arms around her. The ceiling of that dark cell seemed to be full of stars, and she spontaneously slipped into a whirlpool of memories. Reminiscing about the nights she had spent in his arms at Amber Fort, she could smell the fragrance of night jasmine and hear notes of soft music that the musicians had played for them. She remembered how she wandered on the ramparts of the fort, hand in hand with him, discussing the problems of Jai Nagar. She smiled thinking about that game of chaupar that they had played on the full moon night, the one she won. Everything was so vivid, as if he was there with her, and then suddenly, she was haunted by the thought of him not being there ever again.

Raskapoor could not envision him lying in state in Preetam Niwas. She shivered with a chill in her bones, but the very next moment she felt the heat of the fire. What was happening to her, she wondered? She did not wish to die before the last rites of the man who had defied all the traditions to not only shower love on her but accord so much respect to her. She did not want to lose out on all those beautiful moments only because of the one terrible moment of her conviction. Though tormented with her unjust conviction, she treasured their fairy-tale romance. Her eyes closed, and she fell on the bed sensing his warmth around her. That momentary sensation made her wonder if her lover's soul had come to her before leaving the world. It was a long, sad night as she tossed and turned in her cell once again, thinking about why she could not protect either of the men she loved so dearly.

It was a different sunrise for her with no light to lead her on. All she could feel was darkness, even when the winter sun radiated on Sudarshangarh. Her only solace was in her devotion, and she wanted to pray one last time at Shiv Mandir to free the soul of her beloved and to free herself from the guilt of Rudra's death. She was waiting for the cell lock to be opened. Having bathed early, she chose to put on the same saffron attire that she wore the day she left Ras Vilas. Raskapoor was anxious to head to the temple the moment the prison chief arrived and hastened to collect all the ingredients for her ritual.

As she was assembling her pooja thali, the tray for the ritual, she could hear her mother's voice echoing in her ears. 'Ras, watch out, use kapoor (camphor) "judiciously" . . . not too much, just enough for effervescence . . . and never swallow it, it can kill you . . . Watch out my daughter.' The mother cautioned her baby girl each time she hurried to the Gupteshwar Mahadev near the glass palace, realizing how fascinated her daughter was with camphor. With the same determination with which Raskapoor used to defy her mother, she placed a handful of camphor pieces on her tray and a pink lotus. Just then, there was a creaking sound at the gate, and the cell lock opened.

The prison chief smiled. 'Here is some water from the holy Ganges. I knew that my devotee prisoner would be ready to offer special prayers at the Shiv temple. The last rites of the Maharaja will be performed at dusk near the cenotaph of "Bado Maharaj", his father.'

She did not respond and slowly walked towards the Shiv temple, softly chanting 'karpur gauram' repeatedly, as if in a trance to free the soul of Jagat Singh from this world. 'He was a passionate man full of love that was meant to rule a heart not a kingdom. I come to you one last time to pray to release his soul so it can dwell in peace.' As she stepped onto the temple steps, she had the same glow on her face that had captured Jagat Singh's heart when he saw her for the first time on the steps of the Brijnidhi temple. She had just lit the oil lamp, and she was radiating in its soft glow. An ardent worshipper of Shiva, the Neel Kantha, she knew that he drank halaal, the poison that killed instantly. That poison came out at the time of samudra manthan—when the gods and the demon churned the ocean.

She poured the water of the Ganges on the Shivling, praying for the peace and tranquillity of the troubled and tortured souls of her two men. She sat down and chanted 'Om Namah Shivay . . . Om Namah Shivay . . . Karpur Gauram . . .' for hours altogether, as if to say she was cleansing every cell in her body of guilt; as if to say she was craving for the emancipation of all three souls; the souls of Rudra, Jagat Singh and herself.

Amidst the chanting, the chiming of the bells in the temple and the exhilarating aroma of the camphor's effervescence, Raskapoor slipped into an ecstatic trance. She spontaneously reached out for the unused stack of camphor and swallowed it. Within a few seconds, Raskapoor saw herself flying towards the sky. Flapping her wings, she joined the two birds flying high. She recognized the two birds as Rudra and Jagat. She joined them, and they lovingly made space for her between them. She felt protected and dared to change her flying altitude, suddenly spinning in the sky. They flew together, circling over Amber, Sawai Jaipur and Sudarshangarh, taking their last flight of love!

She had asked the guard if he could leave her alone as she wanted to pray till the time the funeral pyre of the Maharaja was lit. The guard granted her wish and sat on the ramparts till the mortal remains were lit. When he went to escort her back, he was stunned to see her lying next to her pooja thali and the extinguished lamp with no residue of camphor left. The words of the hymn were reflecting on her persona as the guard chanted in reverence of Shiva and his devotee, 'Karpur Gauram . . . pure like camphor; Karunavataram . . . the incarnation of compassion.

Sadavasantam Hridayaravinde . . . always residing in the pure hearts who live and preserve their purity against all odds, like the lotus flower blooms in muddy waters.'

The nervous guard tried to feel her pulse and heard the chant fading away as her head rolled to the side with her gaze fixed on the Shivling. Raskapoor had breathed her last as the flames of

the funeral pyre of Jagat Singh reached out to the heights of the
ramparts of Nahargarh Fort. Heaps of camphor had been poured
into the pyre.

And the valley was filled with the essence of camphor . . .
Raskapoor.

Their souls became inseparable as whenever Jagat Singh's
name is brought up, along comes the name of the one and only
Raskapoor—Queen of half of Jagat Singh's empire, and the
Empress Noor Jahan of Jaipur. She left no survivor and was
remembered with reverence only by the Bhatiyani queen, who gave
birth to Jagat Singh's posthumous son Sawai Jai Singh III. Despite
the conspiracy hatched by the eunuch Mohan Ram and his friends,
Jai Singh III was declared heir to the throne. Till he came of age,
his mother held the reins of the administration, which were taken
over by her two confidantes, one of them being the handmaiden,
Roopa Badaran.

Such was the destiny of Jagat Singh that no one even built a
cenotaph for him in the complex of cenotaphs at Gaitor, where
cenotaphs of the successive rulers as well as of the two illegitimate
sons of Maharaja Sawai Madho Singh II were built. Strangely
enough, in sharp contrast, Sudarshangarh stands almost as the
memorial of Raskapoor, defying all efforts of Jaipur to wipe her
out of existence. Raskapoor's name is taken more often than his.
Each time the history of Sudarshangarh is narrated, it unwittingly
reignites camphor—its hallucinatory aroma brings her alive. From
the enclosed ramparts of Sudarshangarh Fort, that ethereal essence
of camphor 'Raskapoor' continues to linger.

Tailpiece

In my wildest dream, I could not have imagined ending up finding not one but three Hindi novels about her during my research, published in 1978, 1980 and 2004 by Dhyan Makhija, Umesh Shastri and Anand Sharma, respectively. Quite uncannily, both Makhija and Sharma felt the presence of her soul, which chose to narrate her story at the same place, Nahargarh. I am not trying to turn Nahargarh into a haunted fort, but the experience of the two authors is a bit too strange for me. However, the two authors differ on the end of Raskapoor. While Makhija describes her escape from prison with the help of her soulmate, Anand Sharma gives a detailed account of her performing sati. But how strange it is that both see her change her attire to disguise herself to embark upon her last journey.

I got hold of these books after being well into my narrative. I was only hearing the voice of the woman in me moving through the corridors of history! In fact, Shastri's book came my way after finishing the first draft, and that too, by sheer chance, for I had not even heard of yet another book on my lady. I got Anand Sharma's book much earlier and chose to discuss the view with him on her performing sati. I still went ahead to verify the same in 'Dastoor Comwar', the source given by him and available at the Archives Department of Rajasthan in Bikaner. It gave the account of Jagat

Singh's last rites, but there was no mention of her being present there. He was still helpful in sharing what a history professor, Shyam Singh, wrote in his work, mentioning Raskapoor's name in the list of those who immolated themselves with Maharaja Jagat Singh. When I tried to contact the Professor, I got to know that he had passed away just a couple of years back, leaving her mysterious end a mystery. In any case, Ranbir Singh of Dundlod had already brushed aside the theory of her committing sati. Dr Chandramani Singh, with long experience at the City Palace, Jaipur, too, had not come across any such mention.

Just recently, the former Superintendent of Amber, Mr Zafar Ulla, came up with the most bizarre theory of Hadira in Handipura, Amber, being a monument built in the memory of Raskapoor when there was none built for her lover, the Maharaja himself. I immediately called him to find out the basis of his theory. He too gave the story of her committing sati and felt that the architecture of Hadira was of that period. However, when I set aside the story of her committing sati, referring to the records, he conceded that his theory came up because of the period of the architecture and the popular belief that the monument was raised for a dancer. Since Raskapoor was the only legendary dancer who could have deserved that monument, he drew a logical conclusion.

Acknowledgements

It has been an interesting journey to work on this book. It all began when I was sitting over a cup of coffee in Delhi with Milee Ashwarya discussing the idea for the next book. We had worked closely on my big book *India's Elephants: A Cultural Legacy*, a Penguin publication. She suggested I take up a historical fiction as I had a deep connect with the history and culture of Rajasthan, the Indian state that is known as the land of forts and palaces. I pondered over her suggestion for a few minutes and the first character who came to mind was Raskapoor. It was a spontaneous reaction but as I narrated her story in brief, I was sure that I wanted to write it, unfolding a history replete with splendour, intrigue, battles and, of course, romance. The story of the nineteenth-century dancer was also going to reflect on the arrival of the East India Company that gradually shifted from trading to the tactical handling of the conflict between the princely states of Rajputana, Marathas, Holkars and the Pathans.

After listening to my narration intently, Milee asked me to start writing. I returned to Jaipur and started researching and reading. Finally one day, I got the idea of where to begin and as I wrote, the characters started appearing. I was compelled to write the full story and not just a few chapters before going ahead. I researched and wrote at the same time, sitting at the desk for hours together.

My first draft got ready with the constant support of my sister who lives in the USA.

Dr Deepa Dixit, who not only read chapters as I sent them, but also added information, researching on her own and we spent hours discussing the development of the story. I cannot but be thankful to her for the incredible backup. I then shared the first draft with yet another doctor in the family, a voracious reader herself. After reading it on her return flight from Canada, Dr Swati Pai called to give her reaction, 'This will definitely be published.'

I was encouraged and worked on my first draft for months together. Then came the most important moment for me when my writer brother Piyush read it and handed it over to a team who could get it edited to finally present to the publisher. Thereafter, Milee had a first look at the few chapters, shared it with her team, and Penguin decided to publish it after the final round of editing by their editor. I am thankful to all who set the stage ready to unfold the most dramatic story of a real life person turning into a fable, which includes the offices of the Rajasthan Archives Department and the Archaeological Survey of India. I need to thank my friend Archana Julka, yet another doctor, to join me in my research, driving me around as I followed the footsteps of Raskapoor visiting the places connected with her story.

References

Asopa, J.N., *Cultural Heritage of Jaipur: Symposium: 11th Session: Rajasthan History Congress: Papers*, United Book Traders, 1982.

Bahura, G., & Sinh, R., *The City of Sawai Jaipur*, Publication Scheme, 2009.

Byley C.S., *Chiefs and Leading Families in Rajputana*, Office of the Superintendent Government Printing, India, 1903.

Bhattacharyya, S., *The Rajput States and the East India Company: From the Close of the Eighteenth Century to 1820*, Munshiram Manoharlal, 1972.

Hooja Rima, *A History of Rajasthan*, 2006.

Lal, B., & Prinsep, H.R., *Memoirs of the Puthan, Soldier of Fortune, the Nuwab Ameer-ood-Doulah Mohummud Ameer Khan, Chief of Seronj, Tonk, Rampoora, Neemahera and Other Places in Hindoostan, Compiled in Persian by Busawun Lal (Translated by Henry Thoby Prinsep)*, G.H. Huttmann, 1832.

Malcolm, J., *Sketch of the Political History of India, from the Introduction of Pitts Bill, AD 1784 to the Present Date*, printed for William Miller by James Moyes, 1811.

Malcolm, J., *Political History of India*, John Murray, 1826.

Minto, G.E., & Minto, E., *Lord Minto in India: Life and Letters of Gilbert Elliot, First Earl of Minto, from 1807 to 1814, while Governor-General of India: Being a Sequel to His 'Life and Letters' Published in 1874*, Longmans, Green, 1880.

Misra, S.C., *Sindhia-Holkar Rivalry in Rajasthan*, Sundeep, 1981.

Ross, J., *Fall of the Maratha Power and the Marquess of Hastings*, Sunita Publications, 1985.

Sarkar, J., & Simha Raghubìra, *A History of Jaipur: c. 1503–1938*, Orient
    Longman, 1994.
Singh, N., *Thirty Decisive Battles of Jaipur*, JEP Works, 1939.
Tod, J., & Paul, E.J., *Annals and Antiquities of Rajasthan*, Roli Books, 2008.
Publications of Rajasthan Sangeet Natak Akademi, LokKala Mandal as
    well as Gazetteers of Jaipur, Jodhpur, Jalore and Udaipur.
Thakur Mohan Singh Kanota, *Champawaton Ka Itihas*, vol. II.
Siya Ram Natani, *Kachchwaha Rajgharane Ki amulya Virasat: Amber*.
Nand Kishor Parekh, *Rajdarbar Aur Raniwas*.
Manisha Choudhary, *The Royal Household (Rajlok) of Kachhawa Kings of Jaipur*.